er
ad
he
sang, the Sunday drives we used to take, and how, away from my mother, he seemed younger, more frivolous and debonair, the nights he'd sat up with me when I had pneumonia, his disproportionate pride in my every small achievement.

Trains ran direct from Manchester to London. A few hours there and a few hours back. One day I'd acquire the money and the opportunity. I'd be on my way to Beauchamp Road, to the half-timbered house with the bow windows and the rhododendron bushes in whose gracious blue-carpeted drawing-room Olivia Murray dispensed china tea and cultured conversation. If and when my mother found out, it would be too late to stop me.

MY FATHER'S HOUSE

Kathleen Conlon

Hamlyn Paperbacks

MY FATHER'S HOUSE

ISBN 0 600 20146 5

First published in Great Britain 1972
by William Collins Sons & Co. Ltd
Hamlyn Paperbacks edition 1981
2nd printing 1982

Hamlyn Paperbacks are published by
The Hamlyn Publishing Group Ltd,
Astronaut House,
Feltham, Middlesex, England

Printed and bound in Great Britain by
Collins, Glasgow

The flat was described to us as having a fine view of the sea, but that's just estate-agent's licence in full flower: on our first visit to Montpelier Crescent we discovered that the sea, judging by the tracery of cranes on the not-too-distant skyline, could legitimately be called the estuary.

This is our second visit. We reach number nineteen and step backwards into the road to get the full glory of it. But we're half a century too late for that. Once it must have been a perfect wedding-cake of a villa with its fretted balconies and porticoes like white icing against the pale-pink stucco. Fifty years of creeping neglect have reduced it to an almost comic state of disrepair: the stucco is no longer pale-pink, but that glum shade, always worn by your maiden aunt, known as 'dusty', the shutters hang awry, the balconies retain their grip of the wall by sheer will-power, or so it seems. The overall impression is of a relic of French colonialism fetched up on the shores of Lancashire; you half-expect a Creole beauty wearing an inviting smile and little else to lean out from an upstairs window.

Berenice, my sister-in-law, straightens her shoulders and says, 'Well, at least it's got character,' in her beggars-can't-be-choosers tone. Not that she doesn't find it appealing in a nostalgic way; she's reminded of college days and crumby rooms in houses such as this, clothes-lines and giggling and the water-heater that always ran cold. Even so, she wouldn't touch it with a ten-foot barge-pole herself, not now; now she has joined the army of attack against the demon dirt, with her vacuum-cleaners and impregnated polishers and squeeze-dry floor mops.

'Let's get in,' she says irritably. 'I can't stand the heat out here.'

It's the hottest June since God-knows-when and she's suffering. I'm a sun-worshipper, but she's the fair, temperate type.

Inside it's cool enough, too cool, almost dank, as though the walls are weeping. Perhaps they are impregnated with the tears of tenants past who have cried woe and alas and put their heads into gas ovens only to find they've run short of shillings.

Berenice puffs and pants up the stairs. I make a feeble joke about the rarefied atmosphere, anxious to retain her good-fellowship, aware that she didn't have to accompany me and aware also that this afternoon is merely her duty; I'm reduced to the stray-dog category. I can imagine her telling Maurice, my brother, that she must, simply must, see to it that Anna gets settled.

The top floor is my prospective domain: one bedroom, one kitchen and an enormous living-room which boasts two floor-to-ceiling windows and from which, a thousand apologies to Messrs Parker and Jones and their high-flown prose, we can actually glimpse water.

We look about us, attempting to find pros to weigh against the many cons among which are those same windows, badly fitted and certain to rattle with the merest breeze, the size of the room – large enough to warrant a camp-fire for heating purposes – and the floor which seems to be not quite on the horizontal; we should have brought a marble to roll, like real prospective purchasers of property. Maybe it's riddled with woodworm and seething with dry-rot as well. Still, the beams are attractive and the rent's moderate.

'It's amazing what a few cushions will do – a touch of brightness,' Berenice says. She's going to start her woman's magazine philosophy any second. I interrupt hastily.

'Who's downstairs?'

'The middle floor's empty. Mr and Mrs Robson live on the ground floor. They're retired people.'

'Very definitely not rushing upstairs with neighbourly smiles and cups of tea.'

'You can hardly expect them to,' she says, eyes wide with reproof. 'Retired people!'

She's in the same category herself, of course. Special dispensations for retired people and nursing mothers.

'*I* could make a cup of tea.' The removal men have dumped a crate of utensils in the kitchen. My mother's china cups are at the top of another crate, wrapped and wrapped. Pale faded pink they are, like the house, like eggshells or sugared almonds. A wedding-present, she'd kept them intact as she'd wanted to keep everything intact.

I *could* make a cup of tea, but I've run out of matches. I can see that Berenice believes this to be deliberate. Our social manners form only the tip of a dark and ugly iceberg composed of spite, intolerance and fundamental dislike.

She pauses with her hand on the doorknob. 'We'll be round on Sunday. All of us.' It's as much a threat as a promise. She has to go now. Harriet and Roland and Jessica have to be collected. Maurice's dinner has to be prepared. She has to return to the life that normal people lead.

I smile and make all the right noises, watching her, marvelling that Maurice, my brother, should be able to summon the desire that accounts for Harriet and Roland and Jessica. I marvelled years ago, when he used to bring her home to tea on Sundays, all clean white peter-pan collars and clean pink nails and never speaking with her mouth full.

The heavy, dusty silence in this place is a delight. So too is the smell, a *mélange* of damp and geraniums. My predecessor has bequeathed me a window-sill full of them, as well as an encrustation of grease on the stove and a gilt-framed picture in the bedroom portraying a 'Rustic Beauty' taken from the Pears Almanack of 1923. Dust motes shimmer in the air as I pass from room to room, the only sound my breathing and my shoes when I move from the carpeted bedroom into the linoleumed kitchen. Unpacking can be done later, after I have savoured all this territory of space and silence that is to be exclusively mine.

My bathroom is opulence unstinted – all gilt and mahogany and Dutch tiles. Perhaps it was once an adjunct of the nursery; numerous Harriets and Rolands and Jessicas having their chubby little well-bred limbs soaped before being ushered in to bid good night to that benign but distant couple, Mama and Papa.

I look at myself in the mirror above the bath, comparing the present image with that of nine months ago. Then, I was ill and ugly and wretched, desiring only sleep and mental inertia; now I am healthy, ready to start all over again, ready to resume where I left off. Chris Ross told me that you can't close doors behind you for good and all. Life, he said, is like exploring a house: you go through the same rooms twice; sometimes the occupants change, but the settings remain constant. It seemed to me that it was a prison sentence he was describing, but then there's nothing to say you can't open a few windows en route.

Part One
Signposts

CHAPTER ONE

My father left home when I was eleven years old. In a way, his going was something of an anti-climax. I had summoned my resources against the contingency two years earlier and when it finally occurred I was almost acclimatized to the idea.

Comprehension had dawned gradually. There were the rows of course, and though it wouldn't be true to say we got used to the rows – we'd tiptoe down the stairs and listen at the keyhole for the first ugly word, the first crash – at least they were so frequent as to be a part of life. This was something different.

I had heard hints and allusions, I had been aware of conversations that ceased suddenly when I entered the room, of sideways glances and glances that contained elements of both pity and curiosity. The neighbours, the social acquaintances, the local shopkeepers, all had contributed to creating a vague unease in my mind. I was a child and I did not understand, but I could sense the scandalized delight, the disapproval, the expectation of imminent shaming events. Hadn't I, two years ago, known that Aunt Kitty's departure in haste and silence was in disgrace also and had something to do with Sex, even though neither comprehensible gossip nor information had sullied my ears?

It was Maurice, my brother, who filled in the gaps. Down in the garden shed where six neglected mice propagated their species and then ate them because their cage was too small, he told me that Dennis Wintergreen's father had told Dennis Wintergreen's mother that Alec Blake, who was *our* father, had a woman, which piece of information Dennis Wintergreen had duly passed on to Maurice.

He stood with his hands in his shorts' pockets, kicking at the floor and ruining his shoe-toes. His shorts were too long. He looked like a Barnardo's Boy, not the son of a prosperous businessman.

'Stone the crows!'

It was Maurice's latest expression and it seemed as good a comment as any to use at the time because I hadn't the least idea what the sombre phrase 'had a woman' was supposed to mean.

For Maurice, imitation was far from being the sincerest form of flattery. He told me I sounded stupid saying 'Stone the crows!' He told me that I was just like a parrot, copying what everyone else said without knowing what it meant. He told me he'd bashed Dennis Wintergreen and then I knew the gravity of the situation and that 'had a woman' was something very dreadful. As he told me all this, he kicked harder and harder at the earth floor of the shed, driving loamy sprays into my hair and over my newly-whitened sandals.

'What will we do?'

'I could go away. On a ship.'

But I dismissed that. He'd tried it twice before. The first time my mother had bolted the door behind his retreating back and he'd turned round promptly and howled to be let in. The second time he'd fallen on a broken bottle in the park and ended up in the heady excitement of Casualty having four stitches put into his knee.

'I'll go and you'll be left on your own.' He came up close to me. My eyes were level with the row of pens he had clipped to his jersey. I could see egg and gravy and other remains of school-dinners on his tie. His rage had not worked itself out upon Dennis Wintergreen's nose, so he was venting it, as always, upon my obtuseness.

'Why should I be left alone?' I could see no possible connection between my father having a woman and me being abandoned. While he'd been talking, the idea of 'having a woman' had finally crystallized in my mind. I imagined she, whoever this highly-favoured woman might be, and my father, taking tea, eating cream-horns and unwinding brioches, my father saying 'Please have some more', and wielding a silver tea-pot then gallantly paying the bill with no thought for the expense.

'Because Dad'll go and I'll go and Mum –' I don't know to which shore of oblivion our mother was to be banished because then his face stiffened into the rigid lines which always preceded tears. You clenched your teeth and swallowed and pinched your nostrils together. That way you could stifle the sobs, but your eyes usually betrayed you, you couldn't control your eyes. Nor could Maurice. I could see wetness trembling on the lower lids where the yellow sleep was in the mornings. He turned away into the corner. 'Quasimodo's dead,' he said, through the blue check handkerchief.

Quasimodo was one of the latest mice, a black, hump-backed, twisted creature which, by rights, should have been the first sacrifice of the litter, but which had managed to stay alive when its healthier brethren were lying around in decomposing lumps.

He opened the cage to let me see. He didn't give a hoot about Quasimodo and neither did I, but it was a respite for both of us. Across the bars of the exercise-wheel lay a headless, legless abomination of hair and tail. The other mice, startled by sudden daylight, scurried behind cotton-wool and newspaper, but the biggest, glossiest one, more debonair, sat and looked at us and licked his chops.

We closed the door upon this Saturnalia. We were bored rather than disturbed. Mice were only mice, after all, and we could recognize the divine logic in their activities. 'He had a good run,' Maurice said. 'He was a game little beggar.'

His tears were now mere snail-tracks on his cheeks, his sparse fair eyelashes now completely devoid of shame.

'Perhaps Dennis Wintergreen made a mistake,' I said.

'Sod Dennis Wintergreen.'

His language was dreadful since he'd started at the grammar school. My mother had wanted to send him to St Anthony's, but my father said they were a lot of little pansies in straw hats and if Maurice couldn't get through on his own merit then he didn't deserve to get through at all. And my mother said what about all the scruffy children from the estate, with lice in their hair and heaven-knows-what-else, and that if he didn't take trouble over his son's education, who would? And my father called my mother a snobbish bitch and wished he could go back thirteen years.

All of which ended in Maurice donning a maroon blazer and seeming no worse off for it, except of course for the language.

'I must go. I must go.' He'd waylaid me as I was on the way to Madame Flavia, late of the Ballet Russe, who worked wonders with the knock-knees and bow-legs of the neighbourhood.

'Don't you say anything. Not to anyone.' He shook me by the shoulders until my teeth chattered.

I had no intention of saying anything to anyone. What could I have said? The information related to me only in that it confirmed my long-held belief that we were a family set apart from other families. I walked slowly up Tennyson Avenue, pulling leaves from other people's privet hedges, despoiling other people's fuchsia bushes, looking in through other people's windows. I saw pretty wallpaper and nice furniture, curled-up cats and preening birds in cages. I saw the embodiment of tranquillity. To step into one of those rooms would not be to anticipate disaster, as stepping into my own home meant tensing oneself to interpret the atmosphere. The people who lived in those rooms did not apply themselves to destroying one another, did not need to pull the covers over their ears to obliterate the ugly clangour of quarrelling and, worse, the mystifying empty silences.

We were set apart, we were different. But there was a crumb of comfort: I had an ally. I was nine years old and for nine years Maurice, my brother, had been cast in the role of persecutor, had symbolized everything I longed to be and was not, everything beyond my scope. My bed-wetting, my fear of the dark, my lack of physical co-ordination, all had been grist to his mill. For nine years, by various metaphorical means, he had convinced me of my inferiority, had pushed me too high on the swings, had pulled back the sheet to expose me, blue-striped and steaming slightly, had doubly set me apart. It was over now. There was misery in store for us, for both of us, and in the garden shed the first seeds of truce had begun to germinate.

*

The woman my father had had when Maurice was thirteen and I was nine was not the same woman he left home for. That lady's charms were apparently just not sufficient to arm him against the moment when all hell would break loose; Olivia Murray's undoubtedly were. That we all knew Olivia Murray made it that much more puzzling. She was a real, flesh and blood woman whose tea we had drunk, whose roses we had admired, who had once taken Maurice and me to see *Jack and the Beanstalk* at Christmas, not some shadowy husband-stealer to whom distance might have lent a romantic enchantment.

We were puzzled, but we were not surprised. We thought it very odd that our parents should have married in the first place. It was misalliance, pure and simple. He was high-spirited, sociable, impatient, she was cautious, suspicious and always looked on the black side. He had ambition, confidence, great charm. He left her behind with every footstep. She ought never to have aspired so high.

I loved my father, during the lulls between the periodic storms – despite the misery of his marriage, he had a quality of undimmed youthfulness, a gift for invoking a magical atmosphere as though, like me, he too was discovering excitement for the first time. It was only during the storms that I learned to hate him also.

He left one July evening. I had been for a bicycle ride and returned too late to witness the big scene. Scenes, for Maurice and I, had long ago lost their horrid fascination. We'd discovered that, inevitably, they rebounded upon us, so at the first warning signal we'd bolt down our lunch or our tea and speed away to the placid auras of other people's homes. In that way we built up our social façades much earlier than is usual. We were popular, we had to be popular in order to ensure that there would always be a refuge when the missiles started flying.

All unaware, I put away my bicycle and went into the sitting-room. What I saw astounded me: my mother, writhing on the sofa ('Take your feet off, you'll dirty the covers'), a cushion gripped against her stomach, howling like a dog.

I thought she was in pain. I had never seen my mother

cry. Silences were her forte. She could be silent for a week. Doors would slam and plates would crash and the old rocking chair would creak as she drove it to and fro, setting your teeth on edge, but not a word would pass her lips until she'd worked him up into a frenzy and he threw something. Never at her though, always at the ground. Sometimes I thought he might achieve more if he altered his aim.

My mother moaned and rocked herself, pummelled the gold satin cushion, drew breath in great gasping lungfuls. 'He's gone. I didn't think he would. But he's gone.' She was beyond pretence or restraint. Words like whore and harlot, which I had thought were used only in Shakespeare and dictionaries, came from between clenched teeth. The howling subsided into an anguished moan. She'd see him in hell. See how long he'd stay with that whore. It was the only thing he could think about. That! And she used a word I had seen written in chalk on the air-raid shelters in the school playground, but never heard spoken. My mother! Please God, let the Langleys next door be out. And the Adamsons on the other side. Please God, let Maurice come home.

But Maurice didn't return until ten, so for two hours I bore the brunt of her desperate ravings. She'd thought she could play a game with him, stretch him on a piece of elastic to see how much he could take and then draw him back again. But this time the elastic had snapped and he'd fallen into one of Olivia Murray's immaculate tapestry arm-chairs and Olivia Murray had raised a smooth ivory hand to beckon him away to London.

Piece by piece I filled in the jigsaw of events that had led up to his defection. He had sold his property, sold the garages, sold Olivia Murray's house, negotiated to buy a place in London. His departure alone caused her agony enough, but the fact that he had plotted and managed to disguise his plotting from her until it was too late made it unendurable. If he'd stormed out impromptu she could have coped better.

I could do nothing to solace her, and I was terrified to my soul – my father gone, my mother a wailing lunatic.

Between crying and cursing, she'd call for Maurice, or suddenly reach out and clutch me to her and call me pet names she hadn't used for years. I almost wished that nosy Mrs Adamson or stuck-up Mrs Langley *would* come in – they were at least adult and in the presence of adults she might feel the need for some restraint.

Later, when she'd crawled up to bed, full of sleeping pills, Maurice and I sat side by side, whispering to each other. You whisper after a death and it was a kind of death for us. He was pale that night, whispering and pulling his cuticles ragged. It wasn't until afterwards that he could pass it off with a sneer as 'The old man's gone off with a rich widow – it's too corny to be true.'

What rankled most was that he had gone without informing the son of the house. But I knew, in retrospect, that he had said his goodbyes during the previous, deliberately idyllic week end. And I should have known it was too good to be true.

He had brought a car back to the house at the crack of dawn on Sunday morning. He was taking us to the Lakes for the day. My mother had immediately begun to worry about sandwich fillings and vacuum flasks but he'd halted her in midstream with an upraised hand. No moth-eaten sandwiches for us. We were going to lunch at the Old England and dine at the Lakeside. She was bundled into her best coat before she had time to envisage snags. Even Maurice was seduced into a degree of the enthusiasm that was foreign to his nature at that time. The car purred along, the tar bubbled on the road, he sang as he drove – something he hadn't done for years. He had a fine tenor and his songs were touchingly nostalgic. They'd met at an operatic society; he was dressed as a Ruritanian officer: high-collared red jacket and tight black boots, while she was a flower-seller in white muslin with a basket of paper violets. They couldn't fail to be enchanted with each other. When the play ended its run it was too late. The next time she saw him he was in airforce blue, the lustre quite dimmed.

The sky was blue, the sun was yellow, the trees were green – every colour in the spectrum was intensified that day. We rowed on the lake, we climbed a hill and told ourselves it was a mountain. In the hotel, he ordered wine which sparkled topaz in its bottle. It was a wine they had had before, during a day which should have been remembered often – I saw her flush and look away and a momentary flicker of pain on his forehead – it was a small sentimental gesture to the way things might have turned out.

It was all bound to change, Maurice and I agreed on that. All meant all we could take in with a glance around his room – the pen and wash pictures of boats on the wall, outgrown Arthur Ransomes and *Biggles* in the bookcase, the virginia creeper that grew in at his window, the tea-stain on the rug – plus other things.

'I'm not leaving school. He's not having that, the bastard.' Maurice looked across at his textbooks, he who had once desired to run away to sea.

My first reaction too had been to wonder whether or not we were now penniless waifs, dependent upon the parish, or whatever people were dependent upon. But we were to be well provided for; Olivia Murray had her late husband's substantial fortune to fall back upon.

In fact the changes were not nearly so radical as we had anticipated. Two months elapsed between my father going and Aunt Kitty coming back, coming back plus a four-year-old child. During those two months my mother went into purdah while the town chewed and digested the juiciest steak of scandal that had come its way since the mayor went berserk and put a bullet through his brain. And Maurice and I went into purdah with her. Luckily term had ended and come September we were to have different schools. I was to be transferred to Beechwood, a private school ten miles outside town, where I knew none of the other pupils and where my father would never be mentioned, but Maurice, given a second chance of St Anthony's, firmly declined. There were several boys at the grammar who had errant fathers. They didn't give a damn. Neither did he. She gave in eventually, assuming he was thinking about her financial situation; actually he was deliberately weaving himself a crown of thorns. And perhaps it was a wise decision: having withstood those first few hideous weeks of the autumn term, he found he could withstand anything.

My transition, however, was one in the eye for my socialist papa. She sent him the bill, together with various bits and pieces he'd left behind him: odd cufflinks, out-of-date diaries, ghastly ties he'd discarded to the back of his wardrobe years ago. His photographs, all those glossy mementoes of his dashing operatic roles and the blurred snapshots showing teeth and hats at a rakish angle and captioned 'Me, Mac and Tiggers, Tangmere, '43', she tore up and burned. All except one, which I filched and locked in my jewellery box. I had to keep the key in my desk at school – she had no scruples about diaries, letters or left-around keys – so I didn't get to see it all that often, but I knew it anyway, by heart. I could close my eyes and see it: me, a shapeless dumpling of two years or thereabouts, anybody's child in my woollen bonnet and buttoned gaiters, and him, Alexander Blake, a fair-haired, blue-eyed man whose hideous demob suit couldn't totally disguise his fine bearing. This was the image of my father which I carried with me until I saw him again. It would have been better if she'd burned that photograph too.

CHAPTER TWO

'Is that you, Annie?'

However many times she said it, it never failed to grate. I grimaced in Aunt Kitty's direction and slung my lacrosse stick into the hall cupboard. Lacrosse was one of the mysteries of Beechwood. There were other mysteries: an entirely new vocabulary of slang, a certain irregular angle for wearing one's school hat, a code more rigid and complex than I had known at my previous school. One thing I learned quickly: to melt insignificantly into the background when other girls talked of their fathers.

'Had a good day, Annie?'

I went into the sitting-room, clearing my throat loudly.

Nothing, short of asking her point-blank to refrain, could intimate to her my loathing of this familiar liberty being taken with my name.

Five years had wreaked an incredible alteration in Aunt Kitty's appearance. She'd left our house a slim, nervous young woman with fear in her eyes, she returned to it fat, placid and indolent with a new name, four-year-old Jamie, and no husband.

'Deed poll,' Maurice explained laconically. 'You go somewhere and pay a few bob and you can call yourself what you like.'

'So she's no husband at all?'

'Nope. Just the brat.'

Maurice called Jamie the brat, or the poor wee fatherless cheild. I think the over-emphasis was to distinguish his own status as one who, though not having a resident father, certainly knew who that father was. I reacted no more strongly to Jamie than to regard him as a nuisance.

In the sitting-room he was discovering how many curtain-rings he could detach from their hooks with one tug. Aunt Kitty knitted on, impervious to the rending sound behind her. I removed his hands and gave him the button-box as substitute. The worst he could do with that was to swallow its contents. He was now five years old, and we all knew that normal five-year-olds should have outgrown curtain-tugging and button-swallowing. There was something wrong with Jamie. The child-psychologist, the same one who had failed so dismally with my bed-wetting, had a fancy name for it, but Maurice called him plain retarded.

'Kitty,' my mother called from the kitchen, 'will you come and give me a hand?'

My poor, houseproud mother – Aunt Kitty drove her to distraction. She was by nature slovenly, leaving dirty combs and rimed washbasins and miscellaneous débris in her wake, and Jamie was growing up into the same pattern. The pair of them remained, I think, because Aunt Kitty was my father's sister and my mother got a peculiar satisfaction from opening her door to the sister he had never been able to tolerate in the house.

'What is it tonight?'

'It's the Mesopotamians.' I had spread out my homework and was ruling out a nice accurate ziggurat into my history book.

She nodded sagely, though I'm sure she didn't have the faintest notion about the Mesopotamians. She'd often told me that my father had received her share of the brains, so to make up for her lack she took an inordinate interest in my scholastic career. 'Cissie, this girl of yours has got talent. She'll make the grade, you mark my words.' (My mother was called Cecilia, a beautiful name, I thought, and this philistine diminution of it annoyed me more perhaps than 'Annie'.) And my mother would nod and say that we'd see what we'd see. She was a good deal more shrewd than Aunt Kitty, realizing that there might be a germ of truth in my assertion that I was always top of the class because the others were thick.

At that moment she came in, a duster in her hand. All the day long she brushed and swept and polished and used her odd moments to dust what had already been dusted. A Lancashire woman, inherently houseproud, but there was something neurotic at the root of it.

Over the top of my ziggurat I compared the two of them. Or rather I contrasted them. Both were fair-haired, blue-eyed women, but my mother, at thirty-nine, five years older than her sister-in-law, had a slim figure and strong bone structure to her advantage. She'd be one of those women who look handsome at seventy, frown-lines, downward-curving mouth and all. Aunt Kitty was as shapeless as the garments she knitted. I longed to know what had changed her from the trim-ankled, narrow-waisted, pretty Aunt Kitty we'd known into a frump whose spare flesh spread over her inadequate corset.

Jamie had purloined a ball of wool and was busy winding it round the chair-legs and the table. 'Give up, Jamie,' Aunt Kitty said affectionately. He ignored her. Someone, later, would have the happy task of unwinding it. I could see my mother's fingers twitching and knew that she must be longing to give him a good crack. She daren't though; Jamie would roar like seven bulls and Aunt Kitty would pet him and say 'You've got to let children express themselves, Cis.' So in the end she left the room for the sake of her nerves.

Jamie stepped back, gazing with pride at his handiwork. With his long eyelashes and dark curls, he would have been a beautiful child if it hadn't been for the look of vacancy stamped ineradicably on his features. Maurice and I often speculated about his parentage, whether whoever-he-was had been a loony.

'But Aunt Kitty wouldn't go about with a loony.'

'I don't mean a raving loony, you idiot.'

Maurice made cretinous faces, eyes rolling, tongue hanging out of the side of his mouth. 'I mean someone who seemed OK but had a vital bit missing. It would have been better if he'd had another vital bit missing.'

He often spoke like that just for the sake of witnessing my discomfiture. My knowledge was limited: sex was something to do with the drawings of eggs and sperms with wriggly tails in the book my mother had once snatched away from me. It was something silly and disgusting one's parents had done once. It had no bearing, nor ever was going to have a bearing, upon my life, if I could help it.

Over dinner, the subject of Jamie cropped up again. Weren't there special schools, my mother wanted to know, placing the words in inverted commas, *resident* schools for children like Jamie?

'He's just a late developer,' Aunt Kitty said, calmly spooning apple crumble. 'Dr Spenser says he may take some time to catch up, but when he does there'll be no holding him.'

'That's precisely what I mean,' my mother said, jabbing at her pudding. 'In a special school they'd know how to encourage his development.'

'Cis, there's no substitute for a mother's love.'

She was like a pneumatic cushion. Tact just bounced off her. Maurice, who was reading *Antic Hay* under cover of the table-cloth, caught the tail-end of the conversation, looked up and said 'Jamie's just plain bats'.

Her countenance crumpled. She got up slowly and walked to the door. She paused and looked over her shoulder. 'You wouldn't have let *your* child be taken away from you, Cis.'

My mother's face went ugly and crimson. She launched into Maurice: 'Get out, get out!' And Maurice, for whom this was no hardship as he'd finished his meal and was getting out anyway, got out.

We were left together. I stared at my plate in case she decided to start on me just to prove that there was no favouritism.

She tapped her spoon on the edge of her saucer. 'Your Aunt Kitty's had a hard time,' she said. 'We've got to be kind. Bringing up a child on your own is bad enough but when you don't even know where the father is –'

'But I thought her husband was killed in the war.' That was the authorized version put about for the benefit of the neighbourhood. *Which* war was unclear. The big one had been over for seven years when Jamie was born.

She became aware of me. 'Shouldn't you be doing your homework?' she said.

'I've done it.'

'You can help me with the washing-up then.'

'I wanted to go to Mary Leslie's.'

Mary Leslie was my soul companion. Mary was a grammar school girl and therefore more worldly than most of the pupils who were being educated behind Beechwood's chaste, ladylike portals. Though three months younger than me, she had two pairs of nylon stockings and a bust.

My mother frowned and began to bang plates together. 'I wish you wouldn't go there so often. That house is like a tip.' The rhythm of the banging accelerated. I escaped. The Leslie household might be untidy, and what would you expect with five children and two adults in residence? But there was no plate-banging. Mr Leslie, who was Scottish, called me a bairn, and Mrs Leslie stuffed me with food to compensate for having no Daddy. And, all the while, the four younger Leslies rampaged around the room, kicking the furniture and each other, spilling food and tearing off wallpaper. Jamie would have been in heaven.

I went up to the attic. Since the reappearance of Aunt

Kitty, my mother had given up the matrimonial bedroom and moved into mine. Aunt Kitty now slumbered noisily in the big double bed, Maurice had refused to move, so I was quartered under the rafters. Not that I minded. It was a chance to be right away from everybody else, to pore over my treasures without interference. These treasures were: my father's photograph, a Woolworth's lipstick called 'Miami Pink', two somewhat blurred pictures torn from a newspaper of Pancho Gonzales in athletic pose, and a silk nightdress edged with white lace, my father's Christmas present to me, selected no doubt by Olivia Murray, which my mother had immediately confiscated and thrown into the boxroom and which I had retrieved.

Unlike Aunt Kitty, my mother knew where her husband was. We all did. He lived at 24 Beauchamp Road, Hampstead, N.W.3. 24 Beauchamp Road loomed large in my imagination: it had a long curving driveway, rhododendron bushes and bow windows. I had never seen it. Nor had he seen us since his departure. I believed this had something to do with him having to comply with her wishes in order that she would one day give him a divorce.

At the corner of the street I met Maurice, re-winding his bicycle chain. It had begun to rain and I was in my blazer. 'You'll get your death,' he said.

My health and the necessity to worry about it was impressed upon the whole family. I had had pneumonia three times and could subsequently summon up a sepulchral cough at will. It was a great asset during boring lessons. For a year now I had been emancipated from the liberty bodices and thick orange rolls of Thermogene which went between my vest and my chest and got up my nose and made me sneeze, but the jars of cod-liver oil and malt and the Vick Vapour Rub prevailed, even in the summer.

I continued to stand still. 'I've grown out of it.' Beechwood had worked marvels; it must have been all that lacrosse. 'Where are you going?'

He wiped his oily fingers on his blazer. 'Somewhere where little girls like you aren't allowed. Where are *you* going?'

'Mary Leslie's.'

'Mary the mare. Why do have such funny friends?'

My friends were funny! His were all called Les or Kev or Trev, huge loutish youths who rode motor-bikes and cat-called after me, 'Sister Anna will carry the banner,' then, falsetto, 'But I carried the banner yesterday and I'm in the family-way.' Then the final resounding 'You're in everybody's bloody way, but you'll still carry the banner.' They were destined to become haulage contractors, travelling salesmen in cheap flashy lines, electricians. My brother had a loftier destiny. Under the lamplight, he looked like my father must once have looked. None of his blemishes showed up.

'Would you like to go to the pictures?'

This offer was totally unexpected. Normally, he never accompanied me anywhere except under duress, his explanation being that, as we didn't look alike, people might not realize we were brother and sister and suspect him of cradle-snatching.

I had half a mind to reject him on principle, but I was gradually realizing that my secret, sedate, undemonstrative brother sometimes needed me. I accepted the offer. I needed him too.

CHAPTER THREE

On her fortieth birthday, while inspecting fish in the market-hall and comparing the relative merits of haddock and halibut, my mother passed out.

At half-past eleven I was summoned into the presence of the headmistress and as the words were leaving the messenger's lips my chest muscles tightened. Only death or catastrophe warranted that summons, unless you'd just gained a scholarship to Girton or somewhere, and I hadn't.

Maurice was standing in the corner of the study beside the long silk parchment-coloured curtains, just right of the John Piper. The headmistress's study was a completely different world from the rest of the utilitarian school; it shrieked the size of the fees from the Persian rugs on the floor to the crystal chandelier on the ceiling. All the time she was talking, I was looking over at Maurice and wondering why I hadn't noticed he was a grown man before and how stupid grown men looked in school blazers.

There was a taxi waiting outside to take us to the General Hospital where my mother was lying with an ulcer haemorrhaging away inside her. It could have been diagnosed long ago, but she hadn't been near a doctor since I was born.

Maurice stared out of one side window and I stared out of the other. To communicate our fear would be to give substance to our terrible imaginings. Deep down, we bled together but we were unable to touch on the surface.

Inside the hospital, a sharp-faced, red-haired nurse started to ask him about next-of-kin. I could positively hear the resentment bubbling up inside him and knew he wanted to hit her.

'Us,' he said. And she looked up from her form-filling and said briskly, 'Haven't you got a father?'

That was when his fists began to clench and unclench. 'We have a father,' he said, spacing his words in a way that made them sound like calculated insults, 'but he lives in London.'

'It's just a formality,' she said in a different kind of voice; you could tell she was unused to anyone challenging her authority.

It was Aunt Kitty, arriving breathless from the solicitors' office where she was now employed, who provided the necessary responsible adult signatures.

'Well, Sister, what's the situation?' She adopted her 'just watch and see how good I am at getting through to the nursing profession' face. The Sister was impervious to it. 'You are?' she said.

''Mrs Pendlebury, her sister-in-law.'

'They're going to operate,' the Sister said. 'Is there any chance of contacting the husband?'

Aunt Kitty fumbled in her handbag. Before she could find what she was looking for, Maurice had supplied the telephone number. I was quite taken aback; I hadn't thought Maurice was that interested, at least not interested enough to memorize the telephone number.

While Aunt Kitty went off with the Sister to her office telephone, we waited in a little room painted that colour, favoured by all establishments for its dreary neutrality, known as *eau-de-nil*, reading posters that advised us about free teeth and orange juice and the hazards of smoking. Through the glass doors we could see into the casualty department whose clientèle boasted nothing more alarming than crutches and bandaged thumbs. I still had in my hand the paperback copy of *The Tempest* which I'd been reading when I was called out of the classroom. Maurice sat with his thumbs in his belt and his legs extended, studying the zip of his trousers.

'What's the old man supposed to do?' he said. 'Charter a plane? Or give thanks to heaven?'

But the old man wasn't able to do either of those things. A moment later we learned from Aunt Kitty who had got through to a charlady, or whatever the posh Hampstead equivalent called herself, that Mr and Mrs Blake were on holiday, touring in France and had not left any address.

'This could be a case for Interpol,' Maurice said. 'Message to all mobiles: "Stop on sight middle-aged Englishman travelling with fancy lady, as his lawful wife is dangerously ill." Of course, middle-aged Englishman might just say "So what?" but that's the chance you have to take.'

Aunt Kitty looked at him askance. She didn't realize that his only alternative was to cry. My alternative was to read Act 1, Scene 1 of *The Tempest* over and over again even though the words ran into each other and made no sense.

'How long do we bloody wait here anyway?' Maurice asked no one in particular.

'Until the operation's over. And wipe that look off your face, Maurice. The best thing you could do would be to pray.'

We looked away from the embarrassing spectacle of Aunt Kitty, who had never professed any religious beliefs, sitting with her hands clasped and her head bowed, praying for a woman who wasn't all that fond of her and who would have been as embarrassed as we were if she'd known.

It seemed like a year of my life in that room. The only indication of time passing was that Maurice's stomach began to rumble and, later, a WVS worker brought in cups of tea on a trolley. I tried to adjust to the idea of being an orphan, or as near as dammit. Would we stay with Aunt Kitty, or would Olivia Murray take over our welfare? Who would there be to care that feather pillows gave me asthmatic attacks, or to come and console me when I woke up from a nightmare, or to kill the spiders which drove me into screaming hysterics? All the things, over and above the call of duty, that my mother did came flooding into my mind. Maurice wouldn't do them, merely because it wouldn't enter his head to do them. Aunt Kitty wouldn't do them, being too embroiled in her day-to-day slovenly chaos. Olivia Murray certainly wouldn't do them because she'd hate me for being me. My father, though doubtless willing, would not be capable. So I would end up in an orphanage, having my hair chopped short and ugly and wearing other people's cast-offs.

It was the surgeon himself who came to tell us that everything was going to be all right. He had been a boyhood friend of my father and kept Maurice talking for ages about cricket.

We were allowed in to see her that evening. She looked smaller and older and kept dozing off as we sought for conversation. A dreadful embarrassment had us all in its grip. It was difficult to adjust to the idea that our mother, whom we looked upon as being invulnerable, could betray us by thus exhibiting her mortality.

During the times when she was awake, her main concern was to inform Aunt Kitty of those domestic chores she'd left unfinished. Aunt Kitty smiled and patted her hand and said 'Yes, yes', but you could tell that not one word about the butcher, or the ironing, or the clean shirt for Maurice's speech day was penetrating; she was still in some kind of mystic daze due to the success of her appeal to the Almighty.

She came out of hospital the day term ended. I went to meet her in a taxi, my arms full of plimsolls and shoe-bags and flowers kindly donated by the school. I hoped that in the confusion she'd forget about my report which showed good marks but an unpleasant general remark to the effect that I was too easily satisfied.

She had other things on her mind. The doctor, in his pre-release summing-up, had told her that she must have a holiday. He'd suggested a proper convalescent home, but she wasn't going to be bossed around any longer by little chits of nurses and said so. He said all right then, go privately if she preferred to, but go she must or he wouldn't be responsible.

At home we held an awkward conference. Aunt Kitty immediately began to coo about the salubrious delights of Hastings and Hove. My mother drew mental frontiers between Morecambe and Llandudno. They compromised at Colwyn Bay. My mother hoped that we would be able to book sufficient accommodation for all of us. Maurice and I let out groans in unison. His refusal was adamant, mine was tentative. He was almost eighteen, quite capable of opening a packet of cornflakes or frying a piece of steak. He had absolutely no desire to walk the sandy boulevards of Colwyn Bay. He and Trevor Owen were going to spend the whole of the Easter holiday building a sports car out of bits and pieces in Trevor Owen's brother's garage.

At that her face stiffened. Trevor Owen's brother's garage had once belonged to my father. But she couldn't take Maurice by force, so she turned on me instead. Did I seriously think that she'd leave a thirteen-year-old alone in the house?

'I'll stay and look after them, Cis.'

Aunt Kitty had not yet emerged from her state of grace. Sacrifices were very much her line of country. I thought joyfully of a fortnight's total freedom to come and go as I pleased. Aunt Kitty would never notice whether we were in the house or not.

But my mother, very properly, regarded that suggestion as worse than leaving us alone. Also she needed Aunt Kitty's moral support, not having the self-confidence to be able to stay comfortably in a hotel on her own. The vistas of glorious licence faded and were succeeded by the narrow confines of Colwyn Bay.

My role, as I knew it would be, was that of nursemaid. While my mother and my aunt sat shivering in deckchairs on the forecourt of the Highlea Hotel, I was ushered forth to show the sights to Jamie. It was a wet, blustery Easter. There wasn't a young person in sight. I always walked rapidly, head down, hands deep in my pockets, but never succeeded in leaving Jamie behind. Passers-by said, 'What a sweet child,' because, at first glance, he did look a bit Mabel Lucie Atwell; it was only closer acquaintanceship that revealed his unattractive qualities.

After a fortnight's boredom, home seemed a place of absorbing distractions. In my absence Mary had become friendly with Rachel Conway, the doctor's daughter, and I wondered if I would be *de trop*, but after a slight initial coolness I was received back into the fold. Maurice was debonair, slapping me on the back and saying 'How was Colwyn Bay?' making Colwyn Bay sound as exotic and sinister as Casablanca – and out till all hours, wearing his best clothes and an aroma that lingered in his wake.

But Maurice had either not my native cunning or had underestimated the thoroughness of my mother's habitual prying.

The bomb fell one Saturday morning while she was sorting out what needed to be sent to the cleaner's before we went back to school. I was setting the table for lunch. Maurice, sprawled in an arm-chair, was flicking through a scientific magazine. Whenever he was in the house he sprawled. When it was time for him to be off he became a dynamo of brisk activity.

We heard her feet come running down the stairs, thudding on each step. We raised our eyebrows. She didn't run down the stairs unless there was a very good reason for doing so because of raising dust. She stood in the doorway, every line of her face turned downwards, her eyes glittering, a small packet in her hand.

'I want you.'

One look at Maurice's face and I knew it wasn't me she wanted. He was blushing. I hadn't seen Maurice blush since he forgot his lines during a Nativity Play when he was ten.

She stood there, motionless, while he crossed the room. Then I heard their footsteps re-ascending the stairs and his one comment that broke the silent tension: 'I'm not twelve years old any more, you know.' After that I could make out nothing comprehensible from their raised and mingled voices, hers strident, his staccato and resonant. Five minutes later there were footsteps again, two at a time, his footsteps, and then a shuddering crash as the front door banged behind him. She didn't reappear until she smelled the potatoes burning and then she was wearing her *mater dolorosa* face. She and I ate our lunch together and not one word did she utter and, for the sake of self-preservation, neither did I.

Every Saturday afternoon, without fail, she went to the library. She didn't allow the present state of alarm to change her routine, and it was obvious that Maurice had waited for her departure before returning to the house.

I followed him into the kitchen. He was raiding the fridge.

'What was all the fuss about?'

'I'm getting out of this rotten hole, just as soon as I can, that's what all the fuss is about,' he said, dismembering a cooked chicken with more fervour than finesse.

'But what was up with her?'

'She found something nasty in the woodshed. And serve her right too.'

'But *what*?'

'Never bloody mind what. Her trouble is that she can't get it into her head that I'm no longer the little boy in the sailor-suit who used to recite nursery rhymes. She called me a sexual maniac, not just a sex maniac, a *sexual* maniac. It killed me. Said I was just like my father. It seems the old fellow was always after his oats.'

'Was it something to do with Jenny Abbot?' I said hesitantly. Jenny Abbot was the loosest girl in the grammar school. Rumour had it that Jenny Abbot had had sexual intercourse with five different boys during one night at a party. I had seen Maurice talking to her a few days ago at the corner of the street.

'Jenny Abbot!' he said scornfully. 'I wouldn't touch Jenny Abbot with somebody else's.'

He leaned against the kitchen table, devouring his chicken leg. 'She'll be seeing the back of me just as soon as I can get somewhere else.'

'What do you mean?'

'I could get a flat with Trev. He's been wanting to get out too.'

'And what would you live on?' The whole idea was too preposterous to be a threat. And what about those twin gods, 'A' levels and university?

'There are plenty of jobs,' he said calmly. 'Eric Owen would take me on tomorrow. And you can take exams externally, you know. We've done the whole of the syllabus. It's only a question of revision.'

So it was all quite feasible. Maurice could go and I could be left here in this house of gloom listening to my mother's sighs and helping to wind Aunt Kitty's knitting wool. It was chiefly the thought of that dire fate that allowed me to voice what I'd discovered a long time ago: 'It's only because she loves you that she carries on so. She loves you far more than she loves anyone else.'

'Well, if it's love that makes people behave like she does,' he said, 'I'd rather do without it.'

He didn't go. It wasn't really worth the effort. There were only a few months left before he would leave for university. After a week of silence and avoiding each other, they reached a state of uneasy truce. She threw what she'd found into the dustbin. I saw it when I was disposing of some potato-peelings. The packet contained only one where, I gathered, there should have been three. (I'd asked Rachel, the doctor's daughter, who proved to be surprisingly ignorant; it was Mary Leslie, with all those brothers and sisters, who had enlightened me.) I replaced the bin-lid. There was a queer fluttery feeling in the pit of my stomach. How strange it seemed that Maurice should be initiated into that privileged society whose behaviour was still a total mystery to me.

CHAPTER FOUR

Berenice Butler was the most mature girl in Beechwood's Upper Sixth. She was of medium height and medium size with short curly fair hair and the kind of social comportment that made parents believe that Beechwood might work wonders for their daughters too.

Maurice met her during a week-end field-study course at Flatford Mill. I imagined them, walking side by side through the salt marshes, their intimacy deepening with every bit of silver goosefoot and sea lavender that was collected, docketed and analysed, perhaps even sharing a test-tube in the laboratory of an evening. At any rate, I was certain that intimacy with Berenice Butler would not extend as far as sharing the contents of small square-ish packets.

She was the first girl he'd ever brought home to tea; her predecessors had enjoyed his patronage at the cinema, or the tennis club or, quite conceivably, on a bench after dark in the municipal park. One or two had progressed as far as sitting stiffly on the edge of the sofa making polite noises at Aunt Kitty's monologue while they waited for him, but none before had been magnified by the official stamp of being worthy of Sunday afternoon tea.

It was not an occasion that I viewed with rejoicing. Firstly, Berenice was my senior in every respect: age, status and authority; secondly, I didn't see why my Sunday afternoon should be disorganized by having to pass the scones while my mother made use of a golden opportunity to draw her out upon the subject of my scholastic progress.

'Are we expecting the Queen Mother?' I asked as, yet again, she took the dustpan and brush to the area around my feet. 'Or is it the Archbishop of Canterbury?'

'Oh, didn't you know?' Maurice hovered over her as he looked in the mirror to adjust his tie. 'We've invited the sanitary inspector. I can see a crumb, Mother, by the bookcase. It won't do. We shall be evicted and put into the care of the council.'

She just carried on sweeping. 'If you don't care what impression this girl gets of your home,' she said, 'I do.'

Aunt Kitty and Jamie had been shooed out to the park until tea-time so that they could confine their messy activities to the great outdoors. I looked around me at the room that was so meticulously washed and polished. If it had been beautiful, I could have understood her obsession, but it was just an ordinary room in an ordinary Accrington-brick house filled with rather bulky, nondescript furniture. When I got a house I'd carpet it from wall to wall in blue six inches thick and have long cherry velvet curtains at the windows and lie on the floor sipping amontillado sherry and scattering cake-crumbs with joyous abandonment.

We'd got ready much too early. It meant that we had to sit around, bored to tears, in our Sunday finery, all longing to occupy ourselves but knowing that the moment we picked up a book or started sewing she'd appear.

I'd spent a long time tarting myself up. It was the fashion that year to wear layers of stiffened petticoats under one's skirt, ropes of plastic beads down to one's navel and shoes with long pointed toes. I must have looked like an opened parasol. Berenice was not fashion's slave and looked all the better for it. I would have looked dowdy wearing a plain skirt and blouse like hers. She looked impeccable and had struck exactly the right note for Sunday afternoon visiting.

Her first diplomatic act was to make a play for Jamie who, to my amazement, didn't stick out his tongue at her as was his usual wont with strangers, but allowed himself to be questioned, about his school, his interests, his toys. Within minutes he was demonstrating how one hitched on a goods-wagon to the back of a locomotive. Aunt Kitty was in raptures. My mother, Judas that she was, smiled fondly.

'I didn't see you in church this morning, Anna.'

That wiped all fond smiles from my mother's face immediately. Mary Leslie and I had lately forsaken morning service in order to hang over the rugby field fence. Our mothers imagined we were chanting the *Te Deum*; the rugby players were much too old for us.

'I was at the back, in the gallery.'

Her eyebrows shot up and I knew that she must have been at the back in the gallery too, and for once in my life I thanked providence for Aunt Kitty who launched into an account of the exciting new policy of free-expression that prevailed in Jamie's school.

'They're encouraged, you see, to do exactly what comes into their heads because every one of us has some talent. That's a lovely thought, isn't it? If only we could recognize it, of course –'

It seemed to me that what came into Jamie's head was chiefly anti-social behaviour – peeing down the outside drain or throwing lumps of Plasticine so high that they stuck to the ceiling. But that afternoon he was transfigured, gravely handing round plates and using his table-napkin with an excess of zeal for the correct purpose instead of wiping his nose on it as usual.

I consumed jam tarts and star-shaped buns (we'd had a baking jamboree), and thought what a little traitor he was and how I'd been looking forward to seeing Berenice's discomfiture if he'd wiped sticky fingers on her skirt or said 'Bugger'. Not that I hadn't *attempted* to be well-disposed towards her but the remark about church, though doubtless devoid of evil intent, had weighted the scales.

'I see your mother sometimes in the library, Berenice,' my mother said. And Berenice said yes, *her* mother had reported seeing *my* mother in the library sometimes too. Which remarks just about summed up the general sparkling level of the conversation. Berenice's mother was a very grand lady who sat on a great number of committees and had the kind of shatteringly refined accent that made you wince and run for cover. Her father was the local property magnate and had just about learned to tack on his aitches, which probably accounted for her mother's enormous over-compensation. Berenice was promised 'a little car' if her exam results came up to scratch. They were that sort of family.

'Are you beginning to get nervous?' my mother asked her.

The results were due in a fortnight. One was asked to leave a stamped, addressed envelope at school so they could be sent on. I remembered the other occasion, two years ago, when Maurice and I had awaited the lunchtime post, his face white with apprehension and my stomach churning in sympathy.

Berenice, however, seemed to anticipate no such traumas. 'Oh, I don't think I've done badly,' she said, eyes cast modestly down upon her slice of Dundee cake. 'I was lucky with the papers.' She had a tentative university place already, at London.

Maurice wasn't making any great contribution to the conversation. I caught his eye and winked. Perhaps we would launch into our renowned double-act: 'Knock-knock.' 'Who's there?' 'Peter.' 'Peter who?' 'Peter night before you go to bed.' But he pursed his lips and shook his head. Berenice, no doubt, would consider it vulgar and extremely childish. And Berenice was not to be offended.

I looked from him to her, wondering what affinity they could possibly have beyond a common interest in that infantile specimen-collecting. What had Berenice got that the others hadn't had? Poor Frances Mottram who had begged and begged me to invite her to tea just so that she might have a glimpse of him in his natural habitat; he'd taken one look at her, sitting shyly at our piano, picking out 'Claire de Lune', announced that he felt his allergy coming on and disappeared to his room until she'd gone. Valerie Something-or-Other whom he'd stood up two nights running outside the Odeon cinema while his friends walked up and down shouting, 'Will I do instead, love?' The Caroline girl to whose splendid ancestral home, five miles out of town, I had been sent on my bicycle to deliver the note that severed all connection. Others, who had come and gone and disappeared into the mists of obscurity. This was different. I just wished that the instrument of his alteration had been somebody other than Berenice Butler.

Long before that wretched afternoon came to an end, it was obvious that she was all that was to be desired from my mother's point of view: a polite, nicely-brought-up girl without a dirty habit in sight. Just the sort of girl she would have liked for a daughter instead of the one she had who refused, on principle, to be charming to people she didn't like and who cleaned the finger-nails of one hand with the finger-nails of the other.

Then came the crowning Sunday of them all. It was a celebration-cum-wake. The results were out. Both Maurice and Berenice had passed everything they should have passed, brilliantly. Berenice had been awarded a Major and Maurice a State Scholarship. My mother did everything but put up a plaque on the front gate to commemorate the occasion. Her son, Maurice, the boy she'd brought up single-handed through his difficult adolescence, succeeding where other boys with every advantage in the world had failed.

'I thought you said you'd done stinking papers,' I said to him crossly when he was going about crowing.

'I did,' he said. 'By my standards. Their standards obviously aren't so high.'

But my mother's maternal pride was soon too much for him. 'Put another record on,' he'd say as she invited in yet another of the neighbours to behold the magic piece of paper that proclaimed him to be a genius, or as near as made no difference.

She pretty soon did put on another record. Maurice had applied to three Universities: Oxford, London and Manchester. All three were prepared to welcome him with open arms.

'You'll accept Manchester, of course?' she said. Manchester was an hour away by train. He could live at home where she could keep her eye on him. London was unthinkable anyway. If she'd known he was going to apply to London she'd have nipped it right in the bud. London, as well as containing a University, contained number 24 Beauchamp Road. I believe my mother envisaged the metropolis as being no larger than a good-sized village where every one of the inhabitants was bound, sooner or later, to turn a corner and bump into the others.

But, entreat and weep though she might, it was for

London he was bound. He attempted, patiently, to explain: London offered the course that best suited him, he had absolutely no ulterior motives, least of all number 24 Beauchamp Road, or even Berenice, who was going to Bedford College.

But privately he told me that she must be round the twist if she imagined he was going to come home to Mother every night. Why did she think people went to University? I wasn't very sure myself, but since delving into the literature he'd received concerning societies and recreational facilities and Freshers' Balls, it seemed a somewhat more alluring prospect.

Since he'd left, three years ago, my father had corresponded with us solely through Christmas and birthday presents. But, soon after Maurice's success, a letter arrived for him bearing a Hampstead postmark, a letter which was left ignored, in chilly isolation on the mantelpiece, until he got back from cricket practice.

I believe handwriting to be as good a representation of character as anything else. My mother's was small and cramped, my own was enormous, not yet formed, Maurice's was like my father's: clear, devoid of frills, very masculine; to receive a letter from either of them was to receive a well-considered compliment. The Hampstead letter was no exception. There was no woolly generalization, no facile insincerity, just a few straightforward paragraphs of congratulation and an expression of the hope that Maurice would realize that our father's house was to be regarded as his home, now that he was coming to London.

'How did he know?'

'I wrote him.'

'And *will* you go to see him?' At the end of the letter there was a line, scored out until it was indecipherable, followed by 'I think of you and little Anna always'.

'I might just pop in to see how the extra-marital ménage is progressing, if I have the time,' he said with false panache. Of course he would go, Olivia Murray or no. In London he would be his own master, while I was stuck at home, imprisoned by a child's dependance. I was filled with an acute rage. Other people's parents were separated but other people's parents could still be civilized. Why didn't he contact us more often? How could some woman mean more to him than his own flesh and blood?

I wished the letter had never arrived. It evoked all the memories I had thought were safely buried: the way he sang, the Sunday drives we used to take, and how, away from my mother, he seemed younger, more frivolous and debonair, the nights he'd sat up with me when I had pneumonia, refilling hot water bottles and plying the Lucozade, his disproportionate pride in my every small achievement.

Trains ran direct from Manchester to London. A few hours there and a few hours back. One day I'd acquire the money and the opportunity. I'd be on my way to Beauchamp Road, to the half-timbered house with the bow windows and the rhododendron bushes in whose gracious blue-carpeted drawing-room Olivia Murray dispensed china tea and cultured conversation. If and when my mother found out, it would be too late to stop me.

CHAPTER FIVE

There was a 'For Sale' notice in the front garden of the house that used to belong to Olivia Murray. I made a detour on my way home from school one afternoon to look in at the ground floor windows and see what changes the previous occupants had wrought since Olivia Murray entertained in her Wedgewood-blue drawing-room and no doubt committed adultery upon the rose-pink bed.

The house was situated in the centre of town at one corner of a quiet square of Regency houses, an oasis between the railway station and the market-hall. It had the ideal position for a house of assignation in that a narrow lane ran beside it, an artery connecting the busiest areas of the town, making it impossible for anyone to distinguish whether Olivia Murray was being visited or merely side-tracked for the sake of a short-cut.

Trinity Square looked at its best in the early autumn: eight houses and the railed-off plot of grass between them, a profusion of golden rod and guelder roses, an aura of stillness and dignified wealth. No children played in Trinity Square; it was a select residential area whence came childless widows to live upon the interest of their late husbands' fortunes.

The windows were grimed with dirt but I could still make out the blue of the walls, the Adam fireplace, the white icing-sugar cornices and the shelved alcoves each side of the chimney breast upon which used to be displayed fragile figurines of jade and porcelain, a silver-framed photograph or two and a perpetually-nodding Chinese mandarin. I wondered if the bedroom still smelled of jasmine. I remembered the glinting array of glass bottles on the white lacquered dressing-table, the rose velvet curtains and the picture of Pierrot on the wall, a papery yellow tea-rose in a narrow copper jug, the alabaster nymph who supported an almond-coloured lampshade, the white rug bedside the bed, so luxurious you slipped off your shoes for the sensual delight of digging your toes into its depths, the frilled pink peignoir that hung behind the door. All this under the pretence of going to the lavatory.

Our association with Olivia Murray had begun with a car. Her chauffeur had been paid off and the Bentley was too big and lumbersome. She needed something small and quick and easily garaged. During the period while she dallied between the MG and the Sunbeam, the Blake family were added to her visiting list.

She was a tall, small-boned, pale-skinned woman in her middle thirties with hair that contained every colour of autumn. Usually she wore it coiled into a chignon, but once I saw it down over the shoulders of her green crêpe dress; she looked like a Botticelli maiden: creamy, round-bosomed, ethereal.

But drowsy boredom was my chief memory of those teas in the garden: the bees' drone, the roses' winy scent, the fat golden fish that flopped idly in the pond around the sundial, the elongated navy-blue shadows on the grass, my green-stained knees patterned criss-cross with the pressure of kneeling, sucking cream soda through a striped straw, listening to my father being urbane and my mother, shy and uncomfortable, striving to join in the silvery small talk that was *de rigueur* at Olivia Murray's tea parties.

Trinity clock chimed five. It was time to stop loitering without intent. I turned my back upon the white and blue house that had witnessed the beginning of something that was to change the lives of five people, seven people, if you were to count the re-housing of Aunt Kitty and her son.

Trinity Square looked prosperous and elegant; Tennyson Avenue looked prosperous and ugly – an endless vista of red-brick houses squared off with privet, distinguished only by the daring use of blue paint or vermilion here and there. Good solid residences, well-constructed, unlikely to depreciate in the property market, built for good, solid, unimaginative people. I stood at the gate and surveyed our particular specimen: bay windows, green drainpipes, stained-glass fanlight above the door, brass doorstep, bleak, regular laurel bushes. I thought of the back garden where once raspberries and sharp tangy blackcurrants grew, now a wilderness overgrown with briar and willow-herb and a riot of dandelions, because nobody could be bothered with it and little old men with spades and trowels were so hard to get. I put my key in the front door and envisaged what awaited me: shepherd's pie and rhubarb tart and Aunt Kitty calling me 'Annie' and Jamie thrusting some grotesque drawing executed at school under my nose for inspection and my mother's sharp, nervous comments as though expecting calamity to strike at any moment, the florid carpets and bulging, bow-legged oak furniture, the dark at the top of the attic stairs and the damp stain on the ceiling, the square patch on the bedroom wallpaper where once the wedding photographs had hung, still clean, still bereft.

Maurice had been gone a year and I missed his leavening presence in our muted household. He wrote infrequently and had spent all but two weeks of the long vacation 'leaning on a spade' on a building site in West London. During those two weeks he'd been reticent about his life in the great metrollops, as he called it, and got me to answer the phone for fear it was Berenice in which case he was mostly out.

'Is it all off then – the grand passion?' I'd asked him.

'Not so much off as in abeyance while I get some living done.'

He was also reticent about his visits to Beauchamp Road. I drove him distracted with my oft-repeated queries as to the nature of the house, the state of their relationship, the appearance of Olivia Murray. 'It's quite a nice house, they seem quite happy, and they both look the same as ever. At their age people don't seem to change much.' The things I really wanted to know: whether they kissed each other, whether they laughed at one another's jokes, whether there was an atmosphere of serenity in that house, he either couldn't or wouldn't tell me.

I'd received a letter from him that morning. It was brief and very nearly to the point:

'Dear Anna,

Are you yet a big enough girl to jump on to a train at Manchester and jump off it again at Euston? If so, how about the week-end after next? You could stay at Pat and Rona's place on the Saturday night and go back Sunday. It's about time you saw how the other ninety-five per cent lives and what's in store for you if you're a good girl and pass all your exams. If the idea appeals, let me know and I'll write and smooth it over with Mama, so she won't get into a fever about it.

Yours etc.,

Maurice

P.S. Don't forget your rubber sheet.'

I'd scribbled a reply during the first period history lesson and posted it on my way home. I trembled just thinking about it. I knew it wasn't Maurice who was anxious to see me, Maurice was merely a go-between. The question was, would my mother realize that too? However, if he wrote by return of post, which was unlikely, she wouldn't get it until Thursday at the soonest, and sufficient unto the day . . .

*

'What silly nonsense is this?' my mother said, putting on her reading glasses the better to see just what silly nonsense was propounded in Maurice's letter. 'Going to London. Staying with somebody whose name I can't make out. Maurice ought to know better.'

'Her name's Rona,' I said, peering over her shoulder at Maurice's list of half-truths.

'Rona. That's a funny sort of a name. And who's she supposed to be, anyway?'

'It says. She's a student in his department. She shares a flat with some other girls in Fulham.'

I kept my fingers tightly crossed behind my back. I had been extra charming and helpful ever since I'd received Maurice's letter, read my horoscope daily, observed and attempted to translate all omens, rehearsed sensible answers to all objections she might raise. In fact, so well-rehearsed was I, the words of justification trembling on my lips, that she quite took the wind out of my sails when she said, 'Well, I suppose Maurice has got enough sense to see you don't come to any harm. Though why you should want to go there and what you'll do, I can't imagine.'

'But I've never *been* to London. I've never seen the Tower, or the National Gallery, or the Victoria and Albert. Everyone else at school has been to London *millions* of times.'

Neither had she seen the Tower and so on, and she was none the worse for it. I played my trump card: how did she think I *felt* when all the other girls could boast about where they'd been and I had to keep silent?

'You've been to the Lake District,' she said, 'and Llandudno and Colwyn Bay.'

But the seed was sown. A little while later she was saying I hadn't any underwear fit to be seen and was I aware of all the pitfalls inherent in entering empty railway carriages? The proviso came later: 'You'll stay with Maurice all the time? You won't go wandering off on your own?' And it wasn't the idea of homicidal maniacs or slave-traders that was bothering her. I had practised sincerity in the mirror. In my two monosyllabic replies, affirmative and negative, I managed to convey that, although she couldn't say it, I knew exactly what she meant and that I wouldn't be found dead within a mile of Beauchamp Road.

Aunt Kitty came in as we were discussing train reservations and vests and whether it would be warmer or colder in London.

'Give my love to Piccadilly,' she said, rolling her eyes in an expression of sentimental idiocy, before launching into an account of her life and times in the big city: Horseguards' Parade, the Crown Jewels, Buckingham Palace, tea at Lyons. I had visions of Aunt Kitty, with her maps and guide-books and inane comments, the laughing-stock of everybody within earshot.

Saturday morning didn't dawn, it emerged, through a low-lying pall of thin yellow fog. The laurel bushes, ghostly through the window, dripped tears of moisture, footsteps in the road were muffled, the postman's wet coat steamed as he trundled up the garden path.

'You'll never get there. You'll never get there. They'll stop the trains and you'll be stranded. I'd better ring up and call the whole thing off.'

I fiddled with my cornflakes and wished to God that she'd be quiet. My heart was pounding and my stomach jelly as it was without her predictions of catastrophe. 'It'll clear. It always does when it's this early.'

'Well, I'm coming with you to ask someone at the station whether the trains are getting through. And if it's at all doubtful, you're coming straight back.'

At the station, I stood away from her, beside the bookstall, mortified, while she questioned a porter who said, 'Lady, if you're going to be on it, we'll get it there in half the time.'

'It's not me,' she said stiffly. She hated that sort of facetious familiarity. 'It's my daughter.'

'All the same, love,' he said, looking around for some helpless infant child, no doubt. 'We'll get her there.'

'Well it sounds all right,' she said doubtfully, coming over to join me. 'But don't forget, I want a telephone call just as soon as you get there. And be sure to get on the right platform at Manchester.'

I stared fiercely at the *Guardian* headlines. I tried to

pretend she had nothing at all to do with me.

'It's all very well looking like that,' she said, 'but it's happened to better people than you. People who thought they were going to Scotland ending up in Devon.'

'It's in, it's in,' I said frantically, gesturing vaguely through the barrier. It wasn't in, but my urgency convinced her. 'Goodbye. I'll phone you.' I kissed her and rushed through to the platform. She was still talking about making sure the sheets were aired after I'd gone.

By the time we reached the Midlands the fog had dispersed – we left it behind in shreds, adhering to trees, fences, bridges, like scraps of rotting cerement – now there was sky to be seen and the gentler, lusher characteristics of England's southern half. I craned my neck to try to catch the names of sub-stations, but the train flashed by too quickly and I caught only the first or last two letters. My stomach was at peace; it would remain that way until Euston loomed and then it would begin to churn as I reached down my case, wondering whether Maurice had mistaken the time, the station, changed beyond all recognition, or had just plain forgotten about me.

He was there of course, prominent, unmistakable, among the throng of waiting welcomers. I saw him before he saw me and I thought how nice-looking he was, how tall and straight and superior he stood in the nondescript ranks of humanity.

'So you made it.' He relieved me of my case and we walked uphill towards the exit, a little shy of each other yet, a little afraid of showing too much enthusiasm.

We were making for the Tube entrance when I remembered the telephone call.

'Oh, Jesus,' he said. 'Can't she get it into her head it's two hundred miles you've come, not two thousand? Over there.'

After I'd assured her that I was actually in London, in one piece, and she'd told me to watch my purse and see that nobody cut the strap of my shoulder-bag, and Maurice and I had embarked on the dreadfully complicated network of escalators and tunnels and trains and pretty-coloured maps that led eventually to Fulham Broadway, he read me a long lecture about independence and breaking the cord. Which was all very well for him; he'd escaped.

As we neared our destination I asked him nervously about Rona and Pat.

'They're both post-grad,' he said. 'Pat is a bit of a nutter, but Rona'll see you're OK. And they'll never notice another one in the flat. The place is crawling with females.'

The information did little to alleviate my misgivings. I imagined hordes of very elegant, superior girls either ignoring me totally, or being too up-stage for words.

In Fulham we found the decaying front door of the tall terraced house left open and proceeded straight up the lino'd stairs. Maurice called, 'Ro-na, Ro-na. Come out from wherever you are.' And a door opened and a voice said, 'Who is it? Is that you, Maurice?'

'No. It's the moral welfare.'

The voice materialized. Small, limpid-eyed, with dark hair cut in Dutch doll fashion, that was Rona, running down the stairs to welcome me, saying, 'Anna, how nice to see you,' evoking immediate liking for her impulsiveness, her prettiness, her light put-you-at-your-ease chatter.

We went into their huge communal sitting-room; there were four distinct areas of occupation, one meticulously tidy, the other three strewn with every kind of aid to good living imaginable: Lautrec posters, bundles of material in various stages of dress-making, painted mugs and wooden bowls, an easel and a jam-jar full of brushes, an electric kettle, three grimacing Negro masks, balls of wool, one knitting needle, a gold brocade tunic, a vase of dried grasses, and books – books everywhere, expensive art-reproduction books, ancient and dilapidated textbooks, paperbacks with lurid covers. I breathed in hard through my nose. I had never before in my life been in such a mess of creativity.

'It's a bit of a pig-sty,' Rona said. 'But it's the only way we could live.' She removed a paint-encrusted palette from a chair-seat. 'Janet's the painter. She's gone to the West Country for a couple of days.'

'Oh yes?' Maurice said slowly. 'She's a bugger for

punishment, isn't she?'

'Well.' Rona stroked the fringe of an Indian shawl that was thrown over the back of the sofa. 'She thinks they ought to talk it out.'

'*Talk* it out? That's a laugh. If I know that git, it's not talking they'll be doing.'

He spread himself elegantly into an arm-chair. 'Where are the other two wise virgins then?'

'Trimming our lamps, of course. What else?'

Through the open doorway came a stunning, olive-skinned beauty wearing a flame-red coat and a matching scarf tied turban-wise around her black hair. 'Don't you be calling me a virgin, Maurice Blake. It's a downright slander. Oh. Pardon me.' She registered my presence. 'Nobody announced guests before I opened my trap. You're Anna, I take it? I'm Pat and this person behind all the shopping is Trixie. Come and say hallo, Trix.'

Trixie put down her baskets and her bags and stuck out a hand in my direction. She had very short hair, a square, unmade-up face, horribly tobacco-stained fingers and wore what appeared to be a two-piece boiler suit. I couldn't take my eyes off Trixie.

'Well, girls, what's on the me and you for today?' Maurice said after he'd greeted them with 'Hallo, Trix. How's tricks?'

Pat took off her coat to reveal a white dress of some silky stuff that fitted like skin. I lowered my eyes from those splendidly-contoured thighs and breasts. She made me feel like a stick-insect.

'I take it you're staying?'

'We-e-ll, it makes a change from the Savoy, doesn't it? Who else are you expecting to drop by?'

'Frank and Eddy, probably, pro*vided* they bring along the vino. And Jake of course. Of course Jake. It just wouldn't be mealtime without Jake.'

'I'll show you your bedroom and things, Anna,' Rona said quickly. 'You've got Janet's bed. I've changed the sheets.'

'I should *hope* so,' Maurice said. And Pat winked at him and exposed her teeth in a curving cat-like grin.

Lunch, which consisted of watercress soup, stew dignified with the name of goulash and pieces of shop-bought Swiss roll, all washed down with some kind of red wine, so sour it set my teeth on edge, passed in a series of sharply-glittering images, my head turning from one to another in such quick succession that my neck ached.

There were eight of us seated round the scarred oak table, elbow to elbow, foot to foot. The three newcomers were Eddy, who talked like a lord and ate like a navvy; Frank, who slumped over his food and who was either drunk or naturally inarticulate – and Jake. Jake smiled at me and filled my glass. 'Are you lost in this asylum?' Jake said. 'It's no fit place for big-eyed girls.' Jake brought over an art book and said, 'You're the spitting image. Did you know?' flicking through the pages until he reached a Madonna by Bernardino Luini, a Madonna with curving cheeks and heavy-lidded, modestly downcast eyes. Jake looked away so that I could blush unheeded. 'What do you like doing?' Jake said. 'What will you be?' And straight off, without qualm or preamble, I told Jake what I hadn't told anybody else: that I was going to be the most celebrated actress since Bernhardt.

At the other side of the table, Maurice, leering, said, 'What *is* that word that means an unhealthy interest in young girls?'

'Nymphet-mania,' Eddy supplied.

Jake said, 'What *is* that word that means having the right-shaped nose for searching out bad smells?'

Rona started a conversation with him about a production of *Macbeth* they'd all been to see the previous night. I listened to him – he talked of 'nuances' and 'dramatic ploys' and 'pale representations' – and watched his emphatic profile. He had greenish eyes and a chin that was not quite strong enough to sustain his dominant nose and definite mouth. His hair was long and black and his skin was smooth and pale. I looked at him and thought of russet velvet and mandolins and white ruffled shirts, open to the waist. I longed to know everything about him.

Trixie sat on my left, hacking great lumps off a roll of French bread with which to mop up her stew. She'd rolled up her sleeves and you could see the muscles rippling along her faintly-tanned forearms.

'Are you at the university?' I ventured.

Her eyes were red-veined. 'Wouldn't you say,' she said, 'that I was a little old for that?'

'How old *are* you, Trix?' Frank said, surfacing from his torpor to seize the largest piece of Swiss roll.

'Trix is ageless,' said Maurice, 'infinite like the universe. Age shall not wither Trix, nor custom stale . . .'

'Thirty-two last birthday,' Trixie said prosaically.

'Tell us about your rotten childhood, Trix.' It was Maurice again, leaning avidly across the table. There seemed to be a certain malice in his amusement. 'About the nasty time before the war when your mum used to have to entertain soldiers in order to buy you new shoes and a few crusts of bread.'

'Shut up, Maurice,' Pat said. But Trixie didn't look at all discountenanced. She merely said, 'You've heard it all before,' and continued to mop her plate.

Then the general conversation turned to the affairs of the absent Janet and what an unmitigated fool the absent Janet was proving herself to be.

'I just hope she's saving up her pennies,' Pat said, 'because the same thing's going to happen. I can see it coming.'

'Perhaps she'll manage a marriage licence this time,' Eddy said.

'You're joking, of course. You weren't here at the time. It was Trix and I who had to do the mopping-up – literally. The first and last time too.' The expression on Pat's face was probably the nearest she ever got to looking ugly. 'I wouldn't mind, but all because of that –' She sought for the word.

'Randy runt,' said Maurice. 'Slimy, unwashed, randy little runt.'

'Careful,' Jake said. 'You are not in the Union bar now, brother.'

'You're right, of course, as ever. Jake Stavely, the Diplomatic Service needs you. They'll get you too, I shouldn't wonder. Well, folks,' he said, patting his stomach, 'that were a grand bellyful, as they say down t'pit around where I come from. If there's nothing else coming, you will please to excuse me as I am going to wheel *ma petite soeur* around the town, leaving the rest of you to co-habit in peace. Come on, kiddywinks, grab your hat.'

'What time will you be back?' asked Rona. 'I can put a bottle in for Anna.'

Everybody except Jake guffawed. 'Put a bottle in for Anna,' Maurice said. 'Christ, Rona, you're lovely. I love you. Get fixed up and some day I'll marry you. There'll just be you and me and a pink hot water bottle.'

Jake looked across at him. 'You put in your request too late,' he said.

'Oh, do-o-n't have him, Rona,' Maurice sang. 'He'll corrupt your smile and pervert your happiness. I know him.' He caught hold of my arm and, kicking his legs out and waving his hand, pulled me out of the doorway as though we were the tail-end of a chorus line. They applauded us as we receded. I wondered if my brother Maurice wasn't playing the court-jester just a little too whole-heartedly.

'What's on the time-table then?' I asked him, as we went down the stairs. I hoped he wasn't going to abandon me in some museum. I was completely overawed by London and those of its denizens I'd met.

'Well, first of all I thought we'd go and see whatever you want to see. Then, at six o'clock, you're expected at Hampstead, to stay to dinner. I shall deposit you there – it's Berenice night tonight, some stinking Italian film shown with sub-titles on white backgrounds – pick you up afterwards and deliver you to Rona and her hot water bottle.'

My knees began to quake at the prospect. But I had four hours' grace. I could defer total panic.

We did a sketchy lightning tour, taking in Westminster, the Embankment, Fleet Street and St Paul's and ending up with a dash through the National Gallery, prior to sampling their tea and buns. Everything seemed more crowded and smaller than I'd imagined it to be and, anyway, I was far more interested in hearing about that curious group of people we'd left behind us. Who were they? What were they? What was their relationship with one another? My naïve questioning irritated Maurice, but he bore with it.

'I told you: Rona and Pat are post-grad; Janet, the other girl, is at the Slade; Eddy's in my year doing the same thing as me – who else is there? Oh yes, Frank's final year English.'

'And Trixie?'

'Trix works in a factory. She makes valves.'

'A *factory*?'

'Yes, a *factory*. There are people, you know, who actually work in factories. And Trix is one of them.'

'Does she like it?'

'She loathes it, but the money's good and she does all the overtime God sends. She's saving for a share in a garage. She's the best blooming mechanic I've ever come across.'

'You haven't mentioned Jake.'

'Ah, Jake. Jake always reminds me of what the old headmaster at the Grammar used to say: "It's not personality that counts, boy, it's character!"'

'You mean Jake hasn't any?'

'Not visible to the naked eye.'

But I didn't care. Anyway, that remark was probably occasioned by jealousy. Jake would be certain to have all the success with women. 'I suppose he's Pat's boy-friend?' I asked wistfully.

Maurice hooted. 'My dear little girl, Pat doesn't have boy-friends. Trixie is Pat's boy-friend. Can't you tell? Surely you must have come across it in that convent where you're incarcerated? It's *Rona* that Jake's after.'

There were instances, of course, at Beechwood. Girls who were fiercely faithful to one another and held hands in secluded parts of the grounds. I was glad though. Rona didn't seem the fearful adversary that Pat would have been.

'It's a quarter to six,' Maurice said. 'We're late already. And we don't want to muck up Olivia's cheese soufflé, or whatever, do we?'

So it was Olivia now, not 'that old tart my Dad's knocking it up to'. I followed him outside. All the way in the Tube I was praying, 'Please, God, let me be just what he expects, let me not be a disappointment to him,'

CHAPTER SIX

There were no rhododendron bushes, the windows were not bow but tall and thin, the driveway did not curve but ran straight and narrow, flanked with stone urns, to the door; worst of all, it was not half-timbered but built of dirty yellow glazed brick like the frontage of a grocery shop – my father's house was a body-blow.

'You said it was nice.' But then I wasn't really certain about Maurice's aesthetic sensibilities.

'So it is – for the average city dwelling. The sort I expect you'd call "nice" are occupied in the main by tycoons and film stars.'

The door was opened before he had a chance to ring the bell and, softly-contoured, dim in the dim light of the hall, stood Olivia Murray. 'Anna,' she said, and made as if to kiss me (though she'd never kissed me as a child, not even as a social gesture), then awkwardly altered her impulse to a touch on my arm. And she was the same Olivia Murray of the summer teas, not altered one whit by remorse, regret or the ravages of time.

'We're late,' Maurice said, 'and a thousand apologies. But the time has been spent in a good cause – enlightening Anna's ignorance about the finer points of life.'

I was thankful for Maurice and his facetious chatter. Between that and taking unnecessary pains over divesting myself of my coat, I managed to seem to be at ease. It was only when she ushered me into that same blue drawing-room that I'd assembled in my daydreams that my heart began to knock in my ribs and my voice when I said, 'Hallo, Dad,' came out weak and throaty.

He was standing beside the window, his thumbs in his trouser pockets, leaning back on his heels. He looked like a man preparing to face a firing-squad. His hair was longer but going grey and his suit and shirt were smarter, more fashionable than those I remembered him wearing. I wondered if she bought his clothes, as my mother sometimes had done, but she'd bought things to last: flannel and worsted, dull greys and browns, not for the sake of their beauty.

When I was small it had been his habit to swing me up in his arms until our faces were level and our noses brushed together. I was eleven years old when he left; despite that fact I think he was prepared for the child in the white organdie frock and frilly knickers. Fifteen years he knew, theoretically, but he hadn't really envisaged fifteen years as being height and breasts and a face that had lost its childish candour. His embrace was almost as obvious in its last-minute compromise as Olivia's had been.

'You can offer me some sherry, if you like, Dad. I can't stay long. I'm due for foreign edification at seven.'

'I didn't think sherry was your drink, Maurice,' Olivia said, but started to pour all the same.

'Anything's my drink when it comes free of charge. I'm a professional scrounger.'

They could banter, he and Olivia. It flowed effortlessly. Olivia proffered the glass and he, the boy with the ugly knees who'd once knocked flakes off her paintwork with his heavyweight shoes, took it with a small suave bow. My father and I sat beside each other on the sofa, silent, graceless.

'So it's Berenice's turn tonight on the duty roster?'

'That's right. We have an understanding: every Saturday night and no questions asked.'

Their laughter mingled. They stood together, sipping their sherry. They matched: he, tall and unmarked, as my father must have been before seventeen years with a woman he couldn't love; she, ageless, changeless, with her abundant leaf-coloured hair and strong slim legs.

'Tell us about all the things you've seen today, Anna.'

Maurice had now had a large enough ration of Olivia's exclusive attention. I recited place-names in a mechanical voice which made my tour of the sights sound about as exciting as a walk down the village high street. They smothered what vitality I might have mustered, Olivia and Maurice, between them.

'If you could only stay,' she said, perching herself on the arm of the sofa so that I could see one small milky-green drop ear-ring, a long delicate sweep of collarbone and the beginning of a promise of plenty down the front of her dress. 'I'd love to show you the real places, the places that don't get into the guide-books.'

Of course, she was at home. A Londoner who'd married a Manchester cotton-king and been an alien during all those years in Trinity Square. I remembered how *different* she'd seemed – her clothes, her voice, everything.

'I have to go back to school on Monday,' I said, instantly summoning up an ink-stained, gym-slipped juvenile who usurped my place on the sofa and effectively put paid to any vestige of urbanity.

'Are they teaching you to be a lady?' my father said. He'd always been a supporter of state education, equal privilege, death to discrimination.

'Oh, *I* went to one of those places,' Olivia said, before I could reply, 'where I was called a "gel" and everybody was in love with her pony. Not,' she hastened to add, 'that there are schools like that any more. They're all most democratic and free-thinking and so on now, aren't they?'

I didn't know whether to say yes or no. We weren't 'gels' at Beechwood and it wasn't done to show off but, on the other hand, any thinking was supposed to be conducted between fixed lines and the constitution was about as democratic as Stalinist Russia.

'But I'm forgetting my duties.' She rose and deposited her glass into Maurice's waiting hand. 'I must show you the house. Excuse us for a moment, you two. Discuss the economy, or the Test Match, or something.'

I followed her out of the blue drawing-room, into the hall and up the stairs. There were Pre-Raphaelite prints all the way up: tubercular damozels with crinkly hair and long throats reclining on tapestry couches. One or two of them looked a bit like Olivia. She talked of builders and decorators and materials. She caught hold of a heavy damask curtain and fondled it in her hand: it had been specially shipped from some exotic place. She deplored the modern trend in furnishing: all those garish colours and hard edges. What did I think? I was still inarticulate to the point of being mute. She showed me the four bedrooms. Three were decorated in boudoir, Trinity Square style, the fourth, which shrieked the fact that it was the matrimonial bedroom, or rather the extra-matrimonial bedroom, from his black silk robe behind the door to her pots and jars on the dressing-table, was neutral territory: polished wood surfaces and deep clear colours. She didn't need the rose-pink satin and the alabaster nymphs of the mistress period any more; she was established now.

Downstairs was dining-room and kitchen – straight out of the Provençal cookery book: copper and scrubbed pine and earthenware pottery – and a small Italianate conservatory with a mosaic floor and a fountain which flowed soundlessly into the deep mossy well that surrounded it. Pale-blue carpet and cherry velvet curtains and me sipping amontillado – I remembered and thought how lack-lustre they seemed compared with all this.

When we returned Maurice was putting on his coat. His knowledge of the surroundings and the informality of his manner made me realize that he must be used to dropping into this house whenever he felt like doing so. Whatever tensions there might once have been had altogether melted away by this stage. I envied him enormously: his assurance, his light, easy conversation, I envied him the year's advantage he had over me.

'Pick you up later then,' he said. 'Lucky you. Olivia is Escoffier reincarnated. Think of me, won't you, watching half-clad Eye-ties communicating their passion in grunted monosyllables?'

Olivia saw him out and then came back and looked round the edge of the door. 'I'll leave you two together while I get the dinner. It's one of those occasions when three is an absolute multitude, isn't it?'

She was kindness and tact personified. If only I could thaw out sufficiently to allow myself to accept all she was offering, how easy it would be.

Again we sat side by side, father and daughter, estranged by ties of blood. Eventually he reached out a hand towards mine. I allowed it to make contact but I gazed at the opposite wall.

'It's difficult,' he said. 'I'm shy. If I open my mouth I'll say all the wrong things, not what I want to say.'

'What do you, then?' I still couldn't look at him but was aware of the cloth of his sleeve, the sheen of his tie, the speck of towelling that adhered to his cheek from when he'd shaved.

'Oh, I want to ask you whether you're happy – although I know it's a stupid question to ask anyone, I want to know whether you realize I love you just the same as if I were at home with you. I suppose I want to know your opinion of me or, to be honest, I want to know that you have a good opinion of me.'

I gazed at the wall still. He said, 'Of course this visit is secret, isn't it? I don't even have to ask.'

I tugged at my skirt with both hands. 'Why? Why won't she let me visit you, above-board, properly?'

'Because she's afraid of losing you, that's why. You've got to understand, you two are her universe. And you more so than Maurice because he's a man and adult. She wants you to love her, not to love me.'

'Love!' Maurice had once said. 'If that's love, I can do without it.'

'Then why don't you come to see us? You're not divorced yet, are you?' I blushed; I was in a house of sin – the very idea! 'I thought you hadn't to see us or she wouldn't give you a divorce.'

He tightened his hand upon mine. 'No, we're not divorced,' he said. 'And don't look like that, Anna. I love Olivia. I love you and I love Maurice. Divorce isn't of paramount importance. Some day perhaps you'll understand that seeing you against her wishes would be the final insult. Another year or two and you'll be able to see whom you please. But don't break her heart. For my sake.'

I was the child of a broken home. It was pure melodrama. 'You don't care about me,' I said. 'Or else you'd never have left.'

He turned my face to his. 'Can you deny that home's a more peaceful place since I left?'

There was no full-scale rows now, no pieces of shattered plate on the floor, no strident voices reverberating night after night. I had always believed the rows to be her fault, because of her difficult nature, but since he'd left there was no one worth provoking. Not to the same extent, anyway. 'No,' I said, 'I can't deny it. Except that Aunt Kitty gets on my nerves.'

'Your Aunt Kitty,' he said, 'is a cross that we have all had to bear at one time or another.'

Olivia came back in time to hear us laughing together. She smiled, rather triumphantly, as though she'd achieved her object. Wearing an apron and her face flushed with the heat of cooking, she looked more ordinary, less formidable. I found I could even offer to carry plates without feeling I'd betrayed myself.

We sat down, the three of us, at a round black table upon which there were straw-coloured table-mats and a white bowl filled with bronze dahlias. I broke bread and drank tawny soup. Even that matched the general scheme of things. Had he been seduced away merely by good taste?

My hand trembled a little and my spoon clicked on the side of my dish. She noticed. She talked to me without looking directly at me, for which I was grateful. Had I any ideas for when I left school? I opened my mouth to tell her. I was as ready to confide in her as I'd confided in Jake that morning. Whatever else she might be, Olivia was the sort to understand an ambition to rise out of the rut, to enter a members-only magic circle, to be something more than Anna Blake, a girl whose father hoofed off.

'She'll go to University, of course.' My father's affectionate, proud face opposite me. 'I don't believe in wasted brain-power. Maurice says she's very bright and Maurice would be the last person to exaggerate.'

My jaw closed. Just like my mother. Wanted to flaunt

me as a success. Wanted to be able to say, 'This is the child sprung from my loins, the one with all the diplomas testifying to her brilliant heredity.'

'But perhaps that doesn't fit in with Anna's plans, or hopes,' Olivia said. And I didn't know whether to be astounded by her perspicacity or suspicious in case she was trying to suborn me. 'University wouldn't have suited me. I just hadn't the necessary powers of application, which is quite a different quality from ability.'

They fell to discussing the precise value of further education. Their views clashed on many aspects and this resulted in an intelligent debate not a mindless row as it used to do when he had a different protagonist. For the time being they forgot about me and, no longer the focus of attention, I began to relax and admit to myself all Olivia's sterling qualities: her tact, her quick perception, her kindness. Perhaps she was good with young people because she'd never had any children of her own, never been disillusioned when they didn't turn out to be robot paragons.

'Maurice says you're staying with some of his friends,' she said quickly, in case I was feeling neglected. 'Are they nice? Are you comfortable?'

'I haven't really had much chance to get to know them. Rona, the one whose bedroom I'm sharing, seems nice, and there's a boy – well, I suppose he's a man really – called Jake who came to lunch.' I couldn't resist mentioning his name and I was delighted when Olivia said, 'Oh we know Jake. Jake Stavely? He's been here a couple of times. He *is* charming, isn't he? Though Maurice says he's too charming. But then Maurice detests anyone who doesn't make at least one outrageous remark per sentence.'

'Maurice is finding himself,' my father said. 'And when he does, you won't find a more sober, conventional citizen of the realm within miles.'

I thought Maurice had found himself years ago, when he'd decided not to run away to sea but apply himself to biology text-books instead. But I supposed my father was the authority on people finding themselves; he certainly had, at any rate.

'You've only to take as an example the way he sticks to this Berenice. He has his flings, but it's always the girl-next-door he goes back to. I believe Maurice has that fine old-fashioned moral sense which distinguishes between the sort of girl you marry and the sort you don't.'

My breath caught in my throat. I thought his remark a bit near the knuckle in view of the circumstances. But she only laughed and said, 'More men still think like that than you'd ever imagine, dear.'

It was that 'dear' that did it, I think, a familiar year's-long-married kind of dear. It made me think of carpet slippers and woollen waistcoats and nodding off together in front of the television set. I saw that my father and Olivia were not involved in some romantic sinful liaison, but formed a unit of two who had their fair share of the unpleasant, the dull and the workaday.

Afterwards, in the kitchen, when she was washing and I was wiping, she said, 'Your father may not be very demonstrative but – please believe me – he hates the idea of your being away from him. If he didn't realize that you're happiest where you are, he wouldn't have a moment's peace.'

By that stage of the evening – I had drunk a little wine too – I wasn't at all certain about being happiest where I was. I allowed myself to envisage life in London, in this desirable residence, having one of those four bedrooms for my own, pouring sherry for Jake when he came round of an evening, undergoing a total metamorphosis of personality. But all she said was, 'You must come again soon, if you can, if it's possible.' And later, sitting quietly in front of the fire, he echoed those sentiments. He talked again about my soon being old enough to choose. He said this was home, too, whenever I felt that I needed it. If Maurice hadn't come in, all banging and breeziness, no doubt tears would have been shed. As it was, we exchanged appropriate, meaningless phrases, we embraced. Only our eyes gave us away to one another, only our eyes spelled out our mutual suffering.

In the Fulham flat, Rona and Jake waited. He sat on the

floor, his head against her knees, playing the guitar. He played 'The Streets of Laredo'; it was the saddest tune I'd ever heard. He said, 'How did things go?' looking through my eyes and into me. He didn't need an answer.

For a long time afterwards the glimpse of dried grasses in a tall jar, the smell of oil paint and the memory of that tune would combine to squeeze my heart in a spasm of regret for what was wasted.

CHAPTER SEVEN

Love and respectability came to Aunt Kitty in the neat and narrow shape of Henry Bute. It didn't come in an instant flash of recognition, but germinated and ripened for two years in the solicitors' office, in between the yellowing files of conveyances and tithes, under the grim gaze of long-dead Joseph Etheridge, the firm's founder, beside the clacking typewriter and cups of cooling coffee. It spread its roots so surely and gradually that no sudden frost could wither it. It blossomed only in due season. And it was only when this blossoming had taken place that it became public knowledge.

Aunt Kitty's evenings out had certainly caused no speculation; she made friendships like a fly-paper picks up flies – if Aunt Kitty had been an Arab she could have made friends in a kibbutz. No one ever thought of Aunt Kitty and men. The idea was just not congruous. Aunt Kitty belonged with women who talked about knitting patterns and prolapses. Consequently we were dumbfounded when she told us the news.

And she was as tongue-tied and timorous as a young girl asking permission of forbidding parents. I blinked. This was Aunt Kitty, whose vocal chords were rarely at rest except when she was eating and sleeping – and not always then.

It had not been an easy decision: she felt as though she were deserting my mother after all her kindness and generosity – I could see my mother tapping her foot with irritation: Aunt Kitty had only ever been with us on sufferance – but she had to think of Jamie and it would be good for Jamie to have a settled home and a father-figure now he was getting to be a big boy.

I had to agree on that. Perhaps a man's hand might have some effect on Jamie's perpetual perversity.

'And when is this event due to take place?' my mother said. She was extremely peeved that she, the professional ferreter-out of other people's shabby secrets, had detected no indication of the state of affairs.

'Well, we've only just decided. Henry says any time that suits. It's only a matter of getting the licence, you see.'

'Henry?' my mother said coldly. 'I presume we are allowed to know which Henry you're talking about?'

'Didn't I say?' She was all pink cheeks and confusion. I snorted. She looked across at me with a nervous smile, uncertain whether my snort might be interpreted as sympathetic. 'Henry Bute. Mr Paulson's clerk. We've got to know each other very well since I went to work there.'

'You don't say?'

'Well, yes and well, he's been a widower for twelve years now and he thinks it's silly us being on our own when we could be together – not that I'm exactly on my own, of course, but in a manner of speaking –'

'He does know what he's taking on, I gather?'

I suddenly felt very sorry for Aunt Kitty. 'Congratulations,' I said. And: 'When are you bringing him round for inspection?'

I had often mocked her, been impatient with her, sometimes downright rude to her, but I was willing to be her ally against my mother who was a past-master at the comment that diminished happiness, the phrase that punctured the cloud of euphoria.

'He's very shy,' Aunt Kitty said. 'About meeting people's families, I mean. I've often said recently, "Why not drop by for a cup of tea and meet Cis and Anna?" But he always says, "Wait till we're properly established, Kit." So I don't like to press it. Jamie's quite taken to him though. And that's half the battle, isn't it? He lost a little boy himself at three years old. He says he's always regretted not having a family.'

It occurred to me that Henry Bute must be privileged to know all. Obviously she couldn't keep up the nonsense about Mr-Pendlebury-killed-in-the-war when it came to the stage of registrar's office or church records or wherever the marriage was to take place; she would have to be described as spinster of the parish. I wondered if Henry Bute minded about the long-gone loony. At their age I suppose it wasn't worth bothering about.

'I'll be sorry to leave here, Cis. It's been home to me for a long time now, and I think we've managed to get along all right, despite our little differences.'

I looked at my mother's face as she sat, needle poised above her sewing as it had been ever since Aunt Kitty made her announcement. The 'little differences' formed huge ravines between herself and Aunt Kitty; the mere presence of Aunt Kitty in the house got on her nerves. With Aunt Kitty gone, there would be no more débris, no more messes to be cleaned up, no more inane comments to be answered. Yet she realized it was one more step towards isolation: my father gone, Maurice gone, Kitty going, it left only me – and for how much longer could she be sure of me? She felt herself to be a sinking ship.

Eventually she summoned the grace to add her congratulations to mine, to say stiffly that Henry Bute would be welcome to partake of a cup of tea whenever he felt ready to do so. But it cost her an effort. And I knew that, like the shot at Sarajevo, the effects of this occurrence would be far-reaching and could only bode ill for my freedom.

Three weeks passed before Henry Bute felt he could 'drop by' for introductions. I had imagined all kinds of faces and figures to fit his name, but I was nowhere near the mark. He was smaller, thinner and more dapper than anyone would have expected of a man who might appeal to Aunt Kitty.

'And this is Anna, my niece, although you must feel you know her already after all I've told you.'

He looked unsure. I wondered what kind of wild overstatements Aunt Kitty had been making. His hand felt like warm emery paper and his suit was so stiff and sharply-pressed it seemed as though it would stand up without him inside it.

He smiled briefly and sat down again. Aunt Kitty kept sugaring his tea. I hoped his metabolism could stand it. My mother, after a few minutes' mutual embarrassment, had found an excuse to leave the room. I think she was surprised to find he didn't have two heads or a club foot.

'I've been telling Henry how clever you are. Show him that book you put together about Elizabethan England. Beautiful it was, Henry, all with illuminated letters, like monks' manuscripts, you know, and drawings she copied out of history books. You couldn't tell the difference – except I think hers were better.'

That was two years ago. I looked at Henry Bute and, by the merest flicker of his mouth, he managed to convey to me that he realized Aunt Kitty was over-enthusiastic and simple and that he didn't mind at all and that we must both bear with her.

'Don't drag up school at the week-end, Kitty,' he said. 'I'm sure Anna doesn't want to think about school. I'm sure you didn't when you were her age.'

'I was never very good. Could never grasp it. They used to say I was a willing worker. It's the same with poor Jamie. No matter how hard you try, if it's not in you, it's just not in you.'

It certainly wasn't in Jamie. I could see him through the window, flicking stones with the aid of a piece of elastic tied to a forked twig. Mrs Langley had already lost a pane of glass out of her veranda that way and had told Aunt Kitty he needed re*straining* in tones that embraced the idea of straight-waistcoats and fetters.

Physically, Jamie compensated for what he lacked in intellectual ability. His babyish good looks had developed into sturdy boyish handsomeness. Anyone seeing him in his blue-striped tee-shirt and shorts, with his hair falling over his forehead into his eyes, would have thought him an excellent specimen of breeding. At school he held his own by brute force. Aunt Kitty mopped and moaned over his bloody knees and black eyes, but Maurice said, out of earshot, not to worry because where there was no sense there was no feeling. I could see Jamie growing up into one of those gangster film toughs who break open men's heads at the drop of the boss's hat. I wondered what plans Henry Bute had for him.

As if he'd read my thoughts, Henry Bute, brushing crumbs from his lap into the palm of his other hand, said, 'What Jamie needs are the wide open spaces where he can channel his energies into something physically satisfying. Have you ever thought of an Outward Bound school, Kit?'

'Dr Spenser says there's no substitute for a mother's love.'

Dr Spenser was God. But I don't think that particular maxim had issued from Dr Spenser's lips; it sounded much more like an extract from one of her magazines.

'But surely a mother's love aims for the good of the child?'

I looked at Henry Bute with a new respect. Perhaps the old-fashioned uniform, the ladylike way of drinking tea, the narrow-eyed, rather furtive expression, perhaps they were all components of a disguise and the real Henry Bute was a man of firm conviction.

They decided to plight their troth in the Town Hall. As she told us, I saw in Aunt Kitty's face a fugitive glimmer of longing for all those experiences she'd forfeited: choir-boys and 'O perfect love' and 'Lohengrin' and silver horseshoes; ten minutes closeted with dyspeptic Mr Evans, the chief registrar, just wasn't the same thing at all.

We must have looked a somewhat pathetic entourage assembled in the ante-room at the Town Hall: me, my mother, Jamie wearing his first suit with a carnation in the button-hole and kicking the polish off the chair-legs, Henry's widowed sister who was still in mourning to judge by her woeful expression, and the prospective bride and groom. Aunt Kitty wore pink, which I didn't think was all that becoming in view of her mature years. I don't think she was entirely certain herself but it *had* looked mouth-watering when clothing a long lean dummy in the shop window. Henry wore a wedding-cum-funeral suit and had hoisted his braces so high that the trousers were almost up around his neck. We were waiting for Mr Paulson who had agreed to act as best man, but who had to appear in the adjoining magistrates' court first.

I had been looking forward to meeting Ruby and Phyl and Jo, Aunt Kitty's old friends from her ATS days, who wrote such long and ebullient letters, but Aunt Kitty said they were working girls scattered in various parts of England and, anyway, she wanted it to be a quiet affair.

It was that all right. Ante-rooms in Town Halls are not renowned for their arresting décor or provision of amusement and if it hadn't been for Jamie who rhythmically hacked at my shin with his swinging heel I'd have dropped off ages ago. But Mr Paulson soon altered that. He came trotting in, consulting his watch, smoothing his fine wavy hair and patting his pockets, presumably to make sure no one relieved him of one narrow twenty-two-carat gold ring.

'*So* sorry,' he said. 'I've been straining at the bit but one can't hurry these things. Now, all present and correct? Come on, Henry. Force a smile. It happens to the best of us, you know.'

After that the whole thing took on the air of court proceedings. Aunt Kitty, as Maurice would have put it, made a complete town halls of the responses and Mr Evans, whose ulcer seemed to be particularly active that morning, clicked his teeth like castanets when forced to reiterate the same simple phrases. My mother, standing forward as a witness, gripped the handle of her handbag so tightly that her knuckles showed white. Mr Paulson located the ring all right but dropped it in a bowl of roses as he was handing it over to Henry. Jamie communicated a whispered desire to be excused and, when this was denied him, wriggled in his seat like one possessed. I gave thanks to God that Maurice was not present, otherwise we'd have been prostrate on the floor with hysterics.

Eventually, however, it did come to pass that they were pronounced man and wife and we repaired to the restaurant where the reception was booked.

Red soup, ham and tongue salad and individual trifles which had one glacé cherry stuck on the top like a nipple. My mother and the widowed sister who was called Alice and had a glint in her eye didn't speak throughout the meal except to reiterate 'Speech' when the time was right. Neither did Jamie; he abandoned himself to the more primitive pleasures of eating and drinking. Mr Paulson turned his florid face to me and talked about education, or rather one aspect of it: what a damn shame it would be if Latin and Greek were to be scrapped on the school syllabus because learning Latin and Greek was the finest mental discipline anyone could ever have. Henry said a few quiet decorous words when called upon to do so, but for the rest of the time contemplated his knife and fork. It was Aunt Kitty who saved the day, talking on and on, to the waitresses, to the manager who popped in to see if everything was as it should be – 'Yes? Good. Splendid' – to no one in particular. There was nothing you could teach Aunt Kitty about the powers of rhetoric.

There was a mirror on the opposite wall. While Mr Paulson droned on, sprinkling his monologue with classical quotations which were alien to me, possible because he pronounced them in old, church Latin, I ogled myself. I'd had my hair done for the occasion: a smooth bob with a big kiss-curl at either side that had been secured to my cheeks with Sellotape all through the night. I was wearing a new silk dress the colour of ripe chestnuts which rustled with my every movement and new shoes of soft black leather, so soft that they creased whenever I bent my toes. I thought I looked a vision of beauty and was filled with an overpowering sense of humiliation at having to be associated with this motley crew. I should be sitting in the Café Royal (which figured very frequently in my reading matter) drinking apéritifs, making all heads turn to wonder who I was as I waited for Jake Stavely to arrive in his white dinner-jacket. I could feel the glass in my hand, taste the ice-cold liquid, see the silver knives and the heavy white tablecloths. 'The Bride and Groom!', someone said. And we stood up and raised our glasses and drank something that reminded me strongly of Sanatogen tonic wine. The waste!

And the sense of anti-climax, after they'd been driven to the station to catch the 3.10 for Bridlington, grew worse. The widowed sister declined all offers of transport and trundled away with her raffia handbag and white gloves to wait for a 39 bus. Mr Paulson drove us home, said, 'Ah well, back to the grindstone,' and shot off in what looked suspiciously like the direction of his golf club.

My mother took off her hat. I went to hang up the chestnut dress inside polythene until the time when a more suitable occasion to show off my charms should present itself. When I came down she was back in her pinny, down on her hands and knees in the kitchen, cleaning the stove.

'The radio says good weather on the East Coast.'

'Well, I'm glad of that,' she said. 'For Jamie's sake at least. If he can't run his wildness out on the sands he'll drive them mad. Let's hope Mr Bute's nerves are in good order.'

I'd thought it a putrid idea to drag Jamie along on the honeymoon, but Aunt Kitty said, 'Henry insisted. He wouldn't have a minute's peace knowing that boy might be pining for me.' Not that it would be a honeymoon as such, I supposed; Aunt Kitty was so large and Henry so small I couldn't see how they could possibly fit together.

'It'll be queer without them.'

'Hm,' she said. 'It'll be a blessed relief, I know that. This place might just begin to look like a home again instead of the council refuse dump.'

'D'you think they'll be happy?'

'Happy? It's what she wants, isn't it?' she said, as though people must automatically be happy when they got what they wanted.

I nearly quoted Shaw to her, but what would be the use? And she'd had one bad moment during the wedding reception when Mr Paulson read out the telegrams. After 'All the best' from Ruby, came 'Much happiness' from Alec. I had watched her crumbling the tiny slice of wedding cake, watched lines deepening into furrows round her mouth, observed her silent agony. At least he had had the discretion to restrict it to his name only.

I left her wielding Vim and the scourer and went up to my attic. The little window opened on to a view of all the back gardens for miles. The cherry trees were in blossom, their petals made circular pink rugs on the grass. There was a week-day, mid-afternoon hush over the whole neighbourhood. I could see the Leslies' house: the only house where the curtains didn't match.

I thought of the long steel road to Bridlington carrying Henry and Aunt Kitty and Jamie to bed and board and 'please leave the bathroom as you would wish to find it' in the Chalfont Hotel. I ran my amber wedding beads through my fingers. Why didn't my mother meet a Henry Bute and marry him? Why didn't she instruct her solicitors that Alexander Blake had been committing adultery with Olivia Murray since 1956? Why didn't she at least make a life for herself and free me from the crippling burden of her love?

CHAPTER EIGHT

Mark and Jonathon Lawrence were related to Rachel on the distaff, aristocratic side. They weren't Honourables like her mother, but you'd never have guessed.

In the twilit school cloakroom, among the green tiles and grimy roller-towels and chronically empty soap-containers, I first made their acquaintance. They slipped from between the pages of Cicero *In Verrem* chapter twenty-eight, as Rachel was organizing her homework. We both bent down to retrieve the photograph, but my eyesight was keener than hers.

'Who are these?' I took it over to where the mesh-covered bulb cast its dim nimbus of light and saw two curly-haired young men, brothers obviously, one each side of the Conways' jowly golden retriever. Whoever had taken the photograph had concentrated on the dog – its companions were cut off at the shoulders at either edge.

Nevertheless, it showed sufficient to inform me that they were two extremely attractive young men.

'My cousins,' said Rachel, continuing to pack her satchel.

'You've been keeping them very dark.' I looked at her accusingly. One, perhaps yes, but two – that was sheer gluttony.

'They've been living abroad. They came over last week-end. Dad took the photograph.' She came over beside me. 'It's turned out quite well, hasn't it, considering Dad?'

'And why are you carrying it round with you, Rachel Conway?'

I had never seen Rachel blush. She didn't oblige me on that occasion either. I think her nerve-ends and blood vessels were constitutionally incapable of combining to produce a blush. 'They are rather super, aren't they?' was all she said.

It was Christmas before pasteboard was made flesh. I had squeezed out every particle of information concerning the Lawrences from Rachel. Mark was eighteen, Jonathon his junior by eleven months. 'Mummy said Auntie Jo actually believed that old wives' tale about not getting pregnant while you're breast-feeding. Isn't it quaint?' Rachel was fast making up for lost time in the field of obstetrical knowledge. I steered her back to the subject in hand. They were both at school in Wiltshire; Mark was destined for Sandhurst, but Jonathon was artistic. My heart leapt in my breast. All that and artistic too! They were spending their Christmas holiday with the Conways.

Throughout November and the first three weeks of December I paid special court to Rachel, reminding her, sometimes subtly, sometimes downright bluntly, how long we'd been friends. It was a very necessary piece of strategy; other girls had seen the photograph and Rachel was well on the way to becoming the most popular girl in the class.

I had spent parts of Christmas with Rachel and her family before – sometimes Christmas Eve carol-singing, sometimes Boxing Day lunch followed by noisy games of Monopoly and drowsy games of draughts and hot mince-pies. But an invitation to spend the whole of Christmas at their house was something new.

My mother liked Rachel. Rachel was a quiet girl and quiet girls were good girls, or so it followed in my mother's philosophy. Rachel was the 'right sort of friend' for me. And this invitation was the 'right sort' of invitation too. Almost in the nature of a royal summons.

'You don't mind me going then?' I had laid out my dresses over the back of the sofa and was surveying them with increasingly vehement expressions of disgust. For a new way of life one needed a new outfit of clothes.

'No. Not at all. It'll be very nice for you. We'll get you a new dress and you'll need some new shoes too.'

Like Maurice's State Scholarship, this was a vicarious triumph for her: 'My daughter, spending Christmas with the Honourable Mrs Diana Conway and her family.' It wasn't simple snobbery. It was just that our achievements were the only means by which she could glean a crumb of self-satisfaction.

I got a new dress and shoes, and a new coat too – all in scarlet. I kept them on all evening, they were so beautiful. Maurice, sloping downstairs in bleached jeans and denim jacket, said, 'You look like a set of traffic-lights jammed on stop. Oh, and by the way, before I forget: the Butlers are going to the Imperial for Christmas. They're booked in for the period. So Mummy won't have to soil her lily-white hands stuffing a turkey, I expect. Any road up, as they say on the BBC, they've booked me in too. So I suppose I'll have to hire a what'sit from what-not's.'

'DJ from MB.'

'That's right. I've left it too late to borrow from Dad. He's leaving London at the end of the week.'

'For where?'

'For the wild Hielands. Olivia has a brother-in-law up by Loch Rannoch or Loch Awe – one of those places that sound as though you're throwing up when you say them – so it's going to be wee drams and slàinte var and the rest of that barbarian nonsense.'

I stopped stroking my coat and breathing on the silver buttons before polishing them with my sleeve. 'She'll be on her own.' This was the first Christmas she'd be totally abandoned.

'She could go to Aunt Kitty's. I'm sure Henry wouldn't mind extending the hospitality of his festive platter. Why didn't the Conways invite her, anyway?'

'She's too shy to make friends with them. I believe they think she's stuck-up, unfriendly. What about the Butlers for that matter?'

'Ma and Pa Butler haven't got to be where they are today by considering anyone other than Ma and Pa Butler and progeny.'

'You could have hinted, delicately.'

He groaned. 'That's right, start disturbing my conscience. God, Anna, can't you imagine what sort of Christmas that would be? She's be asking me if I needed hot water bottles and saying, "Now, Maurice, don't you think you've had enough?" when I started on my second sherry.'

'It's rotten, though, isn't it? Christmas is the one time it's perfectly foul being on your own.'

'She'll enjoy it,' he said decisively. 'Just thinking about us mixing in high society. She'll be really made up – sitting here with her chicken sandwich and the Queen's Speech.'

I tried to persuade her to go to Aunt Kitty's, and so did Aunt Kitty, arriving boisterously with her arms full of gifts, but Maurice was right: she would be happier in solitude, living our lives for us at a distance.

All the same, it was not without a pang or two that I picked up my overnight case and left her sitting beside the artificial silver tree and the dish of apples and tangerines that would go bad before they got eaten.

There was a reception committee at the Conways' front door: Rachel, in green velvet with her hair piled high in precarious Victorian ringlets; Doctor Conway, wearing one of the shrunken, V-necked jumpers that seemed to be his regulation mufti; the Honourable Diana, looking more dun-coloured than ever and two young men almost identical in height and colouring, until you looked more closely, unrolling and twisting yards of violent purple crêpe paper streamers.

'How lovely to see you, Anna.'

I leaned forward to receive the customary brush of her cheek. Mrs Conway always smelled of Johnson's Baby Soap and her skin felt cool and granulated due to the beige-coloured powder she applied with more liberality than discrimination.

'You haven't met Mark and Jonathon, but I'm sure you've heard about them.'

The two young men inclined their heads and grinned, consecutively. Mark had a wide, heavy-boned face and eyes like a young kitten's; Jonathon was altogether thinner and sharper, his hair grew lower down and his eyes were a curious opaque shade of flecked hazel.

'Take Anna upstairs, Rachel, and she can get settled.'

'And don't be too long,' her father called after us. 'We're due at St Luke's at eight and I've got to round up the stragglers.'

I dropped my case on the camp-bed in Rachel's bedroom. 'What are they like?' I said. Preamble would have been wasted on Rachel.

'Mark's nice.' She sat down carefully on the *petit-point* seat of a little round chair, spreading her dress behind her. It was a well-cut, restrained, elegant dress; I suddenly felt uncomfortable in my bright scarlet that had looked so gay and eye-catching in the shop.

'Jonathon's a bit funny.'

'What do you mean – funny?'

'Well, he always seems to be laughing at you, even when he's looking perfectly serious. I heard Mum telling Dad that Auntie Jo had had a lot of trouble with him, about schools. She had to take him to a child-psychiatrist when he was younger because he wouldn't conform. He's good fun though. Dad says he'll go far, one way or the other.'

The more I heard, the better disposed I became towards the mysterious Jonathon. I wanted to pursue the subject, but Rachel was eyeing my case.

'Have you opened them? What did you get?'

The Conways' Christmas presents were always arranged around the tree and opened, ceremonially, after breakfast on Christmas morning. In our family no such ritual prevailed. I had only Aunt Kitty's left to open.

'No. Don't cut it,' Rachel said, as I gave up the struggle with the string and reached for the scissors. 'You should never cut string.' Her practical, patient fingers worked away at the knots, methodically disentangling them. I remembered our one-time passion for horoscope books and palm-reading sessions. They had been unnecessary – Rachel's character and future were intelligible at a glance.

'I don't know what it's supposed to be. A big scarf, perhaps?' She held up a large rectangle of knitted fluffy wool which could only be described as being of that obsolete shade: helio. 'It's too wide for a scarf.'

'It's a stole.' I draped it round my shoulders. It looked catastrophic against the scarlet. 'It's what girls used to sport at dances when Aunt Kitty was in her heyday.'

'Is she colour-blind too?'

'It'll go with my purple silk ensemble.'

'You haven't got a purple ensemble.'

'No. But I'll buy one specially to go with it. When I get invited to the Mayoral Ball.'

We fell about on the camp-bed, imagining the happy pride on Aunt Kitty's face as she wrapped it up and stuck on the Scotch tape, remembering all the other gifts-with-love: the garish brooches, the Film Fun annuals, the pungent green bath-salts, the handkerchiefs that said 'H' instead of 'A' because she hadn't got her reading glasses with her when she bought them. 'I think your Aunt Kitty's tremendous,' Rachel said. I supposed she was, from afar.

'Ladies! We're leaving. So if you're not down in two minutes you'll have to hoof it.'

It was a starlit, bitterly cold night. Rachel wore a white fur hat. Jonathon called her Nanook of the North. I had come without gloves. In the back of the car, he took off his own sheepskin mittens and fitted them on to my numbed hands. I sat between him and Mark. They generated heat each side of me. Dr Conway looked round from the driving seat and said, 'Are we all in good voice?' I thought of my father's easy, tuneful tenor, 'The Fair Maid of Perth', 'Maiden My Maiden', the tight, high-collared red jacket, his smile, the shouting and the fragments of Willow Pattern on the kitchen floor, Olivia Murray and her rose-coloured, oval finger-nails, my mother, sitting alone, listening to the choir of King's College Chapel, sitting alone and thinking.

'You're very quiet,' Jonathon said.

'I'm sorry.'

'Don't be sorry. I like quiet girls.'

I looked at his smiling face. It was a dangerous face. On the other side of me, Mark, in profile, gazed through the car window. His profile was stolid, open, entirely trustworthy. I turned back to Jonathon.

After assembling at St Luke's, the carol-singing route was plotted through two hotels, three hospitals, one maternity home and then back to congregate around the fir tree in front of the church. During 'O Little Town of Bethlehem' an old woman died, in the second verse of 'The Holly and The Ivy' a baby was born. A nurse, hot-foot from the labour ward, informed us that 'baby' was going to be called Noël; 'Why not Jesus?' Jonathon murmured. The clientèle of the saloon bar in The Grapes got very sentimental and proposed 'Three cheers for the boys and girls'. At the Queen's, which was posher, an inebriated old gentleman tried to get off with the curate's wife. Dr Conway could be heard, long after everybody else's breath had given out, hanging on to '. . . new born King' or '. . . saviour is born'.

The last carol, outside St Luke's, was *'Adeste Fideles'*; Jonathon and I stood next to each other. The stars were many and precisely defined. You could almost imagine them having the same pointed shape as the one on top of the Christmas tree. The concerted choirboys' treble, at the end of the line, rose clear and triumphant above the indifferent noise issuing from the rest of us. I felt tears come into my eyes. It was the singing, purely, and not the religious aspect that moved me. Nevertheless, at that moment, I could believe that there was innocence and truth and good in the world. Jonathon reached out his hand for mine.

'Cantet nunc io
Chorus angelorum,
Cantet nunc aula cael-e-e-stium,
Glo-o-o-oria in excelsis Deo . . .'

Our grips tightened upon one another. Together we were transfigured under that dark-blue, glitter-perforated sky.

In the Parish Room – mince-pies and hot Vimto – the glow faded somewhat. But Jonathon was still beside me and still individual among the mass of uniform faces that surrounded us.

Rachel came over, proffering a plate of mince-pies. 'You look like holly, you two,' Jonathon said.

'And I'm the prickly one, I suppose?' she replied. The ringlets had come adrift during the course of the evening, but looked less artificial, her eyes were bright and her cheeks were glowing from outdoors. I wondered how any man could not find Rachel attractive. Beside her, I felt sallow and lethargic. But Jonathon stayed.

'Your brother's very quiet.' I gestured to the corner where Mark stood between Dr Conway and the vicar, balancing his glass and his plate and gazing into the middle-distance. Apart from saying hallo when we'd met, I don't think he'd spoken to me all evening.

'It's all part of his image. If you don't say anything people often assume you're thinking profound thoughts. At school they regard Mark as the young Plato. Intellectually of course, I mean.'

'And isn't he?'

'I have a better brain,' he said with engaging conceit, 'but Mark has superior powers of application. Ergo, he's brilliant and I'm a thick-head, according to popular conception.'

'Doesn't it bother you, being thought a thick-head?'

'Why on earth should it? Do the opinions of your intellectual inferiors bother you?'

They did. To a great extent. But I wasn't going to admit it to him. 'I think school is a total waste of time anyway,'

I said in a world-weary way.

'Oh, I don't think so. It's probably the greatest amount of freedom we'll ever get. Just think of it when we're bunged somewhere where we'll actually have to do something or starve. It needn't be wasted, you know,' he said earnestly. 'I read my way through *A la Recherche du Temps Perdu* during the history periods alone last term.'

'Oh.' What else was there to say?

He surveyed the room from beneath drooping eyelids. 'I love it,' he said. 'It's like a scene out of a book that you read and then think, "Ah, but life's not really like that": everybody being matey and jolly and superficial. I think we ought to join in.'

'Don't let's.' I was glorying in the fact that, for once, I was apart – from the vicar who always called me Mona, from the more earnest of my school-fellows, from the predictable, boring, jam-making, jumble-donating ladies of the parish.

'OK. But I adore being charming.'

We stayed together, isolated from the inconsequential chattering masses. He talked. I listened, and looked. I admired the virile weight he gave to his statements, the firm hard line of his mouth, his neat lobe-less ears, the beautiful symmetry of his hair. I tried to compare him with Jake. I thought back to the conversation I'd had with Maurice during his summer vacation.

'How are your funny friends?' I'd said. 'And Jake,' I'd said casually, 'how's Jake?'

'Jake left for foreign parts at the end of last term. Didn't I tell you? British Council thing. Leipzig or Zagreb or Danzig. Somewhere with a "z" in it anyway.'

And with that, the little kernel of hope that had been slowly ripening in my heart withered abruptly. How, among the millions of dark young men in the world, would I ever make contact with him again?

And now, standing beside Jonathon, I found that Jake's bright image had faded.

At one o'clock the assembly dispersed. Going home in the car, Mrs Conway dozed, her head drooping from her neck like a flower from its stalk. 'Come on, old lady, nearly there,' Dr Conway said, extricating her gently from her seat. We stood in the hall, laughing at the infirmity of middle-age, as he conducted her, still half-asleep, up the stairs.

Rachel let out several jaw-splitting yawns and followed in their wake. Mark stretched his arms above his head. 'Me too,' he said. And then noticed we were standing under the mistletoe. I noticed it, too, and he saw I'd noticed it, so gallantly made a quick snap in the region of my mouth. The attempt was totally mismanaged. I was left, looking foolish, my lips still apart.

'Not like that.'

He turned me round on the spot. The other one. His face came down upon mine rising to meet it. There was no question of noses. They might not have existed. Everything fitted together. Lips fused, teeth receded. A warm, sharp, almost painful shudder from from my mouth down the centre of my body. We broke away only when suffocation threatened. Mark's face was flushed, Jonathon's eyes were wide open and sparkling. I clung to the banister for support; it had happened – the time, the place and the person, at last.

CHAPTER NINE

There was a moment when I woke up next morning, before I was able to ascertain where I was or what had happened to me, when it seemed as though this was just another grey day and I might as well turn over and seek to re-enter the more exciting domain of dreams. Then I remembered and was out of bed in a flash.

The window was thick with ice sculptures. The carpet was cold and hostile underfoot. One tuft of dark hair was all that was visible of Rachel. I pulled away the eiderdown and shook her. Still asleep, she readjusted it and muttered. I shook her again. This time her eyelids opened over an uncomprehending stare. 'Merry Christmas,' I said. 'Go away,' she replied. Eyelids came down again like shutters. 'It's Christmas, Rachel.'

'Oh, is it?' With one heroic heave she made full transition into consciousness and was out of bed immediately. We were still eight years old when it came to Christmas mornings. But I had another reason.

Breakfast, though delicious, was gobbled. It was the bright collection of square and rectangular shapes around the tree: be-ribboned, rosetted, mysterious, that made our mouths water.

Dr Conway was first, wonderfully affecting surprise as he pulled apart green and red paper to reveal gloves, a scarf, a road atlas, a watch that told you the date, the month, the year – everything, apparently, apart from the common or garden time, because the winder was stuck. Then it was Mrs Conway's turn and hers was the lot of mothers the world over: useful presents, sensible thirty-denier stockings, household effects. Her restrained gratitude was immediately overshadowed by Rachel's shrieks of delight. It was really Rachel's occasion. Everything else just led up to or tailed off from that moment. 'The "Prague" and the "Jupiter". How marvellous! And the "Choral" too!' Records galore in their shiny albums emerged from concealment – the bright laminated covers were almost as beautiful as their contents. Within five minutes the floor looked like a pulp-merchant's dream of home, and set out around the folds of her green velvet dress were records, books, a bottle of perfume, a pair of pink feathered slippers, a nightdress too beautiful to wear, an antique ring – jet mounted in silver – that had once belonged to an Edwardian ancestor of great charm and doubtful virtue.

'I think,' Jonathon said, under cover of the rapture, 'that all we need now is a good old-fashioned human sacrifice to round off the frenzy. How about you, Anna? Are you eligible?'

I thought I knew what he was getting at and blushed. I was most definitely eligible and very aware of the fact. One day someone would relieve my eligibility, competently, painlessly, as if in a dream.

The rest of us had not been excluded from the orgy of

giving and receiving; in particular, Jonathon was now the possessor of an edition of modern American poetry and announced his intention of going to his room and reading aloud until dinner was ready. I felt a pang – that I should be forsaken for the sake of a few lines of pseudo-intellectual unintelligibility. But when Jonathon left, Mark took over. I had observed it before: the way that brothers and sisters could appear as quite different personalities when they were apart.

'Let's have a bit of intellectual exercise,' he said. He fished out the ancient, scribbled-upon Ludo board. 'It may not be *avant-garde* American poetry, but we can't all have sensitive souls. Now, I'm red, Anna's blue, Rachel's green and, Uncle Phil, will you be buttons?'

'It's a bit childish, isn't it? Couldn't you make it Scrabble or draughts or something?'

'But that's the whole *point*,' we chorused. Parents had really no comprehension of what constituted adolescent enjoyment.

'In that case you must give me a bye,' he said. 'I shall go and deliver a food hamper to a poor old lady.'

'That's his nice way of saying a couple of drinks in the Eagle and Child with the other fugitive husbands,' said Rachel. 'He'll bring Mum back a little bottle of Cherry Brandy. He always does. She was drinking it when he met her. It was the only liqueur she'd heard of at the time and actually she detests the stuff, but she couldn't bear to disillusion him.'

I shook a six. That a trivial pretence of that sort could be kept up through the years just to preserve someone's sweet misconception was beyond my understanding. Was it on those little, apparently unimportant foundations a marriage was built?

After the Ludo we ate nuts and tangerines and discussed what we were going to do when the seemingly endless prison sentence of school was over. Rachel and I were still young enough to have vague but grandiose ambitions; Mark was two years older and had his future mapped.

'Yes, but is it what *you* want to do?' Rachel said. 'The fact that your father was in the army doesn't mean you're necessarily fitted to do the same thing. *My* father's a doctor, but that doesn't mean *I'd* make a doctor.'

She was right about that; Rachel, Beechwood's most famous fainter.

'I've never really wanted to do anything else,' he said. 'One odd-ball in the family's enough.'

'Just because he reads poetry it doesn't mean to say he's an odd-ball.'

'It's not just the poetry reading. It's the way he knocks everything. Not because he dislikes whatever it is, or it's against his principles. He knocks it just for the sake of knocking. He's got no logic. Take this business of my going into the army: according to him, I'll turn into a mindless automaton, unable to think beyond the parade-ground or the loyal toast. He has no rational basis for drawing those conclusions. He's read Evelyn Waugh and *Catch 22* and that's the fashionable sort of attitude to take.'

He didn't know it but he'd just described a kindred spirit. I, too, was over-sceptical, I, too, mocked what I couldn't be bothered to understand, I, too, had formed my ideas from the books I read. I prepared myself to spring to Jonathon's defence, then I looked at Mark's face – a nice, average face, the face of one born to conform, to accept, to never dream of questioning the status quo, to make the best of any circumstance – and I realized it would be pointless.

Rachel was more direct. 'Aren't you being a bit rotten,' she said, 'criticizing someone who isn't here to defend himself? I shan't play Ludo with you any more.'

Rachel was positively the only person I'd ever met who never talked behind anyone's back.

'No. It isn't cricket, is it, Mark? Not what you'd expect from the Head of the House.'

Rachel and I started. Mark went red. We wondered how much Jonathon had overhead. But he didn't seem to be offended. He merely rattled the dice-shaker and looked at the Ludo board and said, 'Well, this should be jolly good practice for all that strategy and tactics stuff you'll have to learn.'

'We've been talking about careers,' I said. 'What are your plans, Jonathon?'

He flashed me a quick brilliant smile. 'You remind me of my Dad. "What are your plans, Jonathon? Army? Navy? Make a man of you." I haven't got any plans.'

'But you've got to do *something*.'

'Why? Why can't I just be me, full stop?'

'And who would support you?' Rachel asked with supreme logic.

He ignored such an obvious query. He perched himself on the arm of the sofa beside me. 'As far as I can see,' he said, 'everybody squanders themselves *being* something – a lawyer or a stockbroker or a street-sweeper – just so that they can be docketed and pigeon-holed and told how stockbrokers or street-sweepers should behave. They let their life-force drain away in little drops pursuing their pointless little goals instead of expending it in one great effort on what they *really* want to do.'

Rachel started in with the 'but somebody's got to sweep the streets' argument, but I perceived what he meant. 'Who do you admire, Jonathon?'

'Baudelaire,' he said instantly. 'Gaugin, Byron. Even Hitler, perhaps. And, before you say, "But what about the eight million Jews?" Rachel, just remember the ideal – it may have been evil, but it was an ideal.'

'Oh look,' Rachel said. 'It's Christmas Day not the philosophical society. How about my ring, everyone? Daddy says Great Aunt Flo got it for being a good girl as good girls go.'

Dinner was gay: crackers and hats and corny mottoes, the threepences in the pudding, the brandy that wouldn't flame but spluttered damply around the holly leaf, the delicate way in which each of us tried to disguise our indigestion, the long poem which Doctor Conway, after a glass of port, was prevailed upon to deliver called *Christmas Day in the Workhouse*, the way Jonathon deliberately let his hand brush against mine when we reached for the sugar; it was Christmas written by Dickens and if I was alien, Little Emily perhaps, then Jonathon was my Steerforth.

We tackled the washing-up with our eyes closed, except for Rachel who kept saying, 'Glasses first, then crockery, *then* cutlery. And *don't* put the handles in the water. They go yellow.'

'For God's sake, woman, shut up.' Jonathon gagged her with a tea-towel and proceeded to tip everything into the sink at once and then wondered why the plug-hole was bunged up.

'What now?'

We hung our grimy, sodden drying-up cloths on the back of the door. Mark pushed the oven dishes, which we'd forgotten, back under the oven. Jonathon made one last futile plunge at the plug-hole.

'Let's listen to my new records,' Rachel said.

'Let's not,' said Jonathon. 'The half-dozen most popular works in the world. Ugh. Let's go out.'

'Out?'

'Yes, out,' he mimicked. 'If it's still there. It's the only time outdoors is fit for human consumption – Christmas day, when everyone else is inside sleeping it off.'

'There's only the *park*,' Rachel said, pulling on her fur cap. She was annoyed about his remark concerning her records. Jonathon looked at her face and changed her name from Nanook to Dostoyevsky.

The park was forged out of the reclamation of a disbanded estate. The lake had been preserved and the natural twisting tracks that led between the open spaces. Some of these were so narrow that we had to walk in Indian file: Mark leading, Rachel, still recalcitrant, behind and then Jonathon and myself. Where the hard frost hadn't penetrated, all was dampness and decay. Our feet squelched through mounds of rotting leaves, skated on patches of ice, were ever more chilled with each footstep.

'The woods decay, the woods decay and fall,
The vapours weep their burthens to the ground.'

Jonathon matched the metre to the rhythm of our progress. For once I could match him, quote for quote:

'Man comes and tills the field and lies beneath,
And after many a summer dies the swan.'

Rachel rolled her eyes heavenwards and walked on to catch up with Mark. There was a sudden bend in the path which separated us, couple from couple. 'Let's lose them,' Jonathon said.

We doubled back. The path rose steeply. He gave me his hand to assist me and there didn't seem to be any reason to let it go afterwards. Our climb brought us to the edge of a clearing.

'What's over there?'

'The observatory. And a kind of summer-house thing.'

'Let's go and have a look.'

We made our way across the space. Each blade of grass was separately defined with a silver rim. Each footstep was eradicated as the stiff trodden turf sprang back into shape, The sun hung, bloody, between two stark trees. My stomach quaked. An attractive stranger held my hand, urging me towards the unknown.

But Jonathon was accomplished. Sufficiently accomplished to sit beside me on the bench that ran round the inside of the musty wooden pagoda and make easy, inconsequential conversation. The windows were grimy and the light was dim; I could feel him more easily than I could see him.

'Your nose is cold.'

The tip of his nose, cold too, brushed mine back and forth. During this gentle, warmth-infusing contact, our lips met and opened, shaping themselves to each other. One arm came about my shoulders, the other around my waist. His kisses were light, exploratory. I was no longer afraid. When his mouth hardened upon mine I was ready. Ready, too, for the prising and jabbing of his insistent tongue, for the hand that unbuttoned and parted and eventually found flesh beneath the unwieldy layers of my clothing. He kissed behind my ear. I shuddered. His hand pressed rhythmically to my breast. My eyes were tightly closed. All was touch and taste: scratchy tweed, ribbed wool, soft skin, heat-arousing tongue, and the sound of his shallow breathing. My body recognized his, drawing close, dovetailing joint to joint. We were lying on the seat. It was no longer cold. Zips and buttons fell apart without resistance. A momentary withdrawal of contact and then there was the heat and the sweetness in another place, the pressure in my groin, the sudden fright and his not-to-be-denied potency. And then, through the hot and swirling blackness, our names, faintly echoing, growing louder and clearer: 'A-a-nna. Jon-a-thon.'

A flurry of arms and legs, a trembling of hands upon buttons, a brushing of hair out of our eyes and then walking blindly out of the gloom towards two inquisitive faces.

'We were just snuggling up to keep warm.'

He made it sound as innocent as a childhood game of Sardines. My cheeks were stinging, everything under my coat in disarray. Rachel said, 'Well for heaven's sake, come on. We're going home.'

Their faces were innocent of comprehension. How could they not realize what had almost happened?

He held out his hand to me, the hand that had lately wrought fire in forbidden places. He smiled. We began the long walk back. Rachel said, 'We mustn't be late for church tonight.' I thought, 'I have just been saved from the fate that is worse than death.' His lips moved in the darkness. I read them. They said, 'You're lovely.' It had been strange, and wonderful. It would not be strange the next time.

CHAPTER TEN

I kept Jonathon Lawrence's letters in an old shoe-box. By the end of July they amounted to twenty-nine. I read and re-read them until they fell apart at the creases. I thought it a criminal waste that they were written in ball-point pen; ball-point pen was only supposed to have a legibility span of thirty years. Even my undiscriminating eye could detect that they were largely exercises in lyrical prose, not addressed exclusively to me, but to the world or perhaps even to posterity. Some of the quotes and references were entirely out of my range: I spent a good deal of time in the library consulting the Oxford Dictionary of Quotations, usually to no avail. I couldn't help feeling that I was an excuse rather than a reason, but nevertheless they existed and they said 'Darling Anna' and 'Dearest Anna'; I drafted my replies so carefully and so many times that I nearly bankrupted the school stationery department.

Mr Langley might well play the 'Eroica' upon his gramophone. I had just received the twenty-ninth avowal of devotion – a good deal of it by kind courtesy of John Donne, but never mind. Downstairs Mr and Mrs Butler finalized wedding plans with my mother. Maurice and Berenice seemed to have little to do with it. I didn't need to go downstairs; I knew exactly what their attitudes would be: Mrs Butler would be sitting on the edge of the sofa, her square feet planted parallel, her jaws moving up and down with metronomic regularity while Mr Butler stood with his heels on the hearth, massaging his Harris tweed stomach. 'They built the pavement too near his arse,' Maurice said, 'and he's never stopped trying to make up for it.' There would be the occasional hesitant word from my mother. There would be tea and biscuits. I could see Mrs Butler's teeth going crunch, snap, crunch, snap, through digestive and shortbread, I could hear the drain-like sound that was Mr Butler imbibing liquid. As well as having ducks' disease, Mr Butler was dreadfully common.

The chief protagonists were in Manchester being measured up for their regulation fancy-dress. I had been done locally, together with one of Berenice's college friends: pale blue silk shantung with lace appliqués – expense no object. D-Day was August 4th and hysteria was mounting accordingly. As often as I could I retired to my attic with my letters. I saw the whole proceedings as a dreadful error, a black farce: Maurice and Berenice, Berenice of the clean nails and the good sense and the Scripture Union. Berenice the conventional, the parents' delight, the girl with no dirty habits and no imagination. I thought my brother must be unhinged and had told him so.

'You'd better start getting used to the idea. You're going to be sisters-in-law. You'll be washing one another's hair, chatting over cups of coffee, pinning up each other's hemlines. What fun it will be!'

'But you don't love her. You *can't* love her. You used to go out with other girls.'

'You've got an awful lot to learn haven't you, kiddo?' was all he said. He said it very gently.

My protestations notwithstanding, the marriage was arranged, the honeymoon hotel in Torremolinos was booked, the invitations were issued. I observed my mother closely during the intervening weeks. Six years. She was edgy, bemused, her hands shook conveying food to her mouth, or pouring out tea. I wanted to say something that would banish the desperate spark of hope in her eyes when she bought her wedding outfit, arranged to have her hair done, applied creams and lotions to her face. I wanted her to know that she couldn't compete in that way, not then, and certainly not now.

Mr Butler had hired the Imperial for the wedding reception. Perhaps not so much hired it as taken it over from cellar to garret. There were droves of Butlers booked in there for the night – and my father. I wondered what the droves of Butlers would think when they realized the bridegroom's father was not on residing terms with the bridegroom's mother.

In my attic I was spared the repetitive discussions about flowers and taxis and wines. The Maurice of a year ago would never have been conned into a morning-suit or the high-church rigmarole of St Luke's. The Maurice of a year ago had been a full-time knocker of every institution generally, but marriage in particular. I remembered my father talking about Maurice finding himself. Apparently he had now achieved that object. 'I have put away my college scarf and my CND badge and my rag magazines,' he said. His questioning of values too, by the look of it. There was a job in research and a dear little house in Middlesex awaiting him. Berenice was to teach biology at

St Winifred's School for Girls for a while and had visited the Family Planning clinic to ensure that this would be possible. They had become caricatures.

August 4th dawned misty, unseasonable, with a distinct nip in the air. I slept late and went downstairs into pandemonium.

'I've called you three times.'

'I'm not getting married,' I said, calmly placing slices of bread under the toaster.

'Don't be clever. There's enough to think about without having to put up with your cleverness.'

I set my face. Someone was going to suffer before the day was out and the likeliest candidate was me.

'Where's Maurice?'

'Getting ready, of course, as you should be doing.'

'I am ready. I have only to slip on my pretty blue dress and that's it.'

'And where's Trevor?' she said. She was darting about with cream on her face, doing absolutely nothing.

'Perhaps the army's cancelled his leave.'

'What! They wouldn't do that. Would they?'

'*Mother*. He was here, last night. It's only ten o'clock. You can't expect him *yet*.'

'And then there's what's-her-name, Ruby, the bridesmaid.'

'Jewel. And we're picking her up from the Butlers'.'

I took my tea and my rounds of toast and escaped to Maurice's bedroom before I could be infected with her madness.

'Mon Dieu!'

I leaned on the jamb of the door and laughed. He turned round from the mirror to display his full glory. He'd been trying on his topper.

'I know, I know. Like a pox-doctor's clerk. Don't say it.'

'Oh, Maurice.' I spread out my breakfast on his bed. 'Couldn't you have made it special licence and the Town Hall?'

'Why didn't I just?'

'I have to wear a funny little coronet of flowers stuck on

top of my head. it's sure to fall off during the most dramatic bit. And that Jewel girl walks as though she's been forty years in the saddle. I'll get the giggles. I know I will.' It was bubbling up inside me already, the nervous hysteria.

'Don't you bloody dare. I'm just about ready to rush off and board the nearest freight-train as it is.'

'Actually, looking at you in a cool, impersonal way, the effect is quite stunning. I bet you could get a job modelling for Moss Bros. But what will Pa Butler look like in this rig-out?' The very thought of it set me off giggling again.

'Here, take this.' He put a little white capsule into my saucer.

'What is it?'

'Tranquillizer. I got them off a bloke for the Finals.'

'And have you taken one?'

'You bet. In a few minutes I shall just float away on cloud nine.'

I swallowed it down with my tea. 'Have some toast?' I said.

He made a grimace of disgust and turned to adjust the grey topper again.

'A little more to the left. Don't stick it on bang in the middle. You look like a funeral director. There! That's it. Very Rex Harrison.'

Half an hour later I was in my blue and my flowered coronet, feeling as though I daren't move in case something gave way. The bouquet and the button-holes had arrived. But not Trevor. My mother, pale-lavender and Ascot hat, paced the floor. We'd be late. They'd call the whole thing off. She might have known everything would go wrong. I could see the sweat standing out in tiny beads on the surface of her powder.

'They can't start without Maurice, that's for certain.'

Maurice was shredding the spare button-hole into fragments.

'I thought Trevor, as best man, was supposed to be organizing everything?'

'Trevor,' he said savagely. 'Trevor couldn't organize a

piss-up in a brewery.'

He was just starting to dial Trevor's number when there was the sound of footsteps on the path and then a sharp bang at the door. I let him in. He was in uniform and looked bigger and rougher than ever.

'Hallo, folks,' he said, breezy smile, rubbing his hands together.

'You're bloody late, you half-wit. Now, here's the ring and don't sodding lose it.' Maurice picked up hat and gloves in a flurry.

'But I thought that was the whole idea of weddings,' he said, with innocent astonishment, 'being late.'

'That's the bride, you misbegotten son of – *Come* on.'

Maurice went. And then my mother went. It seemed a very long time before the taxi came for me. I knew that, by rights, I should have been round at the Butlers' all morning, helping to adjust Berenice's veil or something, but neither she nor I had mentioned the matter and, besides, Jewel Thing was there, who looked like the veil-adjuster of all time.

Jewel Thing was quite pretty in a fluffy, ill-defined way. Her coronet seemed to sit a good deal more happily upon her shining hair than mine did. 'I've got the jitters,' she said, stepping into the taxi. 'Have you?'

Maurice's tranquillizer must have been a big con. I did have the jitters, but for a different reason than Jewel.

'And Berenice is so *calm*,' she said. 'You wouldn't believe it. She looks *lovely*.'

And, when Berenice finally arrived on the arm of her father who looked like a drawing by Phiz, I had to admit it – she did look lovely: pale and assured but with the pensive, heroic air of one going voluntarily to sacrifice.

We took our places at the door. We waited for cues to be passed from Mr Butler to the vicar to the organist. My legs were quivering. Jewel sneezed. In front of us, Berenice was straight and still. The organist got the message and switched from the muted 'Water Music' to an ear-splitting 'Bridal March'. There was a great scraping and rustling as everyone stood up. I saw Mr Butler squeeze Berenice's hand. There was a lump in my throat.

How could I ever have imagined that I would giggle? I had to do Maurice's old trick with the upper lip in order to forestall the tears. I looked ahead of me, but into the corners of my vision flashed faces, turned towards us, strange faces, then a familiar one – could it be Rona? Then Aunt Kitty smiling and Jamie shifting from foot to foot. On the other side were massed ranks of Butlers and their relations, a riot of colour, headed by Mrs Butler in cerise brocade. Up to the front, the second pew on the right, my mother, and beside her the unmistakable morning-coated back of my father.

It was a protracted ceremony, interspersed with hymns and psalms. From the back, Maurice and my father could have been interchangeable. Even their voices were alike in timbre. There were no Aunt Kitty-type blunders during this service; both Maurice and Berenice responded loud and clear. 'Do you, Maurice Anthony . . . Do you, Berenice Mary . . .?' My eyes filled, were glazed over, with tears. I kept telling myself the the whole business was uncivilized, pagan, ritualistic: Maurice, who hadn't set foot inside a church since he was fifteen, making a pact in the sight of God – an absolute farce. But my tear-ducts paid no heed to my rationalizations.

At last the vows were made, the names were signed, the organist began the rousing prelude to the 'Wedding March'. Mrs Butler was weeping openly. Her husband kept pinching her elbow and whispering in her ear. I turned my head. My mother was gazing steadily at the stained glass above the altar. Had it been like this twenty-three years ago in the church of St Simon and St Jude? I didn't know. The wedding photographs had been either hidden or destroyed. My father was smiling at Maurice. He stood in a stripe of sunlight. His grey silk tie shone and his pearl tie-pin flickered. He looked very elegant. I tried to catch his eye but he was intent upon the bridal pair. I felt a sudden resentment at playing only a minor role in the proceedings. It should have been me, up there in front, wearing Swiss lace and wild silk. It should have been me upon whom his eyes were fixed in tender admiration.

The Imperial awaited us. Pa Butler was in his element, bossing waiters and dashing around, tails flapping, making sure everyone could understand the seating plan. His wife seemed to have mastered her tears by the third sherry. I squeezed my way to a corner where I consumed bushels of salted peanuts. 'Did you know your head-dress was slipping, dear?' Somebody's reptilian-necked great aunt assailed me in mid-mouthful. 'Here, let me do it for you.' A pair of wrinkled, bangled, old arms reached up and secured it at what I felt sure was a most unbecoming angle. 'You're Maurice's little sister, aren't you?' I slid rapidly away. That was quite enough of that. She smelt of that stuff you put on bitches' behinds to deter dogs from mounting them.

I couldn't see my father or my mother or Aunt Kitty or any other familiar face. Maurice and Berenice were in the centre of the mêlée, holding court. It was curious how the company seemed to have split up into distinct groups: the Butlers, the university crowd – all out-shouting one another, the local people; it was only my own family who seemed to have dematerialized.

'Anna.'

I felt a hand upon my arm and turned round, prepared to be told that I ought to be circulating.

'Rona!'

She was wearing a white coat and a white big-brimmed hat. She looked like a milkmaid.

'Gosh, it's nice to see you, among this awful mob. Are you still in London then? In the flat?' It seemed such ages since I'd sat at their round table, drinking in their puzzling conversation.

'Oh no. We have the flat up some time ago. Trixie got her garage and Pat got a job in Brazil. And I'm getting married myself in a fortnight.' She called over a small, thick-set man with a wrinkled Gallic face. She put her arm through his. She looked very happy and I was glad for her. I was glad, too, that she hadn't got Jake.

'Shall we go and see the presents? Simon?'

Simon made a noise that might have meant anything. We went through anyway. In the wedding-present room were a few anonymous lookers-on, and my mother and father. They were both gripping their sherry glasses and didn't appear to be talking. I remembered my manners. I performed introductions.

'Oh, I've met Mr Blake,' Rona said, beaming at him.

Of course, I should have known, it was on the cards she'd have met him.

My mother went rigid. It followed that Rona had met Olivia too. I started to chatter about the presents. Weren't they delightful? Had anyone ever seen such breath-taking glassware or gleaming stainless steel? I sounded very foolish.

Rona was gallantly attempting to converse with my mother who was looking at her as the Maquis probably looked at collaborators. My father said, 'Hallo,' very quietly and drew me away from them.

'You're sitting next to me,' he said.

'Am I? I feel like sitting somewhere entirely different just to confound Mr Butler's well-laid plans.'

We laughed conspiratorially. I saw my mother's head jerk sideways to see what we were up to.

'How's it going?'

Six years. How had they greeted one another? How had she managed to control the trembling of her hands? That hat looked fussy, pathetic. My heart ached for her.

'It's a bit grim. What can you expect?'

There was a sudden crash of gavel on block and some sergeant-major shouted, 'Ladies and Gentlemen, the wedding breakfast is served.' We rushed to take our rightful places before Mr Butler had an apoplectic fit.

'Mr and Mrs Butler. Mr and Mrs Snodgrass. Mr and Mrs Bursting-Reaching.' It couldn't be true. The sergeant-major chap was probably hard of hearing. He couldn't do much with Blake though. A lot of heads turned to see my mother making her entrance on my father's arm. They separated at the top table, she to sit beside Mr Butler, he to take his place between me and Mrs Butler who was casting a hard eye over the knives and forks – to make sure that they were clean, I supposed.

'Sam Butler has certainly gone to town,' my father said,

remarking the expensive flowers, the numerous glasses awaiting different wines.

'He probably gets it back off his income tax. Did you see all the photographers? There'll be a picture in every paper in the land next week.'

The table curved round in a horse-shoe shape. He had only to incline his head to see my mother, enduring the finger-clicking, bouncing proximity of Mr Butler. Maurice was attacking his melon as though he hadn't eaten for weeks and Berenice was smiling very prettily as the head waiter adjusted her veil over the back of her chair.

On my right sat an usher, Nicholas Bentley by name, who kept saying, 'So you're old Maurice's sister,' which I thought was hardly what you'd expect of a BA in English, so I turned my attention to an Italian waiter who was much better looking and who kept winking at me and refilling my glass to the exclusion of everyone else's.

Mrs Butler had claimed my father. She was talking about London and how it had changed since she'd done her season – I suspected that the only season Mrs Butler had done was serving teas at the end of some pier – and going all coy with her hand up to her neck. My father had a reputation; I expect she fancied her chances.

The cake – tiered and arched like a miniature Doge's Palace – was cut. A dozen cameras recorded the incision. Trevor read the telegrams – a mixture of old restrained and young *double-entendre*. Trevor spoke. Mr Butler spoke. Maurice spoke. There seemed to be a tacit understanding that my father wouldn't speak: after all, 'My wife and I' would have sounded somewhat preposterous under the circumstances.

We rose and dispersed. The waiters began to clear away the débris. Nicholas Bentley and the other ushers were rushing about with toilet-rolls and tin-cans and lipsticks. I followed them into the car park where they proceeded to despoil Pa Butler's Rover, amid much idiot hooting. They didn't know it, but Maurice and Berenice were leaving by taxi for the airport. Pa Butler would have a stroke.

I went back into the hall. Berenice, at the top of the stairs, changed into her going-away clothes, threw her bouquet over the banister. I missed it.

'And you know what that's supposed to mean,' Maurice said.

He was wearing the new gold signet ring on the third finger of his left hand. I wondered if he envisaged a time when he might want to take it off.

'We might as well say goodbye now, before the massed grand farewells,' he said.

I suddenly felt very embarrassed.

'Take care of yourself, kiddie. I'll send you a postcard.'

'Saying "Wish you were here"?' I replied automatically. But the days of the double-act were over. He was being deliberately hearty and adult, telling me that I would always be welcome in Enfield whenever I chose to jump on a train, telling me to be sure to attend to my schoolwork and look after my mother. He could have been my father. Except that he had really little time for me. I stepped aside to make way for the other bon-voyagers and well-wishers. The separation seemed total, irrevocable.

'That's that,' my father said. We stood among the empty glasses and the cake crumbs. My mother had disappeared. Perhaps to have a good cry. That dreadful after-the-ball feeling had already descended upon us. There was much consulting of watches and talk of traffic conditions. Some of the resident Butlers were sneaking upstairs to pack their cases. Mr Butler was drinking Benedictine and talking drainage with the borough engineer. Trevor and Jewel were exchanging addresses. I couldn't see *that* optimistic gesture amounting to much.

'Do you have to go straight back?'

'It's better if I do.' He was starting to say something else when the Butes converged *en masse*. He winced. He'd been escaping from Aunt Kitty all day.

When he finally extricated himself, it was my mother he looked for. They met in the hall. He put his hand on her arm and then drew her into the now empty wedding-present room and closed the door behind them.

I said my goodbyes. To the Butes, to Rona and Simon, to Trevor and Jewel. The Butlers I avoided, one and all. Nicholas Bentley had offered to drive us home. In the car park his little MG stood next to my father's dark-blue Lotus. I let him talk at me while I waited. I believe I allowed him to take my telephone number. He kept talking about 'old Maurice'; I kept my eye on the door at the end of the hall.

They emerged. Her eyes were hard and bright. My father contemplated his waistcoat buttons. They walked apart. No prayers had been answered, no miracle had occurred. Their desolation hovered about them like an infection. Mr Butler appeared and hailed my father and they both went to the reception desk to attend to the financial details. My mother remained where she was, excluded, as it seemed she always would be excluded.

CHAPTER ELEVEN

The day after the wedding Rachel came back from Spain. I was overjoyed to see her. The atmosphere in our house was unbearable. My mother didn't say a word but her eyes had gone deep-set with crying. He wasn't coming back. He'd asked her again for a divorce. I knew it. She didn't have to say a word. The very walls dripped with melancholy. I said, 'We will now have three rousing choruses of "Abide With Me".' She looked at me with such anguish that I was spurred to cruelty.

Rachel brought me back a leather purse appliquéd with pictures of Flamenco dancers.

'Did you get seduced by a señor?'

'No. Not really.'

'What do you mean – not really?'

But she brushed it aside. 'Listen,' she said. 'You're not going on holiday, are you?'

I never went on holiday.

'Auntie Jo rang up last night. You know they have a holiday cottage in Northumberland, near Seahouses? Well, Mark and Jonathon are spending a week there. And she wondered if we'd like to go too. Mrs Bartholomew, their old nanny, who lives in the village is staying there to cook and clean et cetera, so it'll all be perfectly respectable. Mum said she'd ring up *your* mother and assure her of your moral safety – well, she didn't say that exactly but that's what she meant. *Do* come. It should be great.'

My insides started to quiver as they always did when I wanted something so desperately that I couldn't believe it would come to pass. I could think of a dozen reasons my mother would have for refusing permission. How was it that mothers like Rachel's could allow privileges without batting an eyelid, while mothers like mine saw pitfall and gin in the most innocuous activity? Not that this was likely to be an innocuous activity. I remembered Christmas. My insides quivered frantically at the thought of seeing him again and him seeing me, after our short-lived passionate encounter, after all those lyrical letters. I'd never have to face the problem though. She'd never let me go.

But I had reckoned without Mrs Conway's persuasive powers or, more particularly, her prestige.

'Is it that boy who writes to you?' she said, replacing the telephone receiver.

'Yes.' That much I'd had to concede, passing it off as a casual pen-friendship. She'd never managed to get at the letters. I transferred my cupboard key from pocket to pocket of whatever I happened to be wearing. If she'd read them she'd either have assumed he was mad or packed me off to a home for delinquents. There certainly wouldn't have been any idea of a holiday in the offing.

'Well, you haven't had a holiday for a long time and Mrs Conway says their old nanny will be looking after you and Rachel seems to have her head screwed on the right way and the sea air should be good for your chest –' She put down her duster and looked at me. I had a horrible feeling that I was about to receive a long-overdue enumeration of the facts of life. We'd never discussed anything remotely to do with reproduction before – when I'd started my periods she'd merely said, 'I suppose you know what it's all about?' – if she began now I'd die with embarrassment. But she only said, 'Just be careful.' Being careful ranged from how you crossed the road to wearing clean underclothes in case you had an accident, right through all aspects of the forbidden subject.

The following Saturday morning I was waiting in the station, my case packed with all manner of antidotes against coughs, colds, wounds, wheezes and insect-bites. 'I'm going to Northumberland,' I'd said. 'Not up the Congo.' All of Rachel's luggage fitted into a canvas air-line bag slung over her shoulder. She was wearing fringed jeans and her new Spanish suède jacket. Somehow Rachel, like Berenice, always succeeded in looking just right for the occasion.

The journey passed in a swirling haze of travel-sickness. Rachel ate chocolate biscuits while I sat rigid, fighting back the nausea. It wasn't until I hit *terra firma* that the green waves receded, and it was just as well they did because Mark and Jonathon had come to meet us.

They were off-hand, shy of making any demonstration of affection in a public place. And we were shy too. Six months had passed. It was possible that we might have nothing in common any more.

Jonathon and I exchanged glances and looked away quickly. He seemed taller, broader, a stranger. The letters were an embarrassment: easy outpourings in which we'd written what we'd never dare to say, face to face. We were right back at the beginning; all the ground we thought we'd covered would have to be re-trod.

The wooden bungalow was situated right on the edge of the beach. We would be sleeping with our toes almost in the North Sea. 'Tide's out, Jonathon,' Mark said. 'And it's your turn.'

'Your turn for what?'

'Well,' Jonathon said, 'due to the lack of plumbing arrangements, certain homely accommodations are necessary, entailing a trip down to the sea at low tide. Volunteers are welcome.'

We made exaggerated sounds of disgust. One tended to forget that rustic living included all sorts of distasteful features.

Mrs Bartholomew was up to the elbows in flour. The table in the tiny kitchen was arrayed with pies and flans and jam tarts. Rachel and I looked at one another, silently vowing to return to the Ryvita régime with a vengeance next term.

Mrs Bartholomew was a small flat woman with no apparent bosom or child-nursing lap and a cloud of fine silver hair through which you could see large pink patches of skull. I discovered later that she suffered from something called alopecia – 'Comes out in handfuls.' Next to Diana and Josephine, it was her favourite subject.

She showed us our sleeping quarters: a double bed which took up the whole space of the bedroom; you had literally to climb through the threshold. Jonathon and Mark had a similar arrangement at the other end of the bungalow. Mrs Bartholomew herself slept on a let-down studio-couch in the living-room. 'Bags by the wall,' Rachel said. 'Do you still talk in your sleep?' She'd told me that one night, during the Christmas holiday, I'd carried on a somniloquy in two different voices. 'Just like *Psycho*,' she'd said. The idea had intrigued me ever since, the idea of a totally different personality struggling to escape out of my subconscious.

'Dear Mrs Bartholomew, how about some nosh then, for four growing bairns?' Jonathon said, putting an arm around her frail shoulders. She started to chuckle. It was a foregone conclusion that he'd be good with old ladies. He had only to say 'Why aye', with his head on one side for her to start falling about with mirth.

We ate, and listened to Mark expounding his plans for the week. He had lists and maps and guide-books at his elbow. Names dotted his conversation like islands in a stream: Beadnell and Bamburgh, Warkworth and Lindisfarne, Coquet and Cheviot, they sounded like the background to an old romance saga.

'Watch it, or he'll have us on a commando course,' Jonathon said.

'Which could only be to the good, as far as you're concerned. If you didn't happen to have a thin nature, you'd be flabby – all that lying around reading.'

'Yessah. Immediately, sah.'

'Isn't there an abbey or a priory on Lindisfarne?' I asked him in an attempt to relieve the tension.

'I simply can't do with famous ruins,' he said. 'They're always full of adenoidal guides and enthusiastic shiny-faced women in flowered cotton frocks.'

I could see that it was not going to be a very profitable activity suggesting anything to Jonathon; all the ideas would have to emanate from him or else be considered worthless.

Mrs Bartholomew, who had been dreaming above her ginger pudding, suddenly came down to earth. 'I haven't congratulated you yet, have I, pet?' She smiled fondly at Mark who made modest, dismissive gestures. His examination results had been excellent.

'You might as well congratulate me while you're about it,' Jonathon said. 'I don't suppose there'll be much cause for congratulation next year.'

'Don't tell me *you* won't get on in the world, Jonathon, because that I won't believe.'

'Say it again, say it again,' he said. 'I *adore* the way you say "won't": "wu-ant"; say it again.'

'Get away.'

He imitated that too. Within a few days Jonathon had Mrs Bartholomew off to a t, Geordie and gestures and all. It helped to enliven our ruin-touring. While Mark and Rachel religiously inspected every perpendicular arch and flying buttress, he'd regale me with imaginary duologues between Mrs Bartholomew and his mother who, he said, spoke in exceedingly friable upper-class tones.

To a certain extent I shared his philistine views about ancient monuments.

'I prefer people to things,' he said.

'But people *made* these places,' Rachel said in exasperation.

'They just don't speak to me. Heaps of stones. Monkish cells. Who *were* those people? I don't know. I don't care. They don't impinge on me or my concerns. And don't start rabbiting on about heritage, Rachel. I know my attitude's wrong according to every cultural principle in the book, but it's how I am. Utterly egotistical.'

It wasn't until the third day that I realized what he meant about places speaking. We were walking to Amble, the beach upon our right, a colliery upon our left-hand side. It was a cloudy afternoon. Stillness stretched before and behind us. The pit wheel was static, etched black against the grey sky. Rachel shivered. Mark said, 'And a deathly 'ush descended upon the earth.' I stood stock-still, watching them, listening to their conversation, as though mesmerized.

'What's the matter with you?'

I closed my eyes, I tried to close my ears to shut out their voices, but it was too late; I had lost it.

'This place. I've seen it or dreamed it before: the sea down there and that slag-heap and all that scrubby ground overgrown with weeds. And I knew that Rachel was going to shiver and that Mark was going to say what he said, just as though I'd read it or seen it previously.' I opened my eyes. It was the same scene that I saw, but transmuted to normalcy, to meaninglessness.

'*Déjà-vu*,' Mark said. 'Paramnesia. It's just a momentary time-lag between two sensory nerve-centres that normally work simultaneously, so when one finally catches up with the other it seems as though you're remembering something, not experiencing it for the first time. It's quite a common occurrence.'

Jonathon came over beside me. 'Don't let him rationalize your magic,' he said. 'That's the explanation put forward by scientists who simply can't do with an enigma or a loose end. Perhaps you *were* here – in another life. Perhaps your consciousness escaped and visited this place. Who knows?'

'Perhaps it's my Celtic blood.' I felt very cold and slightly shaky. The clouds were low and seemed to be bearing down upon me.

'You're not Celtic. You've not got Celtic colouring and you're not tall enough. You probably mean Iberian. They were the very first British settlers. Those dark-visaged, shaggy people who painted themselves with woad.'

'Pardon me.'

He grinned. 'Don't mention it. It's a common misconception.'

Mark began to sing, to the tune of 'Men of Harlech':

'Going up Snowdon with your woad on, never mind if you get rained or snowed on, go it, ancient B!'

We joined in and proceeded, in unison, to Amble where, after a glass of lager, I felt warmer but could not entirely dispel that strange internal chill. Jonathon drew in the slopped beer, pulling out liquid points from the centre puddle to form a star.

'D'you remember those stars? Christmas Eve?'

How could I ever forget them?

He looked at me and then smiled, very sweetly. And for the first time in three days I felt completely at ease in his presence.

The pub began to fill up with old men, capped and mufflered. High, thin, plaintive, Northumbrian accents filled the room. Mark and Rachel were reading about Hadrian's Wall. Jonathon and I sat back in an alcove, partially obscured by a red woven curtain. He entwined my fingers in his. 'That summer-house thing,' he said. 'You were lovely.' He looked round into my averted face. 'I wish those two would just drift away with their historical facts and their five-mile hikes. I wish it was just us.'

I remembered those parts of me with which he was familiar, those affected, passionate phrases we'd written, and the chill feeling in my inside was swept away before an upsurging stab of desire. Nothing was changed.

On the morning of the fourth day Rachel awoke with a sore throat and a high temperature. I vacated my side of the bed very promptly, away from her germ-ridden presence and fetched Mrs Bartholomew who, armed with a teaspoon, pushed down Rachel's tongue and reported inflammation at the back of her throat. 'Perhaps someone could get some antiseptic lozenges,' Rachel croaked. Her face was flushed and she was bathed in sweat.

'Throat lozenges'll not shift that lot. That's tonsillitis, or I'm no judge.'

Unfortunately Rachel confounded this glib diagnosis by informing us thickly that she'd had her tonsils removed ten years ago.

'Perhaps it's flu. Perhaps you picked up a Spanish bug.'

She groaned and lay back on the pillows, eyes closed, uttering imprecations against fate which chose to strike her down during the holidays when it had the whole school term to go at.

'You ought to get back to your father.'

'But it might be gone by tomorrow. Twenty-four hour flu. I've had it before.'

But Mrs Bartholomew had not reared generations of infants without knowing how to turn a deaf ear to arguments. Besides, Rachel was too weak to be obdurate. We left her, swallowing aspirin and hot lemon, while we held a conference.

'If I could get hold of a car,' Mark said, 'I could get her home. I suppose she'd be all right here, kept in bed, but one doesn't like to take chances.'

'Well, there's our Billy, isn't there?' said Mrs Bartholomew, sniffing a bit because that fact hadn't sprung to our minds immediately.

Of course, 'wor Billy' who owned the local garage. Billy would lend us a car, a good car too, that we could be sure of.

It was arranged, despite Rachel's half-hearted squawks and they were really only protestations for form's sake; you could tell she was longing for her own bed.

'When you come to the end of a perfect holiday,' Jonathon said, sitting on the edge of the bed and pretending to take Rachel's pulse though, as he freely admitted, he hadn't the faintest idea what the pulse rate should be.

'There's no need for you and Anna to leave. I feel bad enough as it is, dragging Mark away.'

'No there isn't, is there, when you come to think of it?'

We faced one another, each side of the bed. His wish had come true: Mark and Rachel were fading away.

'After all, Mrs Bartholomew will still be here.'

I could go home, in the front seat, next to Mark's sturdy dependability, home to safety, to routine, to boredom. We might write a few letters, then the correspondence would tail off: a Christmas card, a view of some foreign beach, silence.

'Will you kill my spiders?' I said. 'It was always Rachel's job.'

'I'll kill your spiders.'

‘Oh, stop making such a big issue out of it. There’s no earthly reason why you shouldn’t stay.’ Rachel’s voice was fading fast. It would be notes on pieces of paper by the time she got home.

We waved them off. Mark was going to bring the car back the next day. Rachel looked very small and child-like wrapped in her rugs. I saw Jonathon’s face as we turned to go indoors. He looked pleased with himself, triumphant. I thought of tales I’d read: voodoo, people who could impose their will upon other people. They no longer seemed quite so fantastic.

It rained that afternoon. Mrs Bartholomew started another batch of buns. The bookcase contained a few paperbacks: standard Neville Shutes, and Agatha Christies. Jonathon and I read, the silence broken only by the occasional striking of a match when he lit one of the evil-smelling Gauloises he’d taken to smoking that summer. The clock ticked. In the kitchen, Mrs Bartholomew wondered, quaveringly, where oh where, her Highland laddie had gone. I was pleasantly bored, but hoped that this wasn’t going to be the pattern for the rest of the week.

Summer flu can strike viciously and unexpectedly. At lunch-time Mrs Bartholomew was quite fit, by tea-time her legs wobbled under her and her head felt ‘stuffed up with cotton wool’. Jonathon placed a professional hand on her forehead. ‘You’ve got it,’ he said cheerfully. ‘Rachel’s lergy. Who’ll be the next, I wonder? We’re dropping like flies.’

‘Maybe if I just put my feet up for a while,’ she said, but without conviction.

‘You’re going straight home to your Marjorie,’ he said firmly. ‘Anna’s going to pack your things and I’m going round for your Billy and one of his fleet of cars. So you can just stop your arguing before you start.’ He was as deaf to her excuses as she’d been to Rachel’s.

‘What about you two?’ she kept saying. ‘I promised Rachel’s mother I’d look after you.’

‘We’ll settle all that when we get you tucked up in bed,’ he replied.

I threw grey cotton stockings and long vests and pinafores into her hold-all. I didn't look at him. It was all a bit uncanny.

Billy and Marjorie duly arrived with the car and lifted their mother, still protesting, into the back seat.

'Back in a flash,' Jonathon said. 'Just get things sorted out.'

I paced the floor. My forehead was wet and my hands were damp, but it wasn't the flu. Everything was happening much too fast. I had the wild idea of packing my bag and vanishing before he came back, but the mad, adventure-hungry part of my nature rooted me to the spot. I was so absorbed in my interior dialogue in which my cautious, frightened self was losing out that I didn't hear him come in.

'You are a jumpy bird, aren't you?'

'You startled me. You've been a long time.'

'Had to have a cup of tea. Two cups, in fact. All they seem to do in the barbarian north is make tea. Announce earthquake, plague or disaster and on goes the kettle for tea. You should see that house! She has photographs of her forebears ranged round the walls, glaring down at you. They all look like Ramsay Macdonald – and that's just the women.'

'So what's happening?'

'You're going home. I'm putting you on the bus for Newcastle and thence the train and then I'm waiting until tomorrow for Mark to bring back the car. At least that's the authorized version, as told to Mrs Bartholomew to put her mind at rest. The point is – are you?'

'They'll come and check. Somebody will.'

'Not on your life. Marjorie will be too busy making sure her mother doesn't budge an inch and Billy's going to Berwick for his big night out.'

It seemed as though he was leaving me with the whole burden of decision. Then he said, 'Stay, Anna. Please. I want you to stay.'

Of course I would stay. Why should the cycle of coincidence have been set in motion otherwise? It was ordained.

We heard the sea that night. It sighed as I sighed. It plunged and receded as he did. It filled my ears, rushing and roaring, and I cried out. His face was grim at first and very young afterwards. It was not at all like the books, like I had imagined it would be. The books made it seem a slow, easy, smooth progression; they did not mention the halts, the fumblings, the pain or the embarrassed breaking-off to ensure against conception. Nor did they mention that the climax, when it came, did not draw you together but thrust you apart, making you seem, during its brief span, mere instruments of one another's enjoyment. He smiled in his sleep, he looked like a wicked choirboy. I thought of my father and Olivia, Maurice and Berenice, all the millions of initiates whose ranks I was now qualified to join. I thought of all my fears and speculations and convictions that I'd make a mess of it. I thought forward to the morning and how we'd appear to each other in the light of this new knowledge. I slept.

CHAPTER TWELVE

The homeward-bound bus jerked and bumped over the country roads. Each and every bump and jerk was a small agony, but I cherished my aching soreness; it was physical proof positive of my altered state.

We'd had the statutory farewell at the station: promises to write, mutual determination to meet again as soon as possible. We kissed and exchanged all the proper sentiments. From the bus window I watched his still figure diminishing. I wasn't sorry to be on my own; I had so much to think about, so much to re-live. His presence would have been extraneous. The pangs of separation would come later.

Tennyson Avenue slept. I could almost feel the tangible descent of torpor as I turned the corner. I was returning to another world, the real world of hot dusty summer afternoons where nothing ever happened.

I had expected her to be at the front door, ready to

welcome me. She was nowhere to be seen. I pushed open doors, calling 'Mother!' Like a small child, I had the panic-stricken idea that, in my absence, she might have died or gone away.

And then she appeared at the top of the stairs.

'You've come home then.'

'Yes. We had a great time. The weather was glorious. Look at my tan.'

'Did you?'

It was then that she started to descend the stairs, one step at a time. She was very pale. I could see a tic beating in the side of her cheek.

'What about last night? Was that glorious too? Was that glorious too?' Her voice was going higher and louder, her face breaking up into sharp planes, her eyes burning, her mouth spewing the words.

'What do you mean? What's the matter?'

She reached the bottom. She had me by the shoulders. Our faces were level. There was no way I could avoid her hateful gaze.

I started to gabble: 'Have you heard from Mrs Conway? About Rachel? Mrs Bartholomew started to feel peculiar too this morning, so I decided I'd better come home –'

'You filthy little bitch. You filthy, lying, little bitch!' Her control had snapped. Each word was punctuated by a stinging slap on the side of my face. 'Rotten little bitch.' She flung me away from her. My ringing head struck the banister. Through the mists and stars I saw her coming for me again. There was murder in her face.

'Rotten. Liar. Bitch.'

I shook with terror. It wasn't so much the violence as the sound of those dreadful words. The telephone rang. At the third ring she went to it. I heard her terse replies. I went into the sitting-room. I couldn't get my breath. I knew I'd have been dead or maimed for life if the telephone hadn't rung.

'You thought you could deceive me and get away with it. You haven't lived long enough to do that.' She stood in the doorway, her hands on her hips. Violent rage had given way to cold hate. 'That was Mrs Conway on the phone. She said Mark had just rung from Northumberland to say you were on your way home. You thought you'd been so clever, didn't you? Well, everybody knows just what you are now, the Conways, Mark – a filthy little whore. How many times has it happened before? How long have you been carrying on like this? A boy you hardly know.'

Slam, bang, went the door behind her. She crossed the room and stood over me. I cowered into the back of the chair. I couldn't speak. I couldn't cry. I was numb.

'Mrs What's-her-name's daughter rang Mrs Conway this morning to explain about her mother being ill and to make sure you got home safely last night. My daughter. Common knowledge that she's a little tart.'

She was working herself up to the pitch of physical assault again. I didn't care. If only the stream of obscenity would cease. She was soiling me, defiling me, sullying what had been pleasant and simple and straightforward, deforming it into a kind of perversion.

'Nothing happened. Nothing *happened*. We just stayed there. Because I missed the bus.'

'Liar. Liar. I know when you're lying. You slept with him. You were intimate with him. We'll soon find out when I take you to the doctor. A boy you hardly know.'

'He loves me.' Just to hold on to that: Jonathon loves me. Just hold on to it and come through, somehow.

'Loves you? You think that's love? You were just easy access for him. He'll laugh about you. A dirty little tart.'

'Shut up. Shut up!' I was shrieking now, the tears pouring down my face. I couldn't bear to hear it any longer. 'You make everything rotten. You always have done. You hate anybody to be happy. You don't give a damn about me. It's the Conways knowing that drives you mad. I hate you. I've always hated you. You should be glad somebody likes me, because after living with you for all these years I'm not very likeable.' The words ran into one another, were distorted with sobbing, were as raucous and mindlessly aggressive as hers had been. But to attack was my only hope of defence. 'You want to make my life a misery like yours, like you tried to make Maurice's, like you made my father's till he left you. No wonder he left you. Anybody would have done. My father was happy and gay and you made him miserable . . .' I subsided as a sob caught my breath. I was trembling from head to foot, awaiting the blow, ready to flinch.

The blow didn't materialize. She began to smile. It was more horrible than her face of fury. I felt that I was being turned to stone.

'Your father,' she said. 'He's not your father. Your father was like you, no good, rotten. You've got the same bad blood.'

They were just words, words used as weapons to inflict pain. Bitch and whore and tart had become blunted with repetition. It was only when they were said that she seemed to realize their composite meaning. Her smile evaporated, she looked bewildered. As though she found it incredible that after all this time she should be the agent of her own betrayal.

The tears were still running into the corners of my mouth and my chest shook rhythmically with sobs. The mirror on the opposite wall was not exactly parallel with the shelf beneath it. It annoyed me. More than anything, I wanted to go over and straighten it. My hands were folded in my lap. All along my forearm tiny hairs, sunbleached to white, lay flat and regular against my tanned skin. In the winter they weren't noticeable. The electric clock ticked vibrantly. In the other room the telephone gave out the whirring sound that was usually preliminary to it ringing. We waited, but nothing happened. It often did that: whirred, making you start from your seat, then didn't ring. 'Who knows,' Maurice had once said, 'what potential beautiful friendships have withered in the bud due to a misdirected telephone call?' Even our breathing was audible in that silent room, mine echoing hers: inhale, exhale, inhale, exhale. The beginnings of sentences kept forming in my head but, always, voicing the first word was the stumbling-block. Nor could I look at her. Perhaps if we could keep up this motionless silence for long enough the words would be drawn back into the depths of her unconscious as if they had never been.

But there was a knock at the front door. Thursday. My mind automatically registered the fact. The butcher, or the insurance agent. She picked up her purse and went to answer it. I went upstairs. There would be no more shouting and assault now. We had come far beyond such simple straightforward solutions. I dropped my suitcase on the floor and took the cupboard key out of my pocket. I removed my secret store, object by object. Treasured tokens they'd been, representing me, representing my life, my experiences and my identity: 'Anna Blake, aged twelve, Anna Blake, her blue period'; they were meaningless. I was Anna Somebody-Else.

I took out my savings book. My clothes were already packed. I undid the suitcase and pushed in a few favourite books and records on top of the clothes. There was nothing else I minded leaving behind me. I began to write on the back of an old envelope: 'Don't worry. I shall be quite safe. I am going away.' Then I crossed out the 'Don't worry', signed the note and stuck it into the side of the mirror between glass and frame.

I came down the stairs unobserved. The insurance agent was a garrulous man, immune to signs of impatience and the front door was closed behind her back. I avoided the bottom step which creaked and went through to the kitchen. As children, Maurice and I had made a hole in the hedge which divided our back garden from the Langleys'. The hole was child-size, but just possible to squeeze through if you crawled sideways. I pulled my suitcase, on its edge, behind me. The Langleys were cruising in the Mediterranean. I crossed their smooth cultivated lawn where Mr Langley sat in his canvas chair, drinking tonic water and wielding the gramophone needle. I might never hear the rising strains of Scarlatti or Mississippi Delta jazz on the summer air again. Round the side of the house to the front gate, a quick look left and right – no sign of the insurance man – and I was off down Tennyson Avenue, round the first corner into Browning Road and on to a fortuitously-timed number 9 bus in the space of three minutes.

At the GPO I withdrew as much money as they would allow me to withdraw at one time. It was sufficient, anyway, for my present needs; I looked no farther ahead.

I cut through Trinity Square to get to the station. Olivia Murray's old house had been bought by a high-class doctor, a very smooth man with a sinister, totally bald head and rimless glasses. There was a Daimler and a Renault Floride parked outside. I wondered if illegal operations were now being performed where once Pierrot had gazed poignantly down from the pale-pink wall.

'Just missed it, love,' the porter said, as I arrived at the barrier brandishing my ticket. 'The next one isn't until 16.30 – that's 4.30 to you and me – you might as well go and stretch your legs.'

I cursed British Railways and their timetables and went into the buffet. I attributed my giddiness and trance-like feeling to hunger. I hadn't eaten since – Seahouses, breakfast-time, years ago. Around me were the various old tramps and decayed-looking talkers-to-themselves who always inhabit station buffets. The dispossessed. I was now one of them.

I divided my money, putting some into my case, some into my bag and the rest into my coat pocket. I was my mother's daughter. Hadn't she always stressed the affinity between railway stations and pickpockets? The minute hand of the clock above the doorway moved in jerks. As long as I watched it, it remained stationary, whenever I looked away then looked back again, I found it had moved. But not quickly enough, not nearly quickly enough. I still had more than two hours to wait and I didn't know whether or not she'd have the police out searching for me.

An old, grey-bearded woman, held together precariously with safety-pins, seated herself opposite me and fixed me with an eye of such glassy malevolence that I picked up my belongings and fled. I would put my case in a left-luggage locker and ride on buses until the train was due.

The bus station was just around the corner. I boarded a number 7 – the 7 had the longest route. The conductor looked at me queerly when I said 'There and back', as though it contravened omnibus regulations. I sat upstairs in solitary splendour, smoking cigarettes. My thoughts kept slipping away from what should have been their main preoccupation. My head ached frantically. It was like that period just before sleep when you can't hang on to a lucid train of thought because stupid irrelevancies keep breaking in.

We moved out of the town centre, along Queensway and up Glebe Hill. It was only then that I realized this was Aunt Kitty's bus, Aunt Kitty's district. I rushed down the stairs as the bus drew level with Osborne Drive. The conductor rang the bell and shook his head in bafflement. 'You must be in love,' he said. I thought briefly of Jonathon. He seemed very vague and far away.

Aunt Kitty was in the back garden weeding the rockery to the tune of 'And this is my beloved'; she'd rinsed her hair – it was now a thoroughly incongruous shade of strawberry-blonde, more strawberry than blonde. She put down her trowel, got to her feet and launched into her welcoming routine: Had I forgotten the address? It had been so long. I would stay to see Henry, wouldn't I? Otherwise he'd be so disappointed. Why hadn't I brought Cis with me? I curtailed her in full flood. I had to say it immediately or I would never say it.

'We've had a row. She says my father isn't my father. Is that true?'

The stream dried up abruptly. She stood with her mouth open. Aunt Kitty was not like me to whom lies came more fluently than the truth. You could almost see her brain ticking over through the windows of her rapidly-shifting eyes.

'It is true. Isn't it?'

'Come inside. We'll have a cup of tea. I'm gasping.'

She busied herself, filling the kettle, lighting the gas, sorting out cups and saucers. She didn't look at me once. Inside was surprisingly tidy: all the spoons in the spoon drawer, all the plates stacked uniformly in the cabinet.

'I have a right to know. I'm seventeen.'

She measured milk into the cups with great precision.

On the wall above her head hung a chart of recipes for every day of the week. Thursday was steamed tripe. Poor Henry.

'Why did she tell you?'

'We had a row. I stayed in a cottage with a boy. Alone. She found out and called me some horrible names and then said that.' The cottage with the boy part no longer seemed important. I didn't care whether or not Aunt Kitty was shocked.

She didn't appear to be shocked. She put down the milk jug and the oven-glove and everything else she'd been using to create a distraction and looked at me. 'She's a bloody fool. After all these years. What difference does it make?'

'It makes a difference to me. She said he was rotten – my real father – that I had inherited his bad blood.'

'Well, she would say that, wouldn't she? We all blame somebody else.'

The kettle whistled. We let it whistle for a full minute before she turned to attend to it.

'But you knew?' I said to her flowered back-view.

'I was there.'

'And what about my –' I didn't know what to call him – 'her husband. Did he know?'

'Not to my knowledge. You see,' she said, flustered now, 'he was home on leave just afterwards. He had no reason to be suspicious. You could have been –'

I finished it for her: 'I could have been his. But when I was born and you saw my hair and my eyes, you knew I wasn't. Why did she tell you? Why didn't she just keep it quiet?'

'She had to tell somebody, love. She was going mad.'

'And I suppose she tried to get rid of me. I suppose she took things and jumped off tables and hoped I'd die.'

'No. No. Don't ever think that. Here.'

I collapsed against her bosom. Aunt Kitty, a silly woman whom I despised. 'Go on, cry,' she said. And I did. Like summer tempests. The tea went cold and still I cried. She eased me into the living-room and on to a sofa. 'Bloody fool,' she kept saying, 'bloody fool,' as she

pushed the hair out of my eyes and rocked me to and fro.
When my tears had diminished to mere sniffing and blowing she went to make fresh tea. Jamie came bounding in, shouting, 'What did the captain of the Foreign Legion say when he saw the Arabs coming?' Pregnant pause, and then, '"Here come the Arabs."' I thought vaguely that Henry Bute must be working miracles with Jamie.
She shooed him out and fed me with sips of tea and pieces of Marie biscuit. I wanted to stay on her sofa for ever, but knew it was impossible.
'Who was he? What was he like?'
'It's no good asking me about it, love, because I don't know much. He was somebody she'd known when she was a girl. They bumped into each other accidentally. He was on leave – from the Navy, I think. It was over as soon as it began.'
'Except for me.'
She looked into the depths of her tea cup. 'The war was a funny time, Anna. Everyone coming and going and you never knew if you'd see them again. People did things they'd never dream of doing normally.'
'What was his name?'
'Best. Frank Best. But don't ask me any more because I don't know what happened to him or where he is. And it doesn't matter, you know, Anna. It's *you* who matters, not your father. All that silly stuff about bad blood, that would just be romancing. You see, she never stopped blaming herself and she ended up by making him a devil. It was just ships that pass. Alec's your father. He brought you up. He loves you. Like Henry's Jamie's father now.'
That reminded me of something else. 'She was eager enough to turn you out, wasn't she?'
She sighed. The days of the phantom Mr Pendlebury were over. 'It wasn't a turning-out. I had to go. He couldn't marry me, you see. He already had a family. And every minute I was in that house was agony for her, her having been in the same boat, as you might say.'
'What did you do?'
'I went down to Suffolk and stayed with my friend Ruby until Jamie was born. But there was her mother. She

was ill and couldn't do with crying babies in the house. So I went into digs. I got a job in a clothing factory and the landlady looked after Jamie. Then she got a job herself and couldn't do it any more. I went upstairs after she'd told me. There was Jamie in his cot. I thought, "All you've got to do is switch the gas fire on and not light it and all your worries are over." Then I picked him up and he was so little and helpless, and I couldn't do it.'

'My father would have helped.' I called him that unthinkingly. 'Surely?'

'Ah, but you get funny and touchy when you're like that. He used to send me money. But he had all of you to look after and I didn't want to impose. Things worked out. I got some work from the factory to do at home. And I used to paint toy-soldiers – that was fiddly: red jackets and black boots, ever so tiny – and curl dolls' wigs. Then I got a typewriter on the hire-purchase and taught myself to type. I used to think "If I can only hang on long enough, something good will happen some day." And it did.' She gestured around her to the plant on the window-sill, the pipe on the mantelpiece, the poker-work motto above the fireplace.

I started to cry again. Not for myself this time, but for that little germ of hope that had stayed alive in Aunt Kitty's heart all through the time of the toy-soldiers and the dolls' wigs. 'Oh, God,' I said. 'Why couldn't we be an ordinary, normal family?'

'There aren't any ordinary, normal families, love. Some get off lighter than others, that's all.'

'I don't understand why she was so horrible to me. After all, she hasn't much room to talk, has she?'

'That's why. When you've been through something yourself, you don't want to see it happening to somebody else, you don't want to be reminded.'

I caught sight of the clock and began to mop my face. 'I'll have to go now.'

She misunderstood me. 'Yes, you get back. I know it's hard, but try to forgive her. She loves you so much. She only wants to keep you safe. Try to make her understand that what she said isn't important.' She smoothed my hair and patted my shoulder. 'Cis doesn't know what she's saying when she gets into a rage. She's said some pretty rotten things to me in her time. But I've always tried to remember it's her nature. It's only people who really care who get into rages.'

I thought for a moment of telling her my true destination, but she would try to dissuade me and I wasn't going to be dissuaded. I was going to Hampstead. I was going to tell Alec Blake what I'd discovered. I was going to hand him the weapon he so richly deserved.

CHAPTER THIRTEEN

There had often been times when I'd speculated about illegitimacy as all children do when trying to reconcile themselves to the idea of being sprung from those two strangers, their parents; much more romantic, and feasible, to be the result of a chance encounter with a travelling Romany or a mad love affair with a foreign nobleman. But such thinking is only supportable when it's figurative, and Frank Best existed.

The train lines seemed to be laid through the flattest and least spectacular acreage of England. The landscape merely repeated itself every few miles: fields, a village, more fields, the backs of suburban houses, a goods-yard, a station, and so on; there was nothing to divert me from introspection, not even the group of men who shared my carriage and who kept to-ing and fro-ing between their seats and the buffet-bar and whose conversation increased in volume as the miles flashed by. One or two of the younger ones, emboldened by beer and each other, kept eyeing me up, but I looked straight through them. They reminded me of Maurice at sixteen when he'd just discovered alcohol. He'd only ever come home drunk once. My mother had steered him up to bed, undressed him, pulled the eiderdown over him and never referred to it again. Drink didn't bother her. It was only sex that bothered her.

I tried to imagine her at twenty-six, participating in the brief encounter that had led to my conception; it was impossible. In the window I saw my faint and distorted reflection. Presumably Frank Best had been a dark-eyed, dark-haired man. I remembered all the old allusions: 'You're not brother and sister, are you? Well, I don't know who she takes after – you must have had a Dago in the family. Anna Blake, we're giving you the part of the gipsy girl, the Eastern princess.' Allusions made innocently, at which everyone had laughed, except, it would seem, my mother.

Many things seemed to fit into place now: my relationship with Maurice, not entirely a normal sibling relationship, my mother's preference for her son, her legal child, my peculiar feeling of impermanence in Tennyson Avenue. I was a bastard. An unwanted child, conceived – where? In the back of a car? Inside a partly-demolished house? During a rushed, unsatisfactory afternoon while Maurice was farmed out to be looked after?

Jonathon and I had done the same thing. But we weren't married to other people. And I wasn't pregnant. I felt the familiar preliminary twinge in the pit of my stomach even as I thought about it. If only it could be possible to go back ten hours, to Seahouses, to lying curled together in bed while the lemony early-morning sun illuminated our faces, ignorant, believing ourselves to be in love and safe from anything the world could throw at us. It was as if a page had been turned obliterating all the normal, happy Anna Blake experiences that had gone before. Jonathon, who might have meant everything, meant nothing. My altered state meant nothing. What was a lost virginity except a thankfulness that it was over with? Nothing mattered, except my renaissance. After seventeen years of being one person, I would have to learn to be somebody else.

Euston to Hampstead was surprisingly simple: just down the Underground and five stops along the black line. Beauchamp Road was hot and still and quiet. It suddenly occurred to me that they might have gone away for a holiday and all I'd find would be empty milk bottles and closed curtains. I went cold all over. And then, through the front window of the house, I saw Olivia. She was arranging flowers in a blue bowl with the dedicated precision of a Japanese. I thought, 'Olivia, I have come to bring you glad tidings of great joy.' She could be Mrs Olivia Blake without more ado; I was the bearer of the marriage licence, the human sacrifice.

She looked exactly the same but it took her a few seconds to recognize me. When she did place me, her welcome was as gracious and coolly affectionate as it had been two years before.

'You've come to stay?' she said, taking in my suitcase. 'You can't be going to Maurice's. Maurice is still soaking up the Spanish sun. Have you had a card yet? We haven't. The wretches. Though one should hardly expect postcards from a honeymoon couple.'

'I don't know.'

She looked at me queryingly, head on one side.

'I don't know whether I'm staying and I don't know whether we've had a postcard. Is he in?'

'Your father? He's just having a drink with some business contact, along the road.' She led me into the drawing-room and sat me down. I thought of all the other drinks with business contacts, years ago, that had actually been visits to Olivia. I looked at her face and I knew that this time they were genuine.

'I'll get you something to eat. I think salad, don't you? It's still so hot.'

'I don't want anything to eat, thank you.'

'But you must. Travel is so debilitating. I don't know why. Maybe great speed affects the nerves and digestion.'

She was off into the kitchen before I could stop her. One thing about Olivia: she never asked questions. I supposed it was the result of being in a position herself where certain questions could be embarrassing.

There was a new photograph on the occasional table: the two of them in bright holiday clothes against some exotically tinted scenery. Last summer, the Algarve, probably. I wondered how they managed about passports. Or had Olivia changed her name for the sake of propriety, just like Aunt Kitty?

I heard a key in the lock and then his tread in the hall. I was sitting opposite the open door. His face lit up with surprise and pleasure. I let him embrace me. I was awkward and embarrassed but it might be the last time we could embrace each other.

'How lovely,' he kept saying. 'Much nicer than if you'd made arrangements. Nice surprises do happen, after all.' He hugged me again. 'Twice in a month. It's too good to be true.'

He looked younger and better-looking every time I saw him. He was happiness made manifest. I was going to cloud that happiness, I knew, but I was also offering him what he needed. But before I could open my mouth, Olivia came back with a tray full of food and I had to make eating motions to satisfy her.

'How were the post-wedding blues?' he said. 'Bad?'

'Pretty bad. I went away last Saturday though, so I escaped a good deal.'

'Somewhere exciting?'

'A place called Seahouses, on the Northumberland coast. With Rachel and her cousins.'

'Conway's girl? How are the Conways?'

And then it was 'How is so and so?' and 'How are such and such?' I answered impatiently; I wasn't here for an evening of cosy reminiscence. 'I've got to talk to you. Something private.' I appealed to Olivia. However I tried to put my request, it sounded boorish. But she said lightly, 'Of course. I've got plenty to do. Just call me if you want anything more to eat,' and left the room.

He looked annoyed. 'Did you have to do that? Olivia would like to feel she could be taken into your confidence. We have no secrets from one another. It may be awkward for you but she is one of the family, your family.'

'No. Not my family.'

'Oh, I know what you mean. Not in the eyes of the law. But the eyes of the law don't mean as much as two people's regard for each other.'

'You don't know what I mean.' I closed my eyes. It didn't seem quite so difficult when I couldn't see him. 'We had a row at home this morning. She told me you weren't my father. And it wasn't a lie because Aunt Kitty confirmed it. She said my father was someone called Frank Best who was on leave from the Navy. I didn't want you to know, but I think you have a right to be told. She won't divorce you. So now you know, you can divorce her and marry Olivia.' It wasn't the way I'd intended to say it. I had intended to be subtle, to be adult. I kept my eyes shut. I could hear faint sounds of Olivia from the kitchen. He didn't speak. Perhaps I'd killed him. I opened my eyes. He was looking at me.

'I could murder her,' he said, 'for telling you.'

'Perhaps I shouldn't have told *you*.' It had seemed to be a straightforward matter. Now I wasn't so sure.

He took a cigarette out of his case and tapped it on his thumb-nail. He stared with great concentration at the clock, a china clock ornamented with scrolls and curlicues and pot-bellied, grimacing cherubs. 'You didn't have to tell me,' he said. 'I knew.'

'You *knew*?'

He nodded. 'I got to know in the same way that you did – during a flaming row. She wanted to cut out her tongue afterwards.'

I couldn't get my bearings. 'But *when*? How long ago?'

'Oh, years. You weren't very old.'

'And that's why you left?'

'No, no.' He waved that idea away impatiently. 'I left because we just couldn't carry on together any more on any level, because I'd met someone with whom I knew I could be happy, because I reckoned you and Maurice would get on better if we were apart.'

'But if you knew, why didn't you do something?'

'Such as?'

'Leave straight away. Divorce her.'

He smiled a bit. 'Funnily enough, as you'll find out as you grow older, you don't always split up because of the big dramatic things. They're not usually as important as the little day-to-day aggravations that pile up on top of each other. Besides, I looked upon you as my own. I loved you.'

'But I'm not yours.' Couldn't I get it into his head?

'It's not that simple, Anna. Say you'd been adopted, as a baby. Wouldn't you regard me as your father? It's exactly the same thing. Your parents are the people who rear you, the people you grow to love.'

'There are such things as genes, you know.'

'I know. I think the world was possibly a better place before somebody discovered such things as genes. Anyway, you know yourself. You know you're good-looking and healthy and intelligent. You must have some pretty top-rate genes.'

'But she won't divorce you. Knowing that you know what she did and she still won't divorce you. Why do you allow her to behave that way?'

'She loves me.' He said it as a sad, simple statement of fact. 'And nothing that I can say or do will convince her that I'm not going back. And I suppose I love her too, in a queer way. You can't live with someone for seventeen years and not learn to love parts of them. You think I should terrorize her into giving me a divorce? Is that it? But why, Anna? What's the point? Olivia and I are all right as things are: we're known down here as Mr and Mrs Blake, we have no financial problems, we have no children to consider, and your mother has her small spark of hope to keep her going.'

'Hope deferred maketh the heart sick.' I must have caught the quoting habit from Jonathon.

'Maybe,' he said. 'But it's something. And can't you see, there's no need to stir up a mess if it can be avoided? Olivia and I have discussed it endlessly. Olivia wouldn't countenance the idea of unnecessary suffering.'

'Does Olivia know?' I looked at him, aghast.

'Yes, she does. I told you, there are no secrets between us.'

Oh, it was all too cosy, too smug to be borne. 'Does everybody know but me? Have I been public knowledge all my life? Why didn't you put it in *The Times*?'

'Anna.' He tried to put his arm round me but I shook it off. I was disgusted with the lot of them, with the whole sordid intrigue. I started to shake again. I clasped my hands together to try to stop the trembling, but my whole body was moving in convulsive jerks. He looked frightened. He went for Olivia and, a few minutes later, she followed him in carrying brandy.

'Come on. No. Come on. Drink it.'

I allowed her to put the glass to my mouth and drank, spluttering as the brandy hit the back of my throat.

She refilled the glass. She sat down and put an arm around my shoulders. 'He's told me what happened. Now listen to me. Your mother was a criminal fool to tell you in that fashion. But she was beside herself. And you're not a child. You know people make mistakes. It doesn't matter. Your mother and Alec and me and Maurice, we're the people who matter. Don't let the thought of him eat into you. You're Anna Blake, in capitals. You are what you've become, will become. You're not just a parcel of second-hand genes. And, believe me, your mother loves you, she worships you. Incidentally, does she know where you are?'

I shook my head. I was beginning to feel muzzy.

She motioned to him and he went out of the room. I heard the telephone bell and then the deep murmur of his voice.

Olivia kept on talking. 'My parents were divorced when I was three. He married numerous ladies afterwards and my mother and I moved round from resort to resort. I'm a walking Michelin: Nice, Cannes, Biarritz, Deauville, you name them, I've been there. Mama had many escorts but no one permanent. I met my father years later. He was a florid, over-indulged man I disliked on sight. We didn't have a word to say to each other. I'd cherished fantasies about him, you see. When I went to school I made up stories about him to tell the other girls – I imagined him as Heathcliff and Errol Flynn and Alec D'Urberville all rolled into one. You can imagine the disillusionment when I did meet him.' She broke off as he appeared in the doorway.

'She wants to speak to you.'

I shook my head violently. I had run away to escape from her.

'OK.' He went back to the telephone. His voice was louder now. It seemed as though he was delivering a harangue which was abruptly terminated and the receiver slammed down.

'She's alerted the police. She'll just have to un-alert them. She's been telling me some story about your staying away from home with a boy. Is that true? I thought you were staying with Rachel and her cousins.'

'I was. Rachel got ill and one of the cousins took her home.'

'And you stayed with the other one?'

'Yes.' Why did everybody keep harping on about something that wasn't important?

'Oh, Anna.'

'I'm all right, I'm all right,' I said frantically. 'I *know* I am.' Did he expect me to be specific?

But Olivia shot him what must have been an explanatory glance and said, 'Leave it, Alec, until morning at least. I'm going to get her to bed. She looks as though she could flake out at any moment.'

And it was quite pleasant to be undressed, to feel the slippery softness of one of Olivia's nightdresses being drawn over my head, to have the sheets tucked in around me and the curtains drawn. I was in one of the boudoir rooms. There was a print of *'Les Parapluies'* on the wall, its gauzy, muted tones soothed my eyes. She'd made me take a pill and it must have been a particularly potent pill because, although I'd imagined I could never sleep again, I knew nothing until ten o'clock the next morning.

He was still at the breakfast table when I came down, reading the paper and raising an empty coffee cup to his lips.

'Would you like some more?'

'What?' He hadn't realized that it was empty. 'Oh, yes. Olivia's in the kitchen, waiting to get yours ready.'

Olivia was in fact washing articles of clothing in the sink. 'I hope you don't mind. I took it upon myself when I realized that, if you'd just come back from holiday, your things would need washing.' She brushed aside my polite protestations, wringing out my nightie with vigour. 'Now, what can I get you?'

'I'll get it. Just coffee and toast.'

'Anna.'

I looked up from the percolator. 'Yes?'

'There'll probably be a lecture this morning. Try to listen and make agreeable noises, for his sake, will you? He feels it incumbent upon him to deliver a lecture, as any father would.'

There was indeed a lecture. I knew he'd lingered at the table for that sole purpose. We drank coffee and avoided each other's eyes while he spoke of love and beauty and how easy it was to misinterpret one's feelings and how difficult it could be to stop once started on the path of moral laxity. He spoke about how, one day, I would meet someone to whom I would want to give everything. Promiscuity, he said, could only ever lead to unhappiness and self-disgust.

He should know. To my mind, it was a case of the pot calling the kettle. And, anyway, none of it had any bearing whatsoever upon what had happened between Jonathon and me.

'You've had a pretty rough time all round, haven't you?'

I eyed him warily. 'Did you know anything about Frank Best?'

'Please, Anna.'

'I have to know. It's my right.'

'He and your mother knew each other as kids. They lost touch until they met during the war. He was in the Navy, a regular, not a conscript. She never heard from him again. For all we know he was blown to pieces. And that's the sum total of my knowledge. He's past history. You're not. What's to be done with you?'

'I don't want to go back.'

'Stay here. When does school start?'

'September 12th.'

'Well, that's all right then.'

'I mean I don't want to go back at all. Not home. Not Beechwood. I just couldn't slip into the same old groove and I couldn't bear to live in that house with her watching me, waiting to catch me out. I'd feel as though I were on parole. I want to get away from everything.'

'But Anna, you've only another year. There are your exams, University. Don't let this spoil your career.'

'What career? There's more to life than exams. And I don't want to go to university. I'm not desperately interested in any particular subject.'

'You must be desperately interested in *something*.'

'Yes, people, and behaviour, and coincidence. Sometimes, oh, just occasionally life seems different and full of mysterious possibilities and I think, "It's not really humdrum and boring, after all, it could be a great adventure and the dullness is only a façade." And some people, somewhere, have managed to break through.'

He only said, 'Education is never wasted upon anybody.' He hadn't thc faintest idea of what I was getting at; how could he? I didn't really understand it myself.

'You've got one genius in the family. I'd be much happier doing something else, until I find out what really interests me, at any rate. I want to be where things are *happening*.'

'I should have thought university was the very place to fulfil that particular ambition.'

'But it's so remote from life, isn't it? So cocooned. Maurice said he was absolutely petrified at the thought of going out into the cold cruel world to make a living after three years of pretending it might never happen. Look, I'll get a very respectable job –' I sought in my mind – 'an art gallery, or the Civil Service – you take exams in the Civil Service – I could always go to university later if I wanted to.' I had visions of myself as a lady tax inspector, reading Chaucer on the side.

'But your results have always been so good.'

'Only because I have a – what-d'you-call it, – photographic memory and a clairvoyant facility for spotting questions and most of the others are dimwits.'

He had to laugh, desite himself. 'Well, you stay here anyway until you've got your bearings. After you're settled you'll think differently about leaving school. You'll think differently about Celia too.'

Celia. I had forgotten he called her Celia, having been so used to hearing Aunt Kitty's inevitable Cis. It conjured up quite a different image: you could almost see the girl with the white muslin frock and the paper violets when he said it. But I wouldn't think differently. Of that I was certain.

CHAPTER FOURTEEN

I stayed a fortnight in Hampstead and Olivia gave me what she called a proper introduction to London. 'This is where real people go, not tourists,' she'd say, ushering me into some little pub or riverside restaurant or quiet backwater that, incredibly, existed between two noisy thoroughfares. She took me into shops and attended to my wardrobe: clothes which seemed plain and dreary on the hangers looked surprisingly flattering when on me. Thus she weaned me from the bright and garish, the obvious, whose attraction soon dimmed. She made me an appointment with a West End hairdresser who cut my hair into a straight swinging shape as precise as geometry. We visited art exhibitions, new films, a theatre in the Strand to see a French singer with a beautiful pale haunted face and hands like lilies. How different it seemed from my mini-guide-book tour with Maurice. We even made the Café Royal, that Mecca of my adolescence.

With him, I walked and talked. Ostensibly about my future, but I learned more about him during that fortnight than I'd done in all the years he lived with us. He told me about the Depression, how he'd seen men becoming apathetic and ugly, women selling themselves, rickety children in rags, how he'd sworn to make money – above all considerations, make money. Education, aesthetic pursuits, they went by the board all the time he was speculating and consolidating and reading his bank statement. He'd started with a friend, building engines for racing cars – not everyone was Depressed, apparently –

and they had a good business going when Mr Hitler intervened. However, he was one of the men who'd had had a good war: gained quick promotion, made useful contacts. When it was over he'd had no trouble in taking up where he'd left off. But the day was to come when he sat back and realized lost opportunities. A businessman meets, in the main, other businessmen. He certainly didn't think of culture with a capital 'C', but he was aware he'd have been happier in a different milieu. I reminded him about the amateur operatics. He said yes, he'd been besotted with a girl called Josephine Gamble who sang the leading soprano roles. She had very red lips and a Veronica Lake hair-do. Whatever happened to Josephine Gamble? She went to Australia and married a gold-prospector, or a sheep-farmer, or possibly an aborigine, for all he knew. So he married my mother instead? She was shy and blushed a lot, so dreadfully unsure; one felt it one's duty to shield her from the grimmer aspects of life. He, so acute in matters of finance and transaction, had received a totally false first impression. Whirlwind courtship and wedding. Before the fun started. There had been no time to think. That had been the great mistake. I must make sure I didn't fall into the same error.

I spoke to my mother, once, on the telephone. It was not a success. I was monosyllabic, cruel. She alternated between half-hearted bombast and a sickeningly pathetic attempt at humility. The fire was gone out of her belly. She didn't mind me staying in Hampstead, as long as I was happy. I hadn't forgotten when term started, had I? I didn't enlighten her. I was leaving that happy task for him.

It was compromise, all along the line. I didn't want to go home. Maurice, who would once have been the obvious solution, was otherwise engaged playing at being newly-married. I was welcome to stay in Hampstead and I would have loved to stay in Hampstead but some perverse part of my nature told me that I had no right, I didn't belong, I was six years too late. The only solution, it seemed, was to get myself some independent accommodation.

He went purple. I appealed, once more, to Olivia. But

this time she couldn't help; at seventeen she was being finished in Switzerland, not living independently.

We skirted the impasse and moved on to discuss school and/or career. Olivia said, 'If you really want to fill in time usefully, how about doing a secretarial course somewhere?'

It was always Olivia who made the sensible, workable suggestions. It was she who followed them through, who sent for prospecti and made the compromise complete by finding a technical college where I could combine shorthand and typing with working for some 'A' levels.

But there still remained the problem of where I was to be domiciled. Pressure was exerted upon me to bury the hatchet, go back to Tennyson Avenue; in a few weeks, they said, it would be as though it had never happened. They didn't realize that that was the very reason I didn't want to go back. They argued, both from my point of view and my mother's. I was adamant. If I was forced to go back, I said, I would leave and keep on leaving. Not that they could force me; I was seventeen. And Hampstead, Aunt Kitty's house even, they were warm and welcoming, but could only ever be temporary refuges.

At the end of the fortnight we drove back to Manchester, he and I, in the Lotus. As always, he drove fast, with a kind of nonchalant expertise. My hair blew about my face. The air was cool and the sky was blue and punctuated with fluffy cirrus clouds. I wanted to drive on beside him, endlessly. But Manchester and the Midland Hotel approached us, inevitably.

He knew a woman, a widow, whose late husband had been an employee of his. She now ran a superior sort of lodging-house for students and the like. She was a good, trustworthy woman who would watch over my comings and goings and doubtless report back to him. That was to be our first port of call. Our second was an interview with my mother who was awaiting us, albeit with her guns spiked, but my heart thumped at the thought of Tennyson Avenue.

Mrs Warburton's house was situated in a very pleasant suburb, on all the useful bus-routes and within hailing distance of the public baths – a boon, as I was to come to realize. Mrs Warburton herself was a short, bun-loaf of a woman, everybody's mother. We stood at the threshold for a full five minutes while she well-I-nevered and asked to be blessed at the sight of him. It was apparently his largesse that had enabled her to purchase this desirable property after Mr Warburton died. I felt a bit like the squire's daughter come on a compulsory visit with a baket of food.

Eventually she stopped blethering and invited us in. I was pleasantly surprised. The Warburton lounge hadn't altogether managed to pull itself out of the present-from-Scunthorpe, china-faun, sewing-basket-shaped-like-Ann-Hathaway's-cottage pattern, but the paintwork was white, the furniture modern and there was a bookcase filled with the uniform editions of some book club. Above the fireplace was one of those convex mirrors which make you look engagingly tall and willowly if you stand at the right distance, otherwise it's like seeing your reflection in the back of a spoon. There was central heating too. And I was a chilly mortal. Altogether, I rather cared for Mrs Warburton's appointments.

Of course we had to have tea. Come straight from the *haute cuisine* of the Midland, we dutifully sipped tea and crumbled parkin. Mrs Warburton's ankles bulged over her very small feet and her hair was permed into regular ridges like a neatly-ploughed field. She reminded me of a tidier, more alert version of Aunt Kitty.

'We wondered,' he said, scattering pieces of cake all around his plate to make it look as though he'd eaten some, 'if there was any chance of your finding Anna a room. She's going to the technical college and it's much too far for her to travel from home.'

Sixty minutes each way. But she didn't appear to think there was anything odd about his reason. She was too busy talking about Providence. It seemed that by the first post that very morning she'd received back word from a student who'd got a place in a hall of residence instead. So there she was, left with her second-floor front on her hands. A lovely little room too. She'd show us.

'Well?'

It *was* a nice little room. There was a divan with a striped cover, a wash-basin, an electric fire, a window on a level with a tall horse-chestnut tree and a picture of 'Beauty Bathing' on the wall.

'There are only four others here,' she said. 'Two boys who share the attic, Virginia who's opposite this one – she's a nice girl – and Miss Partridge on the first floor. I don't believe in filling up every square inch, not like some of these landladies who pack them in like sardines. There's plenty of quiet and privacy in this house.'

He looked at me. 'I like it,' I said. I would have liked anywhere that looked fairly presentable.

'Monday, then, Mrs Warburton,' he said. 'If it's all right with you. She starts college the week after, so she'll need some time to get settled in.'

I left them, haggling, or whatever the appropriate term was for superior boarding-houses. It was the opposite to normal haggling though: she would have taken me for nothing if he'd have let her.

I went into the back garden. In the house's palmier days it had obviously been laid out with loving care. There was a stone archway, a pool, a nymph carrying a cornucopia and two herons, each petrified on one leg, all now overgrown with creeper and rambler and lichen. The pool was scummy and the whole area smelt of decomposition. The nymph had lost her nose in the process of erosion. This lack gave her a plebeian, belligerent expression as though she might hurl her cornucopia to the ground at any moment. The place appealed to me: the calm, the quietness, the sense of endurance despite decay.

They managed to come to a mutual agreement. He was to pay her x pounds per week in return for my board and lodging, my laundry and – implicit understanding – my moral welfare. On Monday I was to arrive with my trunk and I would find my bed aired and my place set at table. 'Don't worry, love,' she said, as we made our farewells. 'I'll look after you.' I had a premonition that may stay with her would be like falling into a feather-bed.

'That's the pleasant part over with,' he said, turning the

car in the other direction, the Tennyson Avenue direction. 'Now just stay calm, Anna. A scene isn't going to get us anywhere.'

But I couldn't see how a scene was to be avoided. I started to shiver. The nearer we got to Tennyson Avenue, the stronger the feeling I had of a sickening miasma of wronged mother-love reaching out to envelop me. I was afraid for my resolve. Once inside that house, I felt I would not be able to harden my heart against the knowledge that she loved me, that she had no one else, that she was unloved and growing old. I dwelt on the wound she'd inflicted upon me in an attempt to weigh the balance. I was the result of a furtive adultery, a malicious whim on the part of nature. Mingled with her love there must always have been resentment. My existence had contributed to her husband's desertion, my existence had been a continual reminder of an act for which she could never forgive herself, my lapse from her narrow, neurotic code had brought back, forcibly, the memory of her own lapse. There had been hate in her eyes when she told me about Frank Best.

The front door was open in readiness for us. She was sitting in the lounge, embroidering lazy-daisy stitch on a tablecloth. Her needle flew in and out and the pattern took shape. Every perforation was a vicarious wound. I had expected screaming hysteria, but this was clearly her martyr's mood.

He lit a cigarette. He'd been smoking like a mill-chimney for a fortnight. There were no ash-trays. He had to cup the ash in the palm of his hand and throw it surreptitiously behind the electric fire. Not that she looked at him, not once, the whole time we were there.

'Anna's got a place at the technical college, as I told you,' he said. 'Did you ring Miss Er-er?'

'No.'

'I'll do it then. She'll want a term's fees, I expect. I'll put a cheque in the post before I leave.'

'I suppose this was your doing. Persuading her against Beechwood. You were always against it, weren't you?'

He didn't bother to reply to that. He said, 'Do you

remember Jack Warburton who used to work for me?'

'No.'

'You do. We went to visit him in hospital just before he died. You must remember his wife, anyway – a little woman who kept apologizing for his illness as though he'd done it deliberately.'

'No.'

It was just like the days of the flying plates. The corners of his mouth were tightening. 'She runs a boarding-house now. A very nice place. Anna can stay there. It's very convenient for her college.'

The needle flew faster and more viciously. She could have been stabbing Caesar. Her voice was toneless. 'I can see you don't care what happens to her, so what's the point of me saying anything?'

'Lots of girls live away from home at Anna's age. Mrs Warburton will see she doesn't come to any harm. You can rest assured about that.'

'I can, can I?' She bit through the thread. 'I thought I could rest assured when she went off to Northumberland and look what happened there.'

'I've talked to her about that.'

'Talked! All the talking in the world won't alter it.'

They were discussing me as though I wasn't there. My voice trembling, I said, 'We've been through all that. You needn't worry about Jonathon Lawrence because I expect he's back at school in Wiltshire. And, anyway, I don't particularly want to see him again.'

'Jonathon Lawrence,' she said, slowly raising her eyes from her sewing until they were level with mine, 'is not the only pebble on the beach.'

'There's got to be a bit of trust, Celia,' he intervened.

She winced at the use of her name, as though he'd sworn at her. 'Trust! Nobody's to be trusted. Don't you know that by now? You should.'

'Anna, go and pack your things,' he said.

I went upstairs. Perhaps he would find it easier without having to expurgate for my benefit.

The relics I had left strewn on top of my cupboard a fortnight ago had been put into a drawer. I no longer cared what she'd thought of them. I tugged a trunk from the box-room and emptied my belongings into it. I could hear their voices faintly, on one note, never intermingling. I wondered if she was still pursuing her yes and no policy.

From my attic window I looked out to the Leslies' back garden. Two of the younger boys had built a tree-house during the summer, but were not in residence that afternoon. The Leslies had always been a family of short-lived enthusiasms. I remembered all the times we had reclined in that garden, fortune-telling, waiting for fate to incline its rosy face towards us. The Conways' house was too far away even to be glimpsed from my eyrie. There was no doubt that I'd have been scratched from the Conways' Christmas card list. One of the reasons I wanted to get away from Tennyson Avenue and its environs was the thought of meeting and being cut by Mrs Conway.

I turned away from the window. I felt no pangs. My whole life had been motivated towards escaping sooner or later. It was mere chance that had made it sooner rather than later.

When I came downstairs with my hand-luggage he was on the phone, explaining to the school secretary that, due to unforeseen circumstances, I would not be returning to Beechwood. He went on to say that I had a place at the technical college, just in case there should be any misconstruction of my departure. He had put a sixpence down on the table. What had once been his home was now no more than a public telephone kiosk. She was where I'd left her, concentrating furiously upon the yellow centre of a marguerite. Whoever was going to look at her tablecloth or take tea off it when she'd finished? Good old faithful Aunt Kitty, I supposed, who had absolutely no appreciation for delicate embroidery.

'I shall be fine,' I said. I knew the first word had to come from me.

'Well, if you think so, that's all right, isn't it?'

I wanted to say, 'I'll come and see you. Don't cry, because I'll only be fifty miles away. It's better that we're apart. We've never really been compatible. You're my mother and I suppose I love you, but I don't like you very much.' But she made it impossible for me to say any of those things. Her face was strained with the effort of keeping up her pose. It was only after we'd gone that she'd collapse, moan and cry and curse and wish she'd behaved differently.

'Are we ready then? Your former headmistress is touring the Greek Islands. No wonder the school fees are so high. Good luck to her, but not out of my pocket. Now, have you got all you want?' He kept up his meaningless chatter until we were out of the house. She hadn't so much as moved out of her chair. The tears were streaming down my cheeks. He took my hand and squeezed it. 'You think you'll never be able to love her again, after this,' he said. 'But you will.'

He didn't understand. I was crying not because I couldn't love her, but because I knew that we would never be able to allow ourselves to effect a reconciliation.

The first Sunday after I'd moved in *chez* Warburton I had a visitor. I might have known. Maurice. Fresh from Torremolinos. So darkly sunburnt that his eyeballs showed brilliant white in relief. We rendezvoused in the lounge. Brother or no brother, Mrs Warburton didn't allow male visitors up the stairs. 'Followers,' Maurice called them, standing in front of the fireplace, turning the present from Scunthorpe this way and that. It was only when he was with Berenice that you realized he was a mature, married man.

'So how come you're living the life of one bath per week and no radios playing after eleven?' he said.

'It's not that bad. Though the bath is a bit of a problem. We have to ablute to a strict rota, otherwise nobody gets any hot water. However, there are some public baths along the road which I plan to make use of pretty frequently.'

He pretended to hold his nose. 'None of which explains why you're here.'

'Surely you've heard?'

'I heard from the old man that there'd been an almighty

bust-up because she'd caught you out doing naughty things, but that's about all.'

'That wasn't the basic reason, the naughty things as you call them.' I wondered why his father hadn't told him. Perhaps he thought it was my business. 'She told me that your father isn't my father. That's why I'm here.'

'Christ Almighty.' He sat down, very quickly, on the edge of a coffee table.

I told him, briefly, about Frank Best, about Alec Blake knowing all along, about the way I needed to be away from her. He listened without interjecting, from start to finish, which was very unusual for Maurice.

'I'm your half-sister. Funny really, isn't it, when you remember how people used to go on about us not looking alike?'

'Hilarious.' He sat silent for a long time and then put his arm round me. 'I just don't know what the hell to say. Except that you're welcome to take up residence in Enfield any time you like.'

'Berenice would love that.'

'Yes.' He looked down at his hands.

'Don't worry. I'm fine here. I've had so many offers of accommodation that I'm beginning to feel like an abandoned pup. I'd rather be on my own. Honestly.'

He didn't look convinced. I couldn't bear Maurice, of all people, to become earnest and conscientious and guilt-ridden. To cheer him up I began to tell him about my fellow-boarders. 'There are John and Roger, above me. They're science students. Mrs Warburton doesn't bother about the time they come in because she acknowledges their masculine privilege to be out on the tiles five nights out of seven. They're back early to do re-sits, whatever they might be. Then there's Miss Partridge who's a retired gentlewoman – do gentlewomen retire? – anyway, she lives on an annuity and is terribly refined and timid. And there's also Virginia – no, don't laugh – who's a second-year languages student and who's due back in a fortnight. And of course there's Mrs Warburton who presides, who is feeding me up and whose apparently short-sighted eyes don't miss a thing. Anyway, I should imagine that you're very well acquainted with this sort of place after all your mad, gay undergraduate years.'

'You've obviously hit upon a one-in-a-hundred boarding-house. Most of them are very dreary and nobody ever speaks to anybody else.'

'You can't *not* talk here. Mrs Warburton sees to that. Oh, stay for tea, Maurice, and you'll see. We have plum tart and what she calls her "oven-bottom" cakes.'

'I've got to get back home. Can't leave my bride abandoned, can I? I only came to make sure you were alive and well and not still doing naughty things. Besides, I've got to pay a visit *au* Tennyson Avenue. Am I supposed to be in the dark?'

'I think it's the best policy. Unless she mentions it.'

And I knew she wouldn't. I couldn't, for shame, deprive her of all her illusions. He was her loving son and she was his mother, beyond reproach. It was all she had left.

Part Two
The Search

CHAPTER ONE

'I'll miss you, Anna,' Virginia said, arranging my garments in meticulous folds and placing them in my trunk. She enjoyed packing; I could allow her to do it with a perfectly clear conscience. 'I wonder who'll be replacing you?'

'Somebody called Alison Fairhurst who's very posh, according to Mrs Warburton, and whose very posh parents came to inspect every nook and cranny of the place before agreeing to let her come. She's doing French and German, so you'll have lots in common.'

'Oh, Christ,' Virginia said. I knew she'd miss me. We'd become close friends, confidantes, during the past year. Virginia was in love with one of her lecturers, a much-married man and, as Mrs Warburton could smell much-married men a mile off, they had to be content with the back of his car on the banks of the Irwell. I knew every detail of the sad affair. Virginia was two years older than me and a lot cleverer, but I could tell she was destined for a repeating pattern of unsatisfactory loving and would always need a sympathetic audience before whom she could analyse it to death.

'For goodness sake, I'm only moving a couple of miles away. It's not as though we shan't ever see one another again.' But I knew, as I said it, that we were bound to drift apart as most people with no important links drift apart when they cease to be in day-to-day contact. Her disconsolate face couldn't temper my resolution though. Mrs Warburton's was all very well but it was time I had some privacy.

'There's a little man coming to collect this later this afternoon.' I secured my trunk with rope. 'Could you supervise at this end, make sure he knows where it's going?'

'Sure.'

She looked around my denuded room. 'I think I'll pack

too and get the night-train home. I might as well. There's no point in staying here.'

No point indeed. Alan, her lecturer, was in Sicily with his wife and four children.

'Mind you send me a postcard from – go on, say it.'

'Pairth,' she said. She had a soft lilting Highland voice. Men fell in love with her over the telephone. I was reminded of Jonathon Lawrence and Mrs Bartholomew: 'Go on, say it again – "wor house" – go on.' I had written to Jonathon once, soon after I came to live with Mrs Warburton, one afternoon when I was feeling bleak and unloved. And he'd written back, a charming letter, but very different from the letters that had gone before. The fire was out. Neither of us mentioned the events that had followed upon our night together. To do so would have been mutually embarrassing. We both realized that we'd over-emphasized. I didn't bother to reply.

I marshalled my belongings. All that remained was to say goodbye to Mrs Warburton and Miss Partridge.

Miss Partridge got rather tearful and gave me three lace handkerchiefs which were lovely and a china statue of a shepherdess which had belonged to her dear mother and which was hideous.

Mrs Warburton, who thought little or nothing of china shepherdesses, gave me a food hamper and listed the perils that awaited people who moved into furnished rooms. I was always welcome, I was to remember that, even if it meant her having to sleep on the put-you-up in the kitchen. She'd never stopped regarding me as some sort of waif and stray whom she'd saved from a disastrous fate.

Ephraim Street: 'Desolation Row,' Maurice called it when he came to inspect my dwelling. 'Ask for directions round here and all you get is "Me no savvy".'

It certainly wasn't the prettiest road in Britain: two long terraces of tall grey houses, a betting-shop on one corner, a fly-blown sweet-shop on the other and the Spiritualists' Meeting Hall bang in the middle opposite the Dog and Falcon which was definitely not the kind of local you'd want to look in at. It wasn't the prettiest house in Britain either. All the name-cards outside the front door had become illegible or were out of date – I wondered long and fantastically about Miss M. Pincher, not to mention Mr M. Petronelli – and the stairs were covered in that kind of shiny oilcloth that makes one person's footfalls sound like a herd of stampeding buffalo. But it was a room – a bed-sitting room with kitchenette and use of facilities, to be exact – and it was dry and relatively clean and it was mine, to be paid for by me.

Alec Blake, needless to say, wasn't exactly overjoyed at the prospect of Ephraim Street.

'For God's sake,' he'd said, playing with his potted shrimps as we lunched at the Midland, 'I can afford something better than that for you, if you're determined to get a place of your own.'

'But you're *not* affording it. I'm going to pay for it. My job, remember?'

I had obtained a job in an import firm, a firm well-known to offer scope. It wasn't the scope that interested me as much as the salary.

'If it comes off.'

'It will come off. Mr Shepherd was very impressed with my results and my speeds. Secretaries are very much in demand, you know.'

'Shepherd? Jim Shepherd?'

'Well, we didn't exactly get on to first names, but it was J, yes.'

'Little, dark fellow with glasses?'

'That's right.'

'I know Jim Shepherd. Known him for years. You'll be all right with him. I must get in touch.'

At least, I thought proudly, I'd been considered on my own merits not just as Alec Blake's daughter, which I wasn't anyway. So sucks to you, Jim Shepherd.

'But couldn't you have found a more salubrious area?'

'It's not a bad area. Lots of students live round there.'

'Anna darling.' Olivia stopped pretending to eat her *pâté*. 'I know it seems to you to be the *Quartier Latin*, but it's not very comfortable, is it? And that bathroom . . .' She closed her eyes and shuddered at the memory of it.

'I used the public baths when I was at Mrs Warburton's. I'll continue to do so.'

'Public baths?'

I doubt whether Olivia had ever heard of the public baths, much less dreamed of setting foot inside them.

'Well it's masochism, if you ask me,' he said. 'I'll give you a month, at the outside.'

But there wasn't much they could say. I had lived with Mrs Warburton for a year, shown my self-reliance, not once blotted my copy-book, done well in my exams. The sins of Seahouses had been fully expiated.

I had written to my mother giving her my new address. I had seen her four times during the past year and each meeting had been strained and false and totally useless. Unhappiness and continual disappointment had made her fine face lined and harsh. It was obvious that she paid only a cursory attention to her clothes and her hair. She never suggested that I return to Tennyson Avenue, never brought up my reason for leaving. I got the feeling that she was somehow in awe of me. Now and then she stayed with Maurice for a couple of days. He was her lifebelt.

My holidays and odd week-ends had been spent in Hampstead. I celebrated Christmas there, uncomfortably aware that, only a few miles away, my mother was celebrating – if that was the right word – her Christmas with Maurice and Berenice. Everything was dependent upon timing and diplomacy. I'd cried that night, opening the present she'd sent me, thinking of her being bossed by Berenice who had an understated, very effective line in bossiness. What was it that prevented me from going over to Enfield and smoking a pipe of peace?

There'd been times when I hadn't thought about Frank Best for weeks; other times the thought of him became almost obsessional. One Saturday it was so strong that I took a train to the town where my mother and he had done their growing up. Ambrose Road. I could remember her talking about it. The Bethesda Chapel on the corner. I tried next door and found, by chance, what must have been the oldest inhabitant. She was obviously glad of someone to talk to. The room smelled of unwashed clothes and stale air. She had tough whiskers sprouting from her chin and no bottom teeth. I endured it while she rambled. The Bests, she said, had left the road long before the war. You could tell that the war was only yesterday in her personal time-chart. They never kept in touch with anyone. A bit snooty. The father was a gents' outfitter who sang in the chapel choir but who wouldn't give you last week's *Echo*; the mother kept herself very much to herself. She remembered Frank though. He was the youngest. Quite a nice lad. A *proper* lad, if I knew what she meant. He used to carry her coal in for her and she gave him sixpence on a Saturday. His sister Vera, she was a right little madam, and his elder brother Terry, well, he couldn't say boo to a goose. But she'd been sorry to see the back of Frank. She wouldn't be at all surprised to find he'd got on in the world.

I went back to the station. I wasn't too downcast. There were other streets, other towns. I had my life before me. I had formulated no plan of what I intended to say. I would probably have retreated in panic if I *had* found him.

Even Olivia had been unable to detect a Left Bank aura about Ephraim Street. My mother, senses not ostensibly attuned to auras and atmospheres, would probably have called it a slum. To my eyes, that afternoon I parted from the Warburton *ménage*, it was the very acme of desirability. I thought of Tennyson Avenue and its florid architectural monstrosities, of Hampstead where I had been so sadly disappointed, of Maurice's new house in Middlesex, all timber-clad and picture-windows, which looked so frail and insubstantial that a strong wind might carry it away. Even Fairlawn Drive, my last address, shouted suburbia, despite the horse-chestnut tree and the grottoed nymph. There was no pretence about Ephraim Street.

My flat, as I chose to call it, smelt like a casualty ward. Virginia and I had used gallons of Dettol and pounds of green soap in a determined effort to eradicate the last lingering trace of the previous occupant. The carpet was puce, but whole, the furniture was strictly sale-room, but sturdy. Water flowed from the taps and the cooker cooked. Mrs Warburton had donated cushions, two table-lamps and three pans. Alec and Olivia were responsible for the shaggy bronze rug, the gold curtains, the ironing-board, the tea cups, the drying-cloths and the copper kettle. Maurice and Berenice had sent sheets. Two boys, doing woodwork at the technical college, had manufactured a free-standing bookcase for me. Virginia had plundered her government grant to provide me with a reproduction of 'Jane Avril Dancing' to cover the discoloured mark on the chimney breast.

I stood in the middle of my kingdom, wondering if there could be anything with which I was not already supplied. The kitchen was stocked with food, I had shillings for the gas meter and matches for the stove. I looked out of the front window: a desultory Saturday afternoon street scene. I looked out of the kitchen window: a complexity of drain-pipes and a collection of dustbins. I felt that I should have invited a few people round to house-warm, but we'd done that last week-end with plastic mugs of wine, all among the detergent and scrubbing-brushes and wood-shavings: me, Virginia and her friend Bridget and Fred and Ted, the woodwork boys. For something to do, I re-read Maurice's letter. It was very brief, really just a note enclosed with the sheets. Berenice expected to be confined at any moment. He'd been flip about it at first: 'Berenice is in pod,' he'd said. But you could tell that he was now very taken up with the preoccupations of imminent fatherhood. Olivia said, 'Berenice will drop babies with as much efficiency and as little fuss as a native woman.' There was a half-scornful, half-envious expression on her face when she said it. And I knew then that Olivia had never been able to have babies.

The man with the trunk arrived. Unpacking it and distributing the contents passed another hour. The house was very quiet. During my previous visits I had caught sight of the back view of a young man ascending the next flight of stairs. Either Mr M. Petronelli or Mr R. Bell. Miss M. Pincher remained a mystery. The woman who lived in the basement and took care – which meant, as I was to discover, swishing a mop up and down the stairs at infrequent intervals – was called Mrs Moore.

I needed the lavatory. The idea of a communal lavatory was the one repellent aspect of my new address. I had used Mrs Warburton's palace of hygiene very gingerly, and I knew this one was unlikely to measure up to her standards. I braved it. I would have to get used to it.

As I came out on to the landing I heard a female voice uttering a stream of ripe curses. I looked over the banister rail. Below me stood a woman who might have been elderly-middle-aged or young-elderly – she wore too much make-up for me to be sure – with her heel caught in the lino. She didn't see me. Her whole attention was focused upon wriggling that very high heel out of its trap. I gazed. Usually I found bad language offensive, but this woman cursed with such a fine, ferocious dignity she could have been the Virgin Queen tearing a strip off a disrespectful courtier. A final wrench, and the shoe came free. She picked up her shopping and put her key into the lock of the room below mine. Miss M. Pincher. Then I heard steps on the first flight and a man's voice said, 'Temper, Tassie, temper.'

'I'm going to see Goldman about this. Nearly went arse over breakfast-time on that lino.'

'Give him my best when you do. The old sod.'

The speaker came into view. He was a small thin young man with very fair hair and very tight trousers. He was carrying a string bag. 'I'm going upstairs and I am going to absolutely *drop*,' he said. 'It's sheer murder on a Saturday. I never want to see another inside-leg as long as I live. You're not making a cuppa, by any chance?'

She said something inaudible and he shouted with laughter. Then the key turned in the lock and they both disappeared.

I went back into my room and pondered. He was the same young man whose back view I had seen ascending. Therefore he lived above me. Miss M. Pincher was underneath, though why 'Tassie' when it was M., I didn't know. If the young man was Bell, then where was

Petronelli? Or vice versa? There was only one set of rooms above and one below, and Mrs Moore had the run of the basement. I had made a quiet reconnoitre to ascertain these facts the week-end before. It was very confusing. I switched on my radio. The clock said six. I could hear the pavement beginning to resound with the footsteps of returning shoppers. In half an hour I would prepare my first meal. It would be the beginning of a pattern. No doubt everything would explain itself in its own good time.

CHAPTER TWO

Tassie was not Miss M. Pincher. She was Mrs Victoria Cheetham. Tassie, the result of some obscure, childish mispronunciation, had stuck. After all, as she said, she didn't look like a Victoria, did she?

After a couple of distant good mornings, we got acquainted outside the supermarket. She was struggling with two large shopping-baskets. I offered to relieve her of one of them and we walked back to Ephraim Street together.

'It's my half-day, Tuesday, you see. I get Ray's groceries as well because he goes to the Turkish on a Tuesday afternoon and the shops are closed by the time he gets out.'

I thought it was extremely Christian of her to do so, but she explained that he did lots of favours in return.

'Raymond's a good boy,' she said. 'Handled in the right way.'

All along Ephraim Street I was forming impressions. Tassie's age was still difficult to determine: she was obviously fighting against encroaching age with every corset-bone and spike of mascara she could muster, but I reckoned her to be about fifty-five. She was smallish and very thin with dramatically black hair and seemed to favour beaded jumpers and upswept, diamanté-studded spectacles. Common, my mother might have said, but her accent was impeccable – even the stream of curses I'd overhead had been uttered in the most ladylike tones.

'Come in and have a drink?'

It was five o'clock and the way she said 'drink' left me in no doubt as to what she meant. 'No, thank you all the same.'

'Oh, come on. Have a cup of tea.'

That seemed harmless enough. And I was curious to see what lay behind her door.

'Excuse the mess, won't you?' she said, as she dumped her baskets and took off her coat. But the remark was made only as a matter of form: there was no mess to excuse. It was a huge flat and very tidy, though uninspiringly furnished. She had two big windows to my one and I could see doors which presumably led to bedroom and kitchen.

'It's lovely,' I said, by which I meant 'It's big'.

'Not bad. And not too expensive either. Only I wouldn't let that shark Goldman know it. I've had more battles with him than you've had hot dinners, already.'

'I haven't met him.' And I wasn't likely to met him. We left our rent in the locked post-box in the hall and an agent collected it and returned our books. 'I think it was his wife I saw.' I remembered a little, pouchy woman who'd eyed Alec Blake and probably upped the rent.

'Jewish bitch,' Tassie said absently, searching her groceries for a packet of tea. 'If you don't mind, dear, I'll have something with more of a kick to it. Ray should be back soon. He likes to join me in a drink about this time.'

Judging by the number of bottles on the sideboard, they liked to join each other in a drink any time. My mother kept only a bottle of sherry for Christmas and funerals; even Hampstead could not boast such a comprehensive array. I didn't know whether to be alarmed at the prospect of alcoholic neighbours, or pleased that I was in such a free and easy, hard-drinking household.

While she was in the kitchen I nosed around. There were photographs everywhere: family scenes with a plethora of babies. And above the fireplace was a portrait of Tassie herself, in black lace with a red rose in her cleavage.

'Your husband?' I said politely, indicating a snapshot of an elderly man with his eyes screwed up against the sunlight. She'd already corrected my misapprehension about her name and status and I'd assumed she was a widow.

She tossed her head and laughed uproariously. 'Cheetham? I wouldn't give that devil's photograph house-room, I can tell you. No, that's just a friend of mine, a Mr Griffiths. He runs a shop in Eastbourne. Wants me to go down and join him when he retires. But I'm not sure though. After you've looked after yourself for as long as I have you're a bit wary of depending on somebody else. Still, he's a merry old so and so, and he's got plenty. That's the main thing, isn't it?'

I said I supposed it was. I gestured to the other set of photographs but I didn't say anything in case I'd made another wrong assumption.

'Oh yes,' she said, 'my kids and grandchildren,' but not with any great enthusiasm. However, she brought them over to me and identified them. There was William who was married to Marjorie and Edgar who was married to Joan and Grace – 'God knows why I ever thought to call her Grace,' Tassie said, 'for she's about as graceful as a cart-horse' – who was married to Brian. Then there were Kathy and Nicholas and Rebecca, Tracy and Craig, Ian and Debbie and – 'the baby. I forget the baby's name. There are so many, you see, and they seem to follow one another so quickly.' She held the photograph up to the light and studied it with her head on one side. 'It's a girl, I think. Though you can't tell, can you?'

'You must be very proud,' I said fatuously. 'Eight grandchildren.'

'Why?' She turned her gaze from the photograph to me.

The wind had been taken quite out of my sails. 'Well,' I said, 'it's – it's an achievement, isn't it?'

'I didn't have anything to do with it, love.' She poured herself a generous measure of brandy. 'I'm just Grandma. Remembered whenever a birthday comes round.'

'But your own children, you must think a lot about them.'

She pulled a wry face. 'Kids,' she said. 'I never intended to have any. But I was only a kid myself. Not much older than you, I dare say. Too young to know anything about stopping them and by the time I found out I'd had three. Funny, isn't it, when you look at William and you think "Well, he wouldn't be having his photograph taken if I'd been successful when I tried to get rid."? He was a tough nut, William, stuck like a limpet. Kids,' she repeated. 'You bring them up and wipe their noses and their tears and lose your looks and your pride and your youth in the process and then they take wing and send you a few photographs and think you should be highly delighted. I just don't see the point of it, do you?'

It was all too dangerously near home for me, however much I agreed with her point of view. To change the subject I asked her about the mysterious Mr Petronelli.

'That was Mario. He shared with Ray for a while, but then I think he had a better offer. Didn't we have tears and lamentation then, though? Thought we'd never get over it that time. And Mario was a regular little cheap-skate. Funny really, I always thought Italians were very much the other way, didn't you? I thought it was the Arabs who went in for that kind of thing.'

Light dawned. I was all agog to meet Mr Raymond Bell of the exotic homosexual tastes. As it happened, I didn't have long to wait – a few minutes later someone beat a tattoo on the door and Tassie said, 'That'll be Ray now. Open the door, would you, dear, while I get a clean glass?'

I obliged her. Raymond Bell, looking rather pinker than when last I'd seen him, gave me a blank look and entered.

'This is Anna from upstairs, Ray,' Tassie said, pouring him a drink.

Ray made a perfunctory greeting. He obviously wasn't very interested.

'You've got to admit she's an improvement on the last one.'

I resumed my tea. 'Who was the last one?'

Raymond raised his highly-arched eyebrows to their fullest extent. 'One of your regular old bags,' he said. His accent too was impeccable; he enunciated each word precisely and clipped off its ending, but I had the feeling that this was acquired and lurking deep below it might be a thick, consonantal Liverpool or Birmingham mother-tongue. 'Used to dry her drawers over the gas fire.' He pinched his nostrils togther. 'The stench was unbe*liev*able. I used to go down and knock sometimes: "Madam, this is a civilized house and I'd appreciate it if you could adopt civilized habits." Then I'd scarper before she could think up any abuse. The old bag.'

'No, it wasn't that, Ray,' Tassie said placidly. 'It was her cooking. She ate a lot of fish. She was one of these food eccentrics. Believed red meat makes people aggressive. *She* was aggressive enough without it.'

I was gazing at Raymond, avid for some physical sign of his propensities, but I was disappointed. He was simply an under-sized, pale young man – the pink glow had faded; I supposed it was as a result of the Turkish bath – of twenty-three or twenty-four. His hair-style was rather elaborate, his fingernails were too long and his eyes were red-rimmed, but you would have passed him in the street without a second glance.

'Perhaps we've met before,' he said.

I blushed. I supposed my staring had been a bit blatant. 'I was admiring your suit,' I said quickly. It was indeed a sumptuous suit made of pale-fawn silky stuff.

'Swedish,' he said nonchalantly. 'Only came in last week. You won't see many of these around. This isn't your chain-store tat.'

'I should explain to you, Anna,' Tassie said, 'that Raymond is in Burtons' black books for ever and only escaped a summons for non-payment by moving his address very rapidly. It's easy to dress like Lord Penthouse when you don't pay for it.'

She supplied this information in a friendly way and he received it with apparent good humour. 'It's so *tempting*,' he said. 'Ten bob a week and you can ponce up to the nines, and could I help it if the misguided Assistance wouldn't settle my debts? I was out of work for *months*.'

'Oh, were you ill?' I felt compelled to make some sort

of conversational contribution, even though it seemed to be my afternoon for the *faux-pas.*

He nodded above his brandy, and sighed. 'Unem*ploy*-able,' he said, 'for *months.*'

'What was the matter?'

'Anxiety neurosis,' he said quickly and, I thought, rather proudly, as though he'd been privileged to be acquainted with some rare and very selective disease. 'I was on dope for ages – tranquillizers – I couldn't *move* without a pill. Tell her what I was like, Tassie.'

But Tassie seemed to prefer not to dwell upon it. 'You're better and that's all that matters,' she said. 'And what's more you *have* to pay for your suits now.' She explained: 'He works in a tailor's. That's where he gets his fancy clothes.'

Raymond closed his eyes again, wearily. '*Not* a tailor's, Tassie, I keep telling you. It's a men's boutique. I'd like to see Neil's face if he heard you call it a tailor's.'

They had more brandy. I listened and learned. Tassie also worked in a clothes shop, Miriam Lewis's clothes shop, a very small, very exclusive and very expensive emporium. I had often had my face pressed up, longingly, against that particular window.

Tassie looked at me, smiling. 'I bet you think we're a raggle-taggle couple, don't you?'

'I think you're very nice,' I replied truthfully. 'Maurice, my brother, said that in lodgings or rooms no one ever speaks to anyone else and you could be lying dead for weeks before someone would notice and then only because of the smell.'

'You've got a brother?' You could positively see Raymond's ears pricking up.

'A half-brother, actually.' They were total strangers; it didn't matter if they knew. 'He lives near London. His wife's expecting a baby any day. I keep looking out for the postman but it can't have happened yet. Incidentally, I must get one of those cards for the front door or things might go astray.'

They both laughed. 'I've been here three years,' Tassie said, 'and never put a card up. If the address is right the postman will drop it in. Haven't you seen the piles of letters on the hall table? We get football-pools, income tax demands, postcards, all addressed to people we've never heard of.'

'And love letters,' Raymond said. 'D'you remember, Tass: "After what has happened between us" and that other one that went into such sordid *de*tail?' He leered. 'I nearly wet myself over that one. We let them pile up for about six months,' he explained. 'And then, if they're not collected, we open them and have a lovely *read*.'

'It's all right here then, is it? No hidden snags?'

'It's not bad,' Raymond said. 'There's no interference, if that's what you mean. You can bring anyone in. Old Moore downstairs lives like a mole – compiling her almanack, probably.' He tittered at his joke. 'And Goldman only makes a royal progress to check the woodworm and the cockroaches once in six months. It's a hell of a lot better than my last place, anyway. Take anyone back there and the old biddy who owned it would shout up the stairs, "Mr Bell, Mr Bell, this house is not a public convenience." Finally I got very riled and shouted back, "No it bloody-well isn't. It would be kept cleaner if it was." I was leaving anyway, so it was worth it.'

They fell to reminiscing about their previous residences. Raymond had lived all over the place after leaving the Merchant Navy. Tassie had spent her childhood in London and come north after she'd married. She'd stuck Cheetham for seven years and then had taken the kids and taken off and she couldn't tell us how many furnished rooms and glorified slums there'd been between then and now. I threw in Mrs Warburton's as my contribution, but it clearly wasn't in the same class.

'Well, girls.' Raymond stretched and shook himself. 'I simply must go and powder my face. I've got to be out of here by seven. If I keep a certain person waiting there'll be hell to pay. A certain person's very temperamental. The cow. Ah, Tassie, my groceries. How kind. You couldn't be even kinder, could you? Just till Friday. With what I've got in my pocket it'd be beer and a packet of crisps and his lordship wouldn't like that at all. He's more your vodka-Martini type.'

Tassie opened her purse and I saw a five-pound note change hands. My presence didn't seem to embarrass them in the slightest. He pretended to kiss her hand.

'And now I must fly. See you anon.'

'I must go too.' I got up and handed over my tea cup. 'Would you come up and have coffee with me some time?'

She looked hard at me. 'It's very nice of you, dear, but don't feel you have to.'

'No. Honestly. I'd really like you to. I don't start work till next week and time drags a bit. Perhaps Raymond would like to come too. Would you ask him? How about Sunday morning?'

'Raymond usually spends Sunday in bed. I'll ask him though. And I'll come. It does take a bit of getting used to, doesn't it, being on your own?'

I wasn't bothered about being on my own. It was simple curiosity that had prompted me to issue the invitation. Raymond and Tassie were outside my range of experience. They were like people one read about: glamorous, odd, amoral. By comparison with their lives – intricately embroidered tapestries – mine seemed composed of very dull stuff.

CHAPTER THREE

'Miss Otis regrets,' Tassie said, when I opened the door to her on Sunday morning, 'or possibly may come down later, depending upon the state of his hangover. You'll get used to Raymond. When he drops in, you know he really wants to. There's no social obligation nonsense about Ray. And Sunday morning's sacred to sleep.'

'Don't you sleep in too?' I said, ushering her into my room.

'Oh no. I go to Mass.'

I must have looked very startled because she immediately chuckled and said, 'Just my little joke, dear. I'm a heathen really.'

The very idea of Tassie, who was extremely décolleté that morning and be-sequinned from collar to hem, attending Mass was side-splitting. Except that I supposed she'd quite fancy herself in one of those black lace mantillas.

Thinking of that reminded me of the portrait in her room. I asked her about it as I made the coffee.

'Oh, that. He would make me have it. I didn't want it, but it's kind of grown on me. That was painted many moons ago.'

'Who painted it?'

'He was an artist, dear. Or he thought so, at any rate. I used to be a model. At the art school. That was when I had something to show.' She looked down at her flat body. 'There's nothing now. Tassie No-Tits, Ray calls me. See what age and decay does to you.'

She looked very rueful. I was struggling between shock and laughter. Her vocabulary changed from prim maiden aunt to ribald fish-wife so rapidly that I was quite bemused.

'You have got it nice, haven't you?' She bent down to stroke my rug. 'Did your mum and dad contribute, dear? I believe I saw them once, just before you moved in. A tall man in a grey suit and an auburn-haired lady?'

'My stepfather and his wife.' It was the simplest explanation I could think of, but it still sounded complicated, even to me.

She didn't pursue it, however. She merely said how nice it must be to have a family who obviously thought a lot about me. Her family, she said, drew lots to determine who should invite her for Christmas, but she always put them out of their misery by refusing. 'I suppose I've always been a loner,' she said. 'The type who never should have married in the first place.'

'Then why did you?' I had the feeling that the most intimate personal question would not discountenance Tassie.

'Well, dear, I had, as they say, no option. Cheetham and I had jumped the gun. I was only sixteen and I was in service – you won't know what that meant, but I'll tell you: it meant being the lowest of the low – even being married to Cheetham was a better prospect than that – and when Madam found me boiling pennyroyal on the kitchen stove, that was it, Yours Truly out on her ear.'

'Wouldn't your parents have helped you?'

'They were dead. They died of the Spanish flu when I was a girl and all of us kids were boarded out with various relations. We lost touch.'

'So you got married?'

She nodded. 'Cheetham was all right to look at, and to go to bed with, I suppose. We should have gone through life with our mouths shut. There was no work and he joined up. When he came back he was a brute. I didn't so much mind the wine women and song and I'd learned to defend myself, but I drew the line when he started hitting the kids. That's when I left him.'

'How on earth did you manage?'

She gave me what my mother would have called an old-fashioned look. 'There was no Assistance, no Welfare, in those days – you went into the workhouse if you had no money. And there was only one way to make money when you'd three kids to look after. I suppose it's as a result of that I went right off men. Never went back on them really. There's my friend, of course, in Eastbourne. But that's only platonic. I just can't seem to work up the interest somehow for anything else. I suppose that sounds funny to you?'

The idea of anyone of Tassie's age even considering a sex life sounded funny to me. But I was still a few sentences behind, my mind boggling at her free and easy admission that she'd walked the streets, or whatever polite euphemism she'd use to describe the activity.

But, obviously unaware that I was shocked to the core of my prim little bourgeois soul, she prattled on, telling me how she'd eventually got a job modelling in an art college: 'I felt terrible that first time. But do you know, they just looked at me as though I'd got my clothes on? And the art master handled me like a side of beef. In fact, one of them once said to me, "I'd no idea you were so attractive until I saw you dressed." You see, in class, I meant nothing more to them than an apple or a jug.'

'Then what happened?'

'A little fellow with a moustache decided to invade Poland. I did a quick change-over from modelling to manufacturing munitions. Made a bit of money too. The war didn't last long enough for me. But I spent it as I got it. That's always been my trouble. I'm a soft touch. I can never tell the difference between the genuine cases and the fly-boys.'

'Raymond,' I said, remembering the five-pound note.

'Raymond's like me. Always taken for a ride. That Mario robbed him of every penny. Took his transistor, too, and his gold watch when he went. I told Ray to go to the police but he wouldn't hear of it. That's the trouble with Raymond's sort, there's always somebody to trade on their affection. I wish he could find a nice person. Some of these homos live quite happily together. I've met a few like Darby and Joan. But Ray doesn't like them established. He likes to turn them, if you see what I mean, and they play along with him for a bit and then throw him over when he's spent all his money on them.'

'It doesn't look as though he's going to come down, does it?' I wasn't sorry. Tassie's autobiography had left me breathless; I didn't think I could cope with Raymond's as well. But perhaps Raymond was not the type to unburden his bosom to mere acquaintances.

After Tassie had left I sat for a long time, turning over what she had told me. I came to the conclusion that it was not *what* she had told me that had shocked me, but the fact that she *had* told me. Secrecy, evasion and pretence had for so long been the rules by which I governed my life that to be suddenly faced with someone else's total frankness was a most disturbing experience. Where did the difference lie between my mother and Tassie, that the one should attempt to atone for a single lapse by adopting a neurotically strict moral code and the other, whose sins had been varied and manifold, should be able to accept them and be unashamed of admitting to them? 'There is no one as strait-laced as a reformed rake,' Alec Blake had once said. Tassie was not strait-laced. But then perhaps she wasn't reformed either. It was just, as she'd said, that she couldn't work up the necessary energy any more.

I supposed that most people accepted Tassie as being unconventional, eccentric, 'a character'; I supposed that they were indulgent but rarely took her seriously. That was the price you paid for expressing distasteful truths. People might admire you for your candour, but they wouldn't respect you, because you hadn't the sense to temper your personality to suit your environment. It was then that any ideas I had of being honest about myself and my family circumstances melted away. Façades were necessary; that others might be able to see through them didn't matter so much, it was the making of them, inspired by an attempt to be civilized, to fit in, to conform, that mattered.

I got to know Raymond more gradually. At first he was either nervous and restrained, or deliberately *outré* in my presence, dithering between the desire to present himself as being quite ordinary and the temptation to prove to me that he was far from being ordinary. Sometimes, when I was taking tea with Tassie, he would come in and make some outrageous remark just to see what effect it had upon me. At other times, when we met on the stairs, or he'd run out of sugar and was too idle to go down to Tassie's, he was polite and shy of me.

Some evenings there would be streams of pretty young men ascending Raymond's staircase, then weeks would go by without him having a single visitor. I supposed that a lot depended upon the state of his finances. I wondered about his family, but Tassie told me he hadn't seen them since leaving home at fifteen. He and Tassie seemed to know everything about each other. He had found a superior, substitute mother, and no doubt Tassie found him more filial than ever her true children had been. Sometimes he called her an old bag and she called him Raymond, the Queen of the Queers, but always affectionately. They were two people to whom life had not always been just, they could understand the sometimes tortuous workings of each other's mind, they clung to each other for protection against the world.

During September the chief of Raymond's pretty young visitors was a youth with a pale, blemished complexion and a full red mouth called Billy. Billy was out of work and had not paid his rent. In due course Billy and his hold-all were installed in Raymond's flat. I saw him a few times in the fortnight that he stayed and was not exactly enchanted with him. He had shifty eyes and a sulky look. Raymond was at work all week, so Billy took himself off to the pictures, or the amusement arcades, or the bowling alley, at Raymond's expense, I presumed. Billy had a weak chest. Extra bottles of milk, pints of cream, cartons of eggs appeared on the door-step. Billy, whose wardrobe when he arrived had seemed to consist of jeans, tee-shirt and baseball sneakers, was rigged out by the kind courtesy and credit facilities of *The Men From The Boys*, where Raymond worked. One morning a man from Radio Rentals delivered a television set. Billy's chief joys in life were television programmes, boys' comic papers and pints of milk. He went, at first unwillingly, to the Manchester clubs where the clan gathered – Raymond must have known it was dangerous but couldn't resist showing him off. At the end of the fortnight Billy packed his new clothes and left, while Raymond was at work, for the more promising patronage of an elderly antique dealer. And then the fun started.

It was Saturday night. I had been to the Butes' house for an evening meal and the combined effect of travel, rich food and Aunt Kitty's overpowering *bonhomie* had rendered me exhausted and longing for bed. There was a peculiar smell on my landing – a pungent, sweetish smell. It took me a few moments to identify it as gas. Horrors! Had I left my fire on? I went to check. The tap was flat against the wall, innocent. I went back on to the landing and followed the smell to its source which, as I should have realized had I not been fuddled with tiredness, would be Raymond's room.

I called him. There was no reply. I rattled the door-knob. It was locked. I panicked. I flew down the stairs screaming for Tassie. She appeared in the doorway, her hair down, streaming over the shoulders of her long white nightgown. She looked like Lady Macbeth in a very bad amateur production.

'Gas,' I said frantically. 'Raymond's room.' But she'd smelt it already and was back into her room and out of it again in a flash, wearing her spectacles and carrying a key. She lifted up her flowing skirts and leapt up the stairs. She looked ridiculous. I followed behind, finding it difficult not to laugh despite the gravity of the situation.

She opened the door. A quick glance showed us an old-fashioned gas fire and Raymond prostrate on the rug in front of it, a cushion beneath his head. Tassie moved like greased lightning. First to the gas tap then to the window which she threw open to its fullest extent. 'Help me.' I took his legs. For a small man he was surprisingly heavy. We dragged him out on to the landing. Tassie sat him up and began to smack his face. I hovered over them, choking and spluttering. 'Shall I ring the ambulance?' She didn't answer. She took a small bottle out of her pocket and held it under his nose. Suddenly he moaned and jerked and was very sick down the front of his shirt. I began to retch sympathetically. 'Oh, God, not you too,' Tassie said. So I swallowed valiantly and took his other arm over my shoulder and we lugged him to the window where he drew in great gasping lungfuls of moist night air.

We used my room for convenience. Tassie sent me downstairs for brandy while she stripped off his shirt. When I came back he was wearing my red sweater. I was none too pleased about that, but could hardly say so. She guided the glass to his mouth and he coughed a lot but got some down. The greenish pallor was gradually fading from his face.

'Won't we need the ambulance?' I asked. I had never dialled 999 and had been looking forward to doing so.

She leaned over him. 'How long had it been on, Ray?' He didn't answer. She struck him on the cheek, lightly but sharply. 'Come on, you can answer me. How long?'

He mumbled. 'Half an hour.'

'No. Not half an hour, Ray. How long?'

'Not long.'

'And had you taken anything?'

He started to cry. 'No pills left. No sleeping pills left. Finished them last week.'

Tassie looked up. 'A nice cup of tea, I think, Anna. Lots of sugar. He'll live. It'd take a lot more carbon-monoxide than that to finish him off.' She shook him. 'Didn't care whether or not you finished off the lot of us, did you? It's a damn good job Anna wasn't asleep tonight. You've got her to thank. Stop snivelling now.'

Just as my reaction was a fit of trembling, Tassie's was one of anger. She reminded me of a mother whose child has stayed out late and who, upon its return, first cries with relief and then slaps it for causing her needless worry.

'Why did he go, Tassie?' Raymond hiccoughed and wiped his eyes on my jersey.

'Because he was rotten. And you're better off without him. Good riddance to bad rubbish.'

'But I never touched him, Tassie. Honest to God.'

'I know, I know.' She cradled him in her arms and rocked him. 'It's over now. You're recovering now.'

'The world's full of rotten people.'

'Are we rotten, me and Anna?'

'No. You know what I mean. People you love.'

'Stop loving them then.'

'I can't.'

'You will. Stop loving them and start loving yourself. No bugger else will.'

We put him in Tassie's bed. His own room smelt reminiscent. Tassie would sleep on the sofa; she'd done it before and doubtless she'd do it again. We left him sleeping, his breathing shallow, one fist tucked under his chin. He looked very young, very vulnerable, like that.

In the kitchen Tassie and I smoked well-earned cigarettes. I no longer felt the slightest bit tired. I think it was only then that I realized the full implication of what Raymond had tried to do to himself.

'Has he tried it before?'

'Once, after Mario. But it wasn't as serious as this. He took some pills that time, then came down and told me. I gave him a glass of salt water. Why he's tried it on now, all for the sake of that little pip-squeak, I don't know.'

'Perhaps he's reached the end of his tether. You know, the last straw. All that stuff he was saying about everybody being rotten. But it can't go on – him trying to commit suicide. He'll have to get help of some kind.'

'Love, he's had help galore – if you can call it that: psychiatrists, a spell in hospital, pills. They're only temporary helps. There's only one thing that can help Raymond.'

'What's that?'

'Somebody decent to love him. And I don't think that will ever happen. He's always attracted to the rotten apples. Some of us are. There's not a damn thing you can do about it.'

'You'd think he'd learn from his mistakes.'

She put her head back and laughed. 'Oh, wouldn't life be easy if that was all there was to it? It'd be like learning the multiplication tables.'

She became serious again. 'First of all, there's what Raymond is – queer. That's difficult enough. Then there's the fact that he isn't sure what he wants to be – give it or take it, if you see what I mean. Also he doesn't want to be associated with the rest of them. That's why he always goes for straight boys. That Billy was no more queer than you or I. He was just a little gold-digger. Probably learned the technique in Borstal. And lastly, Raymond's a virgin, I'm sure of it, despite all his boasting. He's frightened, you see. Real dyed-in-the-wool homos, they don't act up so much or talk about it all the time. They accept it and they're normal in every other way. Ray would be just as unhappy with girls. It's his nature.'

'So what's going to happen to him?'

'He'll go on, picking up pretty little boys, playing the big-spender, buying affection. Then, one day, either he'll grow up as most of us have to do, or else he'll do a better job with the gas fire.'

I stirred my tea. 'But everyone's got problems. You said he'd had a rotten home-life, been pushed round from pillar to post, but then so have other people and they've managed to overcome it. My parents separated when I was eleven years old, and worse than that, but I've never tried to gas myself.'

'You probably know very well that your people love you, however they carry on amongst themselves,' Tassie said, emptying her cup and reading her tea-leaves. 'Ray's father was a drunkard and his mother went off with another man when he was twelve. He never heard from her again. Just upped and went. He came home from school one day and she wasn't there. His dad was one of these he-men, very good with leather belts on kids. Ray left home and went on a ship. Well, you know what ships are like; can you wonder he was influenced by the first people who'd showed him kindness? It's all right saying you've had bad luck. So have I, for that matter. But we're probably tougher. If somebody jilted me when I was young I used to cry for a bit, then I'd think, "Well, sod you, mate. It's your loss, not mine." But if someone does the dirty on Ray, he thinks it's his fault, he thinks there must be something wrong with him. He can't understand that life's like that and that the more you devote yourself to one person, the harder you'll be hurt.'

Tassie talked a lot of sense. She was a cynical woman and perhaps tended to see things too much *couleur de merde*, but her philosophy was more acceptable to me than any foolish rosy optimism. Nevertheless, I lay awake a long time that night going over what she'd said. Surely, despite all I'd been told, all I'd observed, surely it wasn't impossible to love successfully?

CHAPTER FOUR

Harriet Emily Blake made her début into the world as easily and unfussily as Olivia had predicted. Maurice said, proudly, as though he'd had something to do with it, that Berenice had had the shortest period for a first labour in the annals of the history of childbirth. He was with her at the time. I was revolted. 'It was amazing, incredible, I'd no idea –' He kept trying to tell me about it. I kept saying shut up. I'd secretly imagined (hoped?) that Berenice would have made a howling, hair-tearing orgy out of it. I'd seen her once in the later stages of pregnancy; she was so smug and apparently proud of the fact that she'd achieved what millions of people could achieve without any bother that I'd been consumed with disgust, and a kind of envy too.

We were foregathered for the christening which, though less well-attended than the wedding, was daunting enough. I was a god-parent. The other two were Trevor, who had by now taken a wife, and the wife he had taken who was exactly like Trevor: clumsy, well-meaning and brash.

Harriet Emily (I could just imagine Berenice scouring the births in the best papers to find out what the best people were calling their children) was reasonably presentable, as babies go. My mother said she had Maurice's eyes. Mrs Butler, after a stiff look, decided to compromise and said she had Berenice's shape of face. Alec Blake attended the ceremony (no one said that Harriet Emily had inherited any of *his* features) but left straight afterwards, before the bun-fight which had been prepared by Mrs Butler who'd been in residence ever since the baby was born. 'Shop cakes,' my mother said scornfully. She had always maintained, in private, that beneath the airs and graces Mrs Butler would have a dirty neck and no familiarity with a scrubbing-brush. In public, she was the soul of deference.

We ate *vol-au-vents* and little pies and cream cakes. My digestion was not aided by all the cooing that was going on around me. Even my mother had succumbed to the general maternal hysteria. Granted Berenice, the baby in her arms, did have the air of a Raphael Madonna, but the event was not unique. As soon as I could I escaped with Maurice, ostensibly to see the nursery.

'Yes, very pretty.' It was all pink and white and blue and there were coloured cotton-wool balls and soft furry animals and tins of talcum powder all over the place.

'This is the theory,' Maurice said. 'In practice the cradle

spends every night in our bedroom, plus its occupant. Still, people are impressed.'

'Should have thought you'd have had a nanny, you and your big income.'

'Christ! My big income! It seems big at the beginning but you'd be amazed how it dwindles just paying for the basic essentials.' He rocked the cradle with his toe. He looked as though he'd had a good few sleepless nights recently. My brother: twenty-two-and-a-half years old, with a wife, a baby and a mortgage. It was frightening.

'Talking of big incomes,' he said, 'Papa shot off pretty sharpish, didn't he?' He gave the cradle one last vicious push then set it rocking madly. 'Scared of leaving La Olivia for too long on her own, I suppose.'

'You've changed your tune. You were all over her at one time.'

He shrugged. 'We've had Mum here quite a bit recently. Can't you see how she's gone old? He's got everything and she's got nothing. She knows nobody really wants her. Why the hell don't you bury the hatchet and go home?'

'That's right. Sacrifice me on the altar for the sake of your conscience. *You* have her to live with you if you're so concerned.'

'Are you mad? There'd be a massacre. You've never seen Berenice, have you, claws out and teeth bared?'

'They used to like each other well enough.'

'Ah, that was just strategy, until I was in the bag.'

'I still don't see why you've become antagonistic about Olivia. Or perhaps I do. It's funny really. He said you were the sort to distinguish between wives and mistresses, that you'd one day become very proper. Is that what's happened?'

I used not to believe that people changed, but Maurice had changed since his marriage. For one thing he didn't spar with me nearly so much. He merely changed the subject. 'What do you think,' he said, 'is going to happen if he pegs out? She's changed her mind about the divorce, you know. She said she'd put it into the hands of her solicitors when she was here last time.'

'She's been saying that for a while.'

'She means it this time. What if he kicks the bucket after he marries Olivia?'

'What if he does?' I couldn't see what he was driving at.

'The money, I mean. Olivia will be entitled to the lion's share.'

'Olivia doesn't need his money. Anyway he'd be bound to settle something on Mum. He's not that much of a swine.'

'Wills,' Maurice said darkly, 'can be contested. And it's not so much Mum I'm thinking about as us.'

'Us?' I said incredulously. 'What's up with you, Maurice? Are you broke, or something?'

'It was just a thought,' he said with cold dignity. 'I think I, at least, have more of a claim than she has.'

'It seems to you that he's going to drop dead any minute, does it? Or maybe you're hoping that, before he has the chance to remarry?'

'Of course I'm not, silly cow.'

We parted on bad terms. Never having been deprived of it, money meant little to me. And Maurice was certainly not deprived either, judging by the look of his home. I said, before I left, 'If you're so concerned about money, you should have taken more care and not started a family.' He got furious at that. I suspected that Harriet Emily had been accidental rather than planned – they hadn't been married much more than a year when she was born, despite all Berenice's family planning fervour – but he wasn't going to let anyone know that. He said there was no need for me to be so effing clever. I replied that that was just the kind of language you'd expect from a rising young executive, and made my exit. I felt betrayed.

Consequently I was astounded when, a couple of weeks after that, he came up to visit me. And came alone. Berenice and the baby had been dropped off at the Butlers'. For which I was truly thankful.

On Sundays, more often than not, the three of us pooled our resources and Tassie, who was the only one of us who could produce palatable roast meat, cooked the lunch. We looked forward to Sundays, after the spaghetti, welsh rarebit, fish cake routine of the week. Maurice arrived as Tassie was reading tea-leaves, another regular Sunday activity. Hers and Raymond's were always legible, if sometimes grim, but mine were murky. It was the way I swung my cup, she said, searching in vain for swans, trees or clover leaves – there was just a coagulated mass at the rim.

I was not overly-welcoming. There was, I reminded him, a telephone in full working order situated in the hall. I might have been otherwise engaged. To arrive without telephoning was the height of ill manners, somebody had said.

'Did somebody also say that keeping a visitor on the doorstep isn't exactly urbane, either?'

'Bring him in for a cup of tea.' Tassie poked her head round the door, giving one of her wide, all-purpose smiles. Her new teeth didn't fit too well. She thought of going private.

'It's my brother.' They must have watched his arrival. I could imagine the speculation.

'All the more reason.'

I thought Maurice sailed through the introductions with great aplomb. Tassie and Raymond concerted, I imagined, might come as a bit of a shock. Tassie was wearing her kimono – she rarely bothered to dress on Sundays. It was quite respectable, but a trifle Somerset Maugham white-lady-taking-to-gin-in-the-tropics. Raymond, on the other hand, was in full fig: lace-ruffled shirt, gold sovereign cufflinks, hand-made shoes. He'd had his hair blow-waved the day before too. I closed my eyes and prayed that they would not say anything outrageous. It was rather like my London visit in reverse: Maurice was now the shockable party.

Tassie made more tea and chattered inconsequentially. Raymond didn't say much but, whenever he did say anything, spoke in the deepest, most masculine tones he could muster. I almost laughed and spoiled the effect.

There was no doubt that Maurice was a great success. Tassie said afterwards that he put her in mind of that boy who played the guitar, but as she couldn't remember his name, we were none the wiser, and Raymond said, 'What a waste. What a wicked waste,' and shook his head dolefully.

We managed, at last, to excuse ourselves from Tassie's pressing hospitality. In my room, Maurice sat on the bed and laughed till he cried. 'Anna, you have a talent,' he said, between spasms. 'Everywhere you go you manage to pick up a weird entourage. That woman, Sadie Thompson, downstairs, did you hear her? She kept calling me Norman. And the other one! He looked as though he daren't move his head in case his hair fell off, and that *scent* he had on – a cross between Californian Poppy and the ante-chamber of an Algerian brothel.'

'With which, of course, you are well acquainted. They may look odd, but they're very kind. Probably a lot kinder than your posh so-called friends.' I had met a few when visiting Enfield: young married couples with strident voices and opinions, dead scared of doing or saying something that might spoil their progressive young modern image.

'All right, all right. Don't get shirty. I'm quite prepared to believe that they're the very epitome of charitable good-fellowship. It's just the way they look. Have you introduced them to the old man and Olivia?'

'No.'

'Well, invite me to be present when you do. I can just imagine the quick double-take on Olivia's face and the way she'll be ultra-charming ever afterwards.'

'So why are you here? Apart from taking the opportunity to mock at my friends and neighbours?' I offered him a cigarette, then remembered that he'd given it up because Berenice thought it was a filthy habit. But he accepted one anyway.

'I thought I'd better come and repair the little rift within the lute that took place at the christening. I suppose I sounded a bit of a bastard. I was right down deep in the slough of despond. I didn't really mean that stuff about Olivia. Olivia's OK. Things were getting me down: the baby and Berenice and Mum walking about as though she was expecting to be hanged, drawn and quartered at any minute. I was dead jealous, to tell you the truth.'

We smoked companionably for a while. At length I asked him what on earth he had to be jealous about? He had everything he could possibly expect to have. Were things not all right at home? I tried to keep my questioning impersonal. If he thought I was crowing, he'd shut up like a clam.

'I'm too bloody young. I'm twenty-two, for God's sake. I get up, I go to work. I have to bow and scrape because somebody's going to be promoted and it might be me. I have to behave in the way that's expected of me: sober, reliable, respectable. Then I come home and Berenice is fussing with the kid. I might as well be talking to myself for all for response I get. Then she's too tired. Or the baby cries. And to cap it all there's been Ma Butler breathing down our necks for the past couple of months, making her sensible bloody suggestions. Everything's just sort of closed in all of a sudden.'

A dozen suitable replies suggested themselves to my mind: but it's what you freely chose, but everybody's life's like that, but that's the result of marrying without what I think of as being love. 'Do you think you've boobed then?' was all I said.

He grinned. 'Did I sound as though I was knocking on the door of the divorce court? It's not come to that. Never will. I know you're not exactly in love with Berenice, but she's great really. I just wanted to explain my bad temper. That day of the christening, the old man, swanning in for a few minutes, looking oh so prosperous and elegant and isn't the world a delightful place, it was the last straw.'

'I know what you mean. Whenever I'm with them I get the feeling that they've excluded the rest of the world from their private bliss. Relationships are awfully selfish, aren't they?'

'Well, yes, by their very nature. If everybody concentrated on one other person instead of just dispensing impersonal charity, the world might be a better place.'

'But there'd always be somebody not catered for.' Like our mother, I was thinking. But I didn't have to say it; he knew.

Maurice consulted his watch. 'Another hour,' he said. 'I promised to be back by four. I have to fit in my activities with an intricate feeding routine. I often wonder how these native women go on who haven't a clock in sight.'

'They feed them when they're hungry.'

'You're probably right. But that's blasphemy according to the baby clinic. It's to be every four hours, on the dot. The kitchen's like a bloody laboratory what with bottles and timers and sterilizers.'

'Were we bottle-fed, do you suppose?'

'You weren't. I can remember it quite clearly. A most traumatic experience for me. All my toilet-training went for a burton.'

I settled myself on the rug at the side of the bed and leaned back against him. We hadn't achieved this kind of closeness for years. 'I often wonder whether she tried to get rid of me. I've heard Tassie talking about her attempts at getting rid and I wonder if they apply to me.'

'Not her,' he said definitely. 'She's always had too much respect for the mysteries of the human body. Look at the way she used to carry on with you: vests and cod-liver oil and that Thermogene waistcoat you used to wear. The body was sacred, as far as she was concerned. D'you think she'd have risked messing up her internal workings?'

'It's just that it's an awful thought, knowing that people wished you'd never been conceived.'

He pulled my hair, gently. 'I should think that applies to about fifty per cent of the population. If you take the idea to its logical conclusion, then consider the odds against being conceived at all – you're just the result of an arbitrary encounter between one spermatozoon and one egg. A million to one chance. A different sperm, a different egg, and you'd have been somebody else.'

But that was sheer sophistry as far as I was concerned.

'I tried to find him once, you know, Frank Best. I didn't succeed. I wonder if ever I shall?'

'What the hell d'you want to find him for? He might be perfectly foul. Eat with his mouth open. Or be three feet tall with a hump-back.'

'Precisely.'

'It's up to you, I suppose. In your position I'd probably be tempted to do the same thing. But I'm sure it's best to let well alone. For instance, have you considered how he might feel, suddenly being faced with an eighteen-year-old daughter of whose existence he was quite ignorant?'

'That's his problem. I didn't ask to be born.' I tugged at my rug, despoiling its lustrous surface. 'Actually I've never got beyond locating him, in my imagination. I'd probably turn and run if I did.'

He looked at me. 'If you *really* wanted to find him, it would be quite simple. Advertise in the daily papers. One presumes he can read.'

'Perhaps that's why I don't. It has to be the hard way. Fate, if you like. If I'm meant to meet him, I will do. Advertising like that would be tempting providence.'

Maurice helped himself to another of my cigarettes, punched a cushion and put it behind his head. Eyes closed, exhaling smoke ceiling-wards, he said, 'It's amazing, Anna. When I think of all that's happened. You were such a spoiled kid. And here you are, living on your own, supporting yourself, being sensible about everything. According to the laws of psychology, you should be in an emotional turmoil.'

'I don't suppose I'd let you see it if I was.'

'I'd see it, ducks. It's a big fallacy, believing that one's personal façade is impenetrable. I bet you pride yourself on being able to see through other people. Why shouldn't they be able to see through you?'

'Thank you, Sigmund Freud.'

'Not at all. I think you're a credit to me.'

'To you?'

'Who else? Who else's shining example did you have before you during your formative years? Who taught you granny-knots and how to swear in three languages? Who woke you up in the middle of the night to go to the loo?'

I threw a cushion at him. He imprisoned my two hands in one of his and made gentle punching motions with the other one. The longer he stayed, the more I realized how much I missed him. My half-brother who, for most of the time, was nothing more than a distant, related stranger. But at times like this our single tie of blood proved itself to be as strong as a regular one. I prayed then, that whatever the vicissitudes of my life, this at least would remain constant.

CHAPTER FIVE

The following summer I accompanied Alec and Olivia to the French Riviera. They were married now. My mother had capitulated and divorced him. He and Olivia were very circumspect about the whole affair. Maurice said, 'I didn't expect them to invite us to be bridesmaids, but dammit all, we could have been notified.' We hadn't been told until the deed was done. Olivia said it felt like an anti-climax: 'A bit of paper and suddenly I'm an honest woman.'

I had to go to see my mother after that. She knew. He'd had the courtesy to let her know. The house was as spotless as ever, but instead of being continually occupied as she always used to be, she sat for long periods twiddling her wedding ring and gazing into space. There was no hope, no purpose any more. It was a mercy, in a way, that Henry Bute died soon afterwards. After the weeping and wailing, she sold up the Tennyson Avenue house and moved in with Aunt Kitty.

The same events kept recurring, but in reverse. If one lived long enough, I supposed, it would be possible to see a regular pattern emerging.

My job was mere routine, although I was methodical, conscientious and received promotion and a raise in salary. Every Monday morning I thought of handing in my notice, but could think of no attractive alternative. I was in a rut; I needed a push, a new incentive.

It was Saturday, October 28th. My horoscope was dull – and inaccurate. Saturday, October 28th, was a date to be encircled in red for ever afterwards

Eleven o'clock. I was in Boots buying toothpaste. Someone bumped into me, a man. I dropped my change on the floor. 'I'm awfully sorry.' 'Not at all.' We both bent to retrieve the money. He held out two sixpences and a penny in his palm. I looked up into his face to thank him. The man was Jake.

My head swam. It was impossible. His palm was still outstretched. I took the money. My hand was trembling. There was no recognition in his eyes. I said, 'Jake.' My voice sounded in my ears an octave too high. There was a look of polite puzzlement on his face. I said, 'What are you doing here? Maurice said you were in Leipzig or Danzig or somewhere. Though that was ages ago. But why here?'

He grasped the only comprehensible word. 'Maurice?'

'Maurice. My brother. Maurice Blake. I'm Anna. Don't you remember?'

Comprehension dawned. He took my hand and shook it vigorously. 'My word, you must have a good memory,' he said. It was obvious that it was only Maurice's name that had triggered off a response.

'You haven't altered.'

'You have. You were a little girl, a big-eyed little girl. You looked like Daniel in the lions' den.'

'I wasn't so little. You were kind to me.' And you lived in my memory for a long time afterwards, I could have added.

'I wonder what ever became of them all.'

'Maurice is married. Rona got married too. I don't know about the rest. Did you not keep in touch?'

He shook his head. 'I was abroad for a long time. One promises to write, but – Look here –' He put out an arm to steady me as a woman, trailing a shopping-trolley, barged between us and knocked me off balance '– let's go along the road and have a cup of coffee or something. You can fill in all the blanks between now and then. We'll have a good old nostalgic wallow.'

We went out into the street. Years ago I had dreamed up situations like this: our meeting at a time when I'd be adult, sophisticated, in command. I was nineteen years old and none of those things.

With a table between us and two cups of coffee, I was able to look at him properly. I had been too overwhelmed with the shock of recognition to do so before. He looked older, naturally – there were lines in his face that hadn't been there four years ago – but he was still the same Jake who made one think of russet velvet and lace. In fact, he was dressed to match my fantasy: he wore a suède jacket, chestnut in colour, which squeaked whenever he moved, and a silky white polo-necked sweater. They gave him a gipsy-vagabond look.

The café was packed. He'd raised a hand and secured service without so much as taking his eyes off my face. He smoked American cigarettes. His finger-nails were meticulously manicured. His smile dazzled his grave face. His gaze never wavered. I tried to return it with equanimity but I was daunted; my eyes roved from the sugar basin, to the table, to his left ear. Wit, fluency, composure, all deserted me. I could only wait for him to speak.

'So Maurice got married?'

'Yes. To Berenice. They have a daughter now.'

'*I* remember Berenice,' he said suddenly and definitely, cigarette suspended in mid-air. 'The one we used to call Miss Liebfraumilch of 1960. Why was that, do you suppose? Could it have been occasioned by her sparkling and wholesome personality?'

'Miss Lifebuoy, more like.'

'You're good friends, I take it?'

'She's a person I simply cannot like, however hard I try. She has no obvious faults, but she makes me feel – uneasy, makes me feel as though I've laddered my stockings. Can you understand that?'

'Perfectly. Your personal chemistries are just not sympathetic. It applies just as much when we're attracted to totally unsuitable people. Reason seems to count for nothing.'

A sudden burst of conversation, and I was at a loss again. I watched his cigarette smoke curling upwards. Through loudspeakers above our heads floated 'The Isle of Capri', canned, homogenized. It should have been 'The Streets of Laredo'.

'And what about Anna? How big and bad did the world turn out to be? Are you treading the boards?'

'You remembered. I'm not the only one with a good memory.'

'It's an affliction. You'll find out.'

'It didn't work out that way. I'm a secretary. I lost my great ambition.'

'Don't we all.'

'You'd achieved yours, surely?'

'I hadn't one. I mistook it for something else. Or perhaps things came too easily and extinguished the flame. You're a secretary. I lecture to students. It doesn't matter much in the long run.'

'Whatever happened to Zagreb?'

He leaned back in his chair and lifted his cup to his lips. His every movement was graceful. 'Belgrade, to be accurate. I came back. I missed something. God knows what.'

'Your roots?'

'My roots! I was born in Paris, schooled in Sussex, vacationed in London and France and New York. My roots are frail, under-nourished plants.'

A woman at the next table said, 'It was cut off. He wouldn't see reason so it was cut off.' Her companion, jaws clamped round a piece of gâteau, nodded encouragingly. Jake's eyes met mine. 'Poor sod,' he said. I laughed, I began to feel at ease. I dared to lift my coffee cup and found my hand had stopped trembling. In retrospect, my nervousness seemed ridiculous. He did not know that I had once cherished him in my heart. I was just someone he'd met briefly, a small girl, when he was embroiled in a relationship with someone else. Rona. Married now. But not to him. Perhaps he was married. I calculated. Twenty-seven, or thereabouts. It was on the cards. But he didn't look married. If there was such a look.

'Do you have any children?'

'Not that I know of. I'm not married, if that's what you mean. I don't know why not. I expect I should be. Your brother puts me quite to shame.'

The waitress to-ed and fro-ed alongside us. We were bombarded with meaningful glances. Our cups were empty and there was a queue at the cash desk waiting to be seated. He consulted his watch. 'I've an appointment at eleven-thirty.' A woman, I thought. 'A colleague,' he said. 'You must let me have your phone number. You're still at home?'

'No. I've a bed-sitter here. I've been away from home for two years.'

He raised his eyebrows. 'I'd never have expected you to have flown the nest quite so young.' He took a note-book from his top pocket. 'Put it down – your number. You're my only contact in an alien country. I can't lose you again.'

I wrote it down while he sorted coins from his loose change. I went over the two juxtaposed phrases, so unalike in sentiment: 'alien country', 'can't lose you again'; I didn't know which of them came nearest to expressing his true feelings.

Outside the café I lingered beside him, unable to release him with a gracious phrase. What was a telephone number? Except to be disregarded, forgotten?

'I'm in a flat,' he said. 'In the throes. Just moved in. I shall have to have a mammoth sorting session.'

'D'you want a hand?'

'You've better things to do with your Saturday nights.' His look was amused, slightly quizzical.

I didn't deny it. I wasn't going to admit to a poverty-stricken social life. 'I know what it's like moving – the mess –'

'We'll compromise. You sort out my frying pans. I'll buy you a meal.'

I couldn't suppress a rapturous smile.

'I'll pick you up. Tell me where you live and what time.'

I made use of his note-book again. Flat against the wall. His Biro wouldn't function at that angle. I had to finish it, struggling, on my knee. I began a stream of verbal directions. He halted me. 'I'll find you. I promise. Six o'clock. Don't disappear.'

Don't disappear. I boarded a bus for Ephraim Street.

My cheeks were fever-hot. My lips were cracked and dry. When I reached home I would unpack my jumbled mind, set each of my impressions side by side and analyse them. 'The Streets of Laredo' – I heard it, hummed in the air, plucked upon the telegraph wires, I saw his fingers coaxing the sweet notes, prolonging them, causing them to sing and cry. I saw his face, different from four years ago, real, full of secrets. I thought: 'I am happy. This must be what happiness is, hope that is soon to be fulfilled.'

Raymond was descending his staircase as I ascended mine. We met on the landing. 'I'm taking the rest of the day off,' he said. 'I had *raging* toothache, but I've doped myself and it's gone.'

'Psychosomatic.'

'Psychoso we can go to the flicks. There's Laurence Olivier at the Odean and a Horror at the Laugh-and-Scratch. Which?'

'Neither.'

'Neither?'

'I met an old friend in town. I'm going to help him sort out his flat. Jake. He used to be a friend of my brother's.' Jake, Jake, Jake. One precious, surprisingly beautiful syllable.

'Well, bully for you,' Raymond said slowly. He would go back upstairs and sulk. He tried my patience. What did he expect? That I should keep my time free for someone who was no more than a casual friend and homosexual to boot?

'I just hope this one's an improvement on your usual run of fellows. You've got shocking taste in men.'

'Maybe. You seem to forget that I have to wait to be chosen, so I've not much control over the matter.'

'Rubbish. You need to learn a bit of technique, that's all. I'll teach you some time when I've a spare moment. Actually I'm quite glad about tonight. I'd promised to ring up a friend but I thought I'd give you first refusal.'

He went down to the telephone, whistling. It could have been bravado, but I thought it more likely that he was in the process of making another conquest. I was surprisingly annoyed. I hung over the banister and eavesdropped.

It was well nigh impossible to have a private conversation in that house anyway.

Raymond had a distinct telephone manner. He reminded me of a switchboard girl, turning, immediately the phone rings, from normal conversational accents to being ultra-refined and efficient. 'Paul,' he said. 'This is a bit of luck.' His face contradicted the easy nonchalant tone of his voice. 'Are you free tonight? There's the Olivier film at the Odeon and I know you're a fan. I thought we could see it and have a bite afterwards.' Pause. His face was screwed up with expectancy. Then, 'Fine. Seven, Bye bye.'

I went into my room. I had no desire to see him, flushed with triumph and hope. It was I who would have to collaborate in picking up the pieces when that hope had been betrayed.

Jake was punctual to the minute. He caught me off-guard. I thought that men like Jake were entitled to be late, just as beautiful women were entitled to be late.

I knew that Raymond and Tassie would be watching. They admitted to it. Perhaps even Old Moore, in her basement, would be peering behind the curtain. I walked proudly beside him to the car.

I watched his hands putting the gears into motion, and then his face, as he craned his neck to assess the traffic. I had to admit that, taken feature by feature, it was not precisely a handsome face: brows too thick and black, nose slightly out of true, chin not quite determined enough to support the strong sculpture of the mouth. It was the face of a film violinist, a decadent Middle-European aristocrat, a hero bound for self-destruction. True handsomeness implied a breadth, a sturdiness not present in his face. I wished him handsomer, I wished myself more beautiful; I knew that in an hour or two I would see us that way.

'Are you cold?' he said, feeling the vibration of my arm against him.

'A bit.' It was excitement, not cold, that made me tremble.

'This is it.'

It was a house I'd seen before and whose turrets and castellations and recumbent stone lions I'd admired. It seemed a gift of double providence: Jake and that house.

His flat was on the first floor. As he went up the stairs he told me the rent. It wasn't a great deal more expensive than Ephraim Street. I looked at the tiled hall, the panelled walls, the carpeted stairs. 'Trust Jake to come up smelling of roses,' Maurice would have said.

'Why do other people's residences always seem more desirable than one's own?'

'The grass at the far side of the hill, I suppose. I thought your place had a certain quaint charm. The setting for some great Victorian melodrama. And who was the old dame peering from behind the curtains?'

I told him about Tassie, about Raymond, as we began to empty the tea-chests that contained his belongings. I embellished my story, exaggerated it, deliberately made it amusing. He laughed a lot, but I felt a bit ashamed. Tassie and Raymond were not the cartoon characters I had made them out to be, they were real people, they were my friends.

'This flat,' Jake said, 'is what is euphemistically called part-furnished. It means that everything non-essential is supplied.' He picked up a particularly ugly varnished clock between finger and thumb and dropped it into an empty chest. 'That's where the part-furnishings are going to remain until I leave.'

'But it's beautifully decorated.' I looked around at the aquamarine walls, the white mouldings, the wood-block surrounds.

He bowed from the waist. 'If ever I get fed up with teaching Eng. Lit. I'll paint and decorate for my living.'

'You did it?'

'No one else. Those pictures in that crate are to be hung over the bumpy places. If you'd oblige.'

He moved round the room, hammer in hand, his mouth full of picture-hooks, while I unpacked the crate. There were a couple of lithographs, a joky Klee and a print of 'Jane Avril Dancing'. I had come upon an omen. 'We seem to have the same tastes when it comes to disguising bumps.'

He looked round. 'That? It's not surprising. I should think that picture ranks second only to Van Gogh's "Sunflowers" in the popularity stakes. Someone gave it to me.'

He stretched to hammer the hook into the wall. There was no fault to be found with his body: broad shoulders, flat belly, taut buttocks. Its perfection awed me.

'What was her name?'

'Who?'

'The one who gave you the picture.'

'Maria.'

'And was she dark with brown eyes?'

'Yes. Why? Do you know her?'

'No. Just testing a private theory.' Men always go for the same physical type; it's a known fact.

He regarded me, head on one side. 'You remind me a lot of Maurice. Certain patterns of speech. You both use a good deal of stress and you go to a lot of trouble to decide what you're going to say.'

'The opposite of spontaneous, you mean?'

'If you like. But it's a definite talent. How is Maurice utilizing his?'

'He's selling his science degree in the competitive market. That's how he describes it. In plain English, he's involved in researching new drugs, anti-biotics. He thought it was all going to be very academic, but now he finds he has to set the alarm for seven and be nice to the boss just like everyone else.'

Jake smiled. 'It was bound to happen. I saw Maurice as potential chairman of the county council the moment I set eyes on him. All the "Let's have a revolution" rubbish was mere conformity.'

'You sound a bit snide.'

'I'm not. Not at all. I admire Maurice's type. The world couldn't get along without it. It could get along just as well without me. Now. Could you pass up those books?'

I glanced surreptitiously inside each one as I handed it over. The only clue was that J. Stavely had received *Quentin Durward* as third form prize in 1950. At the bottom of the second crate was a packet of photographs. I fell upon it with cries of delight but he divined my intention and took it from me. 'Later,' he said. '*Much* later. Photographs are dynamite. And besides, if you start we'll be here until midnight.'

But one had fallen out as he took the packet. Jake, in front of an imposing piece of architecture. 'Cambridge,' he said. 'A fond mama who had to be sure that everyone would recognize the location and know that Jake was a success, despite everything.'

'Everything?'

'I'll tell you some time.' He stacked the crates in the corner. 'If you go through that door you'll find a bedroom where you can change.'

When I'd finished I was satisfied – there are times when anyone can look beautiful – and he was surprised. He still thought of me as the ungainly fifteen year old I had been; the slightest transformation would have surprised him pleasantly. 'You look lovely,' he said. 'You're going to be a knockout in the Wimpy Bar.'

But he'd booked a table at a very plush restaurant. We sat, either side of candles, and he put his hands together and rested his chin on top of them.

'Jake,' I said. 'Is it a name proper, or a diminutive?'

'Neither. It's an Anglicism.'

'Jake? Oh, *Jacques*. Have you French blood?'

'Mother. Father English. Both live in France. Now you.'

I bent my head and studied the texture of my melon. To lie now would be to make it that much more difficult to tell the truth later on. But there might never be a later on and if there were, Jake would surely understand.

'You know about me. One brother. Parents divorced. Father married again. You've met Olivia, I believe.'

He nodded. 'Just a few times. Fantastic-looking woman. Like a naiad.'

'Yes, she does wear a lot of green.'

'Have I said the wrong thing?'

'No. I like Olivia. It's just that she sets an impossibly high standard for womanhood in general.'

'I wouldn't believe it. Everybody's got a fatal flaw somewhere.

'Even you?'

'Even me.'

I was on to my third glass of wine. I was fluent. Over the candle flame his face presented itself to me as planes of light and shade. Our table was an island amid a blurred sea of faces. I was unaware of waiters, diners, even food – the plates changed at intervals and I ate what was on them but I never noticed what I was eating.

'I'm glad I found you. I thought about you quite a lot. I wondered how you'd grow up.'

Lies. Doubtless lies. But beautiful lies. The atmosphere, the dialogue, they were the important things, more important than the drab truth. Everything about the occasion was as congruous and carefully edited as the films I had cried through in early adolescence. He brushed a lock of hair back from his forehead. I had to clench my hands under the table to prevent them from reaching out to touch him. His eyes and the tender area around his upper lip cancelled out the slight lack of symmetry in the rest of his face. He was all the men, since puberty, who'd ever caused my stomach to contract and my throat to ache – Pancho Gonzales, Sacha Distel, the man who looked like Frank Sinatra and sold shoes in Freeman, Hardy and Willis – but this time translated into fact, into possibility.

CHAPTER SIX

'Ray, is there something repugnant about me?'

Raymond raised his face, purple with exertion, from the floor. We'd been reading keep-fit exercises in a magazine and he was trying to catch up on twenty-five years of indolence all in one afternoon. He patted his sweat-bespeckled brow and considered. 'Well, there's your moustache, of course.'

'I have *not* got a moustache.'

'Like to bet?' He approached me, finger and thumb angled to tweak at my upper lip. I ducked my head.

'I have *not*.'

'OK. Have it your own way. Just don't look in any magnifying mirrors, that's all.'

He resumed his press-ups, every one a muscle-searing agony, while I paced the room and kicked the furniture. I had not heard from Jake for three weeks, three weeks of fretting and attempting to recap upon our evening together, moment by moment; an attempt which always failed, always refused to crystallize the particular out of the general blue of recollection.

Raymond said, 'He doesn't fancy you. Go out and find someone who does.' Tassie said, 'There are two sorts of men, dear, the sort who do and the sort who don't. Unfortunately the sort who don't are usually the ones you want to be the sort who do.' Her cheerful resignation was no help to me at all. When three weeks had become a month, I telephoned Olivia and arranged to go down for the week-end. I could, at least, be miserable in comfort.

Olivia was in the throes of organizing a charity dance. I was co-opted to address envelopes. The names were as improbable as those of Maurice's wedding guests. I wrote them in my new writing: careless, sweeping, savage. I hoped they would be illegible to the post office. 'What's it in aid of anyway?' I envisaged help for an animal sanctuary, or distressed gentlewomen, or something equally outside my orbit and to which I was unsympathetic.

'A decent Christmas for several poor families. That's the first, immediate objective. Ultimately we hope to be able to provide a holiday home for them.'

I retrieved the addressed envelopes and went over them with care, ashamed of the many snide thoughts I'd entertained about Olivia's riches, even though, as far as I knew, this might be only a seasonal sop to her conscience.

Beyond the window lay a dark damp day. I chewed the end of my pen.

'You'll be coming over for Christmas, of course?' Olivia asked, absent-mindedly, rhetorically.

'I'm not sure. Can we leave it open?' I moved round the room, fiddling with ornaments, lighting a cigarette, stubbing it out. I couldn't settle.

She looked up, laid aside her work and folded her arms. 'Whats the matter with you?'

'Perhaps I've got the pre-Christmas blues. The thought of all the preparation and panic. It's depressing.'

'It's precisely the reverse of depressing. That isn't what's making you like a cat on hot bricks. There's nothing wrong, is there?'

Pregnant. That's what she meant. She, my mother, Alec Blake, that was the first idea that entered their heads if they thought I wasn't happy. I could have laughed out loud when I thought just how far from that condition I was. I was not forthcoming. And Olivia dared not pry.

'While you're up, would you mind switching on the light? It's pitch already. I wouldn't change places with Alec this afternoon.'

He was down at the race-track. They were testing a new car, or a new engine, a new something anyway. Olivia said she offered up thanks daily that the opportunity had come to late for him to be personally involved. 'For he would kill himself. He has no caution. He was born without the faculty. I think most peole who take risks have a healthy respect for danger. Alec flaunts it, even taunts it, perhaps.'

Her mother-hen tone surprised me, made me realize that the face of their relationship had swung round to its obverse side. Once, she had been the pursued, he the pursuer. Now he had won her and she was steadily developing that instinct to possess, the lack of which had probably attracted him to her in the first place.

I sat down and resumed my task. Olivia, opposite, in her blue angora jersey, looked so serene that I felt more fidgety than ever. Fidgety and altogether disconnected. From everyone except, briefly, Maurice and, sometimes, Tassie. Raymond was happy and in another orbit. Our timing was rotten.

'Do you remember Jake Stavely?' Perhaps talking about him might exorcize my obsession.

'Jake Stavely.' She put her chin on her hand and studied. 'Maurice's friend? Not that they were really friends, if I remember correctly. More thrown together by the forces of circumstance. There was a girl too, Rhoda, Ronessa . . .'

'Rona. He was going out with her at the time. I met him again a few weeks ago.'

'It's coming back to me now. A very charming young man, very gentle. Maurice used to say, "Don't be taken in. Under that gilded exterior is dross, pure dross.'

'Maurice would say that.'

'Yes. He wasn't the soul of charity, was he? I think he's mellowing a bit with age. So you met Jake again.'

'He's just back from foreign parts. He's at the university. We met quite by chance.'

'And is he still the same?'

'I don't know.' I didn't know. I was different. I had no fixed criterion to tell whether or not he had changed.

'Have you told Maurice? He'd probably like to get in touch with Jake.'

I hadn't. A phrase of Maurice's rang in my ears whenever I contemplated doing so: 'He'll corrupt your smile and pervert your happiness.' Maurice would find out in time. Until then I didn't want or need Maurice's views.

The Hampstead visit was not recuperative in effect. They were both too happy in their happiness, too insulated to be able to diagnose my trouble as being anything more than an obligatory pain of youth, too well content to be able to help even if they had made the right diagnosis. I needed fellow-sufferers. I began to feel like Virginia.

Raymond opened the front door to me. 'Had a good time with Mummy and Daddy?'

'So-so. It's not Mummy and it's not Daddy, particularly in those accents. Did you remember to pay the milkman?'

'Everything has been done that ought to have been done.' He was looking extremely pleased with himself.

'You could carry my case upstairs.'

'Who, me? Might have a prolapse, dearie. Forget your case. There are more important things.' He spread out his hands like a priest giving a blessing. 'Come unto me all ye who are heavily laden and I will give you messages of hope.'

'You're misquoting.'

'Oh? And when were you last in church? Shan't tell you then, if you're going to be shirty.'

'*Ray*. I'm not in the mood.'

'You will be when you hear this. He phoned. Your feller. Last night.'

'Jake?' My heart beat painfully, me knees trembled.

'That's right. Jack. Said he'd ring back at first until *moi*, with a positive stroke of genius, suggested that it would be better if you rang him. Much better that way. You can buy me a dry Martini later as a reward for quick thinking.'

'Oh, Ray.' I put down my case. The corners of my mouth, involuntarily, were breaking into a smile. 'Really?'

'Really. So ring him. Bring back the bloom to your maidenly cheeks.'

But I postponed the pleasure. I smoked a cigarette and drank tea. Happy anticipation was the thing.

How curious it is that all voices, perhaps more so than all faces, are different, memorable, unmistakably unique. If I hadn't seen Jake for twenty years I might have passed him by in a crowd, but the moment he spoke I would have recognized him.

He didn't apologize. He didn't even refer to the weeks that had elapsed since we'd seen one another. He invited me to a concert at the week-end. I was not overtly enthusiastic. I said that I wasn't sure if I could make it. I would ring him later and let him know. He did not seem put out. He would buy the tickets anyway, he said. Which meant, I knew, that if I didn't accompany him someone else would.

'He's a bloodless bastard, isn't he?' Raymond said, as he sipped his promised dry Martini in The Squirrel; he said that in order to disconcert the barman completely, he should drink dry Martinis and order pints of draught Bass for me, but I stuck to a modest glass of sherry.

'Not really. He's just not swayed by emotion like you and me.'

On Saturday evening there was a reserve between us.

We listened to Brahms separately. I glanced at his profile. He was totally relaxed, totally absorbed; he might have been alone. I foresaw a pattern for our friendship: the occasional dinner, concert, afternoon out in the country, all separated by the desolate vacuum of weeks. My whole existence would be based on hope which I would never be able to relinquish even in my bleakest moments because there would always be the chance that he might ring up. I couldn't settle for that. It wasn't fair to ask me to settle for that. And there was only one way to alter the situation, as far as I could see.

During our previous meeting he had mentioned, casually, that he would lend me some books. Could we drop by at his flat on the way home? He agreed and could hardly, without being ungracious, fail to invite me in. Once in, I sat down. It might have seemed blatant, but I didn't care. I had only to sit tight and eventually he would offer me a drink.

'There's whisky and – whisky,' he said, rummaging inside the cupboard. 'Unless you fancy Slivovitz and I don't think, for your sake and mine, you ought to fancy it.'

'Whisky will be fine.' He began to pour. I cleared my throat. 'Are you as busy as ever?'

'Things are calming down,' he said. 'I'm finding my feet.'

I gestured towards the desk, piled high with papers and reference books. 'I think of you, sitting here night after night, stuffing your head with facts until it's fit to burst. I suppose it's because you look exactly how a scholar should look, amongst other things.'

'What other things?'

'A doomed violinist in a jerky pre-war film, doomed because he's tubercular, or because his parents have sacrificed themselves to give him the chance and now they're dying and he's consumed with guilt, so that even the Garbo-like ladies who gaze at him moonily while holding a single white rose can't tempt him.'

'Good God?' He creased with laughter. 'I don't know whether to accept that as a compliment or reject it as being the most outrageous insult I've ever received.'

'It's how I see you.'

'In another age, another setting?'

'I see you in different ways.'

'I don't live up to either of those dream images, you know.'

'Don't you?'

'Nobody ever does.'

'But isn't it necessary to cherish an ideal?'

'At your age it would be very odd if you didn't.'

'At my age! You're always dragging it in. I'm adult. I'm over the age of what's-it. I'm not Maurice's baby sister any more. You don't have to offer to take me out occasionally because of a sense of duty. In fact, if that's the case, I think I'd rather not see you again.'

How quiet it was in that room. I clenched my hands to steady them.

'What do you want?'

'I want to know that you're not maintaining this – association merely because of a feeling of obligation.'

'Obligation? Why should I feel obliged?'

'Why else would you ask me to go out with you at infrequent intervals?'

'Why does a man usually go out with a girl?'

'You tell me.'

He favoured me with the full green lustre of his eyes. 'Are you offended because I haven't made a pass at you? Is that it?'

My mouth was rigid with embarrassment. His eyes were neon, like a cat's.

'It isn't because I don't find you attractive. I suppose you have boy-friends who kiss you and say good night. I'm too old to fool about. I can't hold you and kiss you and then let you go. And that's all you want, isn't it?'

'You know very well I can't answer questions like that.'

He smiled a bit and then leaned towards me and kissed me. Our arms went round each other. Our mouths came apart, for breath. We nuzzled one another's faces, exploring with our lips and noses, each familiar plane, every unsuspected crevice and angle. Our tongues, at first hesitantly and then with fervour, probed the sweet and secret interior passages of mouth and ear. My fingers read his face like Braille, registering the cool smooth forehead, the warmer matt texture of the cheeks, the incipient roughness of his chin, the dry fall of hair behind the sweep of his ear. His mouth tasted of whisky and cigarettes – so very different from the cautious, abstemious breath of the nice young men who had kissed me with lukewarm passion. I drew life from his mouth and poured rapture back into it. His hand moved lightly from the sharpness of my collar-bone to the swell of my breast.

'Do you want to go?'

I let him take my lack of response as a negative. I experienced a sudden premonitory flash: the onus would always be upon me; he would never leave himself open to accusation. But it was no time to digest this knowledge. I would have to accept it as I was about to accept him.

The journey to his bedroom took a lifetime. I was unable to accomplish it with elegance. Technically, I was not a virgin, but now that long night at Seahouses counted for nothing. I did not know what to expect. I did not know how many variations upon the same theme there might be. I felt that this transition was clumsy, that it ruptured a much-needed continuity. I wished that I had drunk more whisky. I wished that it had happened then and there upon the sofa.

His bedcover was striped blue and green. It was the only image that registered upon my consciousness; everything else was out of focus. His face loomed above me. His eyes, so sharp, so green a moment ago, dissolved into lambency. I waited for the assault. That was the only way I could think of our coming together. But when he lay beside me his lips were soft, his kisses light, almost perfunctory. He lay, apparently unexcited, moving his mouth from my mouth to my forehead, along the line of my cheek to my neck. One hand was behind my head, the other stroked, slowly, rhythmically, from my breast to my thigh. The tension flowed out of me through his fingertips. My eyes closed. Just when I was thinking that we might fall asleep like that: comfortable, tranquil, he got up and took off his clothes. Every action was unhurried, almost as though he were performing some necessary but trivial task.

He held me. I was tense again. Thoughts of what I might be forfeiting flashed into my mind: my independence, the chance of growing to like him. It was much too late. 'Let me in,' he said. I let go of the last lingering shred of self-preservation. I let him in.

And he was deft, careful, controlled, even at the moment of release. I opened my eyes to his. He was smiling. I had pretended. I had feigned ecstasy and moaned and scratched at his back. But I didn't care if it never happened for me. It was Jake inside me and that was all that mattered.

He went to sleep holding me but, in his sleep, turned over on to his side. I fitted myself to the curves of his back. He had not drawn the curtains and moonlight flooded the room. I saw the hands of the clock, illuminated, his arm, stretched outside the coverlet, silvered. I leaned over him and saw his face, his lips curved into a smile. I would wake before daylight so that we could prolong the night. I would say his name, kiss him and wake his potency to reinforce the bond between us because I feared the grey daylight and everything it presaged.

CHAPTER SEVEN

Jake was reintroduced to Alec and Olivia a week before Christmas. We all four dined together. The three of them charmed each other. I watched and I listened. It was a charade. I was not going to Hampstead for Christmas because Jake and I wanted to spend Christmas together. They smiled their acquiescence. I despised their gullibility. Because Jake was an old acquaintance, an erstwhile friend of Maurice's, our plans were received with equanimity. Had I announced my intention of spending Christmas with someone strange to them, they would have been suspicious and hostile. It was as if they believed that the mere fact they knew Jake would discourage him from behaving in a normal male fashion. I longed to shake their composure, to shout 'I spend three or four nights a week in Jake's bed and that's probably where we'll be spending most of Christmas'. Alec and Olivia, the two hypocrites, who had once committed adultery on summer afternoons, both now concerned for my moral welfare, both convinced that I would be in safe hands.

'Delightful people,' Jake said, when we finally left them to their liqueur brandies and their expensive hotel suite. I couldn't disagree. The Alec Blake who sat serene, listening attentively to his wife's conversation, was not the same man as the father who had shouted and stormed and arranged furtive encounters with other women.

'They believe that you're merely looking after me, old acquaintance and all that. They're simple.'

We came out into the street. It was a raw night. I pulled my fur collar around my face. I longed to be back in his centrally-heated flat, but he said that it would be better if I went back to Ephraim Street in case the Blakes phoned before they returned to London.

'Your mother,' he said, as he drove me home, 'will she want to know your plans?'

I had told him about our estrangement but had not given him the real reason, therefore I believe he saw it as something trivial and temporary and thought that, basically, we still had a normal relationship.

'She'll think I'm in Hampstead. There's no contact between them now except for Maurice, and Maurice has more sense than to let on.'

'I don't think Maurice would approve. Not that it's surprising. I suppose that if I had a sister I'd want to know that a man's intentions towards her were honourable.'

'I only ever seem to attract dishonorable intentions.'

'You seduced me. Remember?'

'Oh? Is it as easy as that, seduction?'

He gave me a playful cuff. I thought of my cold lonely room in Ephraim Street. I wanted him dreadfully. I was impatient all the time we were out of bed, though the earth had never moved for me, yet.

We parted and I went up the stairs to the strains of *'Parlez-moi d'Amour'*. I couldn't remember whether that record signified delight or despair for Raymond, but I wasn't at all sleepy and was bursting to impart my glad news to somebody.

One look at his face and I knew that *'Parlez-moi d'Amour'* was reserved for melancholy occasions. He let me in without greeting. On the table was an electric razor which had been abandoned half-way through being wrapped with Christmas paper. I went to the gramophone and replaced the record with 'A Night at the Ballet'. 'Remind me to buy you some decent records for Christmas.'

He sniffed the air. 'You smell of booze.'

'Very perceptive. I've been drinking. How do you like my coat?' I twirled round, arms akimbo, to show it off. 'Alec and Olivia bought it me for a Christmas present.'

'What it is to have rich relations.'

'We are happy tonight, aren't we? Where's Paul? Washing his hair?' I picked up the razor. 'Is this for him?'

He snatched it from me. 'What if it is?'

'Nothing. Lucky Paul.' I sat down and kicked off my shoes. I hugged myself. 'This time next week I'll be in Derbyshire. He's booked us into a country hotel over Christmas. He says he couldn't bear the thought of me having a nervous breakdown trying to cook turkey and Christmas pudding. He says –'

'Oh, for Christ's sake! Do you have to report him word for word? You're like a record that's stuck just lately.'

I pushed my feet back into my shoes. 'If you're going to be like that, I'm going downstairs.'

'Suit yourself.'

I got up, but he looked so pathetic that I had to find out what was troubling him. 'You'll be spending Christmas with Paul, won't you?'

He didn't answer for a moment. He wore his child's face: obstinate, threatening to break up into tears at any second. 'He's going away with his bloody family. Sod Raymond. He can like it or do the other.'

I tried to be gentle. 'He couldn't very well do otherwise, could he?'

'Why not? You're not staying with your family. What's the difference?'

I could never make him understand that there was a difference. 'You enjoyed yourself last year, alone.'

'Oh yes, it's very easy to believe that, isn't it? You're off whoring around Derbyshire. Tassie's going to Eastbourne to play Happy Families with that old gent of hers. Raymond's stuck here, having a simply marvellous time, saying Merry Christmas to himself.'

I left him staring morosely into the gas fire. He wouldn't try that again though, not while there was hope. I felt guilty, and angry with myself for feeling guilty. I could hardly invite him along too. He wasn't my responsibility. It wasn't my fault that he had no close relatives or friends. I argued with myself in this fashion for a long time before I went to sleep. They were convincing arguments, but I still felt like a Judas.

Jake picked me up from the office. I left them, without regret, to their party preparations.

He never talked much when he was driving. I lit cigarettes for him and put them in his mouth. I was very nervous. The ring he had bought for me was too large. I twisted it round and round my finger. It was a mistake to have been prim and abstemious. I should have had a few drinks to relax myself. I was suddenly afraid that this excursion might not be a success. Perhaps it would have been more sensible to stay in familiar surroundings with no obstacles to be overcome.

'There's nothing to worry about.'

'Do I *look* petrified?'

'Let's just say you look as though you're riding in a tumbril.'

'I've never done it before.'

'There's a first time for everything.'

It wouldn't be his first time. Heaven alone knew how many other illegal Mrs Stavelys had accompanied him to country hotels, all of them, no doubt, carrying it off with a good deal more aplomb.

'We'll have breakfast in bed.'

I pressed close to him, my mind racing ahead to the time when I would be sitting up in my new nightdress, sipping orange juice and buttering toast. It wasn't until he stopped the car that I remembered all that had to be endured before then.

'Converted coaching-inn. Lovely, isn't it? Let's hope the interior matches up to the exterior.'

He strode towards the entrance. I followed behind, practising different expressions. I had once caught sight of myself when I thought I was looking nonchalant; the effect was one of grim determination. I opted for a half-smile and prayed.

The receptionist was obviously overworked and wanting her dinner. Jake switched on his smile. I stood apart, beside a bowl full of bronze chrysanthemums, willing her not to look at me. Someone answered my prayer. The phone rang. She gave Jake a form to fill in, took it back, glanced at it, signalled a porter and gave him a key, all the while carrying on a conversation with somebody who wanted to cancel his booking.

'Ours,' Jake said. 'Do you like it?' Anxious for me to like it.

'I think it's lovely. All of it. The smell when we came in, a mixture of polish and flowers and pepper and salt and beer. I love the gurgling of the plumbing and the china doorknobs and all those fearsome-looking objects of antiquity they've got hanging about the place and the tankards and the warming pans and the horse brasses. I love you.'

I stretched back on the bed, my arms open, inviting. After a minute he responded and gave me a brief token kiss, but his heart was not in it. 'We'll have to hurry,' he said, 'or we'll miss dinner.'

'And it wouldn't do to miss dinner, would it?'

'Definitely not. I'm here for your traditional English Christmas: mountains of food and crackers and awful people and Fred Bloggs and his Orchestral Quartet.'

He changed into a dark suit. He looked years older and

ten times more serious than the usual Jake of the suède jacket and corduroy trousers.

'Is it necessary?'

'I bet at least ninety per cent of our fellow guests have taken their dinner-suits out of mothballs.'

And he was right. We entered the crowded restaurant. Heads turned, eyes swivelled. The men were almost uniformly black and white, almost all the women had a piece of fur draped over the backs of their chairs. We melted thankfully into a dim corner and waited until the little ripple of interest had died down before turning our attention to those around us.

'Before we leave,' Jake said, peering over the top of a mammoth menu, 'we'll probably be on matey terms with most of this lot.'

'God forbid.'

'You wait and see.'

At the next table sat a family group: mother, father, and two unhappy-looking teenagers. Mother wore what appeared to be a converted gold brocade curtain. Father had a bristly, square-cut moustache and his dinner-suit was old-fashioned in cut, greenish in colour. None of them was speaking to each other.

'Wartime Lieutenant-Colonel,' Jake said. 'Still keeps his rank. Has 'em all up and doing physical jerks before breakfast. Can't abide smut before the ladies.'

'She's utterly bowed down. And Nigel and Caroline would like to poison him.'

'Caroline will run away and never go back. They'll find her one morning when it's too late, in Piccadilly Underground.'

'He'll be called upon to give evidence at the inquest. He'll stand up very straight and be frightfully British. He'll get all the sympathy.'

'Nigel writes poetry.'

'He'll turn queer, just for spite.'

'The old lady will console herself with gin and send him the surreptitious few bob every now and then.'

'Aren't we rotten?'

'We all need someone to despise.'

All through the meal we observed and commented upon those with whom we were to share our festive cheer.

'Martin Bormann lives,' Jake said, of a thick-set, blue-chinned, hunted-looking man who sat alone at a table by the door.

'And look! Irma La Douce. Or Irma La Douche, as Ray would have it. Over there.' I directed his gaze to a woman with dyed red hair and a once-beautiful, ravaged face, also alone, who looked about her with a fine disdain.

'Why doesn't somebody introduce them?'

By coffee-time we had identified two sets of Mr and Mrs Average-British-Family-1964 – all white smiles and exquisite table-manners, Charlotte Brontë and her sister Emily – a gangling, wispy creature with an air of the mystical, and two old ladies of such benign aspect that we simply had to christen them Arsenic and Old Lace.

'I can't wait for the Paul Jones,' Jake said, extending one end of a Christmas cracker towards me.

'You'll get Caroline. She'll fall desperately in love with you and won't be able to eat a thing for the rest of the holiday.' I pulled. He got the bigger piece. It contained a ring which he presented to me with a flourish. I put it on the third finger of my right hand. It fitted better than the one he'd bought for me.

'Finish your coffee. It's time we progressed to where all the fun's supposed to be happening.'

We had been last in. We were last out. There were audible sighs of relief from the waiters when we got up to go. We left them among depressing mounds of débris: nut-shells, empty crackers, tangerine peel, paper streamers, to where Fred Bloggs (Stanley Ellman, to be precise, and his Hawaiian Five) tore the night asunder. All his dance tunes sounded alike, we discovered, merged into one another, had no names; Jake swore that all night long he played the same tune in different keys.

The ballroom had been built on to the hotel proper and therefore had none of the charm of the original. It was a plastic paradise with a floor as glossy and dangerous as a skating rink and lights shaped like Chinese lanterns which made everyone look to be in the advanced stages of *mal de mer*.

'Great God,' Jake said. 'All that, and holly berries too. Oh well, so long as I make the Gay Gordons with Irma La Douce, I don't mind. Meanwhile, let's have a drink.'

He accosted a passing waiter who wove his way through the dancers, tray held aloft, with the air of Blondin crossing the Niagara Falls.

Chairs were arranged around the perimeter of the room. I was reminded of dreadful parish hall socials where the boys and girls divided into opposite, antagonistic lines and the vicar to-ed and fro-ed between them, drawing together unsuitable and unwilling partners.

'And I suppose this is your jovial MC,' Jake said, relieving the waiter of our drinks. 'Tomorrow evening he has the happy task of organizing what is ominously called "entertainment" in the brochure.'

'He looks as though he needs our prayers.'

He was a thin, anxious young man, dashing about to no apparent purpose, sweating profusely. Jake, after making a sortie for cigarettes, reported that his name was Gilbert. Wasn't it divine? I felt sorry for him. He looked like the deputy head boy who, when called upon to cope, has grave doubts about his capabilities.

'Dance?'

We moved on to the floor. I was tense at first, as I had been in bed. But he was agile, circumnavigating any possible errors I might make, so I rested my head on his shoulder and allowed him to manoeuvre me.

'It's a funny sort of a place, isn't it, Anna?'

'The place doesn't matter. It's us being together that matters.'

He looked down at me, smiling faintly. 'Oh, how I envy you.'

'Envy me what?'

'Your youthful optimism, your youthful resilience, oh, I don't know, your youth. You don't know what I'm talking about, do you? How could you? You're just a sweet girl and all I want to do is kiss you and bed you and comb your hair and pretend that's all there is.'

'What else is there?'

Still smiling, he shrugged. 'Nothing, perhaps. I couldn't

begin to tell you. Let's be happy.'

But we *were* happy, there was nothing to cloud our happiness, nothing to break the bubble. Why did he fill my head with little icy thoughts that swam in and out like fish? Why could he just not *be*? Why did apprehension have to be a necessary component of our relationship?

He stroked my fingers. 'Smile, Anna.'

And I smiled obediently. If I could smile enough I might reassure him about our inevitable destiny of happiness.

He looked round the room. 'I can't find Irma La Douce anywhere. I reckon she must have retired to her lonely bed with a bottle of vermouth and the collected works of Colette. I call it a damn bad show. Arsenic and Old Lace are here though, sitting it out, eating *petit fours* and smiling. I shall ask them to dance instead.'

'Which one?'

'Arsenic, I think. I rather care for her silk African violets corsage. And that floating chiffon whatever-it-is. She looks liked a very substantial Daphne about to start fleeing.'

'Well, now's your big chance, because I simply must go to the loo. Ask her.' I gestured to Caroline who sat disconsolate, cleaning her finger-nails on the edge of a brochure. 'She'd appreciate it more.'

'Poor little bitch,' he said afterwards, when he came back to me. 'And it's Fiona, actually. I thought she said Fiona Actually. Her conversation consists mainly of stammers and giggles. You can tell she's hating every minute of it. Poor little bitch.'

She was sitting down again, staring at her knees, bright red in the face. She'd preserve the memory of that dance for years. It would alternately delight and torment her. She'd wish it had never happened because it stirred false hopes, but it was a memory that would keep her going through all the years of rejection and ugly young men. She was me. Oh, I was older and better-looking and had acquired a measure of poise, but she was me, and all women who are born without shells and never receive that precious blend of parental support and dispassion which would result in a small degree of courage and self-confidence.

'Let's go.'

We went. To our room where a radio choir sang carols and a bottle of champagne cooled in an ice-bucket. We left it to go flat. In silence, and with absurd urgency, we undressed each other. Flesh meeting flesh obliterated the world. Across the bed, I cried out, so that he had to cover my mouth with his hand. My cry was not feigned. I could hear his heart and my own, thudding in rhythm. I touched our faces and touched tears. I never wanted to let him go. In that position I had him, he was mine.

CHAPTER EIGHT

I woke before he did. Always I woke before he did. This was a deliberate exercise of will-power, so that I could brush my teeth and comb my hair before he set eyes on me. It should not have been necessary; it was indicative of our fundamental remoteness from one another, but I felt that to refrain from doing so was a chance I could not afford to take.

'Very pretty.'

I started and met his eyes in the glass. 'How long have you been awake?'

'Just opened my eyes. Honest. Merry Christmas.'

I had taken the opportunity to bring out his present from its hiding place in my suitcase. I held it out to him. I felt absurdly shy.

'Damn it.' He clapped his hand to his forehead. 'I knew there was something. Why didn't you remind me?' Then, laughing, 'You have the most beautiful, open, crestfallen expression I have ever seen. Open that right-hand drawer and Merry Christmas and lots of love, Anna darling.'

A small square box, exquisitely wrapped and tied, rosette-fashion, with ribbon. I held it up to my ear, shook it and heard the tell-tale gurgling sound. Nevertheless, I maintained the charade, unwrapped it slowly and manifested signs of growing excitement.

'Did you raid a Sellotape factory?' He abandoned his

futile attempts to peel it off and tore at the paper.

'Oh, Jake.' I held up the bottle of Joy.

'Don't you like it?'

'Oh, Jake. It's the most expensive perfume there is.'

The present business had been a big problem in that I hadn't known how much to spend: whether to be extravagant and hope that he'd been extravagant too, or to buy some token trifle, assuming that that was more representative of his attitude to Christmas. Luckily I had opted for extravagance and bought him an expensive art book which he had admired previously.

'It's lovely, Anna. Come and give me a kiss.' He sat up in bed, lips pursed. 'And then open all your other presents. We'll have a real orgy.'

'I'm wearing them. Dressing-gown – Mother, slippers – Tassie, not nearly so luxurious perfume – Maurice, silver ring – Raymond, powder – Aunt Kitty, plus a few other sundries. Everyone seems to be intent upon my adornment this Christmas. How about you?'

He was concentrating upon one of Modigliani's swan ladies. 'What – Oh, the usual.'

'What did your parents send you?'

'Money,' he said. 'As always. It's the only thing they possess.' He changed the subject quickly. 'What are we going to do this morning?'

I looked through the window. The sky was milky, the trees gaunt, a hedgerow shimmered with frost. 'Sit beside a nice warm fire until lunchtime?'

'And be roped into a jolly game of bridge or bingo? We'll go for a walk.'

Fiona Actually was standing by the reception desk, flicking desultorily through a rack of picture-postcards.

'Had breakfast already?' Jake asked her.

'Oh, just a mouthful. I'm not really a breakfast person.'

Poor Fiona Actually. She wasn't at all pretty and she'd scraped back her hair under a broad ribbon band which was too low on her forehead, giving the effect of a vizor. She was probably sixteen and certainly passing through the most virulent stage of adolescent acne. She awoke in me a pang of sympathetic nostalgia. I had not been quite so unattractive, but doubtless my yearning had been written as plainly across my face as hers was.

'Going for a walk?'

I gave Jake a surreptitious nudge towards the door before she could suggest something ghastly like accompanying us. But she didn't have the courage. We left her, gazing blindly at a picture of a war memorial.

'She's fallen for you. I told you it would happen. And don't look so pleased with yourself.'

'Not pleased. Amused. Why has she fallen for me?'

'Because you're the likeliest object of adoration around.'

'Thanks.'

'I didn't mean to disparage your fatal charm.'

'I should hope not. After all the things you said last night.'

'That was just the champagne.'

'Go on. I bet you say that to all the men.'

'All the same, poor Fiona.'

'Poor Fiona. What agonies we suffer because of our parentage.'

He didn't elaborate. I walked beside him, my arm linked through his, thinking of his father, the humourless historian, sifting through dull grey facts about forgotten men, of his mother, longing to be somebody definite but unequipped – a failed courtesan, a failed actress, a failed mother. What mental disfigurements had they inflicted upon the child Jake that were still carried by Jake the man? He had grown up apart from them, cared for and not cared for by a succession of nurses and nannies and girls, until he was old enough for boarding school. He'd been happier at school. It was a reign of terror but at least you knew what to expect. 'You see, my mother thought that having a baby might be fun. She'd have something to show off to her friends. But I just didn't conform to her idea of babyhood: I cried at the wrong times, I was disgustingly human in my functions, I refused to be cajoled. I bored and panicked her alternately. Eventually she had to hand me over to less finely-wrought women for the sake of her sanity.'

We walked along the High Street, into the Market Square and out of it by way of a lane of cottages. I lingered to drool over the thatched roofs, the rustic fencing, the little, leaded-light windows. I was always coming upon places which I imagined as permanent settings for Jake and myself: mews cottages, Regency houses, half-timbered country residences. Life could not be other than perfect in any one of them.

'Footpath to Primrose Lane,' Jake said. 'Let's try it. It makes me think of hawthorn hedges and blackberries, surrounded on either side by fields of nodding barley.'

'It probably runs alongside a stinking canal and is bounded by the brickworks.'

'For one so young you're an awful cynic.'

'It's a result of the disillusionment, the constant disillusionment.'

'Let me open your eyes to beauty. Look. There's even a stile. Allow me.'

He was right and I was wrong. We had come upon a genuine country lane, rutted, water-logged in parts, with a steep bank topped with spiky grass on either side. I shivered, thrust my hand into his warm pocket, nestled close to him. 'It's supposed to be a pleasurable experience,' he said, 'not an ordeal. Listen.'

Obediently I listened. I couldn't hear anything at first, but as my ears became attuned to the stillness, faint noises seemed to increase and fill the silence: bird mews and croaks, the trembling of a bush, small scuffles and patterings. The longer we stood, the more we became aware of the indications of life about us.

'I bet we're surrounded,' Jake said. 'Crows and blackbirds and moles and voles and rabbits, all anonymous. It has to be a still day like this or you'd never hear those noises. Now aren't you glad I brought you?'

We walked on. The sky, above the line of distant farm buildings that formed our horizon, was smoky yellow. Later, the sun would show itself, low in the sky, blood-red. A copse of trees beyond the bank glowed russet and gold, their branches interlaced. A black bird rose from the field with a shriek, rose straight, swerved and flapped past us.

'Ho ho, the carrion crow,' Jake said.

'It wasn't?'

I shuddered. Aunt Kitty was brimming with folk-lore, had often imparted tales by the fireside to do with crows, pictures falling from walls, death-watch beetles. I was thoroughly indoctrinated.

'No. Too small.' He scanned the distance. 'If we walk to the end we may find another route back. I loathe returning the way I came. It seems so unimaginative, such a waste.'

'You keep confounding my theories. I assumed you'd be the sort for whom central heating and thick carpets would be essential.'

'That was in my other life. When I played the violin.'

'I shall have to revise my dream images.'

'It's never very wise,' he said, 'to make assumptions. That way you simply invite the constant disillusionment you were talking about.'

I didn't have time to ponder the possible profundity of the remark because, turning a bend in the lane, we came upon the Brontë sisters, shod in gum-boots, armed with sticks and wearing little trilby hats.

Charlotte made the introductions. Her sister smiled vaguely, disinterestedly, her eyes focused somewhere in the middle-distance. Their surname was Waters, their Christian names – disappointingly terse and prosaic – were May and Joan.

'It's a brisk morning,' Jake remarked.

'I like a walk. I'm a person of good circulation myself, but my sister suffers. Chilblains.'

It was pure Beatrix Potter and Jake had slipped into the part with an ease that might have been born of long practice. He was sending them up, but sending them up so skilfully that they'd never realize it. There was cruelty in his nature, but he used it in a subtle, almost affectionate way.

We fell into step beside them. Emily, swishing her stick at the undergrowth, smiled and said nothing. Her face looked as though it had been eroded by long exposure to the elements, her teeth were large and regular, almost carnivorous in their gleaming strength, her hair, beneath the trilby, like grey hay, thick and straight and carelessly cropped.

'As a rule,' Charlotte said, 'we go up to the Lakes. Do you know the Langdales at all, Mr Stavely?'

He admitted, regretfully, that he was not personally acquainted with them, but was familiar with all of the Lake Poets and therefore felt as though he knew them by proxy, so to speak.

Of course autumn was the season for the Langdales, she said. Her plain, asymmetrical face lit up with happy recollections as she described their 'jaunts': knapsacks and knobbly sticks and pausing on some hill to look down into a tarn – fathomless, treacle-black, still as death.

'We cried off this year. Joan had the flu.' She looked at her sister accusingly as though she'd had the flu purposely to blight the holiday plans. 'We settled for easy living this Christmas.'

We returned to the hotel by way of the high road. The footpath was narrow and we were obliged to walk two abreast. I was next to Emily. 'It's very cold,' I ventured. She made a noise in her throat that could have been agreement or contradiction. I wondered if she was a little mad, or just desperately shy, or both. At any rate, I abandoned the attempt and listened instead to the conversation in front of me.

Charlotte, not surprisingly, taught classics in a girls' school, while Emily kept house. Emily looked less capable of keeping house than anyone I'd ever met. I imagined her, putting the dinner to cook and then forgetting to light the oven, going out on shopping expeditions and returning with numerous exotic foods but none of the basic essentials, cutting flowers in the garden and locking herself out of the house. At that point, she spoke and I nearly jumped out of my skin. 'Damned cold,' she said, then relapsed into smiling silence. I walked faster, treading on Jake's heels in the attempt to hurry him up.

'A brilliant performance,' I told him after we'd parted from them in the foyer of the hotel. 'Why are you wasting yourself teaching English Literature?'

'It was pretty good, wasn't it?' He unlocked our door and, inside the room, stood grinning at himself in the wardrobe mirror.

'Don't you think it was a bit unkind?'

'On the contrary. It would have been unkind to laugh at them, make them feel freakish, as you were obviously inclined to do.'

'Emily's barmy.'

'It's all those long winter nights at parsonage.'

He was a good mimic; his Yorkshire accent was as true as his Jewish theatrical agent or his Louisiana planter.

'Waiting for Branwell to stagger in reeking of laudanum.'

'Emily sits and thinks and Charlotte writes letters.'

'Oh yes. Those long, long heart-rendingly formal letters to M. Héger. He never replies. The beast. Why did he never reply? She would have been content with so very little.'

'He never replied because she'd have progressed to wanting a whole lot more if he had done.'

'Typical male lack of perception.'

'Well, they do say that there's only one kind of man who really understands women. And that's because he's part-woman himself.'

'I'll marry Raymond then.'

'You do that. You can wear one another's dresses and wash one another's hair.' He tapped his cigarette on the edge of the ashtray. 'You know, Anna, it's a funny set-up: you, a retired old bag and a fairy. Why don't you move?'

He had met Tassie and Raymond and what he hadn't gathered from observation I had filled in for him. I took umbrage at his tone. I told him that he sounded just like my mother who implied that there were two sorts of people: the ones who were worth knowing and the ones who weren't. 'Where would I move to, anyway?'

'The flat above mine is about to become vacant, if that interests you.'

'Jake. That would be marvellous. But it's bound to be too expensive.'

'No. The place is owned by a dear old lady who's so insulated with money and so mistrustful of accountants and agents that she's never seen fit to raise the rents to their proper economic value. There'll be a waiting list as long as your arm – I only secured mine through the intervention of my predecessor – but I could put in a word for you.'

'Would you?' No more having to get up to go home. No more waiting for phone calls. It would be like being married, almost.

'Bob Jefferson's moving out in a month. I'll go round and make a personal request. She lives in a mansion with a drab companion who stands behind her wheelchair. They say she has a soft spot for virile young men. Now, come on, tart yourself up, or we shall miss the *Crevettes Marie Rose*, not to mention the paper hats.'

In the dining-room, apart from us, the Lieutenant-Colonel's family and Charlotte were the only ones who were hatless. Arsenic and Old Lace were respectively Minnehaha and a Scottish soldier, Martin Bormann was Archbishop Makarios and Emily had perched a Victorian bonnet atop her shaggy hair – the ribbons trailed either side of her ears, being too short to tie under her chin. Gilbert White, as a Captain of the Hussars, was moving from table to table, disturbing everyone's digestion.

He reached ours. 'I hope I can interest you,' he said. His glasses were beginning to steam up and the lapels on his jacket were frayed. I wondered what motive, financial or social, it was that prompted him to send his holiday in pursuit of a nervous breakdown.

'Try us,' Jake said.

'This afternoon we're trying to get together a few people for whist. Unless of course you're already involved in the table tennis.' He sounded very wistful.

'No, we're not involved in the table tennis.'

'Well then. We only need one other couple.'

'Sorry,' Jake said. 'Some other time. We're having an afternoon in bed.'

Gilbert White's face matched his hat. He licked his lips. 'Well, perhaps tonight then. There are entertainments in the ballroom.'

'Definitely. We wouldn't miss those for the world, would we, Anna?'

He moved on, to less treacherous ground.

'He nearly had a stroke when you said that. And *is* that where we're going to spend the afternoon? Bed?'

'Would you rather play whist? I need some sleep, anyway.'

The bed creaked. What with the champagne and being tired, we hadn't noticed it the night before. Fiona had the room next to ours. I hoped fervently that she was participating in the whist drive or the table tennis and not sitting with her ear to the wall. Though my attitude was ambivalent; it gave me a certain thrill to think that people might see through the marriage pretence and realize we were having an affair.

'Bugger Fiona,' Jake said. And, a few moments later, I had no thought for Fiona or anybody else.

He lay very still for a long time afterwards. His eyes were closed. It had been one of those occasions when he made love as though he hadn't had a woman for months. I bent over him and traced a line down the middle of his face from his forehead to his chin. I would have known him if I'd been struck blind, by his smell and his skin and the sound of his voice. The window was growing dark. Our intertwined bodies were a study in black and white. I wanted to stop the cosmic clock, refuse the future, make that afternoon our lifetime. It was only when we were joined that I felt entirely safe and confident.

Gilbert White's entertainment that evening embraced everything from elimination waltzes to talent competitions to musical chairs. Charlotte and Emily danced together. Arsenic was dancing with the Lieutenant-Colonel who was found to be wearing blue braces and had to leave the floor. Old Lace with Martin Bormann who was a good seven inches taller and appeared to be steering a course by personal radar because, miraculously, they didn't bump into anybody. Irma La Douce swayed past in the arms of a man I hadn't seen before and who looked like a gigolo but who proved, disappointingly, to be her husband – hitherto confined to his room by indisposition.

A young man from the Magic Circle blinded us with

science, a man with a rubbery face and crêpe-soled shoes told a few mildly risqué stories and a stout woman in puce, with much quivering of the bosom, informed us that Charlie was her Darling. Jake and Fiona tied for last place in the musical chairs. She was too disconcerted by his proximity to be able to move quickly, but he gallantly presented her with the box of chocolates he'd won. Martin Bormann, flown with conviviality, ordered bottles of Golden Guinea for those of us who were sitting near him – he almost said champagne, but bethought himself in time. He said that we would all have overhangers in the morning but what the hell. Jake said he'd never heard such lovingly-preserved broken English in his life.

At ten minutes to twelve, Stanley Ellman *et cie* surged into the last waltz. Mr and Mrs La Douce danced as though they were in the running for the Ballroom Championship of '64. Jake put his arms round my waist, I curled mine round his neck and we swayed on the spot.

'We seem to have stepped into a gallery of misfits,' he had said earlier. But I knew that it was a Christmas I would cherish.

CHAPTER NINE

Cheetham finally shuffled off the mortal coil and Tassie made up her mind. 'I've made up my mind,' she said. She was supposed to be putting rollers in my hair but the mind she'd made up was very evidently elsewhere and she kept jabbing pins into my skull. 'I said I never would again, but there you are. It'll be better than working.'

'Anything's better than working.' I searched my sodden handkerchief for a couple of dry square inches. I had a streaming cold and a profound dislike of life which compelled me to rise at seven-thirty and perform boring tasks until six.

'Cheer up, love. I shouldn't be surprised if you're doing the same thing yourself before long.'

Tassie had decided to accept the hand of her retired shopkeeper. She wanted me to assure her that she was doing the right thing. I did so, but without much enthusiasm. I couldn't understand the reason for her doubts and reservations. She was elderly, she was alone, therefore she might as well team up with someone else in the same position.

'*They're* coming down this week-end.'

'They' were her family. Again I thought she was fussing unnecessarily. 'Why should they want to prevent you from marrying him? They're grown up with families of their own.'

'That may be so, but families are funny. I'm Mum, past it, as far as they're concerned. They'll be annoyed at me doing anything off my own bat.'

The deputation came and went: Grace and Edgar, tall and stout and exuding respectability from every pore. It was incredible that they were Tassie's children.

'Never, never have kids,' she said afterwards, sitting with her legs apart in front of my gas fire and bashing the brandy bottle. 'Once they're grown up they think they can treat you like a backward child.'

'I expect they're concerned for you, afraid you might make a mistake.'

'Concerned, my arse,' she said. 'And as for mistakes – well, I've made that many in my life that another one won't make much difference. I'll tell you what it is: they can't bear to think that anyone has a better claim on me than they have. Fred Griffiths has been a good friend to me for many years now, done more for me than those three put together. I must say I was a bit uncertain before, but I'll damn' well marry him now.'

'Just for spite?'

She grinned. 'Just for spite.'

'Don't they like him, Tassie?'

'They think he's common. We were once at Grace's and he took out his bottom teeth – they were new and they were hurting him. She nearly fainted away at the vulgarity of it. Stuck-up little bitch. She moves in good circles now, you see, she's a big cheese in the town: Bridge parties and coffee mornings and all that caper. Thinks we might descend on her and show her up in front of all her fine friends.' She went to the door. 'I'm going to ring Fred now and tell him yes. Any time he likes.' She paused with her hand on the doorknob. 'Eastbourne,' she said. 'It sounds like the end of the world, doesn't it? But I dare say I'll get used to it. You can get used to anything if you try.'

I would soon be getting used to my new flat. Jake had exerted his charm and convinced the old lady that I would make an impeccable tenant. I was due to move in a fortnight.

'Oh, how *nice*,' Olivia had said when I'd rung to inform them of my plans. She meant that because Jake was nice, my new flat would be certain to be nice and, anyway, it couldn't fail to be nicer than Ephraim Street. She made a date to visit just as soon as I was installed. So did Maurice. His voice, over the phone, sounded lugubrious. Berenice was pregnant again. This pregnancy had been planned, but you could tell that his original enthusiasm was beginning to wane. 'I need to escape,' he said.

My mother received the news gloomily. It seemed as though each of my new addresses symbolized for her a step farther towards whatever dire fate she saw in store for me.

Only one person remained to whom the news must be broken as gently as possible, Raymond. I put it off for days – his romance with Paul was dying the death; he'd received Tassie's news with gloomy resignation; my defection would be the last straw – and while I was putting it off, Tassie forestalled me.

He cornered me on the landing. 'You're going,' he said. It was not a question.

'Yes.'

He turned, went up the stairs into his room and shut his door behind him.

I did not see him again for two days when he knocked on my door.

'I'm moving out,' he said, a hold-all at his feet. 'Here are the records you lent me.'

I took them. I stood and watched as he turned to go. He reached the top of the stairs and then swung round and looked me straight in the face. 'Don't let that Jack bloke bugger you about.' He clattered downstairs. I heard the front door slam.

I went back into my room. I experienced a brief pang of self-disgust that I was too preoccupied to feel more than faint regret; I was yet another milestone for him along the long road of rejection and I was able to put that knowledge out of my mind.

Tassie was flummoxed, flabbergasted. Why? was on her lips as often as it was on my mind. But I was short with her, apparently disinterested.

'Perhaps he felt the call of the wild.'

'He didn't leave as much as an address. After all this time.'

She kept on about it for days. She asked around, but nobody could enlighten her. He'd just left, that was it. She even advertised in the evening paper, to no avail. My guess was that he'd joined a ship, but I didn't let on to her. She was busy with her own preparations to move, anyway, and so, eventually, the topic was closed and the consideration of our own imminent parting came to the fore. She invited me to the wedding, to visit her whenever I chose. I smiled and nodded but I knew that the time had come for our friendship to end. My anxiety to be away from Ephraim Street took the form of acute restlessness. It had been a phase in my life. It was now over. There would be no reunions; Tassie would become entrenched in Eastbourne and God only knew how many gas fires awaited Raymond. The last days were terrible. It was like waiting for someone, whose death has been forecast, to die.

'What a nice flat,' Berenice said, standing back on her heels so that no one could mistake the evidence of her fecundity. 'So much nicer than that other place. I often said to Maurice that it was a pity you couldn't find anywhere better than that.'

I could have strangled her. One day, I promised myself, I would overcome my self-consciousness and be openly, diabolically, rude to Berenice.

Olivia stepped between us, making some graceful comment to do with the end of my Bohemian period. She smiled at both of us. I caught sight of my face in the mirror. It was set and sullen, the face of a child. I knew that Olivia was no more enamoured of Berenice than I was, but Olivia could smile whereas I could not prevent myself from scowling. Sometimes I was appalled by these manifestations of my maternal inheritance: rapidity to take offence, inability to dissimulate. Where were the genes of my father?

The symptoms of Maurice's inheritance were less overt. He envied Jake his academic freedom, I knew it, but he was able to stifle that envy under a blanket of camaraderie. They were at the 'do you remember' stage already. I watched them, thinking that at least women were a good deal more subtle in their hypocrisy.

Alec Blake looked at his watch and said that we'd better get moving or the restaurant would be cancelling our reservation.

'All you think about is your belly,' Maurice said. He was smiling, but all the same it seemed as though there was an undercurrent of peculiar rivalry to his most innocuous remark.

'It's one of the few pleasures I have left,' he replied ruefully. His eyes met Olivia's. No one noticed the look that passed between them except me. I blushed. That they did with each other what I did with Jake was just about supportable, but that they should acknowledge it publicly was not.

'Cars,' Maurice said. 'Will you follow us, Jake? Mine won't hold six. Now if we'd come in one of the paternal limousines it would have been a different matter.'

'I did offer. It was your own free choice.'

'Maurice is like that. Has a free choice and then moans about what he's chosen.' If Maurice wasn't squashed at once, his apparently jolly needling might go on all night.

'Let's go before blood is spilt,' Olivia said, appealing to Jake, the only neutral and therefore civilized member of the party. And, prompt on cue, he held out her coat to her. I was a little bit jealous of Olivia's effect upon Jake. In the car I said jokingly, 'Please stop making eyes at my stepmother.'

He looked at me sideways. 'You're a touchy little thing, aren't you?'

My face stiffened. I stared straight ahead of me. My ears had been attuned to slights ever since our visitors had arrived, and now the insult had come from the least expected quarter.

'What's the matter, love?'

He could change so suddenly to being tender that he always caught me off my guard.

'Olivia is so – adult, and Berenice is so charmingly bitchy. I feel on edge all the time I'm with them.'

'Olivia's on your side. As for Berenice, the world is full of Berenices. Give them their own medicine. Be charmingly bitchy back. Don't just stand there stony-faced.'

'I haven't the knack. Why is she like that, anyway? She's got everything: looks and a home and a husband and a baby. Why does she have to be gratuitously unkind?'

'Perhaps you imagine it.'

'It's not imagination. She's been that way ever since I've known her: patronizing and "we must be kind to funny little Anna".'

He took my hand. 'You'll have to be harder. Believe in yourself. Don't lay yourself open to be hurt.'

'Do you think I'm soft and silly?'

'I think you're young and you're a layer of skin short. You'll alter.'

Oh shut up, I thought savagely. Everybody treats me like a dear retarted child. Even you. My mother tried to tie me back on by the umbilical cord, Maurice is still big brother, Alec and Olivia feel sorry for me, and you, who have no doubts about my womanhood in bed at night, look at me with fond amusement when we're in company.

But my bad moods were as short-lived as they were fierce. By the time I had hung up my coat and had a drink I was seeing everyone in a softer light. And Maurice's news made me forget my grievances. His firm was moving him to Liverpool. He had made this visit to contact estate-agents.

'Great,' I said automatically. 'When?'

'Late summer. What's great about it?'

'Pay him no attention,' Berenice said, sipping her tomato juice. 'He's been promoted and we're tremendously pleased.'

'Just when I thought I'd escaped from the barbarous north.' Maurice adopted a hang-dog expression. But it was a cover-up. I realized what the move would mean for him and why Berenice was tremendously pleased. I hung back when the rest of them were going to the table. He was paying the barman.

'Bad news?'

'Bad news.' He looked despondently at the change in his palm.

'Ma Butler practically on the doorstep.'

'Coming over with her home-made pies and her advice. Not to mention Mum who will drop in very apologetically from time to time as though she had no right to be there.'

'And Aunt Kitty. Don't forget Aunt Kitty.'

'Oh, Jesus. That never-ending chatter and those hairy jumpers.'

'There's me too of course. And Jake.'

He studied me. 'How's it going?'

'It's going very well.'

'Yes, I suppose it must be, for you to move in with him.'

'I have not moved in with him.'

'It's the same thing though, isn't it? Listen, kid, don't have him as the be-all and end-all of your existence. It's not wise with Jake.'

I was opening my mouth to reply when Berenice called us over. I resolved to corner him after the meal and make him substantiate his predictions of doom. Until the opportunity arose I had to swallow my irritation together with my potted shrimps.

Alec Blake was debating the sex of his future grandchild with Berenice. They looked at each other fondly. Apart from Maurice, he was the only one of our family she really liked, and he had never got over the enchantment of seeing her in billowing clouds of white lace. And now her rapid productivity of heirs had made him doubly affectionate.

'Maurice wants a boy.'

'Yes, a boy. A grandson.'

'But I don't mind, one way or the other.'

'A little girl would be equally nice, of course.'

They might have been discussing whether to buy a pink

frock or a blue one. I looked at Olivia. She pretended to be intent on her food but she was taking in every word and was well aware she had no legitimate part in the discussion. Berenice, though outwardly polite, disapproved of Olivia. And Berenice was proudly, prettily, pregnant, a condition which Olivia, for all her beauty and charm, had never been able to attain.

Jake and Maurice were reminiscing. Maurice began to reminisce for my benefit. 'Do you remember the time, Jake, when you were pursued by a Bolivian princess? That black-eyed señorita. Kept coming to pick you up in a chauffeur-driven Rolls together with two blue-chinned, revolver-toting bodyguards. You were dead lucky to get out of that one intact.'

'It escapes my memory.'

'And then there was the Swede with the chest who threatened to go all Nordic and throw herself from a high building if you transferred your affections.'

'I never liked big women.'

'Come on! I've seen you with some extremely big women.'

'That was when I needed mothering.'

I looked from one to the other. There was about four years' difference in their ages, but it could have been a generation. Maurice, despite his wife and his child and his mortgage, by comparison with Jake who had none of those responsibilities, looked a boy. Maurice provoked and Jake refused to be provoked. He took the banter for just so long then changed the subject to inquire about Maurice's job.

'It's what they call a job with prospects. That means you work like a Trojan until you're forty, enjoy five years of command, then prepare to be pensioned off. Not like you, you lucky sod.'

'You didn't have to go into industry. And if we're talking in financial terms I know who comes off better.'

'You don't look as though you're doing so badly.' Maurice rubbed the lapel of Jake's suit between finger and thumb like an elderly Jewish tailor. 'Of course, you have private means. It makes all the difference.'

'If you're talking about my esteemed parents, all they

provide is free hospitality now and then.'

'You look rich. You always have looked rich. As though you've got a bit of class. Someone you'd be proud to take home to Mum.' He glanced at me. 'Has he had that pleasure yet?'

'No.'

'Well, the best of British for when he does. Though she'll be bowled over. You can say, "Mum, this is Jake whom I met when I was a little girl and he had a touch of the Humbert Humberts. But we've outgrown all that now." Speak ever so nicely, Jake, don't eat your peas off the back of your knife, mention your papa's profession and you'll be in with a chance.'

'Maurice was ever renowned for his tact.' As a child he'd teased me just for the pleasure of seeing me lose control. I had attempted to retaliate but he had always proved to be imperturbable. I knew that I was now old enough to counter his provocation with the same imperturbability, but he never failed to strike home.

I got up to go to the lavatory. Olivia followed suit. Berenice was contentedly lapping up raspberries and cream.

The lavatory was very grand with fluffy orange fitted carpet and wash-basins that gleamed like mother-of-pearl. I studied myself in a full-length mirror. 'Why does my reflection nearly always fail to please?'

Through an application of lipstick, Olivia said, 'You look with too critical an eye. You're very attractive. Really you are.'

She smoothed a lock of hair back into place and touched the skin around her eyes with a delicate finger. Olivia was forty-three years old and still slim, straight and beautiful. Even her few faint wrinkles were becoming. And neither was she vain, which was even more incredible. They matched each other, she and Alec Blake, both well-proportioned, unblemished, desirable.

'Anna?'

'Mm hm?' I looked at her queryingly through the mirror.

'It's serious, isn't it, with Jake?'

I fiddled inside my bag. 'It depends on what you mean by serious.'

'I think you know what I mean.'

'You mean marriage – and that sort of stuff?'

'No. That's what Alec would mean. He likes Jake. You're his daughter. He tells himself that you'll get married eventually. Because you're his daughter it's the only way he can allow himself to think.'

'Oh, God. He's not been having heart-to-hearts with Jake?' I quaked at the thought of it.

'No. He just expects that that's the way things will turn out.'

'And you don't?'

'I know that all relationships don't end in marriage.'

'Just because I move into a flat which happens to be in the same house as Jake's flat doesn't mean to say we're contemplating marriage.'

'No. But it's more than that, isn't it? And I don't want any harm to come to you. Jake's old enough and presumably wise enough to know what he's doing but, all the same, these things happen.'

'What things?' I burrowed deeper in my handbag. I was shivering with embarrassment.

She sighed. 'Don't make it more difficult for me, Anna. I know that to all intents and purposes you've been independent for two years now, but you're still not twenty and I want to be sure that you don't make a mistake that could mess up your life.'

I thought of Jake and his care and his calendar-watching, the way he had enlightened my ignorance about the workings of my body, the times he went to the chemist because I'd have died rather than ask for such things.

'I'm not daft enough to get pregnant, if that's what you mean. I'll leave that to Berenice.'

'She is rather good at it, isn't she?'

We both laughed and the cloud of reserve was dispersed. She was not attempting to guide my moral footsteps; we were merely two women discussing the mundane practicalities of life.

'I thought she had everything under control, family

planning clinics, the lot.'

'It *is* family planning. She tells me she's planning another one soon after this and then that's it. She'll go back to teaching as soon as they're of school age.'

'It must be nice, to have your life all neatly planned ahead of you.'

'Nice, but boring.' She got up. 'When I was young I preferred surprises.'

'But surprises have a habit of being nasty. I'd be content just for life to continue as it is.'

We were going through the door when she said, 'Do you want to marry him?'

I paused, blocking the entrance to a woman who was obviously in desperate need. 'I've never considered it, not seriously. It seems somehow unattainable. I have day-dreams about how it would be, but they're the same kind of day-dreams you have about what you'd do if you won the pools.'

'There's no reason why he couldn't marry you?'

'No. That's why it's so funny. The feeling that it's unattainable.'

She looked straight at me. 'What I said before doesn't matter a jot compared with what you're saying now. It's perfectly possible for you to get married. Don't fall into the trap of loving only when the object of that loving is beyond your reach. It can grow into a hideous pattern until it's almost impossible to disentangle yourself. Believe in your own worth. You're young and you're attractive and you're worthy of love. Don't abuse yourself by imagining that the only safety lies in falling for someone you can't have. It's the most painful easy way out that there is.'

I didn't altogether grasp her meaning, but from her expression and the tone of her voice I gathered that she herself had passed through some similar situation, and I was grateful to her and even humbled that she could expose herself to me like that.

Her husband claimed her to dance when we got back. Jake looked at me and then gallantly offered his hand to Berenice.

'That leaves you and me,' Maurice said. 'Shall we be a

couple of wallflowers, or do you want desperately to dance?'

'If we sit here people will come back, but we can dance for as long as we want and I want to talk to you. Do try to be a bit more gracious about it.'

Maurice's terpsichore took the form of walking about the dance floor in rhythm to the music, with the odd flick of the elbow or twist of the hip to demonstrate that he knew the routine but just couldn't be bothered. We meandered our way to an empty corner and stood on the spot making desultory arm and leg movements.

'What are we being so clandestine about?'

'I think it's about time you explained your cryptic comments. The way you talk makes Jake out to be a cross between Don Juan and Jack the Ripper.'

'Well, facts for a start. Jake's what? Twenty-eight? Good-looking, clever, socially acceptable, heterosexual. Right? Never minus a woman all the time I knew him. Not just casual stuff, deep, serious relationships – but always short-lived. Don't you think that's odd?'

'I don't think it's a bit odd. You might as well say that everyone who isn't married by a certain age is odd. Just because he hasn't rushed into marriage at the earliest opportunity and then moaned about it afterwards –'

'Let's leave the personal remarks out of it, shall we? I'm trying to be objective. And my honest, objective-as-I-can-be opinion is that Jake is insincere. Or perhaps not insincere, but lives in a fantasy world which embraces grand impossible passions but no real-life situations. I really believe that Jake has no capacity for proper loving.'

We both gazed reflectively at Jake's immaculate back view. 'I've seen him,' Maurice said, 'when a relationship reaches a certain point just switch off.'

'But why?'

'God knows. Maybe he's afraid. We all put up our defences but we have to abandon them with people we love and it's not easy, laying yourself open to dislike or ridicule. Jake wants it all to be fairy-tale, covered in shiny wrappings. He doesn't want to see what's underneath.'

'But none of this fits in with *my* Jake. I'll admit that he's enigmatic, but there are times when he's real and honest and unaffected. And what you've said still doesn't explain why.'

'Rona once said – and it's only what Rona said and I don't want to go all Freudian on you – that he'd told her about his parents and they were a right pair of sadistic bastards. I don't mean they were your average jack-boot, rhino-whip, *healthy* sadists, I rather got the impression that they never gave out love. So Jake had no example and perhaps love is something you have to learn.'

We went back to the table. The Jake I knew was not Maurice's Jake. There was nothing else to say. I looked across the dance floor. He was smiling down at Berenice. I tried to see him through someone else's eyes. It was impossible.

'I dare say you'll have to find out for yourself,' Maurice said. 'But forewarned is, as they say, forarmed.'

But I was already in too deep. I had forfeited my armour.

CHAPTER TEN

Jake has a husky voice; he says 'Where are the cornflakes?' and makes it sound sexy. He is a man of even temperament and tidy habits. He never puts his moods on display; you have to guess whether or not he's in a bad humour. His sexual desire is like a woman's: sometimes he's very randy, other times he just wants to turn over and sleep. He is perfectly charming to people he hates and he hates people for trivial, irrational reasons: one of his colleagues can't pronounce his 'r's; Jake hates him. He is totally without personal vanity but super-critical of other people's appearance. He tells me he likes solitude and then holds an impromptu party and is the life and soul all evening. He tells me he nearly got married once, but didn't go through with it. He makes it seem as though the relationship was foredoomed, but puts forward no evidence to substantiate it. He is impatient when I pry for information about his boyhood, his youth, his manhood before he met me. He says he has better things to do than feed his neuroses by recapitulating his past. But he seems to be the least neurotic man I ever met. The only certain thing about being with Jake is the uncertainty.

I received these impressions and filed them subconsciously; I was too busy living to ponder or attempt to analyse them. I knew that I had the Jake of the moment and it was enough. For months life slid by. I forgot the date – dates don't matter when you're happy; happiness has no peaks, which makes it difficult to recall afterwards. When you're sad, the sad times seem to have lasted for ever. When you experience uncertain happiness, each happy day is the first one.

And I was changing, day by day, into the kind of person I imagined Jake would want. I dieted frantically, smoked heavily, stopped reading Chekhov and started drinking gin, taking taxis and laughing a new laugh. Jake liked Audrey Hepburn, so I sucked in my cheeks and lived on lettuce and oranges. I threw up my job and got one which carried more prestige in the office of an international company where all the other girls dressed as though they had private means and lived on air during the latter part of each week. I thought Jake would like me to have a career – sometimes he invited his students round; they were immature and a bit scruffy, but I was jealous of them talking so eloquently about Brecht or Beckett or The Death of The Novel while I, the little typist, sat in the corner dispensing coffee. To make up for it, I began to read in earnest, during lunch hours, coffee breaks, on the bus; I listened to what they were saying and I read what they were reading. I even thought about trying for a university place, but could not see myself fitting in with them; they were children, newly released from the twin prisons of school and home, my age, but I felt ten years older.

My mother told me I was too thin. Alec Blake told me I was smoking too much. Maurice said I looked as though I were being done to death.

But Jake altered not one whit. The months passed and our relationship continued. I spent almost all my nights in his bed. I bit his shoulder and stroked his chest and said,

'Do you love me?' He said, 'Yes, but you wouldn't understand it.'

'Why not? It's simple.'

'What is it then?'

'It's – wanting to give, it's feeling united against anything that can come at you, it's not being lonely, it's an adventure, it's nothing else mattering a damn.'

'It's wanting someone else to obliterate the past and the future and the fear and the insecurity, it's the ego feeding on admiration, it's the death wish, it's knitting yourself on to another person so that when one wants to break away both of you tear at the edges. It's a tall order.'

I was afraid of him for a moment. I talked and talked to overcome my fear and then he loved me and that made nonsense of all he'd said.

Sometimes I thought about marriage and what Olivia had said, but it seemed to be asking too much and I knew that by asking too much you could lose what you already had. I thought of pregnancy as a solution but every month, punctually, I bled and, after the initial relief and triumph at having thwarted nature yet again, there was a pang of disappointment at something wasted, something forfeited – how many children were conceived in love?

But I was lucky. Every day that dawned testified to the fact. I was in love, loved, illuminated. If Jake seemed reluctant to dwell on the miraculousness of our love, well, that was because he was a man and men's lives embrace a broader spectrum. I was suspended in happy limbo and content to be so.

Until Harvey arrived.

We met him at the station. He was a good-looking, fair young man who gave off an aura of wealthy cleanliness. Jake said his father was a real-estate king in New York.

They greeted each other affectionately. I hung back, feeling hostile as one always does when meeting those who have known one's lover previously. Harvey was a friend from way back. They'd met at Cambridge and now he was passing through England on his way to the Continent and simply couldn't miss the opportunity of seeing what Jake was up to.

'He never let on that he'd found a gorgeous girl.' Harvey turned round to me. I was in the back seat with the luggage. 'He always was a mean bastard.'

He smiled at me. He was deeply tanned and the laugh-lines round his eyes showed up white. I smiled back. There didn't seem to be anything about Harvey to which you could take exception. I envisaged a delightful week: two escorts, one of them rich, both of them beautiful; we would go into bars and everyone else would curl up with envy.

'How's Lou?' Jake said. Lou was Harvey's fiancée, back in a place called Westchester. I thought of her as being all the New York girls I'd ever read about: chic, strong and uttering Dorothy Parker lines in every sentence, rolled into one. But Jake had met her and said she was a typical product of an expensive American education, whatever that meant.

'Lou is great. We're meeting in Rome at the end of the month. Until then she has a daily date with the hope-chest.'

'It's not still like that, is it?' Jake had hated America, he'd told me, for all the reasons that I would have loved it.

'What? The tradition? Sure. Doesn't every normal English girl do the same thing? Prepare for her wedding?'

'I don't know any normal English girls.'

I pulled a face at him through the driving mirror. I hoped he didn't intend to display me to Harvey as his little wide-eyed girl-friend.

'I don't think there's quite the same matrimonial frenzy in England,' he said. 'At least, it's not so overt. And there isn't the same stigma attached to being unmarried. Though we do still have people known as the Upper Classes who hold yearly cattle-markets on behalf of their nubile offspring.'

'Yeah. I remember meeting some of them at Cambridge, at balls. The girls with the long chins and big legs. They have names like Victoria and Penelope and they marry Guards officers.'

'That's right. The difference is that over here that way of life is becoming an anachronism. Where you come from, it ain't.'

Harvey turned to me again. 'He always has a dig at me,' he said, 'as though I were directly descended from Paul

Revere or somebody. And I have no retaliation. You know why? Because he's got no country. He's just a nomad.'

'I have a British passport. It's the most remarkable possession anyone could have.'

I looked through the car window. It was June and the city sweltered. The heat beat up through the soles of one's shoes, the mingled odours of tar and sweat and petrol were nauseating. I worked listlessly and longed for the sea, for the country, but my holidays were not due until August. Jake's term ended in a fortnight. We had made no plans to travel. I wondered just how soon he intended to make use of that passport.

I was hot and uncomfortable in the back of the car. The previous night had been sleepless, owing to love and heat, and my eyelids kept closing. Drowsily, I heard conversation passing back and forth between them.

'Gerry sends her love. She said she wondered if you were ever going to honour her with a visit and she said to tell you she's still holding on to your T. S. Eliot and your blue-striped tie, just in case.'

My eyelids opened rapidly. I could see just half of Jake's face in the mirror. The half I could see was smiling, at ease.

'Isn't Gerry married yet?'

'She was married. He had weird habits. She said she didn't mind too much until the pain began to outweigh the pleasure, then she took off. I have to extract your solemn promise to present yourself while she still has her looks and her muscle-tone.'

Jake laughed loudly. Just a joke, I told myself, a joke.

'Asleep?' Harvey said, turning round. It was then I noticed the shape of his mouth: curved and capable of cruelty. But he was Jake's friend and for that reason alone it was impossible to imagine him being suspect.

In my role as châtelaine I offered to unpack his case for him. 'Close your eyes if you come upon anything unfit for ladylike sensibilities,' he said. But the contents of his suitcase were disappointingly predictable. I unfolded pretty shirts and silk ties and pristine handkerchiefs and speculated about that period of Jake's life that had included Harvey. Cambridge, for me, was a blank. I had seen photographs, but they were merely regulation undergraduate photographs: isn't-it-marvellous-to-be-young-and-privileged groups of faces, and yielded no clues. Harvey's case contained only one photograph: Lou, presumably, reclining against a pillar, the shadow of foliage upon her frock, and looking just too fashion-model to be true.

He put his head round the door. 'Put me out my grey pants and my cashmere sweater, would you? I understand we're going out on the town tonight.'

'We're going out into the country actually. Cheshire.'

'Ah. Summer nights and half-pints of bitter, with one leg propped up on the rustic seat outside the village pub. Right?'

'Very nearly. It's a converted farmhouse complete with cobbled floor and hayloft and oil lamps. The tables are made out of old cartwheels and they serve the booze in flagons.'

We had been there a few weeks earlier, in May, which can be the saddest or the happiest month of the year. There was a bridge with a stone parapet. Jake had covered my shoulders with his jacket and we had stood there for a while contemplating the night and the dark coursing river. 'Water under the bridge,' he'd said. 'It's only when you see it that you really understand the meaning.'

'It's my favourite kind of evening,' Harvey said. 'Provided we all get maudlin together and swear undying friendship on the way home.'

'And hate each other the day after?'

'Such cynicism. And you so young and all.' He pronounced the last part in a deep Southern drawl. He said his grandmammy came from 'Noo Orlins' and flew the Confederate flag above her porch. In the next breath he switched accents and assured me that great-grandmama lived in the Bronx, which squared things up a little. I began to get a clearer picture of the affinity between himself and Jake.

Our Cheshire evening was a great success. I thought we looked an exotic trio: Jake with his dark secret face, Harvey with his accent and his cashmere and me, between the two of them, a queen in my new crimson dress and with my new self-assured laugh. Heads turned towards us, the landlord was effusive, the drinks were strong; it was a situation I had dreamed of all my life: to be the focus of envious attention in a public place.

We dined from an exorbitantly-priced menu. Jake and Harvey were having a verbal jamboree with the bastard culinary French. I nibbled grissticks and listened. Jake with Harvey was not the same as Jake with me. He was altogether more vivacious, more profound and more flippant in turn. Despite my euphoria, induced by vanity and drink, I felt extraneous, excluded from their private world, their masculine grasp of affairs. I was aware that people are different depending upon whom they are with, but I wanted to be familiar with all the Jakes, not just the one that was reserved specifically for me. In the car, on the way home, they sang the verses of some witty, slightly bawdy ballad with which I was unfamiliar. Seated between them, I put my hand proprietorially on Jake's knee and he allowed it to remain there but I felt, somehow, that he was making a concession.

The second night of Harvey's stay there was a party at the home of one of Jake's colleagues, the third, dinner and drinks at a club, the fourth, we went to a film, the fifth, we stayed at home and played Scrabble. Jake won every game, disposing of his 'x's and 'q's with effortless brilliance. I made cocoa in the kitchen and looked at myself in the mirror. I had shadows under my eyes and the thought of another day's work made me want to sleep. My boss, the day before, glancing at another sheaf of errors, had suggested, quite kindly, that it might be a good idea if I had a few early nights. I smiled coolly. My job was a matter of no importance.

Harvey, alone all day, seemed to pass his time quite pleasantly, looking up a couple of old friends, driving into the countryside, or just lying prone on Jake's balcony exposing his walnut-coloured limbs to the sunshine. Every evening when I got home he would pull my forearm close to his and compare the difference in hue. 'Get Jake to take you South,' he would say. 'Hey, Jake, you mean bastard, take this child South and get her brown all over.' But Jake refused to make plans. He said that planning made pleasure impossible because of the lack of spontaneity. In August, he said, we would take our passports and make for somewhere. Sometimes I felt that August was a myth and once out of July we would be straight into September and still no holiday.

On the sixth night Jake had an unavoidable engagement with his professor. He would try, he said, to make it as brief as possible. Meanwhile he left Harvey in my capable hostess hands.

'Let's get some of your friends in,' Harvey said, 'and tear the place apart while he's out.'

But I no longer had any friends. Since Jake, they seemed to have withered and died from lack of attention; even Tassie's once frequent flow of postcards had ceased. I thought guiltily of the never-acknowledged wedding invitation.

It was a hot, sticky evening. Harvey brought gin and lemonade from the pub and proceeded to concoct refreshing drinks with quantities of ice and soda. We opened all the windows and decided it was too hot to do anything but sit still, drink and listen to a cool record or two.

'Jake has Bessie Smith!' Harvey said. 'I always knew that boy had taste lurking somewhere deep down.'

'It's actually mine. And you may not be able to hear it for crackle. It's ancient.' And hearing it always makes me want to cry, I could have added: a powerful, authoritative voice cataloguing the inevitable fate in store for a certain type of woman.

But Harvey, being a man, was merely interested in the musical virtuosity. For a while we compared tastes. He was extremely knowledgeable whether I mentioned Bach or the Blues; I attempted to switch the conversation to a more generalized theme – I had no particular justification for liking what I liked.

We had more gin. Harvey moved in rhythm with the record, opening another shirt button. He seemed to be very conscious of the attractiveness of his body.

'How long have you known Jake?'

'I first met him when I was fifteen. He used to be my brother's friend.'

'And how old are you now?'

'Twenty.'

His eyebrows went up. 'Five years and I never got to know about you?'

'Oh no. We lost touch until last year.'

'I see. I couldn't believe it, five years, Jake.'

'Why not?' I went cold as I had done the night Maurice delivered his warnings. Bessie Smith clicked and was silent.

'Well, five years you'd be married, surely?'

It was easy enough to accept what he said at its face value. I busied myself with records. 'When are *you* getting married?'

'This fall, I guess.'

'You guess?'

'I guess it's time I was married.'

He was twenty-six. I supposed that was quite old for an American not to be married.

'I must have been too much influenced by Jake and his arguments for the abolition of the institution.'

Heaven protect us from our friends. But even as I thought it I realized Harvey was not my friend. Harvey was a smiling villain. But why? He was not homosexual, nor was he that close to Jake to be jealous of him.

'People change.'

'People don't change,' he said. 'Circumstances change.'

'So?'

'So people usually adapt themselves to their circumstances. But that doesn't mean there's any fundamental change.'

I could forsee that arguing with Harvey would be like attempting to keep one's balance on a steep, slippery slope.

'Do you like Piaf?'

'Who?'

'Edith Piaf.'

'Uh-huh.'

The harsh, arresting voice rang out, but he didn't listen to it. He said, 'What's the most distasteful thing you can imagine doing?'

I searched my mind. 'Someone said swallowing a toad every morning before breakfast.'

'Something feasible.'

'Putting on dirty clothes after a bath.'

'Drinking gin out of a cracked tea cup.'

I warmed to the game. It reminded me of those long, pleasing self-analysis sessions in Mary Leslie's back garden. 'Handling worms, having a spider crawling over me, touching an eyeball.'

'If you asked Jake,' Harvey said, 'he'd tell you marriage.'

I watched the record rotating under the needle's caress. 'Are you trying to tell me something? Did you talk to Jake's other girl-friends like this?'

'It didn't usually apply. Most of them were my girl-friends also.'

He scratched the top of his chest, leaving an ugly red mark on its even brownness. I raised my cigarette to my mouth. My hand was trembling. 'Shall we just listen to the music?'

'Sure.'

My hands were cold and trembling, but I was sweating under the arms. I wanted to lie down and sleep and never hear his voice again.

'Most of them weren't as pretty as you.'

He got up and mixed fresh drinks. He came close up behind me and reached his arm round to pass me the glass. But, relieved of the glass, the arm remained where it was. I gazed at it, mesmerized. Suddenly, the hand, suspended, came to life and slowly cupped my breast. I froze. As a child I had loathed being touched; as an adult I still loathed being touched, unless it was the touch of someone to whom I was attracted and then I needed to be touched constantly; that was one thing that worried me about Jake: the way he rarely touched me except when we were making love.

The hand squeezed and moved down my body like some large brown predatory insect. He said, his mouth on my neck, 'You're wasting yourself on Jake, you know. Let's have some fun before he gets back.'

I couldn't answer him. I was stunned. Jake's friend! And

I had thought, because of that fact, there was a tacit understanding between us to regard each other as asexual.

I pulled away from him. He looked at me with amusement. 'OK,' he said. 'You're not in the mood. Or maybe it's the wrong phase of the moon.'

If Jake hadn't come in at that moment, I would probably have remained rooted, staring, speechless, for the rest of the evening.

And he didn't notice anything amiss. He didn't think it odd when I excused myself immediately to go to bed. I lay flat, tense, listening to the music and the spasmodic conversation in the other room, praying for Jake to come and dispel my demons with his righteous indignation. Jake would have it out with Harvey and everything would be all right again.

But an hour and a half had passed before they broke up for the night and Jake came into the bedroom, whistling.

He began to undress. He looked over to me. 'Headache?' he said sympathetically and rhetorically.

'No.'

I averted my face. An hour and a half ago I could have held out my arms to him and begged for reassurance, but it was too late, I had endured too much self-torment.

He lay down beside me and patted my thigh preparatory to turning over. 'Good night, love.'

My back was towards him. 'Did you have a good evening?'

'With Willis? Well, I wouldn't call it a good evening –'

'With Harvey.'

'Of course. We've been discussing his honeymoon plans.'

'Did you also discuss the way he made a lunge at me before you came home?'

'What? Harvey?'

'Yes, Harvey,' I mimicked.

'Are you sure? He lunged at you? I can't imagine Harvey doing anything as ungraceful as *lunging*.'

'He came up behind me and put his hand – here.' In the dark, without contact, I did my best to indicate which part of me he had touched.

'I've often told you that white lace frock is a little too *décolleté.*'

I waited for him to continue. I didn't trust my own ears. He was turning it into a joke. 'He touched me – here,' I repeated.

'And you said, "Kindly remove your hand," I sincerely hope.'

'Jake.'

'What?'

'Aren't you going to do anything?'

'What should I do? Punch him on the nose?'

'I don't understand you. He tried to make love to me.'

He settled the covers around us. 'So Harvey made a pass at you. You're a very attractive girl and Harvey's probably missing his home comforts.'

'Don't you care?'

'I'd care if you'd responded. You didn't, did you? Of course you didn't. You wouldn't be telling me if you had.'

The earth was sliding from under me. I gripped the edge of the mattress. 'That wasn't all. He said that you and he had shared girls.'

'Well, of course. As all young men in a small community do. He went out with Mary or Gladys or whoever and then I went out with Mary or Gladys or whoever.'

'That's not what he meant. He meant that you shared them – concurrently.'

'Christ, Anna, have you no sense of humour? He was joking. Harvey was joking.'

'He also said that you had no intention of ever marrying.'

'He said that? And how the hell would he know? Can't we leave it till the morning? I'm shattered.'

Perhaps if Harvey had not been behind the partition wall and we could have had a blazing, free-for-all row, the problem would have been resolved. As it was, we lay silently, apart from one another, and I brooded until I had magnified the incident out of all proportion.

'He's gone?'

'He's gone.'

Eleven o'clock. Saturday morning. Jake seated with the paper among the remains of two different meals.

'Do you feel better?'

In order to avoid Harvey, I had visited my mother and Aunt Kitty, feigned flu symptoms and been eagerly invited to stay the night.

'Oh, yes. It must have been a false alarm.'

'I dare say it was.'

'Did you say anything to him?'

'About what?'

'You know very well what.'

He folded the paper into four neat sections. 'Harvey has left for Lou and the Eternal City. I shall not, in all likelihood, see him again for years. I think that answers your question. Now stop being a twit and give me a hand with all this disgusting accumulated washing-up.'

We never had our postponed quarrel. We never spoke of Harvey again. But I thought about him. Often. Harvey had drifted into our life and drifted out of it again, unchanged, but leaving me an inheritance of doubt and fear. A pleasant, meaningless and, despite his momentary demonstration of lust, probably inoffensive person, seemingly unsuitable for the role of messenger of doom. A catalyst, I read in the dictionary, is an agent which alters anything with which it comes into contact, without there being any alteration of its own nature.

CHAPTER ELEVEN

Lemmings hurl themselves into the sea. Perhaps some instinct informs them of the time to do it. Or perhaps a Harvey appears in their midst and triggers off their instinctual drive. Without him they might never combine for that fatal head-long rush.

August had every prospect of being the best month of the year. I could have accepted the omens and remained passive. Prone upon the Spanish beach, blue foam-flecked wavelets lapping around the browned symmetry of my ankles, it should have been possible, it should have been easy, to be calm, to smile placidly, to enter Jake's arms whenever they were held open for me. Instead, I set about destroying all that mattered to me, deliberately, it would seem.

'You are going to sleep, eat and soak up the sun,' Jake said. I was pale, I was losing weight now without having to diet and he was worried about my cough. I was young enough and silly enough to regard all of these symptoms as being rather romantic and alluring, but agreed to his plans because nothing pleased me more than lethargy and his undivided attention for a fortnight.

We stayed in an undeveloped village where there seemed to be a fixed, cheap price for everything and where one had to stay the barman's arm when he was pouring drinks for fear of one's capacity and liver-tissue. English was very definitely not spoken, the Teutonic hordes with their great bellies and their cameras had not yet descended; there were only a few wily French and Belgians who had ferreted out this blissfully tourist-free oasis.

The view from the window of the *pension* was composed of tints of the same basic hue: gamboge, ochre, olive. I watched the sky turn yellow and violet momentarily before the sudden and always surprising onset of total night. The heat smelled. I breathed it, together with the fine white dust that arose from every espadrilled foot on the unmade village roads. Recklessly I exposed my fearful pallid skin to the burning sky, an invitation to solar rape. I was rewarded, I got sunstroke. Jake prescribed champagne or the nearest equivalent that could be had. Teeth chattering, clad in two of Jake's sweaters, I drank glass after glass and scorned my symptoms away. The morning after, I was able to uncover myself with triumphant impunity; I had been through the ordeal by fire and was now immune.

The beds were hard, flat and narrow. They were also unfamiliar and I was inexplicably shy. The space between them assumed the proportions of a chasm, but he crossed it, in the evenings when the night came down behind the shutters so forcefully that you could imagine it was the onset of the last, the eternal darkness.

We had showered away sweat and sand crystals. We were cool, smooth and fragrant. We had oiled and polished our tanned bodies until they glowed. Those two areas never exposed to sunlight merged. His eyes closed. I watched his face. It was solemn, strained with intense concentration and somehow feline. Feline characteristics suggested themselves to my brain: indifference, disdain, selfishness. When it's over, I thought, he will shake himself and walk away. But I couldn't think for long. I was caught up into his racing rhythm. I cried out. Gently, he put the edge of the pillow between my teeth. Eyes still closed, he smiled a smile that contained elements of tenderness, conceit and self-satisfaction. I held on to him, gripping like a sea-anemone, desiring to prolong in him this state of unconscious reaction. When he didn't think, analyse and draw conclusions, I owned him.

'I love you,' I said. 'I loved you before ever I met you and it would be impossible for me to ever stop loving you.'

It was homage and homage should be received in reverent silence, but he stroked my cheek and said 'Good' and rolled on to his side and smiled and said we must get moving because they'd want to do the beds and anyway he was hungry.

I got up and soaped away the touch, the taste and the smell of him. I turned my back upon him. I ran the water and drowned the sound of his voice. What misguided God, I wondered, created two sexes doomed to be unable to break through the barrier of sexual difference which separates them? Words won't do it and love can do it only temporarily, and then it's back to square one: you separate and you wash off the traces of one another.

The Belgians were gargantuan, mahogany-coloured, deep-voiced. They took over the bar. I was continually surprised to find that there were only four of them, two men and two women; they seemed like a battalion. The most vocal Belgian was the prize specimen: moustached, six and a half feet tall with shoulders that spanned the doorway, the ends of his crisp dark hair sunburnt to blond, his eyes faded blue sailor's eyes. When he laughed the room vibrated. His drinking capacity seemed limitless. He wore a blue and white striped vest that caressed every muscle of his superb torso. He was not married to the woman he called wife. He had confided this to Jake one night because Jake, the Belgian proclaimed, was a sympathetic soul. The woman, Junoesque, bright-eyed and clear-skinned, fingered her chunky gold jewellery and smiled placidly.

They were singing *'La Vie en Rose'* when we went into the bar that night. The biggest Belgian opened his mouth so wide that you could see down the vast tunnel of his throat. His teeth were huge, square and regular, like the teeth of some massive prehistoric animal. He fascinated me, rising from his stool so that I could pass, one and a half feet taller and twice as wide as me. He should have been displayed in a glass case as the most sublime example of *homo sapiens*.

Philippe, the French student, sat in the corner with his portfolio. We were friends. With his thin sad face and flopping dark hair he reminded me of an immature Jake. But, unlike Jake, Philippe was destined to be a failure. Every day, alone, he wandered up and down the coast seeking the perfect view. Every night, in the bar, he showed us the results of his searching. We enthused, but his pictures were merely pretty, accurate sketches. Any proficient second-year art student could have produced them. Philippe talked about Cézanne. He would become a civil servant and sigh over his wasted genius because success would never come to prove him wrong.

He drank little, brightly-coloured, sickly confections, alone, in the corner and was frightened to death of the Belgians. He had chummed up with another French boy for a day or two, but they had soon parted because the other French boy was interested only in girls.

I went over to join him because the Belgian had flung an arm round Jake's shoulders and was regaling him with some story in rapid, incomprehensible French. Jake did not care for Philippe because Philippe was deluded about his capabilities; he liked the Belgian though who had never disclosed his profession and whom we hadn't probed for information because it would have been too disappointing if he hadn't turned out to be a pirate or a gun-runner, the only occupations we could imagine being equal to his stature.

'You got very brown,' Philippe said. He seemed amused by my preoccupation with pigmentation. His own skin was the sallow sort that remains the same colour no matter what the weather.

I looked proudly at the stark contrast between my white lace sleeve and my brown forearm and bought him a drink. He seemed poverty-stricken. Jake said sarcastically that he expected Philippe believed mortification of the flesh would increase the aesthetic sensibility.

'Those Belgians,' Philippe said. Their abounding white-toothed vitality seemed to make him more aware of his own inhibitions and physical limitations; he cringed whenever they laughed or thumped the bar or broke into the chorus of some unashamedly sentimental ballad.

'They're leaving tomorrow.' I looked across to them and to Jake in their midst. They had taken to Jake. They would leave him names he'd forget, addresses he'd never bother to locate. Despite the fascination they held for me, I would be glad to see them go. Whenever we congregated together, they attempted to speak English at first, out of courtesy to me, but it wasn't long before they forgot and began to jabber away in French which did not resemble the French language I had laboured to acquire at school. And it didn't seem to occur to Jake that I might feel neglected. They were an amusing bunch, he said, which meant that they were life-loving, vulgar and tremendously sure of themselves. I was glad of Philippe.

Someone put on the record that was all the rage that summer: a French song about parting and hopeless passion. If it was played at the end of the evening when the big Belgian had had plenty to drink, it made him cry, and the Belgian crying was an heroic sight. But it was too early for him to cry, so he got up to dance instead. His woman, who was not his wife, measured up to him. They circled round in the small space in front of the bar. She placed her firm plump olive arms about his neck and whispered in his ear. He bared his teeth and laughed and the laugh mingled with the chink of her bracelets as they slid down her arm to her elbow. She was calm, poised, absolutely sure of him. She could have been the first woman, secure in the knowledge that there was no competition. I was envious. I wished that we could communicate better and then I could ask her the secret of her majestic serenity; the Belgian gave the impression that he would lay every big woman who crossed his path, with a great amount of disinterested affection.

I danced with Philippe because he was not big and beautiful and because he would soon be leaving. His dancing, like his painting, left much to be desired. Jake winked at me behind the French boy's back then resumed his conversation with the second Belgian who had the harsh, blunted, open-air features of a navvy. I was being taken care of; he could enjoy himself with a clear conscience. Peeved, I moved closer to Philippe and linked my arms round his neck. His eyes opened wide in astonishment. But it was a wasted gesture because Jake never looked round again.

The Belgians bought champagne, bottle upon bottle, to celebrate their last evening. Jake matched them, glass for glass. Philippe slid away to bed. They urged me to join them, but I had to refuse: my champagne sunstroke cure had given me diarrhoea and I dared not risk it again. So, sober and jealous, I sat and watched the rest of them growing merrier, more affectionate and more neglectful of my incomprehension by the minute. At length I excused myself. They protested vociferously. Jacques was not leaving too? *Alors!* I fixed Jacques with a stern and relentless eye. Without being unforgivably rude, he had no alternative but to follow me.

'Are you tired, or something?'

'Yes, if you like.'

'What do you mean "if I like"? It isn't very late and they're leaving tomorrow.'

'Thank God for that.'

'But they're marvellous people.'

'You might think so. I might think so, too, if I could understand a word they said.'

'If you'd make a bit more effort to converse I'm sure they'd attempt more English.'

'What would I converse with them about? Whenever

they do speak English all they seem to talk about is when they were in London during the war. What do I know about the war? I wasn't even born.'

He slammed down his toothbrush. 'What do I know about the war for that matter? I was only nine when it ended and I was in America. That's just not the point. For God's sake, Anna, if you're going to sit around like a mute you can hardly expect anyone to pay you any attention. I was watching you and that poor man's Claude Monet sitting in the corner like a couple of mourners at a wake.'

'He speaks to me, at least.'

'Yes, because you appear to be as miserable and anti-social as he is. What's the matter with you? I just can't keep track of your moods.'

I endeavoured to keep my voice low and reasonable. 'I want *you*. I don't want you and a crowd of Belgians. This is supposed to be our holiday, the only two weeks we can be together all the time and you spend it talking French to a group of strangers. Do you wonder I'm miserable? I love you.'

He pulled down the coverlet and got into bed. He lay flat on his back with his arm under his head. 'So you keep saying, but it's not what I would call love.' His voice was level, logical, cool. 'You want to possess me, devour me. You won't recognize that other people have some small claim on my attention, that I *enjoy* being with other people, that the company of just one person all the time is not sufficient for anybody.'

'You don't love me.' I thought that perhaps if we had a real row we would make it up again afterwards.

But Jake didn't row. 'Christ,' he said, in the same calm, weary voice, 'that word again. I once asked you what it meant and you said caring for someone, giving and asking no return. Well, if that's a true definition, then you don't love me, you love yourself and think of me only in relation to yourself. And please don't start crying. If we can't have a discussion without you starting to cry, then there isn't much point.'

'You've got everything wrong.'

'Have I? Then tell me how you demonstrate that love

you're so quick to define.'

'I just love you. How the hell do I know how or why?'

'You want to smother me. You're jealous of everything that happened before I met you. You go through my things to try to find evidence of something you could be jealous about.'

I couldn't deny it. I thought resentfully that if he told me more I wouldn't have to search to find out.

'You can't stand it if all my attention isn't focused on you. You disliked Harvey because he's known me longer than you have.'

That was too much. 'I disliked Harvey because he behaved abominably and because he made horrible innuendoes.'

'He put his hand on your tit and you had to make a great big drama out of it. Harvey's like that. I would have warned you but I thought you had more sense than to take notice of it.'

'Why do you have friends like that?'

'You'd prefer me not to have friends, I suppose?' His voice tolled across the space that separated us. 'You want me as your exclusive property. You want me as an emotional crutch. If someone loves me I want her to love me on equal terms. I want her to be a whole, independent person. You may be, one day, but you're certainly not now. I know you had a rough time with your parents breaking up but, Christ, we've all got problems and I can't sacrifice myself for the sake of your ego. I'm sorry.'

'And I'm supposed to go through life with people putting their hands on my tits, metaphorically speaking, and never make a fuss about it?' Sobs escaped from my throat. I couldn't hold them back. Every injustice I had ever suffered in my life came into my mind and added itself to this worst injustice of all.

'Tears are worthless,' he said. 'You ask the Belgian. He cries because of a sentimental tune. He knows just how worthless they are.'

'You're unfair.' My voice came in breathy spurts. 'You sleep with me. You use me. You have no intention of marrying me.'

'Marriage. Marriage! It isn't the end, you know, the final glorious wrapping-up, signing and sealing of your life. It's just the beginning. Surely you've seen enough to understand that? Surely you know there's nothing worse than two people who are unsuited to one another having to live together? All the silly little girls, conditioned from childhood into believing marriage is the Holy Grail, the one and only way to fulfil themselves; I didn't think you were one of them. Grow up first and then I'll marry you.'

You love somebody and you allow yourself to believe that he returns that love, so, loving each other, you build up a defence against the rest of the insensitive, cruel, malicious world. It can't hurt you. But you have no defence against attack from within. A country shoots its traitors. I wanted Jake to die for his disloyalty.

'Go to sleep.' His voice was kind, employing the tone you use to quieten a child who is exaggerating his misfortune. I slept eventually and dreamed and woke up crying. If only I could have crossed to him then, held him and made him recant his words, we might have survived, but there emanated from his bed waves of magnetic repudiation which I had neither the strength nor the skill to overpower.

We finished our holiday like two civilized people. 'What a nice couple,' I overheard someone say in a bar one evening. We were very 'nice' to each other. We consulted each other over every small decision: when to eat, whether to stay on the beach or swim, whether to eat this or that. Our relationship was like a rotten tooth cased in gold.

But there were certain compensations. In Spain, I was safe, suspended from the effects of any decision he might make. It was possible to live through the days and nights knowing that he could not leave me until the fortnight was over. The blue sky mocked me and the lush serenity of the landscape. Unknown faces in the streets frightened me with their lack of realization, but I forced myself to behave as though that dreadful conversation had never taken place. We made love in the afternoons when the heat made him feel that way. It was silent, business-like love. When it was over I made straight for the shower and I drank the foul-tasting water to try to rinse away the nausea in my throat.

It wasn't until we were on the plane, homeward-bound, that I began to panic and to attempt to find out where I stood with him.

'Jake.'

'What?'

He was re-reading a paperback he'd bought in Spain. I, too, had attempted to follow a Simenon plot for a while, but my concentration wasn't up to it.

'We're not finished, are we?' I had rehearsed the words for an hour but still they sounded foolish, inadequate.

'What do you mean by finished?'

He would use this get-out clause of evasion whatever I asked him.

'I mean are we going to carry on together?'

For a week I had watched his interest, his tenderness and his regard for me diminishing daily. He could be cruel because he no longer cared sufficiently to realize he was being cruel.

'I don't know. Honestly. If you want me to rush you to the nearest altar the minute we get back, the answer's no.'

A gleam of golden light was to be seen between the banked grey clouds. 'Of course I don't. I just want us to be happy together.'

'You make it sound so simple.'

'It *can* be simple.'

He closed his book. 'I wish you were a bit older, Anna.'

'Why?'

'Then I wouldn't have to feel responsible for you.'

It was a smooth flight. The plane nosed imperturbably onward. Other planes crashed. I thought I could hear the pilot's voice telling us that, due to engine trouble, we were returning to Valencia, but it was only in my imagination. Every minute brought us nearer to England where he would be at liberty to use me as he pleased or didn't please.

The grey rain fell upon Manchester as steadily and incessantly as though it were the herald of the second Flood. We travelled silently. I had forgotten the language we once used to share. The house would be chill and unwelcoming. The office awaited me on Monday. I would have so little time to assemble arguments and stratagems for my survival.

But the arrival of the telegram solved that problem for me.

CHAPTER TWELVE

'My father is ill,' Jake said, staring at the telegram as though the bald words might disclose some further information.

We had been in the house barely half an hour. I had offered to make coffee as an excuse to remain in his flat; I didn't know whether or not I would be banished to my own quarters that evening.

'What does it say?'

'He's seriously ill. They may have tried to phone. I don't know.' He suddenly moved into action towards the telephone. 'I'll have to get a plane booking as soon as possible. It's a damn good job I haven't unpacked. You can drive me to the airport and bring the car back, can't you? Oh, Christ, I forgot, you can't drive. I'll just have to get a cab.'

He started to dial. I hung on to the jamb of the door, the coffee tin in my hand. 'Don't go, Jake. Please don't go.' I scarcely knew what I was saying, except that I believed his going could only be for the worse and I had to try to prevent it.

'Don't be a stupid bitch. I've got to go.' He tapped his foot impatiently when there was no immediate response to his call.

'Well then, take me with you.'

'I can't. It's not a social visit. For God's sake, stop thinking of yourself for a change.'

He was lucky; he secured a seat on a flight due to leave in a couple of hours. He consulted his watch. 'Just time for a shave. And that cup of coffee if you haven't let the milk boil over.' He disappeared into the bathroom. Mechanically, I spooned coffee and poured milk. The walls seemed to be closing in upon me. Jake was going. He might never come back. My reason asserted itself: of course he would come back, he had to come back, he had commitments. His father would either get better or die. It was quite straightforward. Jake would be back within a week or so. Perhaps sooner. The message might be a false alarm. His mother, like me, might be the panicking sort. I carried his coffee through to the bathroom. He drank it in sips between shaving.

'I'll leave you some money. The rent's due and the milk and the rest of it. Oh, and would you phone John Wilcox for me? I was supposed to see him on Wednesday. You'll find his number in that little book. Oh, God, and there's that London visit too. You'll have to ring Jane Drummond as well.'

'London visit?'

'Didn't I tell you?'

'Perhaps you didn't intend to tell me.'

'Oh don't start that. I haven't the time or the patience. Now, can you think of anything I might have forgotten?'

'Nothing. Except me.'

He patted his face. 'There's no chance of that.'

'You'll write to me?'

'Yes, I'll write to you.'

'Are you upset about your father?'

He paused in winding his razor cord. 'I don't know. I expect I'll find that out very soon.'

It was a curious reply. I wished, then, that I knew more about the circumstances of his early life.

'I can't tell you when I'll be back. I'll drop you a card very soon. Take care of yourself.'

'Aren't you even going to kiss me goodbye?'

'Of course.' He bent his head and touched my lips. I tried to prolong the contact but received no answering warmth.

'Oh, Jake, be careful.'

'I will.' He smiled at me, his old smile, full of sweetness. It was my solitary souvenir, the memory of which was to keep hope alive.

A week later I received a brief letter. Jake's father had had a heart attack, he said, but he had recovered and seemed to be on the mend. His mother, however, was playing her role of Greek tragedy queen, so he felt he ought to stay until she got over it. He would write again soon, he said.

It was a letter written in haste and short on endearments, but I was so pleased to receive it that I forgave him the omission. During that week I had devoted myself to getting things into perspective and now it seemed to me that I had looked too much on the black side. Jake was not to blame. The faults were mine and could be remedied. I would try to be less possessive, less clinging. I would start to develop a personality of my own instead of being content to be a pale shadow of him. When he came back it would be the way it had been before Harvey came on the scene. When he came back.

There was another reason for my optimism: my period was seven days late. The deep buried desires of womanhood had triumphed over his male caution. I looked at myself in the bathroom mirror and began to smile. I touched my stomach. Inside there was the speck of life, safely embedded, that was Jake and me and that would bring him back to me for always. I spent my lunch hours in W. H. Smith's having a free read of books about pregnancy. At intervals throughout the day I tried to catch myself unawares to find out whether the symptoms really existed or were just in my imagination. I walked as though on eggshells. Nothing was going to dislodge the speck – if it existed and, surely, eight days, nine, ten days, surely that was conclusive?

On the evening of the eleventh day, while I was searching for a small bottle to contain a sample to be taken along to the pregnancy testing service – two guineas, but I couldn't stand the uncertainty any longer – I discovered that, after all, I might be mistaken. On the morning of the twelfth day I woke up and found that I was definitely not, never had been, carrying Jake's child.

And then the dreams began. Sad dreams. Every night, in my subconscious, he told me that we must part, in tones so calm and words so logical that I had no argument against them. In the dreams he looked so real, so beautifully and desirably real, that I awoke convinced they were true. Every morning I arrived at work hollow-eyed. My boss said jovially that he thought I'd just come back from holiday. 'If I were you,' he said, 'I'd cut down on my sex life.' I smiled politely and reflected upon what one had to put up with because one occupied a subordinate position.

I wrote to Jake, drafting three letters before producing the final version. It was a good letter, devoid of any trace of self-pity or recrimination. It would be bound to remind him of the young laughing girl he had once believed me to be. It would inspire him to put pen to paper immediately to answer it.

The days passed. I began to find excuses for his delay in replying. I had kept a copy of my letter and referred to it constantly in case I had inadvertently included anything to which he might have taken exception. I checked with the post office to see if any letters had gone astray. The dreams continued to occur, as vivid as ever. I couldn't decide whether to write again, assuming the first letter hadn't reached him, or to keep silent and let him realize how much he missed me. This indecision permeated all my actions. I found myself standing in the supermarket staring at a counter, unable to choose between two brands of baked beans.

Maurice and Berenice had moved into their new house in Cheshire. I went over one week-end to assist with getting things straight. Berenice assigned all the rotten jobs to me: the floor scrubbing and furniture polishing, while she tripped round arranging ornaments, but I hadn't the spirit to hate her for it. Harriet and Roland ('it' had turned out to be a Roland) clamoured for attention constantly and got on my nerves. Berenice got on my nerves too, talking to Harriet in the absent-minded way that never supplies a suitable answer to the question that's been put, and uttering streams of gibberish in Roland's direction.

'How do you like it?' Maurice led me through room after room and out into the garden.

'I do like it.'

It was a dream of a house, converted out of two ancient cottages, with all the authentic and pleasing detail left intact. You approached it by means of a narrow lane which at this time of the year was thickly bordered with dog roses. The garden was a wilderness of rose trees that had run wild and weeds that seemed too beautiful to be weeds.

'Mr Butler, I suppose?'

'But for the grace of Mr Butler it would have been a salmon-pink semi in Speke or somewhere.'

'Or a terraced dwelling in brutal Bootle –'

'– where the bugs wear clogs. Right. I'll be paying him back for ever, but it's worth it.'

'It's the kind of place you know by instinct you're going to be happy in. You remember Mrs Warburton's? When I first went there and saw that marvellous garden with the sundial and the nymph I knew I'd be happy there.'

We smoked a companionable cigarette, sitting on a low stone wall and surveying his property. It was a grey stone house with bow windows, beautifully proportioned.

'Houses,' I said, 'become terribly meaningful, considering they're only bricks and mortar. There are houses which give you a pang because you've been happy in them and houses which make you shudder because they represent a miserable period in your life. It's funny, I went to Hampstead looking for bow windows and you got them instead.'

'And how did Hampstead affect you?'

'It didn't. Oh, I know it's very beautiful inside and calm and gracious, but it had nothing to do with me, it never showed me any familiarity.'

He docked his cigarette carefully and put it in his pocket. They were economizing. 'You're mad.'

'Am I?'

'In the nicest possible way.' He crossed his legs luxuriously and leaned back in the sunshine. 'I ought to be putting up shelves in the kitchen or putting down tiles in the hall or painting the loo.'

'Leave it for a while.' The respite was too precious to be wasted. Berenice had gone shopping, taking Harriet with her, and Roland, quiet for once, was sleeping in his pram under a sun canopy.

'Where's Jake then? Is he averse to manual labour?'

'He's in France. His father's ill.' A drifting cloud

obscured the sun.

'You don't look very happy. Wasn't the holiday a success? You should worry. I've forgotten the meaning of the word.'

'It'll be all right, when he gets back.'

'O-oh. Like that, is it? The beginning of the end. Or the end of the beginning, depending upon how you look at it.'

'Isn't this your cue to say "I told you so" or some such comforting phrase?'

'No.'

I drew circles in the earth with my toe. 'I feel like a condemned man waiting for a reprieve.'

'Look, why don't you come to stay for a while and I'll introduce you to lots of clean-living, upstanding, high-income-bracket young men?'

'I can't abide clean-living et cetera young men.'

'Neither could I if I were you. But stay, anyway. A change is as good as a change.'

I shook my head. The idea appealed to me, despite Berenice, but I had to remain where I was, to keep vigil for the postman, to wonder and pray and await whatever was coming to me.

In the first week of October I came home from work in the same way I had done for the past five weeks: dispiritedly, with no more incentive than there might be a letter from the lunch-time post. Instead of making straight for the kitchen to deposit the ingredients for my meagre supper, some mysterious instinct prompted me to go into the living-room and, seated in the arm-chair, smoking a cigarette and staring into the empty grate, was Jake.

He turned his head. He was even browner than he had been in Spain. I looked at his profile. I could trace it in the air from tactile memory. The dreams had not done him justice.

'Hallo, Anna.'

I was paralyzed with shyness. I should have rushed over to him and embraced him and told him how those five weeks had been for me, but I had to wait for him to make the first move.

'How are you?'

'I'm fine. Is your father better?'

'Yes, quite better now.'

It was a conversation out of a phrase-book between two people who have no understanding of each other's native tongue. It was hideous.

'I thought we could go out for dinner.'

'That would be lovely. I'll have to change first, though.'

'Well, I've some things to attend to. I'll book a table. About half an hour?'

He was wearing new trousers and a shirt I hadn't seen before. From their impeccable cut, it was obvious that they were French. It crossed my mind that, despite his father's illness, he must have had the time and inclination to buy clothes.

'See you soon.'

He had not kissed me or touched me. It wasn't Jake who had been sitting in my arm-chair. It was someone masquerading as Jake and now he was gone and in half an hour the real Jake would reappear. I had half an hour to transform myself so that he would recognize my identity: the girl in whose arms he had so often shuddered and moaned, the girl he had called beautiful, irreplaceable; he would remember all of that.

The red dress I flung to the back of the wardrobe as being representative of Harvey and all that had ensued. I would wear the striped dress that symbolized the beginning of our association. I would wear the same perfume and do my hair the way I used to do it a year ago before I felt it necessary to attempt a greater degree of sophistication. He had liked me and desired me then. People's tastes do not change so radically. Why should he not be attracted to me again?

'You look pretty.' He kissed me on the cheek. Be patient, I thought, give him time to readjust, to acknowledge the feelings that exist between us. He's kissed me on the cheek. I'm still me. Before the night's out I can make him love me again. Be sure of your own worth, Olivia said, and Olivia knows about those things.

In the car I was gay and, after a while, so was he. We were behaving like two acquaintances intent on mutual flattery as a preparation for a more intimate relationship. His suit too was new: grey. With his white shirt and black tie it seemed as though he'd determined to appear to be as unlike my Jake of chestnut suède and silk as possible.

'My mother was all prepared for looking pale and brave in widow's weeds. It came as quite a shock to her when they said he was going to recover.'

'What is her name?' It seemed very important that I should get to know every detail of his family background in order that I might have a wealth of knowledge about him even if I couldn't have *him*.

'Marguerite.'

'And what does she look like?'

'Me, I suppose. Or rather, I look very much like her.'

'And why do you hate her so much?'

'I don't hate her. I know her.'

He changed the subject immediately, as he always did. We compared notes on Nice where his parents were staying. He told me of the girls, hundreds of them, so alike with their blonde hair and long legs and big eyes that they seemed an army. How many recruits had become acquainted with his green eyes during those five weeks? I wondered.

The restaurant was grand and so was the food. I wasn't hungry. I seemed fated to be taken to expensive restaurants and then have no appetite. I smiled, I put my chin on my hand, I caressed the wine glass and stroked my smoooth forearm; all of these gestures were meant as tokens of the sensuousness we had shared. But his face was gentle and impassive. What did it take to move him?

'Have a brandy,' he said, when the waiter came with the coffee.

'No, thanks.' Perhaps I wished to impress him with my temperance.

'Yes, have a brandy.'

I obeyed him. He ordered doubles. I saw his expression and I drank it down like medicine.

'Anna –'

You can be prepared, and yet when it happens it seems as unexpected and agonizing as a knife in the ribs.

He had arranged this evening in order to kill me. The food and brandy were meant to be anaesthetics. He could have saved his money and his concern; his knife cut into my conscious flesh.

Rational. That was the word that kept coming into my mind. He is so rational. Everything he says is unquestionably true. But there is no such thing as truth where emotion is concerned.

He says he would be doing me a dis-service – a dis-service, what a word! he sounds like the chairman addressing the board – if he allowed me to believe he would marry me. He doubted that he would ever marry.

He was right about that, too: I would, eventually, have wanted marriage. I wasn't brave enough to manage without it.

I must understand that it was his own nature which made it impossible for us to continue. No blame could be attached to my behaviour.

Perhaps he would issue me with a diploma to that effect, like a certificate to prove one's sanity.

It was better that he released me now before we were both irrevocably involved.

Oh, bad timing, Jake! You're almost a year too late.

He was very fond of me, he *loved* me in his own peculiar, unsatisfactory fashion. He would always be my friend.

The Friends of Jake: me, Rona, God-knows how many more.

He would return to his new flat tonight to make things easier for me.

His new flat?

Yes, he had come back to England a week ago and found a new flat. He had packed his things earlier today while I was at work. They would be removed tomorrow. It was the only way.

Chief among my immediate reactions, stronger than the shock or the twisting pain, was embarrassment. I could not look at his face. The most important thing was to retain some vestige of dignity. When everything is torn away it's the only ally you have. You sit and you drink your brandy and you think, 'Don't look so tortured. You have behaved like a gentleman, sir. You could so easily have written to me or just gone without saying anything. I shan't make a fuss. After all, I'm a lady and ladies don't make a fuss when the executioner comes along to put their heads on the block; they just sit and drink their brandies and stare with misty vision through the back of some harmless fellow-diner at the next table.'

'I stayed in France to try to think of it objectively. I want you to love someone and be happy, not to love and be unhappy.'

It was the masquerader speaking, not Jake. The real Jake had never come back from France. The masquerader had never kissed my breasts and called me beautiful, so it was pointless to say anything to him. The masquerader wanted me to be his friend. How could I be his friend? I didn't know him.

'This is my phone number.' He pushed a piece of paper across the table. I put it in my bag without looking at it. 'After a time, you might ring me. I'd like you to do that.'

That's the moment when you almost break up, between the onslaught of those two warring instincts: pride and need. That's the time when you have to keep swallowing to stop your traitor tongue from saying, 'Don't leave me, Jake. I love you. I can make you love me again. You can't go without making nothing of all these months we've had together: the flat, the love, Christmas, Emily Brontë. You can't want to destroy all that. If this had to happen, why didn't you have the sensitivity to walk under a bus and then I could have blamed everything on good old useful Fate or the Will of God? *I love you* and you don't need a better reason for not leaving me.'

So you keep swallowing and he leaves you and he thinks, 'Thank God that's over. She behaved surprisingly well under the circumstances.'

But you can't steel yourself against one last appeal, one last silent distraught plea. He sees your face and he shifts his eyes and makes a great production of standing up and pulling back his chair. That's the time when, if you had a knife to hand and had not been brought up a lady, you'd kill him.

So you, too, get up quickly and say, 'I'll find my own way home. No, Jake, please. I'd rather.' And he conceals his sigh of relief and then is stricken with remorse and clears his throat a lot and takes your arm. You part at the door. Neither of you can think of a suitable parting remark. At length, he kisses your cheek and turns abruptly. You never get a proper last look because you can't believe that, accidental encounters apart, this drab street is the setting for the occasion of your last meeting.

I walked to the bus stop. As I reached it the rain began to pour down. The bus-queue rushed for the shelter of the shop verandas. I stood alone in my thin summer dress and was regarded with astonishment. When the bus came I was soaked through to the skin. I would contract pneumonia and die. But no, you probably get pneumonia and die only when you want desperately to stay alive.

It takes a while before your reasoning capacity and your emotional reaction combine. You don't fall on the carpet and writhe and cry and tear your finger-nails against its bland surface. You don't weep and weep until your face is sore and swollen and your eyes disappear into the back of your head. Not immediately. There are days and days for you to do all that. First of all, you light the gas under the kettle, you light a cigarette, you huddle beside the fire and your clothes steam on you as you reflect that it's like having a tooth out: immediately afterwards the gap feels as wide as the Mersey Tunnel, but later on you stop probing it with your tongue and it seems to have closed up. It's the meantime that matters. Just what *is* there to fill that great portion of your life that was given over to all things Jake?

CHAPTER THIRTEEN

By the time I have marked off my calendar to November 1st, I will feel better. When I get to December 1st, I might wake in the morning without this ten-ton weight resting on my chest. Come January 1st (you can't count Christmas because you know that Christmas is bound to be hell – you'll just have to get drunk and pull the sheets over your head), and I might be noticing colours and trees and sunshine again.

It's lies, it's all lies.

For the first three months there are records which you play over and over again. They make you cry, but you cry anyway and listening to them helps to sharpen the precision of your mental image of him.

During the next three months you pack away those records in a dark place where you are not likely to catch sight of them because, fundamentally, you are not a masochist and listening to those records is masochism.

You smoke continuously and avoid people for fear of being bruised and spreading your infection.

You can recite almost any serious conversation you had with him, verbatim. Your skin looks grey and lifeless. Your hair grows ragged.

During the second phase you start going to the hairdresser again, you start caring for your body and scrubbing the nicotine off your fingers because enough time has now elapsed for him to have come to his senses and want you back.

The nights you get drunk you lift the phone on to your lap and you dial the first three digits of his number – well, he *said* ring, didn't he? Twice you complete the dialling and then slam down the receiver when he answers because his voice sounds just the same and you find it incredible that *anything* about him should remain constant.

You pray to God with such fervour that if He exists He must be deaf or wilfully perverse. You talk to yourself, you scold, chastise, berate yourself, then him. You say 'Bastard' in the street, loudly and virulently. A woman turns round and then hurries on, afraid of the madness in your eyes. Because you *are* mad, you have acknowledged the fact. You need a quiet white room and a psychiatrist. You will say 'Help me' and he will help you. But you have been indoctrinated to fear madness and you are still too inhibited to behave in a way that would result in your receiving that help.

In May you are alive – fragile, but alive, and sane. He sends you a birthday card. He might just as well have sent you a dose of arsenic.

But, of course, just as every Grandmother, Aunt and Older Person has always maintained, Time Heals. It's a poker-work motto on the wall. When it's finally true, you've stopped repeating it to yourself.

When my telephone-obsession abated – better to go out and imagine he had rung in my absence than to sit in contemplation of the silent instrument – I spent week-ends at Aunt Kitty's house. I told myself that I should have fled to Aunt Kitty's house immediately after the break-up, like all sensible rejected young girls, back to the maternal bosom, the comforting familiarity of the nest. But that also was unreal. I had nothing in common with them except heredity and memories; their tastes, their conversation, their life-style were alien to me. I found it curious and somehow frightening that I had spent what are called the formative years in the company of these two women and yet I could achieve an easier rapport with a casual acquaintance.

There was nothing in my life except a dull job and a set of relations with whom I had no fundamental contact. Hampstead might have come into its own at this stage. I thought of Olivia's solace, her wise, I-have-been-through-it-too-and-so-have-thousands-of-other-women solace. But Hampstead was empty and shuttered; the pair of them were taking a long holiday in the Caribbean. What irony. They had left during those five weeks when I was waiting for a letter that never arrived. They had begged me to accompany them. I could get another job when I returned. It was an opportunity not to be missed. I thought bitterly that I must have been born with no sense of timing.

My twenty-first birthday occurred during this black and grey period. I prepared myself for purgatory; I had vetoed any idea of a party but would not be able to restrain Aunt Kitty from singing 'Twenty-One Today'.

'Happy birthday, love.'

She barged into my bedroom with the mail. I submitted, my lips compressed, to her kiss. Through the opened curtains a shaft of sunlight stabbed its way across the room. It could have been the harbinger of a beautiful, memorable day.

'Look at this pile! And you've been moping around recently as though you hadn't a friend in the world. Now you stay where you are. The birthday girl gets breakfast in bed. Then you can come and open your presents. Your mum's getting them ready.'

It was all I could do to stop myself from vomiting. I stared for a long time at the heap of envelopes on the bedcover. Then curiosity overcame my inertia.

A great many telegrams: Alec and Olivia from Bermuda, Maurice and Berenice, the girls in the office, my boss, Virginia – bless her, a few fairly obscure relations, one or two friends – lamentably neglected of late.

Then the cards: my mother, Aunt Kitty, Jamie – each adorned with some variety of silver key, Alec and Olivia again – restrained and stylish.

I came to the envelope that was, significantly, the last one of the batch.

I should have known: he was the kind of man who would take pains to maintain a civilized relationship. Being friends entailed observing imaginary milestones like twenty-first birthdays. His handwriting was straight, strong, unembellished. He had restricted himself to his signature. The two upright consonants alternating with the two rounded vowels made a pleasing pattern. Did he think that by now I would be recovered? Did he know that the sight of his writing would intensify my longing for him? Did he merely consult his diary, note my birthday, post a card and think no more of it? I could not understand his motivation; I had never been able to do so.

I stood the card in the middle of the sideboard, proof that Jake was living and breathing and posting letters, proof that time, since last October, had not ceased to have relevance for him. Jake was living, in the vicinity. It would have been easy enough to see him by keeping watch outside his flat or his department at the university. Since October I had avoided both of those areas even if doing so entailed travelling far out of my way. Other girls would have kept watch, would have found some excuse to way-lay him in a self-confident, nonchalant manner. Berenice would have done it. So would Rachel. Mary Leslie would never have walked meekly out of that restaurant, knowing it was for always. But then Berenice and Rachel and Mary Leslie had such well-developed instincts for self-preservation that they would have smelled danger and avoided Jake after the first meeting.

'Men are cruel,' Olivia said. 'Even the nice ones. Being men makes them cruel by definition. They don't know it. They can't help it.'

She resumed her distribution of knives and forks around the table. I folded table-napkins with unnecessary precision.

'If only you had come with us.'

'So that I could have met some nice young man who would have displaced Jake in my affections so thoroughly that he might never have existed?'

'It sounds trite, I know. Nevertheless, one's affections are more open to suggestion than you seem to believe.'

With a great effort I changed the subject. Ever since arriving I had bent her sympathetic ear to the tale of my woes. She was the only person to whom I could unburden but I realized there must be a limit even to her patience and understanding.

'Shall I put on my frock?'

It was hung over the back of a chair, the frock she'd bought me that afternoon. I took gifts from her without compunction. I justified it by telling myself that I was giving her pleasure by allowing her to spend money on me.

'No, save it for tomorrow.'

We were spending the holiday week-end in Northumberland with Olivia's brother-in-law and his family. This was the same brother-in-law who had once lived by Loch Awe during that time I had first met Jonathon Lawrence, but the Northumberland fiasco seemed too long ago for me to invest this visit with false nostalgia; I doubted whether Seahouses and its environs would cause me a pang.

'I think you'll enjoy it,' Olivia said, vigorous with the pepper-mill. 'I think you'll like Stephen.'

I wondered why people never realize that the sure way to put two strangers in an antipathetic state of mind towards one another even before they meet is to say, 'I think you'll like each other'.

'I'm sure I shall.' Attractive, athletic, Oxford – I'd find some reason to dislike him.

'Now, if Alec would condescend to come in, we could eat. I've never met a man before who could turn a fifty-yard walk for cigarettes into an hour's expedition. And always at meal-times.'

It amused me to hear her talking about him like that. You'd have imagined that they'd been boringly married for years and years, rather than being only recently legalized illicit lovers.

I slept between London and the North. I felt continually tired and attributed it to the fact that sleep, after Jake, had been my only panacea and it had now become a habit. But the Blakes regarded it, and my cough which had become so persistent as to be part of my personality, as symptoms which should be explored professionally. I lied and told them that I had visited a doctor who had proclaimed me fit. Continual ill-health in childhood leaves you with the feeling that there is a stigma attached to being ill; childhood invalids rarely become adult hypochondriacs.

Olivia's brother-in-law and his wife Annette had become landed gentry and lived near Alnwick. Victor was years older than Annette. I half-expected a disclosure of some *Rebecca*-like history: he, the wealthy mature man rescuing her, the pretty, penniless ladies' companion and introducing her to a life of ease. But Olivia told me that their families had known each other for generations and the match had been practically fore-ordained: he pursuing an army career until she reached marriageable age. Reality seemed to me so dull.

Their two elder children were married and away from home; there was now only Stephen – whom I awaited with less than bated breath – who had not yet taken permanent wing.

However, he was not of the welcoming committee which consisted of Mother, Father and Jack Russells posed on the steps as though awaiting the camera-click that would canonize them for the definitive issue of *Country Life*.

I met him later, on the stairs. 'Hallo,' he said warily – he'd probably been sickened to death with hearing about me – and we proceeded into the dining-room where he immediately made a bee-line for the farthest side of the room.

Olivia looked at me over the rim of her glass. 'He's nice,' she said.

'Nobody's nice. We're all out to tear each other to pieces.' I drank my sherry and watched him.

He was tall, like Jake, dark-haired, like Jake and with Jake's unconscious elegance of stance. There was a resemblance, too, in the way Stephen put one hand in his pocket and his weight on one foot. (Christ! To go through life comparing every man with the one who went before.) But the differences out-numbered the similarities: Stephen's face was rounded, open, his features more regular, his hair had a springy curl in it, his eyes were brown and opaque, Arab eyes.

They had placed us side by side at the end of the table for dinner. He was so exactly like the undergraduates who had frequented Mrs Warburton's establishment that I knew I could handle him easily. No mystery there. A nice, healthy, bright young man, fashionably dressed in just the right studiedly-scruffy yet clean manner, who probably thought of me as a little secretary to be dazzled for the week-end.

He passed me the peas. 'Have you any special plans? Look up old friends, or something?'

'No.' I thought of looking up Mrs Bartholomew or Marjorie or Billy: 'Do you remember when you loused up my introduction to living?'

'If you like, I could show you a few quaint pubs round here. Unless you actually want to stay and listen to these dear old souls walking down memory lane?'

It was a duty invitation, of course. No doubt he had been well primed before my arrival: Anna, down in the dumps, thrown over by some character, be a good fellow, take her out, show her the sights, cheer her up. But, of course, I accepted. There was an evening to be got through and he was presentable and probably intelligent, and quite meaningless.

CHAPTER FOURTEEN

Stephen's voice outside my bedroom door: 'I've been sent up to tell you your cornflakes are getting cold. And if we *are* going out, it's time to be off.'

I surfaced to the sound of his retreating feet. Gingerly, I put one leg out of bed. The room stayed still. Last night it had swung around me as the bed tilted to and fro. Last night I had drunk too much. Driving back, I had been poised on the edge between tears and laughter; it was so reminiscent: the dark night outside the windows, the proximity of someone dark and male and strange. I could have wept, for the sake of a sweet smile, a curved nose and a large white handkerchief initialled with J. Instead I leaned across to be kissed. He was surprised, but obliged. His mouth was wrong: too soft, too hesitant; you can't gauge the quality of a kiss by the shape of a mouth. When he showed an inclination to extend our activities, I gently deterred him. He was quite good-humoured about it. The next day I would yield to something a little more intimate, and so on. It was the behaviour pattern with which he was familiar.

The smell of bacon and egg permeated the hall. The sight of the rest of them chewing and swallowing was too much for my stomach. I poured a cup of coffee and tried to close my ears to the sounds of mastication.

Alec Blake peered at me. 'Aren't you eating?'

I shuddered. 'I feel a bit green.'

'Believe me, you look it. Why on earth do you drink so much when you know you'll feel rotten next morning?'

'*Please*. There are two little men beating out the Anvil Chorus inside my head. Talk quietly if you must talk at all.'

He began his Big-Daddy routine: hangovers are not becoming to anyone, least of all young girls. I closed my eyes and my ears until it was over.

'And what's on the agenda for today?' he asked Stephen.

'Drive, walk, eat, drive, walk and so on.'

'Well I'm holding you responsible to see that she gets a decent lunch and not too much to drink.'

'I can see the advantages of state-run nurseries,' Stephen said diplomatically when we were in the car.

'He's over-compensating for what he thinks of as past neglect, that's all.'

'Was it bad then – your parents being separated?'

'It was bad being different from other people. It's funny, isn't it, half the kids rejecting conformity and the other half – the different ones – striving desperately to be like everybody else?'

'You can only rebel against a status quo. But then I suppose most people have a status quo – of sorts.'

It was easy to talk to him, but just then a green wave of nausea swept over me. 'Just grant me half an hour and I'll be recovered.'

We drove towards Bamburgh, silently. After twenty minutes I found that the blacksmiths had ceased their performance inside my head.

'Better?'

'Mm. At least I can converse upon simple subjects if you want me to.'

'OK. When do you have to go back? That's simple enough.'

'Tomorrow. I start work the next day.'

'Oh yes, your secretary-ing. Do you like doing that?'

'Not particularly.'

'Why don't you do something else then?'

'For instance?'

'What qualifications have you got?'

'The usual – "O" levels, "A" levels.'

'Why don't you try for a university place?'

'At my age?'

'You're not so old. My mate in college is forty-two, married with three kids. Education isn't solely the privilege of youth.'

'I've had enough of universities and their inhabitants.'

'Oh dear. Am I on dangerous ground? Olivia said you'd had some trouble, some bloke –'

And the temptation to speak the beloved's name was

almost too strong to resist. Only by talking could I keep him alive, believe in his existence. But perhaps silence contains the power to obliterate just as language recalls the past, and I *had* to forget.

'It's all over now.'

It was my happiest day for nearly a year. Or, to be more accurate, the first day for nearly a year when I didn't feel actively sad. Our tastes were similar, we talked easily and without much inhibition and also, as ever, I enjoyed being seen in the company of a good-looking man. We held hands. We passed disparaging comments about the tourists. We ate ice-cream. We frisked in the sea air. He was exactly the sort of young man and it was exactly the sort of relationship I should have had if Jake had not materialized and altered the natural order. But even as I laughed and joked I was thinking that I was too old for that kind of thing and that trying to recapture a piece of one's youth was the worst kind of falsehood.

At the end of the afternoon we started to drive back south. I felt pleasantly tired, that nervous, edgy part of my nature dulled.

'I've been in this area before.'

'Oh? Happy memories?'

'It was only four years ago but it seems a lifetime. And yet, I can remember certain things that were said with perfect clarity. On the road, further on, I suddenly had this "I've been here before" feeling.'

'That's just –'

'I know. I had it all explained to me by a very knowledgeable young man. But another one advised me to keep an open mind.'

'Are you prone to that kind of thing?'

'Atmosphere? Presentiments? Yes, I suppose I am.' I thought of Tennyson Avenue and how it had always seemed alien, of the Jake dreams and how they had forewarned but not forarmed me.

'Maybe, in a previous incarnation –'

'– I was a fisherman, or a crab.'

'Oh no, a dear little silver starfish, or a pretty little pebble washed up from some exotic shore.'

'Very poetic, but your geography's wobbly.'

'I dare say,' he said, 'that's because I'm hot and thirsty and I could murder a pint. How about you? Or does the very mention of alcohol bring you out in a cold sweat?'

'No, I'm fine now. As long as I stick to something fairly innocuous.'

'On my right, the slag-heap,' he said. 'On my left, the sea. It reminds me of the Scilly Islands except there they have grass instead of coal. Shall we turn off here and try our luck with the local ale-house? Yes or no, because there's a stream of traffic behind us all ready to start cursing me for indecision.'

'As long as it's *not* an ale-house. I don't fancy being drawn into the dominoes tournament or having to tread briskly to avoid being impaled on the dart-board.'

'This looks quite classy. Carpets and fairy-lights and a shilling on the drinks.'

'I'll buy my own.'

'Great! I've been waiting all my life for a girl like you.'

I remember walking up to the door. He was pretending to count out his small change. 'Half a pint for me and a packet of crisps for you – plain, mind,' he said. We were laughing. I remember glancing upwards – strange, in retrospect, I never did that – and seeing the landlord's name. I remember looking at it for a full minute because my understanding lagged behind my vision. The sign informed the general public that Frank Gordon Best was licensed to sell beer and spirits on the premises. I don't remember what happened immediately after that except that there was a voice saying, from a great distance, 'Are you OK, Anna? What's the matter? Anna?'

When the world slid into focus I was shaking all over. He took hold of my arm. 'What on earth's the matter?' I couldn't answer. My jaws seemed clenched in an awful rigor. He must have thought I was having some sort of fit. 'Come on inside and let me get you a brandy. I thought you were going to pass out.' He put his arms round me and urged me to the door.

'No, no. Please. Let me go back to the car.'

He turned me round. He looked frightened. In the car he

lit a cigarette and put it into my fingers. My hand was trembling so much that I couldn't get the cigarette to my mouth.

'Are you ill?'

He got the car rug from the back seat and wrapped it round my shoulders. It was ridiculous. Any moment he would dash into the pub and ring 999. I had to say something, but I couldn't think what to say.

'I can't go in there.'

'Why not? What's wrong with it?'

'Let's just go somewhere else.'

'OK.' He put the key into the ignition.

'No.' I put my hand over his. 'No, don't go.' I *couldn't* go.

'Look, love, you'd better tell me what's troubling you. If I can't go and I can't stay, I don't quite know what to do.'

I looked straight ahead of me. It was the most difficult speech I had ever been called upon to make.

'Alec Blake isn't my father. The man who owns that pub is my father.'

He didn't say anything. There was nothing he could say.

'I've never seen him. The only thing I know about him is his name. I've known it for years. I didn't know whether he was alive or dead. I searched for him once but it came to nothing.'

He tightened his arm around me. 'It could be a coincidence. Someone of the same name.'

I shook my head. 'That feeling I got the last time. It wasn't nonsense, it can't be explained away in scientific jargon. Stephen, what shall I do?'

'If I were you, I'd drive away and never look back.' He looked at my face. 'But I'm not you. It wouldn't work, would it?'

'I'd be haunted.' I extinguished my cigarette and shredded the filter-tip. 'Will you help me? I haven't the courage alone.'

'If it's what you want, I'll help you. You need a drink anyway. This bloke may turn out to be ninety-five and a eunuch to boot. There must be a great many Anna Blakes and Stephen Murrays in the world.'

'That's why I want you to help me.'

'Talk to him, you mean?'

'He used to live in Lancashire. He was in the Navy. His father was a tailor, or a draper, or something of that sort. Coincidence can't extend *that* far.'

'I'm not in the habit of engaging mine host in friendly chat, but I'll try. As long as you promise not to pass out on me again.'

We walked back to the pub. I hung on to his hand. I couldn't breathe rhythmically and my legs were weak.

The lounge bar was empty of customers. A young, dark-haired, bored-looking girl was polishing glasses. We hoisted ourselves up on to bar stools.

'A brandy and a pint of bitter, please,' Stephen said. The girl put down her cloth and served us. She reminded me of myself before I got thin.

'Business isn't exactly brisk, is it?' The attempt to follow my instructions was costing Stephen a big effort.

'It's early yet.'

'You make your fortune later, then?'

She appeared to be affronted at the suggestion. 'I'm just helping out. It's my father's pub. The regular barmaid's due in half an hour.'

'Have you been here long? I've been in before but I don't remember seeing you.'

'Twelve years. You wouldn't have seen me. I only help out sometimes during the holidays.'

She moved to the other end of the bar, reluctant to waste her time with someone who was obviously spoken for.

'She looks like me.'

He compared us through the mirror-glass at the back of the bar. 'Vaguely. I've seen nearer resemblances.'

The room began to fill up. The girl disappeared and was replaced by a thin, brisk woman. There was no sign of the licensee.

'There's another bar, the saloon. Perhaps he's in there.'

'Do you want me to wander through? Order another round and I'll have a shufti.'

He sauntered through the communicating door. I drank

another brandy. The more brandy I drank, the less important the whole business seemed.

Stephen was back within minutes. 'There is a man in there and I heard someone call him Frank.'

'What did he look like, what did he –?' But Stephen didn't have to answer my questions. The communicating door swung open. 'That's him,' he said.

He was a medium-sized, middle-aged man with dark, greying hair and a broad forehead. He wore a blue roll-necked jumper and a sports jacket with leather patches on the elbows. There was an air of spruceness about him as though he took cold baths in the morning or exercised with dumb-bells. He looked the kind of man who would talk at length and boringly about his favourite football team or his fly-fishing. He looked the kind of man who never forgot his wife's birthday and was inordinately proud of his children's achievements. He looked like anybody else's father.

He went through to the back of the bar, calling 'Chrissie, Chrissie.' The girl appeared with a long-suffering look on her face. 'Will you give Maureen a hand? I'll stay here with Peggy. Now, sir?'

He wasn't Northumbrian. His accent was a *mélange* of many accents, the sort possessed by a man who has travelled extensively in his youth. His manner was slightly peremptory, a man who had perhaps been used to giving orders.

'What can I get you, sir?'

Stephen gave the order. I gazed at an ash-tray which advertised Cinzano.

'One pint, one brandy.'

Stephen leaned across the bar. 'You don't by any chance have accommodation?' he said. It was an inspired opening gambit. He knew perfectly well that there was no accommodation.

'I'm afraid we don't. For tonight, would it be?'

'That's right.'

'There's the Dragon on the main road. They might have rooms. Mention my name – Frank Best – I'm sure they'll fix you up. In fact, when I've got a minute, I'll give them a tinkle for you myself.'

'Oh, don't go to any trouble,' Stephen said rapidly.
'No trouble. Pleased to be of help. Just the one room?'
'Yes.'
I hastily put my hands out of sight beneath the bar.
Customers claimed his attention. 'Be with you in two shakes.'
'Oh, Christ.'
'Well, I didn't bargain on him being the original Good Samaritan.'
We watched him telephoning. 'What name is it, and would you want dinner?'
'Featherstone,' said Stephen. 'Sandwiches would do very well.'
He replaced the receiver. 'Success. Their last room. You'll be very comfortable. It's a small family hotel.'
'You're really very kind. Will you have a drink?'
'I'll have a half.'
He filled his glass. Peggy seemed to be coping without his assistance.
'Holidaying?'
'Just the week-end. We thought we'd explore this part of the coast.'
'Yes, it's a grand little piece of coast. Though I prefer the south myself: Newquay, St Ives. Good luck.'
We raised our glasses.
'You don't come from around here?'
'Oh no, I'm not a native. I come from Lancashire originally. This is where I came into port for the last time, so to speak.'
I turned my head to disguise the colour that had come into my cheeks. There could be no doubt. This average-looking man whose conversation was straight out of the landlord's cliché-book was my natural father, the man who had courted my mother and seduced her affections away from her husband for the time his leave lasted. I had imagined finding him, I had imagined that a point would be reached when I would say, 'I'm your daughter' or 'Do you remember Celia Blake née Armitage?' He wouldn't even recall the name. He had looked at me and seen a strange girl. There was nothing to connect us except a twenty-two-

year-old furtive jump. If I hadn't known, he'd have been the last man I'd have picked.

He excused himself to attend to someone else. I pulled at Stephen's sleeve.

'You want to go? OK.' He swung down from his stool and hailed Frank Best. 'Goodbye and thank you.'

'Not a bit. Good luck.'

I turned round for one last look. There had been no transformation, no intimation that there was any recognition, any affinity, beneath that hail-fellow-well-met-with tweed jacket.

'You're leaving it then?'

'Wouldn't you?'

Stephen shrugged. 'Nice enough bloke. Respectable, settled, helpful. What did you expect? No, forget I said that. You expected someone special, someone who would only need to look at you to know who you were.'

'I'd thought about him for four years, you see. Now it's all meaningless.'

'Tell me, does your mother know about him?'

'She never wanted to know. I couldn't understand how she could put someone so important out of her life. I do now, of course. He *wasn't* important. He just appeared at a certain time when she was in need of flattery or solace or something. If I hadn't happened she'd never have thought of him again.'

'And your old man, Alec, I mean?'

'I've no doubt he went through hell at the time. But he's not like me. He can get things into perspective. Besides, he didn't really love her, not in the way he should have loved her, and when that's the case, when you're just maintaining a marriage for social reasons, I don't suppose it cuts so deep.'

We sat for a long while in the stationary car. I felt disorientated. Part of me had been geared to this meeting. This meeting was supposed to alter my course one way or the other. It had achieved nothing of the sort.

'Let's go home.'

Home, I didn't have one. There was Hampstead, there was Aunt Kitty's house, there was the flat I lived in for reasons of hope and nostalgia; none of them were homes. I let my head fall on his shoulder. In the night, I let him come to me and love me because he was warm and interested and sympathetic. There was no passion. It was simply solace, like a cup of hot milk or an aspirin. I shuddered and he tightened his arms around me. The contact and warmth of his body obliterated the night-fears and the plaintive, unresolved dreams. Any warm, sympathetic body would have done as well.

CHAPTER FIFTEEN

It is easy to read coincidence into events that though linked superficially are fundamentally quite disparate. I had tempted fate by seeking forbidden knowledge and fate had obliged by rebuking my importunity.

When I returned to Manchester with Alec and Olivia my mother was already in hospital. It was the same hospital where, once before, Maurice and I had envisaged the orphanage. It was the same waiting-room where Maurice now looked at us as though we were somehow to blame for being in Northumberland at the critical moment. We sat side by side and silent, except for Aunt Kitty opposite, who cried into her handkerchief. I watched Alec Blake's hands clasping and unclasping convulsively; he was using all his restraint to stop himself from crossing over the room to strangle her. We were the typical family group as captured by a perceptive artist: beneath the conventional surface could be seen the lurking dislike, lack of sympathy and plain incompatibility.

'If only she'd *said*,' Aunt Kitty gasped. 'Why didn't she *say*?'

Because, when it's something as dreadful as cancer, you don't 'say', you daren't acknowledge it, you hope and pray that by refusing to acknowledge it you can refute its existence. That's why, you stupid, insensitive, uncomprehending old woman.

But Aunt Kitty was no mind-reader and continued to sob

and whimper and ask why. After a time, Alec Blake said, 'Be quiet, Kitty. We could all cry.' And, surprisingly, she shut up.

Years ago, a surgeon had walked into this room bringing with him the odour of ether and death and said, 'She'll be fine. As good as new. Hallo, young Maurice, isn't it? How's the batting average?' That surgeon was long gone; the doctor who came in to tell us that it would be pointless to wait – they would let us know when there was any news – was obviously not long out of medical school and unsure of how to deal with distraught next-of-kin.

'Could I have a word, Mr Blake?'

They went into the corridor. Olivia, back at the hotel, meant nothing. At this moment he was Cecilia Blake's husband and had never ceased to be so.

'Will you stay at my place, Maurice?'

'No. I've got to get back. Berenice isn't well.'

He had scarcely exchanged two words with his father. And, as far as he was concerned, I was tarred with the same brush. We had defected, leaving him with the whole burden of her love. We should be taking the whole burden of his suffering. It wasn't concern for Berenice that made him reject us.

'I'll get you a room,' Alec Blake said to me. 'I don't want you to be alone.'

Olivia was standing by the reception desk. I felt sorry for Olivia. Her cleverness, her beauty, counted for nothing in a situation like this.

'Well?'

He shrugged. 'The usual fobbing-off formula. We'll be informed when they have any information. I want a room for Anna.'

'I've already booked one.'

He took the key and glared at it. 'She'd known for a year. Not even Kitty was told. For Christ's sake, why? Martyrdom?'

Olivia looked at him steadily. 'What would you have done? What *could* you have done? Come on, Anna, we'll go and unpack. You're next to us.'

He put out a hand. 'Olivia, perhaps you'd better go back to London.'

She looked as though he'd hit her. But she only said, 'As you like.'

Upstairs, she took her clothes out of their wardrobe and her jars off their dressing-table. She showed no sign of anger or annoyance. Her hands were calm and methodical, folding and packing, smoothing and arranging.

'Why are you going? Why did he tell you to go? *I* wouldn't go. He's behaving like God Almighty.'

'Because he can't distinguish between anger and remorse. He doesn't know how he should feel. At the moment he doesn't know whom he hates most for complicating his life – me, or your mother.'

'My mother? Because she was so inconsiderate as to get cancer?'

'Illness is just about the most effective weapon there is. She has only to say "Come back" and he'd feel obliged to go back.'

'After all this time?'

She looked very near to tears. 'Oh, Anna, there's no such thing as security. You can only go on from day to day, hoping.' She snapped her case shut and recovered herself. 'I hope she'll be all right. I really mean it. He's not the only one who feels real or imaginary guilt. Anna.'

I turned to face her.

'Try to forgive her. She'll need you.'

I didn't answer her. Alec Blake was right: Olivia had no place here. I was sorry for her but every word she said was an intrusion.

The night was long and sleep an impossibility. He didn't sleep either. Through the dividing wall I could hear his pacing footsteps. When I went in at seven he looked grey and the two ash-trays were brimming with cigarette ends.

Maurice was at the hospital. We were to be allowed to see her, one at a time, for a few moments. They warned us that she was drugged and might not recognize us. The nurses were hearty, hygienic and unconcerned. The little room outside the ward was filled with flowers and stank like a graveyard. I was rigid with fear. She was ill, she was dying – they wouldn't say that, but I knew. I wanted her to die then and there and spare me the waiting, spare me the sight of her ravaged body and vacant gaze.

I was the last to go in. I had seen Alec Blake's face and Maurice's face. I had to hold on to the wall, to the door, because my legs wouldn't take me there.

'Come on now,' the nurse said, disapproval in her tone. What was all the fuss about? She'd probably laid out a few bodies before breakfast. She was a good nurse though, gentle, and all her sheets tucked in with knife edges. 'Just a couple of minutes,' she said, and turned to fiddle with the apparatus at the side of the bed. From this apparatus was suspended a bottle and from the bottle ran a tube down to my mother's cheek where it was secured with sticky-tape, and thence up her nose. The little room with its clean primrose walls and flowered curtains tilted and swayed. I clung to the bed end.

There were flowers and chocolates on the locker beside her bed. Such irrelevance. I moved my eyes slowly. I did not want to look. 'She's trying to say something,' the nurse said. 'What is it, dear?' She bent her head to my mother's mouth, looked at me and shrugged her shoulders.

I wanted to open the door and run, for ever, but I was mesmerized by that shrunken, white-faced form whose lips moved soundlessly, whose hand drooped limply over the side of the bed, that parody of my mother.

The nurse indicated that I should take her place. I too bent my head, but her mumblings were unintelligible. It was the morphia speaking.

'Why is she doped like this?'

'To kill the pain, dear.' The nurse smiled cheerily. 'Perhaps it would be better if you tried later. Three people, one after another, are really too many.'

I put my hand to her cheek. It was pale and soft and perfectly still as though the blood had already ceased to circulate. I wanted to drag her by force out of her drugged trance. I would rather she suffered if, by suffering, she would recognize me and re-assume her personality. The creature I touched was merely a female body, any female body, in the disgusting last stages of life.

'Later,' the nurse said, 'later.' Quite a kind nurse really, despite the tight sheets and the joviality. I allowed her to guide me out of the room. Neither Maurice nor Alec Blake looked at me.

'She will need you,' Olivia had said. She never needed me. She died that night without recognizing me.

Unknown relations surfaced for the funeral. After it was over they disappeared back into their holes in the ground to wait for the next one.

Casual acquaintances became bereaved friends. Faces at the graveside speculated about what sort of meal they would get afterwards. There was a little dignified jostling for the privilege of sprinkling earth on the coffin, a furtive comparing of wreaths: 'That's not much of one, is it? Twenty-five bob and look at it – daylight robbery.'

The sky was the colour you see it in holiday brochures. The sun beat on my upturned face. The bearers were sweating visibly. Mary Leslie's mother, on the fringe of the group, was wearing a green jacket. Typical. Then the long slow walk to the ugly sandy plot. Sunlight glinted on the coffin handles. Maurice used to say that, if you were cremated, they took them off and gave them back to the undertaker for the next coffin, just as they scavenged wedding rings and gold teeth. Maurice's lips were clamped together. Berenice was solemn, in faultless black. Voices could be heard, hushed, but carrying on the still air: 'He's got a cheek, I say. Best thing he could have done was to stay away. Where's *she* then? It's a wonder he didn't bring her. What poor Cis had to put up with, nobody knows.'

And then a meal at the Imperial. After the first, hushed course, people at the other end of the table began to unwind. Laughter was heard and summer holidays were discussed. Aunt Kitty talked to everyone and cried into the *consommé*. Jamie, absent-mindedly, began to whistle, then bethought himself and blushed deep red. I kept my eyes fixed on the plates that were put down before me and made eating motions. No one dared speak to me. People spoke to Berenice instead. She was much more their idea of a dutiful daughter.

They ate their cold roast beef and their cherry tart, they drank their Benedictines and Drambuies – one or two drank enough Benedictines and Drambuies to see them through to the next free assembly – and then they made their farewells. They shook Alec Blake's hand and told him that Time Heals, that it was a Merciful Release, and that everything had gone off very well. Outside, they would say, 'Well, you can't tell me it's not a relief to him. She deserved better than that, did Cis.'

The undertaker drank a glass of beer and chatted to the waiters. He kept looking at his watch. Perhaps he had another send-off to attend to, or perhaps he just wanted to get home and take off his shiny black shoes.

'Bury me under the apple tree,' Maurice said, between clenched teeth. He was fuming. The whole procedure was ritualistic, pagan, meaningless, attended by harpies come to gaze upon death and reflect upon their own good fortune.

We left the hotel and went on to Aunt Kitty's because there was nowhere else to go and because we just couldn't allow everything to break up so suddenly. Berenice fretted. She'd left the kids with a neighbour and wanted to get back. Maurice told her to stop whining. Berenice was pregnant again. Fulfilling her quota. She would cry before the day was out because you're allowed to cry when you're pregnant, and your husband is not supposed to be unsympathetic and boorish.

Alec Blake sat on Aunt Kitty's sofa, his hands between his knees, his head bowed. He passed a hand across his eyes and when he brought it away there was a trace of wetness upon it.

I watched him and rage rose within me. He mopped at his face with his handkerchief. His eyes were small and red. He looked ridiculous.

'Why are you crying, Father?' I used the word in the way that Raymond had used it, as an obscenity. 'Because it's the accepted appropriate reaction? It doesn't fool anybody. It's a relief to you that she's dead, you can't deny it, so why pretend grief?'

'Anna.' Berenice rose from her seat.

'You keep out of it. It's nothing to do with you. You were a bitch to her too. It doesn't mean a thing to you, does it? Nor to him. He just cries for himself, because of his conscience. I think you're a lot of bloody hypocrites – a set of reactions for this, a set of reactions for that – you wouldn't recognize a real feeling if you fell over it.'

Aunt Kitty and Maurice appeared in the doorway and watched open-mouthed. It was as though a valve had opened inside me releasing all my pent-up hatred at the injustice of life.

'You married the wrong woman, that's all there is to it. *I'm* not crying. I *might* have cried, but you and she buggered up my childhood too successfully for me to do that.'

They were still staring. No one spoke a word. I left them because I could not bear to see their faces. I went back to my flat where I sat and gazed into the empty grate and thought about the years of my life and how the troubles seemed to outweigh the happy times. I thought about other people. I knew who seemed to have happy, normal lives. I thought about Jake and Frank Best and every betrayal I had ever suffered. I tried to imagine a future but it was hopeless. I wanted to die, to fall asleep and never wake up again.

They phoned me and knocked on my door. They were puzzled, wary. I was polite. I told them I wished to be on my own. Eventually they went away.

The next day, during my lunch break, I collapsed outside Marks and Spencers, causing some inconvenience to the passers-by. In the ambulance they gave me oxygen and when I came to I thought I had died, but the ambulance-man said, 'That's a girl. Breathe in deep.' So I closed my eyes and pretended to be unconscious again.

CHAPTER SIXTEEN

'Haven't you any family, dear?'

The woman in the next bed talked to everyone. The nurses adored her. She was born to be a hospital patient. 'I bet she keeps you all jolly,' the visitors said of her as she cast her cheery smile about the ward.

I turned my face to the wall and ignored her. One night, when the sister went to the drug-cabinet, I would creep out of bed and strangle the cheery one with skeins of her own shell-pink knitting wool.

I spoke to no one, unless it was really necessary. It's amazing what little amount of speech you can manage with if you set your mind on it. The cheery one was on my left, but the wall was on my right so I had only to turn on my side and I was unassailable.

'Well, young lady, how do you feel about another X-ray?' the doctor said. I just smiled. Smiling will often do instead of talking. 'Another little look at your lung.' He was so old that I supposed I seemed a child to him. I half-expected him to offer me a sweet on condition I didn't cry, as Rachel's father used to do.

The other doctor was young, ambitious and brisk. He referred to my medical history. 'No BCG?' He raised his eyebrows. 'And a history of respiratory infections. Pneumonia twice, three times.' He shook his head. 'When will they learn?'

When I was first admitted I didn't know what was the matter with me. I was enlightened by a patient in the opposite bed to mine.

So. TB. I thought it was dead, conquered, like diphtheria and typhoid fever. Poets used to die of it and alcoholics contact it due to their alcoholism, or did they become alcoholics because they had TB? Mimi died of it in *Bohème* – only then it was known as galloping consumption and relieved a good many parents of the burden of having another mouth to feed.

In this ward they had a joke about it making you feel sexy so that the male patients had to be watched. Sexy? I'd forgotten the meaning of the word.

Life is so simple in hospital. You are woken, you wash, you are fed. The high point of your day is your injection and the gargantuan effort that is needed, the revulsion that has to be overcome, to provide a sample of sputum.

The nurses chatted about their private lives. There were the happy nurses and the sad nurses, the ones as hard as nails, the ones who would never make it and the ones who combined toughness with tenderness. They never chatted to me. I was the odd fish, the one who refused visitors. I was responsible for breaking up their orderly pattern of two to a bed. They would have insisted, but I kicked up a fuss and sent my tempeature soaring, so for fear of further lesions in my lungs they acquiesced to my whim.

I wouldn't see them, but I couldn't prevent them from sending things: magazines from Aunt Kitty, books from Maurice, flowers and fruit from Alec and Olivia. I think the other patients believed I was royalty resting incognito.

There were letters too, which I read but never answered. I wasn't supposed to write, anyway. They were sweet, humble letters. They made me cry. I didn't hate anyone any more. It was just that I couldn't be bothered, to talk, to think, to plan. I would stay in hospital. They would feed me, weigh me, inject me and photograph me. My days would be organized and undemanding. I would stare at the ceiling and smile and sleep, sleep most of all.

But one day they told me I was cured. Another week, provided my weight was all right, and I could leave. I ran a fever. Three times they told me I was ready to leave and three times I ran a fever. I was unpopular. I was messing up their records. They said I was better, so I *was* better and had no business to be running fevers.

'I don't know what we're going to do with *you*,' the day-sister said, brandishing a thermometer. 'Do you like it here, or what?'

The cheery one had been discharged and was replaced by a crossword-fiend. During the afternoon-nap periods I racked my brains to think of nine-letter words beginning with 'y'; I didn't mind that kind of restricted conversation. Besides, the crossword-fiend was not amenable to discipline and rude to the staff which endeared her to me. She was called Tessa and, when she wasn't involved in crosswords, spent her time trying to wangle a crafty, forbidden smoke or treating me to a monologue concerning her boy-friend who had put her in the family-way twice. Directly she was through with 'this nonsense' she was going to have her tubes tied. In clove-hitches, preferably. Her boy-friend's fertility knew no bounds.

'*You're* not supposed to be here,' Tessa said. 'You're taking up a bed that's needed for a poor sick person.'

'I know.'

'Bugger the poor sick people. When I'm out of here I'm into gynae, and stuff everybody else.'

She was painting her finger-nails: 'Deep Coral'. Her finger-nails were chewed and pretty dirty, so the finished effect was grim, but Terry, the boy-friend, was due that evening.

'I heard,' she said, 'Arse-Features' (the day-sister) 'talking to one of the doctors. They were saying that your fevers are all in the mind. They didn't exactly say that, but that's what they meant.' She blew on her fingers. 'So if I were you I'd beware the men in the white coats coming with little rubber hammers to tap your knees.'

'I don't want to go out.'

'I get your point. It's only trouble when you get out. A bloody job, a bloody man. It's all trouble.' She looked at me accusingly. '*You've* got a family though.'

'They're part of the trouble.'

'Haven't you got a boy-friend?'

'I did have.' You wouldn't believe it, months and months go by and there's still a pang.

'Oh? Like that? Acute depression, that's probably what's up with you. I had it once. When I broke with Terry. Couldn't stop crying. They arranged for me to see the trick-cyclist. I never went though. I made it up with Terry instead.'

A week later we resumed our conversation. My bed was needed. I was being discharged. My lungs were whole and healthy; it was my mind that refused to acknowledge recuperation. I was being sent to a convalescent home. At least that's what they called it. I supposed Alec Blake was paying. I didn't really care.

'The Yorkshire Moors?' Tessa said incredulously, as though I'd said the Sea of Tranquillity. 'Rather you than me. And a Merry Christmas to one and all.'

They were starting to decorate the ward with tinsel and streamers.

'At least you'll be spared the carol-singing and the bloody vicar coming round to save our souls. Unless of course it's the same there, at the nut-house.'

'It's not a nut-house. It's a convalescent home.'

'Same difference. Oh, no offence, kid. I'm only pulling your leg. It'll probably be the Dorchester with bed-pans, if your old man's paying.'

'He's not my old man.'

She gazed at me over the top of her newspaper. 'The plot thickens. Anyway, give my love to "Ilkley Moor B'aht At". It's where I lost my virginity on a Sunday school picnic.'

The Isabel Armstrong Convalescent Home was situated in what must surely have been the most wind-grieved gash of the Yorkshire Moors. The staff had been there for years – and I wasn't surprised. They probably couldn't face the journey back to civilization. Perhaps in the summer – but it was Christmas and I looked out of the windows and felt as though I were living through a chapter of *Wuthering Heights*.

I settled in easily; one hospital regime is very much like another. I was there to rest, to eat and to be investigated. I should have known when I first went in and saw the woman crying in the corner.

The nurses were all well-bred young ladies who spoke with cut-glass accents. The doctors were all straight out of Harley Street with brushed-back grey hair, charming smiles and immaculate finger-nails. It was a very expensive convalescent home.

The exception who proved this rule was my doctor, Chris Ross, who had the eager air and blunt manner of a scholarship boy who'd made it to the top. I hated him at first because he never asked me the questions I wanted to answer.

'Do I lie down?'

'Do you want to?'

'Not particularly.'

I sat instead, in a huge studded leather arm-chair that looked as though it had been acquired from some gentlemen's club.

'Anna. Is that the name you're known by?'

'It's down there.'

'Yes. But people aren't always known by what's down there.'

'I am.'

It was the first time, and I didn't see why I should help him.

'Do you object to being here?'

'I don't know that yet, do I?'

He rested his chin on his knuckles. He had a thin, humorous face and unruly hair.

'Would you rather be home for Christmas?'

'I haven't a home and I hate Christmas.'

'Why do you hate Christmas?'

'Because it's a time when everyone's supposed to be happy and love one another.' I stirred in my chair, impatiently. 'Aren't you going to show me some ink-blots, or something?'

'Why do you ask that?'

'That's what they do in every corny psychiatry film I've ever seen.'

'Or word-association. I'd be good at that.'

He didn't say anything.

'Go ahead then. Fire.'

'Heat, cold, snow, ice, cold –' I couldn't think of another damned word.

'I only wanted to meet you,' he said gently.

The second time I had it all prepared. I sat down and reeled it off. 'When I was a kid my parents fought so I felt insecure and wet the bed. Then my father left home for another woman and I felt even less secure and allowed myself to be seduced to make up for it. Then I found out he wasn't my father so I hated my mother. I needed a father-figure so I latched on to a man who didn't really love me. After that I met my real father who didn't measure up to my preconceived ideas, and my mother died and I felt responsible. Aren't you listening?'

He stopped turning over the pages of a book. 'You've got it all worked out,' He said. 'I feel a bit unnecessary.'

After that I was more tractable. We had discussions.

These discussions never seemed to touch upon anything personal but after they were over I realized just how much he had got out of me in those seemingly impersonal answers I had given.

One day he said to me, 'You were rejected by a man, you found your real father wanting, your mother died; all these things followed rapidly upon each other, so you got TB.'

'I got TB? Deliberately?'

'Shall we say the time was ripe?'

The conversation often touched upon envy. I said that I had met lots of people whose lives seemed happy and normal.

'Name one,' he said.

'My sister-in-law, Berenice,' I replied promptly. 'Nothing really bad has ever happened to her in the whole of her life.'

'And would you want her life? Would you want to be her?'

Oh no, I wouldn't want to be Berenice. I wanted to be me with Berenice's lack of afflictions.

I got very jealous of the time he didn't spend with me. The other women patients were like that too. We watched each other like hawks to see who was getting an extra ten minutes or a session out of turn. It was ridiculous, like being at school and jealous of one's favourite mistress giving her attention to someone else.

Falling in love with him seemed to solve all my problems. We would marry and he would take care of me. So simple.

Then, one Sunday, they said I had a visitor. I began to tremble. I had thought they wouldn't dare after the last attempt. 'A Mr Murray,' the nurse said. I shrugged my shoulders. *Mr* Murray? I knew no Mr Murray.

His hair was longer and he'd grown a moustache. It took me a minute or two to recognize him.

'Stephen!'

He held out a bunch of chrysanthemums. He appeared to be mute with embarrassment. I drew him into a corner of the lounge and sat him down.

'They're pretty.' I indicated the flowers.

'You like them?' he said eagerly. 'Some people don't.'

'Don't what?'
'Like certain types of flowers.'
'Oh yes.'
I felt wretched. I hadn't combed my hair and my dress was an old one that wasn't particularly flattering.
'You'll have some tea?'
'Please.'
We sat in silence until it arrived. He looked very surprised to see china cups and silver tea-spoons; I supposed he'd imagined we queued up at a wooden table and ate with plastic knives and forks.
'It really is a convalescent home. Some of the people have had nervous breakdowns, that's all.'
'No Napoleons or Mary Queen of Scots?'
'Not that I know of.'
We grinned and started to laugh. He choked on his Battenburg cake. People turned round to stare. He'd caused quite a sensation already in his faded levis and army surplus battle-dress.
'Anna, I didn't – well, I didn't just sleep with you and forget about you the next day.'
I forgot about you.
'I wrote to you twice and then tried to ring you from Oxford. I'd heard about your mother, of course. I'm sorry. But I thought you'd be recovered by then. When I got no reply I assumed you didn't want to know and left it at that. It was only a few weeks ago that I met Olivia and found out.'
'Did she tell you I wouldn't see them?'
'Yes.'
'So why did you come?'
'I'm arrogant. I thought I'd charm my way in.'
'Don't you have girls in Oxford?'
'Yes.'
'Then why me?'
'I liked you.'
I caught sight of myself in a mirror and hastily looked away. 'I wish I'd known you were coming. I'd have tried to look decent.'
'You look nice. Plumper.'

'Plumper?'

'You needed it. Who wants to sleep with a hat-rack?'

Chris knew all about Stephen. They were as thorough as MI5 in that place. I got the impression that he wasn't altogether in favour.

'Why shouldn't I see him?'

'See him by all means. But you should see other people as well.'

'I'd be embarrassed with other people.'

'And you're not embarrassed with Stephen?'

'No. Everything's a bit of a laugh when I'm with him.'

I had requested reading-matter. The second time he came he brought novels and two philosophical works in paperback.

I pulled a face.

'No, read them. I was having a quick gander through my books and I came across these. They say things which might have some relevance for you.'

'Schopenhauer?' Chris raised his eyebrows. 'I'm not sure I approve.'

I put my elbows on his desk and leaned forward. 'I know he's pessimistic, but I can accept that. He's saying "Look, this is how it is and it affects everybody, not just poor little you. It's better not to be born but if you haven't the guts for suicide you might as well press on and make the best of it." You remember when we were talking about envy? He puts it so well. He compares a state of good fortune to a group of trees. When you see it from a distance it looks beautiful, but if you go up to the trees and inspect them individually, that illusion of beauty disappears. They just look ordinary. I suppose it's like that with people. I think Berenice is fortunate but I don't know her well enough to be certain that my assessment's correct and, anyway, it's only *my* assessment.'

I was gabbling in the attempt to communicate my enthusiasm.

Chris leaned back, smiling. 'Carry on reading,' he said.

I made a new discovery. 'He says the state of despair is having no hope and no fear. He says that when you reach the point of believing that what you want to happen won't happen simply *because* you want it to happen, then you're in despair. I don't entirely agree with that. After all, the *will* is still there –'

'It's not gospel, you know,' Chris said mildly. 'It's just one point of view. Try Kant – he was the greatest source of inspiration. Or even Hegel, his arch-enemy.'

I did, but found them both too full of technical jargon for my taste. Nietzche, though, was easy to follow – not that I agreed with him.

My conversations with Chris turned into philosophical debates. I found myself thinking in the abstract more and more.

I looked through a window, saw blossom on an apple tree and realized it was spring.

'When you leave here,' Chris said, 'why don't you try for a university place? You must have got through a year's syllabus in three months.'

'There's nothing else to do. I don't knit, or sew, or play bridge. It's either read or go mad.' We had quite a few good, sick jokes between us by now. The sun slanted across his desk, glinting on the bronze statuette I had gazed at so often and seen differently, according to my mood. 'You reckon I ought to be going?'

'I'm waiting for you to tell me that you can't stand to be cooped up any longer.'

Stephen endorsed his views about my further education. He was back at Oxford, but came over most week-ends, bearing books and a breath of the world. I let him shower me with college prospecti. I might go.

'When Jake broke with me,' I told Chris, 'I used to lie in bed and say "Help me, help me", to God, or a priest, or a psychiatrist. I don't know which. But I didn't believe anyone could. I was wrong, wasn't I?'

'No. You can only help yourself. I've suggested pointers. So has Stephen about whom I was uncertain at first.'

'You thought I'd fall in love with him?' I smiled. 'I am a bit in love with him, but I think it's inspired by gratitude. He's just my friend. You're allowed to love your friends?'

'Feel free.'

'I did have friends, apart from Stephen. There was

Raymond, and Tassie, and Virginia, and a few others, but I let them drop when Jake came on the scene because I didn't want anything to interfere with our relationship.'

'If they were friends perhaps you can pick them up again.' He looked at me narrowly. 'You've just said "Jake" twice without flinching.'

'I'd like him to be my friend, but it's much too dangerous, isn't it?'

'Much too dangerous.'

'I loved him. He didn't love me. I have to accept that. It was just an event.'

'Can you also say "Father" without flinching?'

'Soon, perhaps.'

I closed his door and went outside into the grounds. There were lambs in the fields. Berenice's third child would now be born. Maurice's house would look inviting in the spring sunlight. Alec Blake would be at the race-track and Olivia would be worrying about him as she'd worry until the day he died. Frank Best would be pulling pints and saying 'Good luck', Aunt Kitty would be putting daffodils on my mother's grave. Jake – well, Jake might be anywhere. He was rootless. He was like me, too much an individual, a loner, too suspicious. We were mis-mated.

The wind was warm and wet and fresh, seeming to carry messages from more animated quarters. Under a tree, Marianne Fletcher, thirty-five years old and unwillingly, unhappily, homosexual, cried over the daffodils. I looked down, down to the road below. I saw cars, tiny, like toy cars, coming and going. I thought of the great adventure I had anticipated with Jake; it might still be possible, within the bounds of reality. At any rate, I had no business here, among people who wept over the daffodils. It was time for me to be off.

It's June now and I haven't seen him for almost a year. Maurice tells me he's gone old, that he and Olivia don't go out much any more, that he will always blame himself. But then Maurice has changed too: he is less flippant, he no longer teases me; we talk together with restraint and affection and tacitly avoid certain painful subjects. Only once, in his garden which is now paved and regular, he looks up from pruning the rose bush and says, 'He would very much like to see you.'

So that's why I'm sitting in this flat, watching the clock and the stripe of sunlight changing its position on the wall. He is coming alone, he is trying to recreate the way things were before Olivia, before I left home, before the seeds of my hatred were sown.

I hear the sound of a car stopping and look out of the window. It is a sober family saloon that is parked now outside the gate. He has acknowledged his fifty-two years and put away the sport cars once and for all. Does he sing, still?

At first, I don't see that he looks old – we greet each other cautiously and I go to make tea – it's only when I glimpse him from the kitchen, his head bent to light a cigarette, that it registers: the skin is stretched tight across his cheekbones, the hand that flicks the lighter is yellowish, the hair in front of his ears is almost white.

'It's a pleasant flat.'

'Yes.'

Silence again. The only sound the chink of spoon against china as he stirs and stirs his tea.

'You start in October?'

'Yes.'

I have a place at the university. 'Try for Oxford,' Stephen said eagerly. But that would have been dangerous. I would have wanted him all the time, I would have turned him into another Jake. We will remain friends and he will visit me, but it's necessary that I start anew, and alone.

'You're very brave.'

'Lucky. I've been lucky – to get a place.'

'If this had happened five years ago –'

'No. Now is the right time.'

He crosses and uncrosses his legs, looks for somewhere to put down his tea cup, taps his cigarette on the ash-tray, bites his lip. He is working up the courage to say something. I don't give him the chance.

'How's Olivia?'

'She's fine. She sends you her love.'

'I'm fine too. So are Maurice and Berenice and the kids. They're quite sweet. I looked after them a lot when I was staying there.'

A month I stayed with Maurice. It was long enough.

'I went to your mother's grave.'

Oh, it needed an effort to say that.

'It's very well kept. Your Aunt Kitty goes a lot – Anna –'

'Have some more tea?'

'Anna.'

I must reach out and meet him, I must – but not yet.

'Aren't you going on holiday this year? It would be a shame not to take advantage of this glorious weather.'

'Malta. We've taken a villa. We want you to come.'

'No, I don't think so. You and Olivia –'

'Not me and Olivia. Me. You and me.'

'Just you and me?'

'Yes.'

'For the summer?'

'Will you, Anna?'

I want to, I really want to. 'What about Olivia?'

'She knows that we should be on our own, for a while.'

I pick at a loose thread on my skirt. 'She never went further than Colwyn Bay.'

He winces. 'It was my fault. Your troubles were my fault too.'

I look at him and realize what enormous power I have, to hurt, to destroy, what enormous power every human being has over every other human being.

'It was a bit your fault, a bit her fault. It was my fault, too, and the rest was nobody's fault. I had wrong ideas, wrong values. I wanted something impossible. I wanted to possess people, take them over completely. She was like that. Possessive and jealous and with no faith in herself. And it was your fault and other people's fault and her fault as well. Other people are other people. The only person you have control over is yourself. It's the only fixed, certain thing in life.'

'I failed you.'

'I didn't understand.'

My values were perverted. I know now. There's no

mystique. You and Olivia have a relationship that is quite ordinary, that may endure or may break up. You can't pursue security. It's a by-product.

'Can we try to take up the threads?'

'I'll come with you to Malta.'

And his face is the same. Older, haggard, but the same face as the man who used to feed me with sips of Lucozade and sing me to sleep. All that's occurred in between hasn't altered it.

'We'll have to help each other.'

'Yes.'

He's all the father I have. 'Father.' 'Can you say it yet without flinching?' 'Soon perhaps.' Frank Best is just a man who pulls pints in Northumberland. I belong with Alec Blake. I must love someone. We can try.

FICTION

CRIME/ADVENTURE/SUSPENSE

☐ **The Killing In The Market**	John Ball with Bevan Smith	£1.00
☐ **In the Heat of the Night**	John Ball	£1.00
☐ **Johnny Get Your Gun**	John Ball	£1.00
☐ **The Cool Cottontail**	John Ball	£1.00
☐ **The Megawind Cancellation**	Bernard Boucher	£1.25
☐ **Slow Burn**	Peter Cave	£1.50
☐ **Tunnel**	Hal Friedman	£1.35
☐ **Barracuda**	Irving A. Greenfield	£1.25
☐ **Tagget**	Irving A. Greenfield	£1.25
☐ **Don't be no Hero**	Leonard Harris	£1.25
☐ **The Blunderer**	Patricia Highsmith	£1.25
☐ **A Game for the Living**	Patricia Highsmith	£1.25
☐ **Those who Walk Away**	Patricia Highsmith	£1.25
☐ **The Tremor of Forgery**	Patricia Highsmith	£1.25
☐ **The Two Faces of January**	Patricia Highsmith	£1.25
☐ **Labyrinth**	Eric Mackenzie-Lamb	£1.25
☐ **The Hunted**	Elmore Leonard	£1.25
☐ **Confess, Fletch**	Gregory Mcdonald	90p
☐ **Fletch**	Gregory Mcdonald	90p
☐ **Fletch's Fortune**	Gregory Mcdonald	£1.25
☐ **Flynn**	Gregory Mcdonald	95p
☐ **All the Queen's Men**	Guiy de Montfort	£1.25
☐ **Pandora Man**	Kerry Newcomb and Frank Schaefer	£1.25
☐ **Sigmet Active**	Thomas Page	£1.10
☐ **Crash Landing**	Mark Regan	£1.25
☐ **The Last Prisoner**	James Robson	£1.50
☐ **The Croesus Conspiracy**	Ben Stein	£1.25
☐ **Deadline in Jakarta**	Ian Stewart	£1.25
☐ **An H-Bomb for Alice**	Ian Stewart	£1.50
☐ **The Peking Payoff**	Ian Stewart	90p
☐ **The Seizing of Singapore**	Ian Stewart	£1.00
☐ **Winter Stalk**	James L. Stowe	£1.25
☐ **Rough Deal**	Walter Winward	£1.10

HISTORICAL ROMANCE/ROMANCE/SAGA

☐ **Hawksmoor**	Aileen Armitage	£1.75
☐ **Blaze of Passion**	Stephanie Blake	£1.25
☐ **Daughter of Destiny**	Stephanie Blake	£1.25
☐ **Flowers of Fire**	Stephanie Blake	£1.50
☐ **So Wicked My Desire**	Stephanie Blake	£1.50
☐ **Wicked is My Flesh**	Stephanie Blake	£1.50
☐ **Lovers and Dancers**	Michael Feeney Callan	£1.50
☐ **The Lofty Banners**	Brenda Clarke	£1.75
☐ **The Enchanted Land**	Jude Deveraux	£1.50
☐ **My Love, My Land**	Judy Gardiner	£1.25
☐ **Walburga's Eve**	Elizabeth Hann	£1.35
☐ **Lily of the Sun**	Sandra Heath	95p
☐ **Strangers' Forest**	Pamela Hill	£1.00
☐ **Royal Mistress**	Patricia Campbell Horton	£1.50
☐ **The Rebel Heart**	Anna James	£1.25
☐ **Gentlemen Callers**	Nancy Lamb	£1.50
☐ **Fires of Winter**	Johanna Lindsey	£1.50
☐ **A Pirate's Love**	Johanna Lindsey	£1.25
☐ **Trade Imperial**	Alan Lloyd	£1.35
☐ **Dance Barefoot**	Margaret Maddocks	95p
☐ **The Open Door**	Margaret Maddocks	£1.25
☐ **All We Know of Heaven**	Dore Mullen	£1.25
☐ **The Far Side of Destiny**	Dore Mullen	£1.50
☐ **New Year's Eve**	Jeannie Sakol	£1.50
☐ **The Pride**	Judith Saxton	£1.50
☐ **Heir to Trevayan**	Juliet Sefton	£1.25
☐ **Never Trust a Handsome Man**	Marlene Fanta Shyer	£1.25
☐ **Shadow of an Unknown Woman**	Daoma Winston	£1.00
☐ **Call the Darkness Light**	Nancy Zaroulis	£1.95